CW01064682

HMS CRUSADER

By the same author

HMS *Marathon*

HMS CRUSADER

A. E. Langsford

'Fight on my men,' says Sir Andrew Barton,
'I am hurt, but I am not slain.
I'll lay me down and bleed awhile,
Then I'll rise, and fight again.'
        Anon: The Oxford Book of Ballads

BARRIE & JENKINS
LONDON

To
my uncle
John Drake Matthews,
Apprentice, ss *Magdapur*,
sunk by mines laid by U–13
(Kapitünleutnant Karl Daublebsky von Eichhain),
10th September 1939,

and my great-uncle,
Lieutenant-Commander (E) George Holme RNR,
Chief Engineer, HMS *Laurentic*,
sunk by U–99 (Korvettenkapitün Otto Kretschmer),
3rd–4th November 1940.

First published in 1990 by Barrie & Jenkins,
20 Vauxhall Bridge Road, London SW1V 2AS

British Library Cataloguing in Publication Data
Langsford, A. E., *1959-*
  H.M.S. Crusader.
  I. Title
  823.914 [F]
  ISBN 0–7126–3742–7

Printed and bound in Great Britain by
Mackays of Chatham PLC, Chatham, Kent

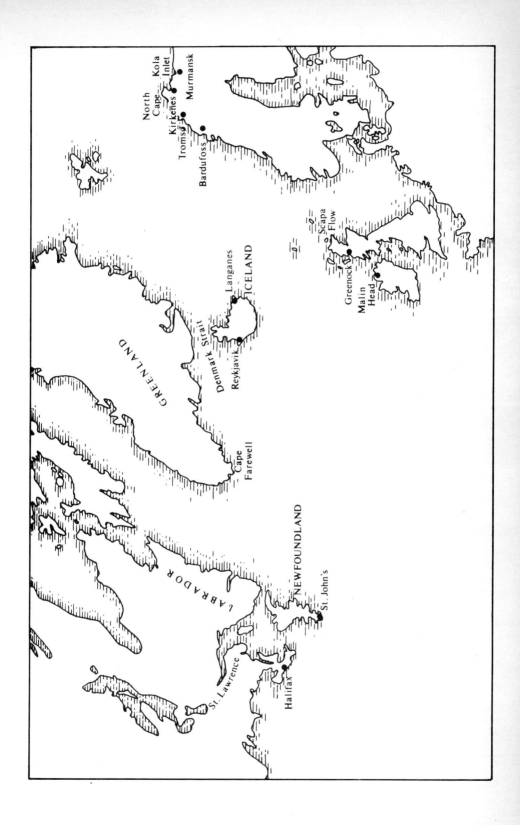

North Cape
Kola Inlet
Kirkenes
Murmansk
Tromsø
Bardufoss

Scapa Flow
Greenock
Malin Head

Langanes
ICELAND
Denmark Strait
Reykjavik
GREENLAND

Cape Farewell

LABRADOR
NEWFOUNDLAND
St. John's

St. Lawrence
Halifax

Acknowledgements:

This book would not have been written without the help and interest of Captain J. F. T. Bayliss, Royal Navy, whose father, Captain H. T. T. Bayliss, commanded HMS *Vindex* in 1944, Mr C. G. Mottram, Curator of the Fleet Air Arm Museum, Yeovilton, and Mr T. K. Norledge, Technical Information Officer of the Institute of Marine Engineers. Professor Paul Brenikov gave me a fascinating afternoon of reminiscences about his time as a Swordfish radar operator, and Dr J. S. Munro once again came to my rescue on the medical side. Jak P. Mallmann Showell was a mine of information on U-boats and Mr Bernard Thompson provided first-hand details of wartime flying training. Stuart Reid assisted me through a fit of writer's block, and was partly responsible for sinking both HMS *Crusader* and U-686. My father read large sections of the book in manuscript and gave much constructive criticism, and also put me in touch with Mr David Rollo, who explained various aspects of naval discipline, but sadly died shortly before the book was completed.

A pleasant by-product of writing this book was making contact with a large number of former escort carrier men who answered my notice in the *Navy News* in October 1989, and gave me enough material for several more books, notably Jackson Brooks, Bruce Burgess, A. E. Charters, C. H. Fowler, Donald Hogg, Dr John Hotchin, J. W. Johnson, W. King, C. Knight, Al Lever, Gerald Lisk, B. McDermott, E. W. Martin, Jack Newall, Bob Porter, Ernie Pringle, Jim Rogan, Tony Tickner, Phil Vine and R. B. Watkin. Those whom I have inadvertently forgotten know who they are.

Historical Note:

The escort carrier was developed by the Royal Navy in response to the heavy merchant shipping losses of the first two years of the war, and the impossibility at that time of providing air cover from land-based aircraft. Various expedients were tried, the best known being the equipping of a small number of merchant ships with catapults and obsolescent Hurricanes, which could be launched against any enemy aircraft that appeared over the convoys, principally the very long-range but lightly armed Focke Wulf FW 200 Kondors. These 'CAM ships' (Catapult-equipped Merchantmen) which went into service in March 1941, and the volunteer naval and RAF pilots of the Merchant Ship Fighter Unit, did achieve a number of successes against the Kondors, the first by Lieutenant R. W. H. Everett RNVR, but they could never be more than a stopgap, as the CAM ships lacked flight decks and each flight ended inevitably in a hazardous baling-out or ditching.

While the CAM ships were providing the only source of air cover over the Atlantic convoys, work was in progress on the world's first auxiliary aircraft carrier, later to be called an escort carrier. This was the German merchant ship *Hannover*, captured by HMS *Dunedin* in February 1940, and commissioned on 20th June 1941 as HMS *Audacity*. *Audacity*'s flight deck was 368 feet long, less than half the length of a fleet carrier, and 60 feet in beam, she had only two arrester wires instead of the normal six, no island and no hangar, which meant that the American-built Grumman Martlet aircraft of 802 Squadron had to remain on deck in all weathers, causing considerable problems of maintenance.

Despite these limitations, *Audacity* demonstrated that the escort carrier was a valuable weapon in the Atlantic war. During her short life – she was sunk on 21st December 1941 – *Audacity*'s aircraft shot down only two Kondors, but their major role was in keeping both enemy aircraft and U-boats at arm's length; indeed, convoy OG76 was able to reach Gibraltar without loss, despite the presence in the same area of eight Kondors and a U-boat 'wolf pack'.

The next escort carrier was HMS *Archer*, commissioned on 17th December 1941, the first of a class of five converted from the hulls of American merchant ships. All five were equipped with diesel engines, and these proved an Achilles heel, as all five were plagued by engine troubles, notably *Archer* herself, which was relegated to the role of stores ship in November 1943. By this time two of her sister ships had been lost, *Avenger* on 15th November 1942 while making a delayed return passage from the Torch landings because of engine trouble. The torpedo ignited the aircraft petrol stored in her double bottom, and as a result there were only twelve survivors. What made this doubly tragic was that her crew included those members of 802 Squadron who had survived *Audacity*'s sinking. The third and last escort carrier to be sunk during the war was HMS *Dasher*, as the result of a petrol explosion during exercises in the Clyde on 27th March 1943. Over 300 men were lost, many burned to death in the water after abandoning ship. One man who had an extraordinary escape was her commanding officer,

Captain L. A. K. Boswell, who was dragged down with the remains of the ship with one foot jammed beneath a stanchion, but jerked free when *Dasher* hit the bottom 300 feet below.

The later, American-built, escort carriers, again conversions from merchant hulls, had steam turbines rather than the unreliable diesels, and as a result were better equipped to play a valuable, if unglamorous, role in the war at sea. In addition to service on the North Atlantic and Russian convoys, several took part in the Salerno landings of September 1943, providing air cover over the landing beaches, but there the limitations of the escort carrier clearly showed themselves; in the light winds of the Mediterranean summer, and with a maximum speed of seventeen knots, they simply did not have long enough decks for their high-performance Seafires and Sea Hurricanes to take off and land safely, and losses were heavy. Rather more successfully, they performed a similar role in the invasion of southern France the following year.

The man in the unenviable position of being the only captain to surrender a British warship since the War of 1812 was Lieutenant-Commander R. P. Lonsdale of the submarine HMS *Seal* on 5th May 1940. While on a minelaying mission in the Kattegat, the submarine was damaged by air attack and then disabled by a German mine while submerged. Lonsdale was forced to jettison the drop keel in order to get her back to the surface, making it impossible for her to dive again. Coming under further heavy air attacks once on the surface, his ship unable to dive, without power and sinking rapidly, Lonsdale ordered an improvised white flag to be hoisted, in order to avoid unnecessary loss of life. On his return from a prison camp after the war, he was indeed court-martialled, on charges of failing to take immediate action to engage enemy aircraft which attacked *Seal*, and of failing to take steps to ensure the sinking of *Seal* when it appeared possible that she might fall into the hands of the enemy. After a two-day court martial he was honourably acquitted on the grounds that his action was justified in order to save the lives of his men, and it is on record that the president of the court martial personally returned his sword. *Seal* herself was partially refitted and towed to Kiel, where she was used by the German Navy for instructional and propaganda purposes, before she was sunk in an RAF bombing raid in 1943.

1

Greenock, October 1943.

Half an hour from the end of his watch the gangway sentry was cold. Not the surface cold which could be countered by putting on an extra sweater, pulling up his greatcoat collar and wrapping a scarf around his throat; this was the deeper cold which dulled the reactions and numbed his limbs, and would take a long time to thaw even after he got below to the warm, tobacco-laden fug of his mess. He moved his rifle to his left shoulder, marched a few paces in each direction, feeling the blood begin to flow inside his boots once more.

Now that his eyes were accustomed to the darkness he could make out the angles and girders of the shipyard cranes against the sky, recognise the deeper stripes of shadow beneath the steel cables which secured the carrier to the dockside, the hawsers themselves, thick as a man's forearm, sagging under their own weight on the steeply angled journey from ship's side to bollard. *Crusader* was an ugly brute, not a real carrier like *Ark Royal* or *Illustrious*, but a hasty conversion from a merchant hull, and spent almost as much time under repair as she did at sea.

He stamped his feet once more, lowered the butt of the rifle to the ground. If he had really wanted to act like a tin soldier he would have joined the army when he got his call-up papers, and if he had wanted to be a seasick tin soldier he could have been a Marine. There wasn't even much point in his being here any longer. The blokes whose leave expired at 2300 – Ordinary Seamen aged under twenty-one like himself – had come straggling back in twos and threes after the pubs shut, smelling cheerfully of beer and chips, and in a rush in the last few minutes before the hour; the Duty Regulating Petty Officer had dealt with a few latecomers, and the lucky blokes with all-night leave would stay ashore until morning. And Ordinary Seaman Charlie Metcalfe was duty part of watch, which meant he had to make do with writing to Dottie, his girlfriend in Morpeth, before drawing a rifle and webbing and reporting for his four hours on. Stuck out here in the rain while Porky Jenkins was snug in the quartermasters' lobby with the *Daily Mirror* and back aft the officers had some kind of thrash going on, with the pink gin flowing. He could have done with a drop of gin or something right now, but the only alcohol the Navy permitted the lower deck was the daily tot, one part of rum diluted with three of water, and there were still eighteen months to go before he was of age to draw it.

Metcalfe blinked some rain out of his eyes and watched the heavy drops slanting into the puddles, noticed an itch halfway down his back and tried to reach it through the constricting layers of his clothes. He cursed and gave up, tried to cheer himself up by telling the stores petty officer in his imagination just what he thought of naval-issue soap which caused itches.

He heard footsteps, started and looked around. Someone coming across the open concrete space on this side of the dockyard buildings. He's well adrift, he thought, with satisfaction, listening to the metallic crunch of steel-tipped heels. But as the man came closer he recognised the officer's-pattern raincoat, noted the line of brass on the cap peak. Commander must've fallen out with his old woman. But it wasn't one of *Crusader*'s officers – wonder what he wants at this hour? He tensed himself, executed a jerky present arms.

The strange officer returned the salute punctiliously. 'Miserable night.'

'Yessir.' It was safest to agree with senior officers, especially when they started talking about the weather.

'Drawn the short straw?'

'Yessir.'

The officer put a hand to the rail, lifted one foot onto the brow, then turned back. 'Just a minute, sentry. You don't know me. Aren't you going to challenge me?' The voice was still conversational, but there was a harder edge beneath. Metcalfe stiffened, jerked forward to level his rifle across the rails, shouted out the challenge that had been dinned into him: 'Halt! Who goes there!' He detected a slight smile as the officer groped in an inside pocket, withdrew his wallet and extracted an identity card.

Metcalfe brought out his torch, turned the card over, saw a name that was vaguely familiar, squinted at it, glanced upwards to make sure the face approximated to the photograph. 'Pass, sir.'

'That's more like it.' The card was taken back. 'Remember that in future.'

'Yessir.' Or should it be Aye aye sir? He lifted the rifle to the slope, stamped his feet once more, grateful that there were only twenty minutes left.

Able Seaman Porky Jenkins slowly masticated the last fragments of a large Cornish pasty, sucked the end of his pencil and considered the remaining clues in the *Daily Mirror* crossword. This was one time when he could put up with life in the Andrew. Boring, but he was warm and dry, not stuck out in the rain with a rifle like that poor little squirt Charlie Metcalfe. Mr Higgins was somewhere back aft, having a look in on that booze-up in the wardroom and leaving him to his own devices; no one to find him odd little jobs that needed to be done now if not sooner, or didn't need to be done but just formed part of the pigs' way of fucking the men about. He heard someone on deck outside. That would be Mr Higgins coming back to check on him and the sentries, and to send him to the galley to make a brew. Jenkins pushed the newspaper into a drawer, removed his feet from the table, set his cap straight on his head. The door opened. Jenkins jerked to his feet, the chair legs scraping backwards, saluted quiveringly, the ease of his watch suddenly gone.

'Where is the Officer of the Watch?'

Jenkins hesitated, shifted from foot to foot. Mr Higgins wasn't a bad bloke, and he didn't want to land him in it. 'He'll be in the wardroom, sir. There's a bit of a party on and he went to check on it. Shall I get him, sir?'

The strange officer gave him a look that meant he had heard it all before. 'Stay where you are. And if you can find the time, the rails need tightening. Get on with it.'

He had not been aboard an escort carrier before, and the layout was sufficiently unlike the ships he knew for it to take some time before he found the way to the wardroom, and then it was mainly the noise which confirmed he was going in the right direction. He pushed open the door, walked into the centre of the compartment. A gramophone continued tinnily to pump dance music, but all other sounds were suddenly stilled. There were several half-empty bottles scattered about, a small pile of broken glass and a dark stain spreading across the carpet, an assortment of unbuttoned reefer jackets and ties at half-mast. That much he had expected, but it came as a surprise to see three or four women sprawled among the men, smell cheap scent above the spirits and cigarettes. The men started getting to their feet; one of the women found herself cradling empty space.

'David!'

'Stand up, you fool!' the man hissed.

They were all on their feet, straightening their clothes, looking sheep-

11

ishly at the carpet like schoolboys before the headmaster, suddenly very sober.

'Turn that noise off.'

The man nearest the gramophone turned it off. The needle scratched to a halt.

'My name is Thurston. I expect you all realise why I'm here.'

'Who is it?' the same woman whispered.

'The new captain. Must be. Didn't know he was coming.'

'Come here, gorgeous, and give me a kiss,' another girl said. She was very young, peroxide fair, with a scarlet slash of lipstick for a mouth, and a pallid curve of breast showing where her dress had been pulled down.

Thurston felt himself flush, collected himself. 'Who is the Officer of the Watch?'

'I am, sir. Higgins, sir,' said someone at the back, hastily tucking his shirt into his trousers.

He addressed Higgins directly. 'Where is the Commander?'

'Ashore, sir.'

'Tucked up in bed with his wife,' someone muttered.

'First Lieutenant?'

'In his bunk, sir.'

'Get back to your post, Mr Higgins. I'll deal with you in the morning.' He looked around him at the various jacket sleeves. Mostly sub-lieutenants, a scatter of full lieutenants, all wavy rings. 'Who is the senior officer present?'

'I suppose I am, sir,' one of the lieutenants answered. 'Shall I get the First Lieutenant?'

'Leave him where he is.'

The lieutenant tried to mollify. 'Will you have a drink, sir?'

He looked round again, at the bottles and smeared glasses, at the young girl's stupid, over-made-up face. 'No, I will not have a drink!'

The young girl sat up. 'Why don' you stop shouting, darling, an' come an' enjoy yoursel' wi' me?'

'Get that female outside.' Her neighbour hustled her to the door. Thurston turned back to the lieutenant. 'What's your name?'

'Bruce, sir.' He looked uncomfortable. He was fair-haired, about twenty-one, with the remains of a barber's rash across his chin.

'All right, Mr Bruce. Before you do anything else you will get these *ladies* over the side and send them back to wherever they came from. Then you can clear up the mess you've made.'

'I'll get the stewards in here, sir,' Bruce said hastily.

12

Thurston's bushy eyebrows drew together in a frown. 'No, you will not! You will do it yourselves, the whole damn lot of you!'

''Ark at 'im,' one of the girls said under her breath.

They filed out, the girls reluctantly, the men with relief. 'Pompous prick,' one of the girls said. 'Proper stuffed shirt,' someone answered. Another giggle, 'Wonder what he's like in bed,' deliberately pitched loudly enough for him to hear.

'Mr Bruce, get them ashore!'

In the Captain's cabin Thurston took a pair of pyjamas from his brief-case, set out his shaving tackle ready for the morning, started to undress. This was not yet his cabin, nor was it yet his ship. The cabin would begin to change once his kit caught him up, and Spencer, his seaman servant, and he could set his pictures on the empty hooks on the bulkheads, fill the shelves with his books, and by the time he had been aboard *Crusader* a month it would be as if he had been here for years. The cabin had been stripped of all traces of his predecessor, so that only the standard Admiralty-pattern furnishings remained, but his stamp would lie over the ship for much longer.

He took his shirt off, ran some water into the basin and began to wash. He smiled to himself. He had certainly given those young officers something to remember him by. He had not intended to arrive as late as this, but the train up to Glasgow had been late, had twice been diverted into sidings to let something with greater priority go past, and the Admiral wanted to see him before he took over.

He knew what the young officers would have seen. Four gold rings, well worn, on either sleeve, a full set of medal ribbons from the last war. Pompous prick indeed! He rinsed off the soap and reached for the towel, then studied himself in the mirror for a moment. A tall man, an inch or two over six feet, who held himself very straight. A lean, rather bony face, marked by a stark white line of scar tissue through one eyebrow and on slantwise across his forehead, and dominated by a high-bridged nose which had been broken in his midshipman days and was angled a little to one side. Dark hair, going grey at the sides, deep-set eyes the bluish grey of slate, a seaman's weathered complexion. An austere face, which could have been stern in repose but for the hint at humour in the creases at the corners of his eyes.

The young officers knew his name and would know him by repu-tation, that in his last command he had been responsible for the sinking of the German heavy cruiser *Seydlitz* in the Denmark Strait, that he had got *Marathon* back to Alexandria under tow through six days of

13

gales when she had seventy feet blown out of her bottom by an Italian aerial torpedo eleven months ago. They would, if nothing else, have seen the red ribbon on his left shoulder and wondered idly what he had done to merit that. But other things they would not know, what it was that had happened to him after that torpedoing, what it was that had kept him ashore and on the sick list for most of the intervening period.

He had expected simply to cross the station and catch the local train to Greenock, but the Admiral's flag lieutenant and a staff car had been waiting for him when the train belatedly reached Glasgow. The Commander in Chief Western Approaches was in the habit of doing his telephoning after dinner, which meant that his local commanders had still to be in their offices even at that hour.

'Sit yourself down, Bob. Do you still drink whisky?' Rear Admiral Herbert Manning-Wilson had been Thurston's Captain when he was Commander of a battleship before the war. He poured two fingers from a bottle he produced from a cupboard, then took a glass for himself, settled back into his chair before speaking again.

'I expect you'd like to know what you're here for?'

'Yes sir.'

'I suppose all they told you was to get up here and take over *Crusader*, and to drop everything else in the process.'

'Just that.'

'I thought I should get you in here and give you some idea of what you're going into. It's not going to be a picnic by any means.' Manning-Wilson paused and ran his fingers through his thinning hair. 'We're finding these Woolworth carriers the answer, or part of the answer, to a good many of our problems with friend Doenitz and his merry men, but unfortunately they're throwing up a good many problems of their own. Some of it is technical, mainly in the engine room, but mostly it's our old friend morale.'

'In what way?'

'I knew you would ask me that.' The Admiral smiled and drank some of his whisky. 'Desertions, defaulters' lists as long as your arm. Air patrols are aborted for engine trouble and the black gang can't find anything wrong. Quite a few flying accidents. All the usual things. Of course, the ship's companies are an ill-assorted lot; T124 ratings, most of them. Bring a man up as a defaulter and he starts to recite the Merchant Shipping Acts. They're still getting Merchant Navy pay and danger money, and the rest of the chaps don't like it.'

14

'Hardly surprising, since it's about three times as much.'

'Quite so, but we can't allow that as an excuse. Then there are the aircrews, and they like to believe they're a law unto themselves. Not that they seem to have much idea what they're doing when they get into the air. *Crusader* and two of the others went out to the Med to cover the Salerno landing – they've only just got back, and from the reports I've seen they seem to have made a pretty poor showing. They were supposed to provide air cover for the Fleet, and from what happened to *Warspite* it's obvious that they didn't do it properly. I suppose you can't really expect aircraft to deal with glider bombs, but they left Jerry in a position to drop the things and guide them on to the target. Shouldn't get so worked up about it, but my nephew's a sub in *Warspite*. He's all right, thank heavens, but it was a near-run thing.'

'So I'm here to sort things out?'

'To put it bluntly, yes. The reason you've had to drop everything is quite simple. I gave your predecessor his marching orders yesterday morning. Tom Owen – do you know him?' Thurston shook his head. 'I had him in to find out what had been going on with the Salerno business, and what he proposed to do about it. Full of alarm and despondency, so to speak. I can't abide a man who's always making excuses, as you probably remember. *Crusader*'s needed at sea – we haven't enough of the things even when they are all available, so rather than wait while the Naval Secretary consults his oracles and sticks pins in the Captains' List, I told him to dig you out from wherever you were.'

'Thank you.'

'Nothing to thank me for. You're available and you can be relied on. You are a bit senior, I suppose, but if you can make *Crusader* work, then that should provide an example for the rest to follow. And you haven't any preconceived ideas about carriers, or about flyers.'

'I don't think I've even set foot aboard a carrier before.' Thurston's tone was rueful.

'Exactly. No preconceived ideas. *Crusader*'s in for repairs – again. Dragged her anchor and bent a few plates against her neighbour. That'll give you a week or so to find your way about, or a bit longer if the dockyard show their usual lack of a sense of urgency. But I want her back at sea. There simply aren't enough of the things. They don't belong to any of the escort groups, for that very reason. They simply go out with them as and when needed. I'm going to give you a free hand, but I'll be keeping an eye on you, and come straight to me if there's anything you need.' The Admiral smiled ironically, finished the

15

last of his whisky and looked at the empty glass with a glimmer of regret. 'It doesn't look as though Max Horton wants to talk to me tonight, so I'm going to get off home. I'm sorry to have delayed your arrival: Charles Beasley will ring and say you're on your way.' He got up, signifying that the interview was at an end. 'It's good to see you again, Bob. Got your mess undress with you? You must dine with me one night, once you've had a chance to get organised.' He moved towards the door. 'How is the beauteous Kate?'

'She's very well.'

'Remember me to her, would you. And the sprogs?'

'They're very well. Quite a lot larger than when you last saw them. George is a snotty in *Duke of York*.' It did not seem appropriate to mention that there was another on the way.

'Lucky lad. I think the last time I saw George he had a black eye from falling off his push bike playing Hopalong Cassidy hits the trail! Jennifer's left me, did you know?'

'I didn't. I'm sorry to hear it.'

'Gone off with an American colonel. With a wife and three children in Indiana or somewhere. She complained that I was too bound up in this job, and that she never saw me, and now the Yank's in Italy. Poetic justice, I suppose. She may yet come to her senses. Enough of that, you haven't come to listen to my problems.'

As he got into the Captain's bunk and turned off the light, Thurston wondered again whether Manning-Wilson knew about his breakdown, whether he would withdraw his faith in him if he were now to learn of it for the first time, or whether instead he had simply wished to avoid embarrassing him. 'Combat fatigue' was the polite euphemism, but the real truth had been that he couldn't take it any more, that it hadn't even been a sudden thing, but he had been on the edge of cracking even before the last operation and the six days on tow, that he had almost died by his own hand, face down in his own blood with an open razor beside him.

They had given him three months' sick leave, and he had expected, naïvely perhaps, another ship or at least a shore job after that, but the damage the razor did in half a second had taken eight months to heal, so it was the middle of July before the doctors finally passed him fit. And even then Their Lordships of the Admiralty seemed in no particular hurry to find him permanent employment. He found himself in demand only for presiding over courts martial and sitting on the board which examined thirteen-year-old candidates for Dartmouth. 'Don't be tempted to rush things,' he had been told. 'There'll be plenty of war left.' But it wasn't an uncomplicated lust for glory which drew him back, nor yet the tedium of enquiring of a succession of painfully scrubbed, best-suited, correctly spoken schoolboys why they wanted to join the Navy, whether they had a dog and what games they played, nor listening to another earnest plea in mitigation in a case where there were no extenuating circumstances. 'Your stupid masculine pride,' was what his wife put it down to, and perhaps she was right. Pride, duty, self-respect, a whole bundle of words which went only some way to defining what impelled him back to sea once more.

Manning-Wilson knew, or did not know, what had happened to him, but he, and Their Lordships, were prepared now to trust him in command once again. Thurston rolled the name around his tongue, spoke it out into the darkness of the cabin. *Crusader.*

2

As he stood in *Crusader*'s stern the flight deck stretched away in a long rectangle, as if a length of road, made of reddish Oregon pine instead of tarmac, had been taken up from its rightful place and thrown down on top of the hull, the white line remaining down the centre. Thurston's first impression was of vastness and openness, the uncompromising squareness of the thing, his second that all that pine was a serious fire hazard. It was early, the cloud which had brought the rain had disappeared to the north-east, and the sun was just rising and breaking through the cloud, shining on the oily waters of the Clyde and the salt-stained assortment of escort vessels berthed alongside. He paced the flight deck, bare-headed, ignored in the proper fashion by a few others also intent on their morning exercise, enjoying the novelty of space after the confined quarterdecks of the cruisers and destroyers he had previously commanded. Five hundred feet from the squared-off merchantman stern to the triangle of bow which protruded beyond the pine and several feet below, sixty-six in beam. At regular intervals there were slots in the deck, at the bottoms of which lurked the lowered arrester wires, ready to be raised by winches at either side. 20mm cannon mounted in sponsons below deck level formed the bulk of the ship's anti-aircraft armament. On the starboard side, three-quarters of the way to the bow, a stumpy island structure protruded asymmetrically, bulging with platforms which formed the bridge and flag deck and batsman's position, and topped by a thicket of radar and wireless aerials.

Not a beautiful ship; an austerity design, pared down to essentials. Laid down and launched as a merchant ship in an American yard, requisitioned when nearly completed, given the basic necessities of an aircraft carrier, flight deck, hangar, rudimentary anti-aircraft armament, radar, and handed over to the British. But she was slow – seventeen knots – and with her boxy shape and single screw she would handle awkwardly; her hull was that of a freighter, unarmoured, less compartmentalised than a true warship, the welded construction as yet barely tested by bomb or torpedo.

'Heard the latest buzz? The new Captain's been appointed.'
  'That was quick. Who is it?'

'Thurston.'

'Not *the* Thurston?'

'The very same.' The speaker reached for his toast rack, removed a slice to his plate and continued. 'Signal came through in the dog watches yesterday, after you'd gone ashore to your floozie.'

'What have we done to deserve this?'

'Isn't it obvious?' the Gunnery Officer broke in, keeping his voice low in the hope that the Commander, sitting at the head of the table, wouldn't hear. 'Their Lordships have decided that you lot are in need of a bloody good shake-up, and about time.'

'You lot? I like that. Since when has the Gunnery Department been so bloody perfect?'

'So what's Wonderboy like?' They all turned to the Gunnery Officer, the only regular within earshot.

'No idea. Never met the man,' he replied unhelpfully.

'Not a gunnery specialist then.'

'I can guess,' someone else said in gloomy tones.

The Commander lowered his newspaper and glared in their direction. 'I understand that, in the best society, breakfast is a meal taken in silence.'

'Actually,' another voice joined in the conversation after the Commander was safely behind his newspaper once more, 'you're a bit out of date. He's already on board. Turned up in the small hours and started creating hell on the spot, or so Geoff Bruce was telling me. Jim Higgins was joining in a bit of a thrash in here, during his watch, when the great man walked in, and it looks as though the sword of Damocles is about to descend.'

The first speaker finished masticating a mouthful of toast and marmalade. 'It seems as though we can abandon all thoughts of a peaceful existence.'

'What peaceful existence?' said an engineer. 'If you could see the state those bloody rotor blades are in.'

The Commander's newspaper was lowered a second time. 'I did say . . .'

Thurston had just completed his breakfast, prepared and served by his predecessor's steward, an elderly petty officer who was not inclined to conversation, and seemed, unsurprisingly in the circumstances, to be sunk in private gloom, when there was a knock on the bulkhead outside.

'Come.'

A compact, square-faced young man with an armful of files. 'Paymaster Lieutenant Scott, sir. Captain Owen's secretary. Good morning, sir.'

'That was nice timing.'

'Actually, I asked Parfitt to let me know when you'd finished eating.' There was an Edinburgh accent which went with his name.

'Is there much there?'

'Not a great deal, sir. A few things Captain Owen didn't get a chance to deal with.'

Thurston sat at the desk, skimmed rapidly through the documents which Scott brought out, routine stuff, signed his name upwards of a dozen times, put away his pen.

'How long have you been aboard, Mr Scott?'

'Since commissioning. About eight months.'

'Before that?'

'*Marksman*, sir. Flotilla leader.'

There was silence for a moment, a mutual sizing-up. Scott must have been aware that, even after four years of war, a post-captain could still largely pick and choose his secretary, which was why Scott had described himself as Captain Owen's secretary. If things aboard *Crusader* were as bad as the Admiral claimed, he could be saddling himself with a dud, but there were advantages in having someone who knew the ship, at least in the early stages while he was working his way in.

'Do you want to stay on?'

'Yes, sir,' with only the slightest hesitation.

They shook hands.

'Is the Commander on board?'

'Yes sir. He has his wife ashore and doesn't actually sleep aboard in harbour, but he's normally in the wardroom for breakfast.'

'Then would you give him my compliments and ask him to come up, and then could you dig out the service records of the heads of department.'

'Made your will, young 'un?'

'No, Stripey, what do you mean?'

'Heard who the new skipper is?' The three-badgeman did not bother to wait for the answer. 'A proper death and glory merchant. VC, DSO and Christ alone knows how many fucking bars. A real head-on bastard. Genuine twenty-four-carat war hero,' he said in sarcastic tones.

Ordinary Seaman Metcalfe's eyes widened, but he said nothing.

'Know what that means, Charlie? Fucker like that won't want to let his laurels go rusty. *Seydlitz* is ancient history. 'E'll 'ave us goin' for the

Tirpitz right up 'er fuckin' fjord, see if 'e don't. So, kid, time you made your will, and see if you can't wangle danger money like those T124 bastards.'

'And now I'd better see the ship.'

'Shall I call the heads of department together?'

'I'd prefer to meet them as I go round. I'd like to see what actually goes on.' Then, knowing that it would be a breach of the usual etiquette to go unannounced, he added, 'But do give them some warning of my approach.'

'Yes, sir,' the Commander agreed diplomatically. 'You may find some surprises, unfortunately.' A faint look of distaste crossed his face.

'This is very much a reservist ship,' he had already told Thurston. 'Apart from ourselves, of course, the only straight-stripers are the Commander (Flying), the Gunnery Officer – Forrest – and young Scott, I'm afraid. The engine room are T124X to a man and a very mixed bag, the aircrew are hostilities only and so are most of the rest. The AA ratings are nearly all Canadians – we picked up a draft of them in Vancouver just after commissioning. Rather different from what you're used to, I expect.'

Thurston declined to be drawn. He had the feeling that Commander Canning already knew a good deal about him, and that Captain Owen's fate if nothing else had warned him to tread very carefully. Canning had apologised profusely for the state of his cabin, and for not being aboard when he arrived. ('That's quite all right. I did warm the bell a bit. But,' to make it clear that things were unlikely to remain as they had been, 'you can give the sentries a shake-up. The man at the gangway when I arrived wouldn't have taken any notice if I'd been Goering.') Canning was in his late thirties, and carried an expensive air about him in the signet ring and heavy gold cufflinks, the handkerchief pressed into three corners in his top pocket; his hair was carefully arranged to cover a thin patch on top.

'We could start with the Air Plot, sir,' the Commander said as they reached the island. 'Ah, here's Wings. This is his territory.'

Commander (Flying) was physically quite different from the Commander. He was very small, no more than five foot five, even with his shoes on, and reminded Thurston more of a jockey than a naval officer.

The Air Plot contained rows of radar screens, facing the bulkheads on three sides of a square. One entire bulkhead was faced with perspex, still marked with several colours of chinagraph pencil from the ship's

21

last operation, numbers of aircraft and names of aircrews entered on a board at one end.

'We keep a running plot of everything that's in the air at any time, both our people and the enemy. We're in radio contact with our own aircraft all the time they're airborne, and we can follow them on radar as long as they're within range of the sets. We should have a Swordfish airborne on anti-submarine patrol at all times – we should have eight in all, and ten Seafires. In practice, we don't usually manage to have them all aboard.' Commander (Flying) was never still, and had a restless, quick way of speaking, quite unlike Canning, who looked on with an air of well-bred boredom throughout his colleague's exposition.

'At the same time, we can pick up any other aircraft that come within range, and the FDO – Fighter Direction Officer – who sits on that throne there,' he indicated a large metal and canvas chair set on a pedestal at one end of the compartment, 'can scramble our Seafires and guide them in to intercept. They usually turn out to be ours nowadays – a couple of years back the Condors gave us a lot of trouble, before we got aircraft with the convoys – but you can't be too careful. The plot is continuously updated, as is the met, and we keep in constant touch with the Ops Room next door, where they deal with the overall picture, and everything that's on the surface.' He grinned. 'It's quiet enough in here now, sir, but when all the blokes are packed in, and they're all on the net talking to different people at the same time, it's pure bedlam.'

The Ops Room; the bridge, which at least was familiar enough, although it would be strange to be pushed out to starboard with the full width of the flight deck to block his view of the port side. No funnels, the engine room gases would be vented out on either side at deck level.

'What comes next, Wings?'

'The hangar, sir. Empty at the moment. The squadron's out at Machrihanish.' He noticed the change in Thurston's expression and hastened to explain. 'It's the usual drill in harbour. They fly off before we come in and rejoin on the way out. The crews get a break from the ship and a chance to get in some flying training, which they can't manage from the ship in harbour.'

Thurston was listening, absorbing what Wings was telling him as they walked the length of the rectangular steel box directly below the flight deck, empty of aircraft now though in the gloom above the wings and fuselages of dismantled Seafires hung as dark shadows from the deckhead.

'This is where we do all the maintenance, though when the weather's good we try to get most of the minor checks and so on done on deck. Again, we're always short of space below. We have a permanent deck park of six, and you can bet your life that when something goes wrong it's always the kite that's furthest from the lift.'

Thurston was turning ideas over in his mind, groping towards a tentative identification of what might be some of *Crusader*'s problems.

'You say the aircrews need a break from the ship?'

Commander (Flying) looked uncomfortable, perhaps wishing he had expressed himself differently, and hesitated before he answered. 'As carriers go, this one is very small. There's only about a third of the deck space of the *Illustrious* class, and believe me, she looks even smaller when you're up there with the light going and ten minutes' petrol in your tanks. And she can be pretty lively in any sort of sea. Of course, she was never intended to be a carrier.' He glanced behind him, saw that the Commander was lagging a little, clearly uninterested in anything that pertained to flying. Thurston noticed, and quickened his pace a fraction.

Wings hesitated again, then went on. 'The aircrews all joined to fly, only secondarily to be naval officers. For some that was a long way second – a good many of them only joined the FAA because they'd have had to wait longer to get into the RAF. I hope you won't get the wrong impression, sir. They're as keen as mustard, but they like to be able to do their own thing now and again, to let their hair down a bit, and to be able to enjoy their flying.'

Thurston looked back at the Commander, now further behind, and asked in low tones, 'Is there much friction between the aircrews and the ship's officers?'

Another wait while Sterling weighed up what he was going to say. 'Not really friction, sir. Nothing overt. Just not much contact, with the seamen officers at any rate. Some of our lads are quite pally with some of the chaps from the engine room. But you know how it's always been, sir: seamen mix with seamen and stokers with stokers. That's what it's like in the wardroom, that's all, and again much the same thing goes on between the seamen officers and the engineers. There's always a bit of flak between flyers and non-flyers. There was in the RAF before I transferred across and I don't doubt there still is. You get all the glory while we do all the work. You're snoozing in your nice warm ready room while we do the work. You're safe in your comfortable ship while we're up there dicing with death.'

The Commander skirted a patch of oil and caught them up, glancing questioningly from one to the other, confirming what Thurston had already come to suspect, that there was little love lost between his second-in-command and Commander (Flying).

'Commander Hodgson, Chief Engineer.'

Chief had obviously had just enough warning of his approach to get out of his overalls and wash his hands.

'I seem to have arrived at a bad time.'

'Not especially. This is getting to be practically a routine job for us.' The Chief glanced at his palms. Despite his efforts they were faintly ingrained with oil, evidence that he took a hands-on approach to running his department. 'If you come this way, sir, you'll find it a bit quieter.'

The sound of hammering, reverberating off the steel bulkheads, died away somewhat after they had moved into the boiler room and the Chief had shut the connecting door behind them.

'We're taking advantage of the repairs to the plates to rip out the latest lot of broken turbine blades, and trying to sort out the boilers. There's a leak in there somewhere – it's been giving trouble for a couple of months – but we haven't found it yet, or as fast as we deal with one, another starts.' There was a resigned smile.

'It sounds as though you have quite a lot of this.'

'I'll be quite honest, sir. I've been a marine engineer getting on for forty years now, and I've never known engines like these. Poor workmanship from the outset. The Americans built her in a hurry and they made a pretty poor job of it, if I may say so. She's given me more problems in a few months than anything else gave me in years. At the moment it's the condensers. We've also had a lot of trouble with the fuel. The Americans use a different system from us. When the tanks are empty, they pump seawater straight in to compensate, instead of having entirely separate ballast tanks as we do ourselves. In theory the next lot of oil should go to the top of the tanks, being lighter, and the water can be drained off, and there shouldn't be any significant contamination of the fuel, but in practice it's causing us a lot of problems.

'I've spoken to various American engineers when I've been able to, and they say that it shouldn't cause any real problems as long as the fuel has time to settle, so that the two are well separated, and we drain the water out before sailing. The difficulty then is that we're in and out so fast we don't have the time for settling. Ultimately, the only way to deal with it is a major modification, converting some of the fuel tanks to ballast or at least improving the links between tanks so we can pump fuel from one tank to another more efficiently and so cut down the amount of ballast we need. But Their Lordships are unlikely to wear that at the moment. Have you time to see where we're working, sir?'

Chief appeared to find it a pleasant surprise that a senior officer of the executive branch was prepared to give him a hearing. He led Thurston back through the door and halted abreast one of the turbines, stripped of its outer casing and worked on by several men with hammers and chisels.

'We got the broken blades off yesterday and we're now taking more blades off the affected rings to even things up. Eventually, it'll all be filed down smooth. Ideally, we would put complete new rings in where necessary but we won't manage that this time.'

'Have you had any trouble getting spares, Chief?'

'Not as yet. The dockyard engineer officer would like to run and hide when he sees me coming, but he can usually find me what I need, eventually.'

They watched one of the men at work with his chisel, cursing under his breath and seemingly oblivious to their presence. His dark hair was lank, his face marked by blackheads, a rag was tied around his head to stop the sweat from trickling into his eyes. Surprisingly, his shoulder straps bore the interlocked single ring of a sub-lieutenant RNR.

'We haven't any ERAs in this ship,' the Chief explained. 'Shepherd here is a junior engineer, Merchant Navy, uncertificated as yet. We have about twenty-five of them. Some are a bit rough and ready, but they're good lads.'

The Commander looked at Shepherd with a pained expression. 'They may be good lads, Chief, but I do wish you would remind them that they shouldn't be coming into the wardroom for meals in their *disgusting* overalls.'

'On the one occasion when that happened, I could only manage to give my lads half an hour for lunch, and even you couldn't expect them to spend all that time cleaning up before they sat down to eat.'

The Chief smiled in a fatherly manner. To have been forty years a marine engineer he must have been in his early sixties, and he looked it, ruddy-faced and a little burly, his cap pushed back far enough to reveal off-white hair and a pair of unexpectedly black eyebrows. His slightly old-fashioned air was further borne out by the wing collar he was wearing and a uniform jacket with the buttons very wide apart and the lapels higher placed than normal. But, old-fashioned or not, he evidently knew his job.

25

When Thurston got back to his cabin he found that Spencer had arrived off the overnight train, and was creating organised chaos first from Thurston's kit and then his own.

'Bit different to what we're used to, sir, innit. Right soft lot, these. Bunks all round, soda fountain on board, whatever *that* is, even a bloody laundry. Just what you'd expect from the Yanks.'

Thurston's tin case and kitbag had disgorged their contents over the available flat surfaces of the sleeping cabin and Spencer was on his knees in the centre of the muddle, sifting through it apparently at random, occasionally rocking back on his heels, musing for a time and then moving something from the carpet to a stowage. It was good to see him again, bulging comfortably out of his blue jumper, cap ribbon tied in a distinctly non-regulation fancy bow over his left eye, three good conduct badges decorating his sleeve, and to listen to him murdering the English language in his familiar fashion.

Spencer had been with him in *Marathon* and in *Connaught* before that, having been allocated to him as a temporary substitute for a steward and been content to stay in the job ever since. He was somewhere in his late thirties, with twenty years' service behind him, had found a niche in the service which suited him, and marked time in barracks while Thurston was ashore, no doubt engaging in a little bribery to ensure that he was not sent on draft unless and until he was ready.

'Don't do anything about the books, Spencer, I'll sort them out myself later.' Spencer moved a pile of shirts from carpet to bunk, placed a sheaf of their collars on top, stood up, and dusted his hands on his trousers. 'How about a cuppa coffee while you're waiting for lunch, sir?'

Without waiting for an answer, Spencer went into the pantry, filled a kettle and put it on, instantly at home. 'Mrs Thurston keeping well, sir?' he called out through the open door.

He hesitated a moment before telling Spencer. 'Very well. She's having another baby.'

'Good for you, sir.' Spencer emerged with the coffee, and a mug of tea for himself.

'It's a bit early for that. It's not due until April.'

A number of his contemporaries had waited for the fourth stripe before embarking on marriage, and were now busily making up for lost time, but even so he had to admit that it wasn't bad going to be a prospective father again at forty-four.

Spencer stirred some sugar into his tea. 'I got some news as well, sir. I'm getting spliced.'

'Are you?' Thurston took a moment to recover from his surprise. 'Who is the lady?'

'Her name's Rose Parker, sir. I call her Rosie. She's a widow – North Africa. Lives up the road from me mum. I've known her since we were little kids. Got two little girls, seven and five. They're gorgeous.'

'And no doubt you spoil them to death.'

'That's just what Rosie says.' Spencer was unabashed. 'When I was on leave after we got back from the Med, I used to go round and see her, and take her out. She likes to go dancing, and to the pictures. I took her to *Gone With The Wind* and she cried all through it, and kept saying it was the most beautiful film she'd ever seen. And then I went round to see her when I went to me mum's on weekends from barracks, and then it got so I was going to Mum's 'cause I wanted to see Rosie. Mum used to babysit for the girls.' He took a dog-eared and already much-studied photograph from his wallet. 'There she is, sir.'

'Very nice.' The photograph showed a pleasant-faced woman in a sensible print frock, standing in front of a garden fence. 'Too good for you, Spencer.'

'Yes, sir, I know. Lovely cook too. You haven't lived till you've tasted her apple pie.'

'You look as though you've been on good pasture.'

Spencer patted his generous belly. 'Could live on that for a week or two, sir. Might come in handy where we're going.' Then, more formally: 'Rosie and me hope you and Mrs Thurston'll be coming to the wedding.'

'When is it?'

Spencer sighed. 'That's the trouble. Rosie says we can't get married 'til I've got me hook back. I did get it back, while I was in barracks, but then I got in a fight with these two RAF blokes, me and another fellow, and I lost it again. One of 'em started saying that all matelots are nancy boys and I couldn't let 'im get away with it.'

'Drunk again?' It was one of several variations on a not-unfamiliar theme.

'Not especially, sir. But it *was* closing time. Rosie wasn't very pleased, specially as I got my leave stopped and couldn't go and see her that weekend. 'Course there was no way of telling her 'til after, and she'd got her hair done and everything. She says it's about time I settled down and thought about my responsibilities, if I'm going to have her and the girls. She says they can't have a stepfather who gets into fights. So we've got to wait another four months at least. But,' he said more cheerfully, 'at least it'll give Rosie time to save up the points to make

27

a proper cake, and to get the dress made. She's doing it herself, the dress, and dresses for the girls so they can be bridesmaids.'

'She sounds quite a paragon. Worth keeping your nose clean for. Though why she wants to take on a rogue like you,' he said affectionately.

'Beats me too sometimes, sir.' Spencer drank the remains of his tea, picked up Thurston's empty cup. 'Better get this lot finished. Proper chatty ship, this. Mind, I was getting sick of barracks. Full of sprogs and barrack stanchions.' He picked up the same pile of shirts and contemplated them once more. 'Glad to be out of it.'

'Clear lower deck. All hands muster on the flight deck. Clear lower deck.'

'Another fucking pep talk. Come on, Charlie. Let's hope this bugger don't go on too long.'

Metcalfe and the three-badger straggled out into the open air, to join the swelling throng of men already there, some extinguishing cigarettes and hastily concealing butts which would be re-used later.

An exchange of salutes. 'Ship's company present and correct, sir.'

They watched the new Captain climb the ladder leading to the 'goofing' platform on the port side of the island. 'So that's the bugger,' the three-badger muttered.

The Captain waited for a gust to pass before he began speaking. 'You've all heard a lot of pep talks before, so I'm not going to keep you for very long.'

'Hope not,' Stripey muttered.

'My name is Thurston and I am now in command of this ship.'

'Thank you for telling us.'

A Petty Officer turned his head and whispered fiercely down the ranks from one side of his mouth, 'If I hear your voice once more, Sutcliffe, you'll be having the pleasure of a personal meeting with Captain Thurston. Across the defaulters' table!'

'Now I can see what you all look like, and you can see what I look like.' His eyes seemed to fix themselves on Metcalfe. 'This ship has gone through a difficult period and she has become almost a byword for things going wrong. But from this point on, that is going to change. What's past is past and we are going to work together to sort things out, and that means a hundred per cent effort from every one of us, and a new spirit that all the gremlins of the past can be beaten.'

'Like the way he says us. The only new spirit this fucking scow needs is a few hundred gallons of aviation spirit and a match!'

'Sutcliffe, you've had your warning!'

The Captain had to raise his voice above the wind. 'You each have a job to do and every one of you has a part to play in making this an efficient and happy ship. The most important thing is that you know your own job thoroughly, and know how it fits in with the man next to you. There is no room aboard this ship for passengers. Unless everybody pulls together and gives that hundred per cent effort, we might as well stay in harbour and play cards.'

'Would that we could,' someone else said.

'You have all come from a lot of different places, and most of you would not be in the Navy but for the war. That doesn't matter. The important thing is that you do your job, whatever that job is, and do it thoroughly, even when you're wet through and chocker and you've just thrown up your breakfast.' The last brought a reward in a ripple of laughter. 'That is all I have to say.'

'Gawd, we've heard all that before,' said Sutcliffe after the Petty Officer had taken his name. 'Pigs sit back and leave us to do all the work, and bleat on about how we must all pull together.' He produced a parody of an officer's voice.

'I thought it was quite good.'

'Short, that's the main thing. But all flannel. You're letting yourself be dazzled by those medals, Charlie boy. I'll believe it when we see him puke.'

Thurston sent for Lieutenant Higgins that evening. He would normally have done it much earlier, but perhaps there were advantages in leaving him to stew for a time.

He pushed a pile of papers to one side. 'Do you know why you're here?' he said at last.

'Yes, sir.'

'It is customary, I understand, for the Officer of the Watch to be at the gangway when the Captain, or indeed anybody else, comes aboard. When I arrived on board during your watch I found the gangway sentry half-asleep, the quartermaster of the watch stuffing his face with Cornish pasty, and you, supposedly the Officer of the Watch, absent from your post and taking part in an unauthorised and distinctly vulgar entertainment in the wardroom.'

Higgins studied the pattern on the carpet. 'Yes, sir.'

'If you have any excuse, make it.'

Higgins swallowed hard. 'No excuse, sir.'

'At least you've got that much sense. Mr Higgins, it is rather remark-

29

able that the first thing I find on arrival aboard this ship is one of her officers in dereliction of duty. I do not intend to take any action against the two ratings since they were quite clearly taking their cue from you. You have made a very poor start, Mr Higgins. This will not happen again.' Thurston was resting his forearms on the desk top so that the four rings were on display. Higgins, standing at attention, cap beneath his left arm, was trying not to fidget.

'No, sir.'

'This reprimand, and the reason for it, will be entered in the log, and will therefore remain on your record. If you had any thoughts of a permanent commission after the war you can forget them. You're lucky that I don't put you over the side here and now.'

'Yes, sir.'

'You will initial the entry in the log when the fair copy is written up, and rest assured that you will be most severely dealt with if anything like this should happen again. You may go.'

'Sir.'

'One other thing, Mr Higgins. When I see you again you will have had your hair cut.'

Higgins gulped. 'Aye aye, sir.'

3

It was not so surprising that Their Lordships of the Admiralty had been in no particular hurry to give him another command. The medical branch might have given Captain Thurston a clean bill of health, but the executive side had every right to question whether a man who had broken down once was likely to do so again, or whether he was capable of turning a revolver on himself during one of those long nights alone in his sea cabin. He had keeled over finally the day after *Marathon* reached Alexandria under tow after the torpedo hit, and been found by Spencer collapsed across his desk in what the psychiatrist's report described as a state of weepy incoherence. Ten days later he had taken his razor into a hospital bathroom and cut his left wrist to the bone. Exhaustion from the six days on tow, coming on top of the accumulated strains of three years' active service and delayed reaction from *Connaught*'s sinking. It could have happened to anybody. But still they were not prepared to trust him again.

It all seemed a long time ago, and longer still across the chasm of hospital and sick leave. He had left Alexandria expecting to be back on duty soon enough. Three months' leave, plenty of exercise and fresh air and the comforts of home and wife. The psychiatrist had been encouraging on the only occasion Thurston managed to pin him down to a discussion of his future in the service. 'No medical reason why you shouldn't carry on your career as before. In any case, the Navy can hardly afford to jettison experienced commanders at this stage of the war.'

But it hadn't worked out quite like that. The orthopaedic surgeon in England decided that another operation was necessary if the full function of his left hand was to be restored. 'We'll simply take a piece of tendon from somewhere you won't miss it, and graft it into place. Come in next week and we'll get it done then.' The surgeon drew him a diagram to show where the graft would go, and assured him it was all quite routine nowadays. 'Nothing untoward. We'll have you out in a week.'

Indeed, the operation itself went as expected. But he who was never ill, beyond a nuisance bout of malaria, picked up some hospital infection, the operation wound went septic and burst open at three o'clock one morning after four days of increasing pain and a fever touched with delirium. They told him later, after the graft had been done again, that had it not been for the M & B they had injected in copious quantities into his left buttock, he might well have lost the arm. So it was that as May and June passed, when he had expected to be fully fit once more and back in harness, he was sitting around at home with his arm in plaster and then going into Haslar every morning for physiotherapy. There were black intervals, perhaps brought on by the M & B, when it seemed that the breakdown was happening all over again, that there had been only a temporary respite and a brittle and illusory sense of recovery, in the depths of which he would wonder whether he should have gone for the throat and made certain.

But as the arm strengthened and the sickness receded, his spirits rose; he went for long walks with the dog and used his son's bicycle to explore further afield. He grew impatient to be back at sea, back in the real world from which he had been separated for so long, but it seemed that all he could be trusted with was sitting in judgement over offenders tried by court martial, and giving those fresh-faced boys the thrill of being interviewed for Dartmouth by Thurston, VC.

'Why do you want to join the Navy?'

'To serve my country, sir,' he had told them at his own interview, togged up in his best suit aged twelve years and seven months, 'and to make something of myself.' It seemed bitterly ironic now.

'What games do you play?'

'Cricket and rugger, sir, and a bit of hockey.'

'What will you do if you don't get in?'

'Have another try, I suppose, sir.'

Nothing much had changed in thirty years. The faces of the selection board were altered, but the composition was the same: an admiral, a post-captain, the headmaster of a prep school and a senior civil servant. The candidates were much the same mixture of the intelligent and not so intelligent, the self-possessed and the slightly shy, and the ones who should never have been there in the first place; those who themselves had decided on a naval career and those whose parents had decided for them. There were timeless discussions on the marks to be awarded to candidates of whom the headmaster thought highly but the admiral had taken against. They were well coached, these aspiring admirals, with the proper answers at their fingertips, having carefully counted the number of steps up to the main entrance, and checked the colour of the hall porter's hair, providing few surprises, apart from one boy who brazenly declared, 'I want to be an admiral,' when asked his reasons for wanting to join the Navy; first fifteen rugby players, first eleven cricketers, collectors of stamps and, less frequently, coins, with fathers who were serving officers or solid professional men, and carefully worded recommendations from the headmasters of their prep schools.

Kate insisted that there was no point in his getting worked up and making himself ill again, that the Admiralty was being thoroughly sensible in easing him back into full duty slowly, after a long spell on the sick list, but Thurston could himself being shunted away to the sidelines, useful only as a kind of figure head on the basis of his past record and his decorations, but not to be trusted any more with real responsibility, whether at sea or ashore. At length he had requested an interview with the Naval Secretary, on a day when the board had finished with a batch of candidates by lunchtime, and asked him point-blank for a seagoing appointment, wondering whether the truth would come out, that the service had no further use for him.

'I don't know how many captains I've got begging me for ships, thinking I can conjure them out of thin air. Hardly a sensible thing to do, slashing your wrists.'

'Sir, I am fit.'

'I also have a continuous stream of crocks through this office, all of whom say just that, and then they beard me at the club when I go there for a bit of peace. Are you sure?'

'Quite sure, sir.'

'Well, I suppose you're not actually foaming at the mouth. What do the medical people say?'

'That I'm fit.'

'You don't have to go back to sea, you know. You've had a lot of sea time and I can find you plenty of work ashore.'

There was a dry rustle of paper as the Admiral unfolded the medical board's report, put on a pair of spectacles and began to read. Thurston knew it by heart now. He glanced at the pictures on the walls, trying to distract himself while the Naval Secretary decided his fate.

'Hm. I suppose they know what they're talking about.' The Admiral took off the spectacles, put them away in their case. 'All right. Go away and enjoy the fine weather and I'll see what I can find you. Any preferences?'

'As long as she floats.'

'Selling yourself a bit short, with a record like yours.' The Admiral's gaze settled momentarily on the red ribbon. 'Still, it makes things simpler. And you'll take a pierhead jump? Good. Now get out of my sight before I think the better of it.'

On the way out he surprised a passing Wren by flinging his cap in the air, and said something encouraging to the Naval Secretary's next petitioner, a fellow post-captain with a disfiguring scar from one temple to the corner of his mouth, and a right eye which was made of glass.

The interview with the Naval Secretary set off a rare serious row when he told Kate about it that evening. He had expected disappointment, perhaps some harsh words, since in the last few months she had made little secret of her opinion that he was long overdue for a job ashore, preferably near home, 'Where I might be able to convince myself that I've actually got a husband,' but he was unprepared for the strength of her reaction.

'You haven't changed your ideas one jot. You won't be satisfied until you're going over the side in a hammock with the bugles sounding the last post over your heroic dead body. You can't even be content with having the Germans try to kill you!' It was the only reference of that kind she had ever made to his attempt to kill himself. 'And nothing but a picture on the wall to show your child who fathered him. Or her, since it's as likely that it'll be a girl.'

He was standing next to the window, changing out of his uniform, taking out his cufflinks and placing them on the chest of drawers. 'What do you mean?'

'You've obviously forgotten how to count, because I'm ten days overdue, and in case you don't remember, the last time that happened it was Helen.'

He came round to where she was standing, and put his arms round her from behind.

She tried to shake herself free. 'Oh get away from me, you great oaf.' But he held on and after a moment she sagged forwards and suddenly began to cry. 'Leave me alone. I'll be all right in a minute.'

He steered her towards the bed, then lay down beside her, settled her against his chest and found her his handkerchief.

' . . . if you knew what it was like, being stuck here by myself wondering all the time where you were, and even sometimes whether you were still alive, and every time I see a telegraph boy, whether he's on his way here. Helen's marvellous, of course, but . . . she's too young, and she's got her exams to think of . . . And everyone in this road is in the same position, so we can never say anything, and now there's George as well.' It was all coming out in a rush.

'It's not like that all the time,' she insisted, more brightly. 'You can forget about it, quite a lot, but it's still there, just under the surface, and when the news is on, and at the cinema and when I open the newspaper . . . As much what they don't say as what they put in . . . All those little notices. "The Admiralty regrets to announce . . ." weeks after it's actually happened . . . I shouldn't be so silly. It's time I was used to it . . . But Mother told me it was just the same when Daddy was in France, even when he was a divisional commander. He used to go wandering about the front-line trenches with his ADC . . . She said that worried her more than anything, the thought of something happening to him when he needn't have been there anyway . . . She never let any of that slip, when we were children.' She was silent for a time, mopping at her face with the handkerchief. 'I wish you'd told me you were going to see the Naval Secretary.'

'What do you want to call the baby?'

She looked up and smiled. 'Esmeralda.'

'Never! That's a name for gipsies.'

'Harriet then.'

He was sure now that Kate was joking. 'I refuse to be the father of a Harriet. And what if it's a boy?'

She considered. 'Horatio, since his father's got the Navy on the brain.'

'Naval it may be, but you're not doing that to any son of mine.' He kissed her, finding her mouth still wet and salty from the crying.

'You are pleased?'

'Of course I am. Just surprised.' Having produced two children within two years of their marriage they had taken precautions ever since, but since George was seventeen and a midshipman, and Helen sixteen, the precautions had become more a matter of habit than anything else.

'You men! It's all your fault, do you realise?'

'I should hope so.' They both laughed, and kissed again.

'Don't go saying we can't afford another child.'

'I still don't know how we managed to afford the other two. And what are they going to think?'

'George will probably think the whole idea disgusting, and Helen will be fascinated.'

'She'll be hoping to try out the drill for emergency childbirth.'

Helen had long ago declared it her ambition to become a doctor. It was a family joke that her dolls had spent all their time in bandages.

'Are you all right now?'

She nodded. He found himself aroused by the contact with her. 'Shall we make sure about this baby?'

4

On his first evening aboard Thurston was invited into the wardroom for a drink before dinner, a formal, rather stiff occasion, however much the Commander tried to pass it off as an opportunity for the officers to meet the new Captain, and for the new Captain to meet them, on a relatively relaxed basis. The Commander introduced each one in turn, in order of branch and seniority, Thurston shook his hand, asked the officer about his job aboard *Crusader*, where he had come from and what he had done in civilian life. He consumed two small whiskies, and departed after the requisite hour for his own cabin and solitary meal, and an hour with the personal files afterwards. Another night he had the Commander to dinner and they cracked a bottle of wine over a discussion of the ship's history to date; he ascertained that his secretary was a keen squash player and had a game with him. That was the extent of his off-duty relations with his officers, and that was as it should be.

A post-captain in command had, in the trite phrase, almost the power of life and death over his ship's company. He could, subject only to rubber-stamping by higher authority, sentence a man to ninety days in a service detention barracks, or ninety days in a civilian prison, deprive him of his rate and/or his good conduct badges, or dismiss him from the service with disgrace; he could sentence a boy rating to twelve cuts with the cane or twenty-four with the birch. Aboard his own ship his power was virtually absolute. He could, if he chose, alter the entire routine of the ship, have every man doing pack drill and justify it on the grounds of physical fitness. He could go ashore whenever he chose; he could, if he chose, never set foot aboard at all when in harbour. He had a personal steward to attend to his bodily needs, and sufficient living space to house a couple of dozen ratings. He could deny access to his ship to the King himself – it had been done. But with that power came responsibility, and the power was only there to make possible the meeting of that responsibility. Battalion commanders surrendered their units quite regularly, but only one ship's captain had struck his colours to the enemy since the War of 1812, and he would answer for his action at a court martial on his return from prison camp.

He want over to Machrihanish for half a day to see the aircrew for himself, discovered there were distinct advantages to commanding a carrier. Machrihanish was at the southern tip of the Mull of Kintyre, only about sixty miles away, but a good hundred and fifty by road or rail.

'No problem, sir,' said Commander (Flying). 'I'll give them a ring and get them to send a Stringbag. Shouldn't take more than an hour, even with the wind against us.'

'Now this is the parachute harness, and it's got to be good and tight because if it isn't you're going to come down singing "Oh, For the Wings of a Dove," sir.' The rating gave a jerk at each of the straps in turn. 'That's better, sir. If you can stand up straight it's not tight enough. Now the G-string hooks on there, so you won't fall out of the aircraft, or if you do, you'll just dangle there in space instead of finishing up on the ground like strawberry jam. The 'chute stows under your seat, and when you need to use it, you just 'ook it on these rings on your chest, and make sure it's the right way up or you won't be able to find the ripcord. And when you jump, you say "Abracadabra, one . . . two . . . three," slowly, like that, so you're well clear of the kite before you pull the ripcord. And if the 'chute don't open, you can bring it back to the stores and change it for another one!'

It was a morning of broken cloud and intermittent sunshine as the Swordfish droned westward across the Clyde estuary. 'She goes very slowly, but she goes on for ever,' the pilot told Thurston through the intercom. He was the squadron's senior pilot, generally a Seafire man, 'but she's good to fly and the CO wanted to send someone who wouldn't get lost.'

Lieutenant James was in his early thirties, with balding fair hair and a beard which was a shade or two nearer ginger, a solicitor in Darlington in civilian life. 'I did quite a lot of gliding before the war – could never afford to learn to fly on powered aircraft – so the war was my chance. The RAF said I was too old and would only take me as a gunner, so I joined the Navy.'

Thurston rested his forearms on the cockpit rim, head and shoulders out in the slipstream, enjoying the keen air and the view unfolding a couple of thousand feet below. The observer's cockpit where he sat was a clutter of radar equipment, leaving him insufficient room to move without knocking against something, but the radar display itself was tiny, barely six inches square.

'I'm sorry, sir, you'll have to get one of the operators to explain it to you,' said James. 'Most of them were recruited specially and they're the only people who understand it.'

Commander (Flying) made the introductions, Thurston shook more hands, had a small petty officer with a degree in Natural Philosophy from Aberdeen take him over the radar set, had lunch, a talk with the squadron commander, a former architect named Bernard Mann, and flew back to Greenock.

'Right, young Metcalfe, you'll do. You've got yourself a cushy little number, if you keep your nose clean and measure up. The Captain wants a sprog OD to be his messenger, and you're not much use for anything, so you fit the description.' Metcalfe hurriedly pulled at the hem of his jumper, hauled his lanyard taut, wondering whether the Master-At-Arms had picked him out specially, but fearing that he had been chosen on the grounds that anyone would do.

'Ordinary Seaman Metcalfe, sir.'

Metcalfe felt the silent scrutiny of the Captain's grey eyes.

'I've seen you before.'

He had thought he might get away with it. After all, it had been pitch dark. 'Yessir,' he said in embarrassment, his eyes going down to the carpet.

The Captain looked at him intently. 'You won't forget again.' It was a statement more than a question.

'Nossir.'

'You know your way around the ship?'

'Yessir.'

'So if I sent you with a message for the Gunnery Officer, you would know who he is and where to find him?'

'Yessir.'

The Captain extended his hands on top of the desk, contracted both into fists before moving them out of sight. 'All right then. Thank you, Master, that'll be all.'

He asked Metcalfe where he came from, how long he had been in the Navy: 'Five months, sir,' what he had done in civilian life: 'Delivered for a butcher, sir.'

'So the Master-At-Arms picked the right man.' The Captain picked up a pen from the desk. 'If you go into the pantry, Spencer will show you the ropes.'

'Don't let the Old Man frighten you,' Spencer told him. 'He can be a bit fierce, but he's all right. Mind, you'd better get your thatch cut,' he looked Metcalfe up and down, 'and you'll *have* to do something about that suit. The Old Man's a terror for turnout.'

Spencer was pressing a pair of the Captain's trousers, satisfying gushes of steam rising from the ironing board, creating a comfortably humid atmosphere in the small compartment, which took Metcalfe back for a moment to his mam's kitchen at home. Mondays she did the washing; Tuesdays when he came home from school and, later, from delivering meat for Milburn's Family Butcher she was doing the ironing, working with one flat iron while a second was heating on the old black range which lined most of one wall. ''Ere, give me that suit and I'll show you how. Go on, once I've finished these. It won't take a minute.'

He stood in the pantry in his flannel, boots and underpants, faintly embarrassed, listening to Spencer's talk. 'Seven horizontal creases, and the difficult bit is getting them the same level on both legs. And if you want the creases really sharp, you go over them again through brown paper, like I did with the Old Man's. *Not* newspaper, 'cos the print comes off. . . . Got the time, Charlie? Right, it'll just be time for the Old Man's tea when we've finished this, and then we'll have ours. D'ye like ginger nuts?' Spencer completed his pressing, unplugged the iron, watched Metcalfe dress.

'There you are. You might look like a matelot in about a million years' time. Now you know how to do it yourself.' He opened the pantry door. 'Toast or cake, sir?'

'Toast, please, Spencer.'

'Good thing too, 'cos I haven't got any cake made,' Spencer confided to Metcalfe. He put the kettle on, cut several slices of bread and put them under the grill, and set out a tray with a teapot, cup and saucer, milk and sugar, a dish of butter, one pot of raspberry jam and one of blackcurrant. 'The Old Man has either toast or cake, never both. I've been with him in three ships now, counting this one, so you might say I know his habits. You got yourself a cushy number, Charlie, but you'll have to work for it.'

It was pleasant to sit in the pantry with a mug of tea, as much hot toast and as many ginger nuts as he felt like eating. Back in his mess there would be no toast, only indifferent wads on good days, and the tea half cold by the time it got to them.

' . . . You don't want to believe everything the papers say, Charlie, but that's all true, at any rate. Got 'is face smashed up and hit in the shoulder as well, blood all over the shop, and he wouldn't have the

39

doctor or nothing. When you see him with his shirt off, he's got one scar in front, 'bout that size,' Spencer indicated with a finger and thumb, 'and a great jagged one at the back where the splinter came out . . . He was in a rare old state afterwards, couldn't talk or do nothing. I 'ad to look after him. You could 'ardly see him for the bandages.'

Metcalfe was impressed, but Sutcliffe poured scorn on him when he returned to the mess.

'Captain's messenger? You poor little squirt. You'll go chasing all over the ship looking for some pig or other, and then by the time you've found the right one the flap'll all be over, and you needn't have gone in the first place. Look at you, Charlie, Captain's bugger boy in return for a few measly ginger nuts! God, they bought you cheap!'

For once Metcalfe didn't care what Sutcliffe thought.

'Captain, sir. I have Inspector Mackay of the civil police on the line. He refuses to speak to anybody else.'

'Put him on.'

Thurston heard the operator speaking to the voice at the other end, then the policeman came on. 'Good evening, Captain. I have four of your men in my cells this meenute and I shall take them before the police court tomorrow morning unless you make the proper arrangements to deal with them. Drunk and disorderly, assaulting the proprietor of the Loch Lomond Hotel – a most respectable establishment. I have their names here: Grey, Leading Stoker; Murray, Stoker First Class; Johnson, Stoker First Class; Watson, Stoker First Class. First Class Stokers they may be, Captain Owen. . . . .'

'Thurston.'

'Captain Thurston. First Class Stokers they may be, but their conduct on this occasion has been much less than first class.' The Inspector continued in his slow West Highland voice. 'I must remind you that all your men are banned from the Loch Lomond, and from all the better establishments in the town, after the trouble there in the summer, but these men of yours went into the private bar nonetheless, and when the proprietor, Mr Douglas Matheson, quite properly refused them service, the man Murray assaulted him. There has been far too much of this sort of behaviour, Captain Thurston, and on this occasion I will not release them into service custody until I have your assurance that they will be dealt with according to the full rigour of the law.'

Thurston sensed the Inspector drawing himself up to his full height.

40

'I'll have an escort sent for them, and they will be charged as defaulters, provided there is sufficient evidence against them, yes.'

'Sufficient case against them? Captain Thurston, you have not seen the face of the proprietor, Mr Matheson; and the man Jenkins has been in my cells not two months ago. For the good of the civil population I cannot release these men without your assurance that they will be most severely dealt with.'

'I will send an escort for them,' Thurston said again, 'and they will be charged if their offences warrant it, but I am not in a position to give any assurances without the full details to hand.'

Mackay seemed to admit defeat, and to make the best of his situation. 'Indeed, and will you be sending the escort at once. I cannot be having my cells filled with drunken sailors.'

'Thank you. Goodnight,' Thurston said firmly, and put the telephone down before the Inspector had a chance to reply.

'And now, what did Mackay mean when he talked about the trouble in the summer?' Thurston asked Scott the next morning.

'That's well known, sir. The Loch Lomond's a very quiet place. Matheson, the landlord, is an elder of the kirk and a councillor and, quite honestly, I wouldn't be embarrassed to take my maiden aunt in there for a drink. And because it's so quiet, some of the men took to going there so they could have a drink in peace. Most of the bars in the town are pretty rough.'

'I know. I have been here before,' Thurston said gently.

'Yes, sir. Well, some of the rougher elements found out about this – it didn't take them very long – and went over there one night looking for trouble. They thought the Loch Lomond needed livening up.'

'I can imagine.'

'It was quite a lively evening by all accounts. Matheson sent us a huge bill for broken glasses – said he couldn't get replacements in wartime, all the sob stuff. One of the stokers knocked another down on top of the provost's wife. The civil police got there before the patrol and took the whole lot into custody, including a couple of our telegraphists who'd managed to sit there drinking lemonade or something while the riot went on around them, once the troublemakers finished resisting arrest. Matheson banned every matelot from the place, and all his pals did from theirs, of course, but there is one element which seems to take a ban as a red rag to a bull, there have been a few incidents, and Mackay's been gunning for our people ever since. He only has to hear the word *Crusader*, sir.'

41

5

'Hands to stations for leaving harbour. Special Sea Dutymen close up.'

The tannoy clicked off audibly at the end of the pipe. Ratings began to assemble on the flight deck, chinstays down, the wind flapping their collars, a slash of cold rain coming with it. As yet it was barely light and a lowering sky, with cloud dragging across the hills beyond the Clyde, promised more rain.

'Single up to the stern wire.'

Waiting to take *Crusader* away from the dockside and out of harbour for the first time, Thurston felt a mixture of excitement and tension, both of which had to be concealed from the bridge personnel around him. *Crusader*, with her single screw, would handle quite differently from any other ship he had served in. She lacked a cruiser's reassurance of sixty thousand horsepower in reserve, though she was twice *Marathon*'s displacement, and her high sides would act as a sail in any crosswind. The Navigator had quietly suggested that he take her out, this time only, so Thurston could see how she handled, but to do it himself was another part of the pattern.

Years ago he had broken his right leg in a fall with a young horse of his father's, and had afterwards to steel himself to get back on the animal and put him at the same gate again. It took most of an afternoon, because the horse also remembered. So he had thanked Lieutenant Beveridge for his offer, and chaffed him gently that he hoped he wouldn't spoil his paintwork. Beveridge was standing at his shoulder now, a solid presence bulked out by duffel coat and other foul-weather gear. Unlike many, who were badged RNR simply because they were Merchant Navy officers in peacetime, and so professional seamen, Beveridge had served his year as a midshipman RNR and a few weeks' training with the Fleet every subsequent year, mostly spent, surprisingly, in submarines. He was about thirty, and due for his half-stripe in the next few months, then possibly a command of his own.

'Singled up to the stern wire, sir.'

The Officer of the Watch, on the other hand, was an RNVR sub-lieutenant, commissioned six months and qualified as a watchkeeper more recently still. He sounded nervous. No more nervous than his captain, if he did but know it.

'Thank you, Mr Vincent. Carry on.'

'Aye aye, sir.'

After a week aboard Thurston was becoming able to put names to an increasing number of faces, but most of *Crusader*'s six hundred-odd men were still no more than names on the muster roll. As usual, the ones who came most easily to mind were the troublemakers: Lieutenant Higgins, and the four stokers who had fallen foul of Inspector Mackay.

'Chief Quartermaster on the wheel, sir.'

The repairs to the damaged plates had been completed the day before, and hardly were the dockyard workmen ashore when *Crusader*'s sailing orders arrived, by hand of an attractive Wren Third Officer who had to brave a barrage of wolf whistles. The ship was to rendezvous with an escort group sailing from Londonderry and co-operate with its Senior Officer in a search for U-boats. 'We want to deal with the blighters before they have a chance to get near the convoys,' the Admiral told Thurston. 'You won't be constrained by having to stay with the merchant ships, and you can concentrate all your energies on sinking U-boats. If anything does get past you, the escorts with the convoys will be there to deal with them.'

In response to his orders *Crusader* cast off the final wire joining her to the land, the water turned to discoloured foam as she began to move away from the dockside. Take it gently this time; remember you can't steer this one with engines. Thurston felt the crosswind catch her, put on a nudge of port wheel to counter it. He heard the calm voice of the Chief Quartermaster check back the order, felt the ship respond. Down on the flight deck the bo'sun's call sounded the Still, returning the salute of a corvette which was remaining in harbour.

'One-one-oh revolutions.'

'One-one-oh revolutions,' repeated Vincent diffidently.

Past an old battleship, *Oudenarde*, in which Thurston had spent eight months as a bored, restless and finally rebellious midshipman after Jutland, and whose Captain was senior to him by six years and must be saluted. The Still sounded again, he raised his right hand to the peak of his cap, heard the bugle's deeper note coming back, made ragged by the wind. He made a mental note to find out whether *Crusader* had a competent bugler on board – the establishment did not provide for one, but there was probably a man aboard who knew the calls – then moved to the voicepipe again as the Firth began to bend.

'Port twenty.'

'Port twenty, sir.'

Rounding the bend, *Crusader* met the first swell coming in from the open sea and began to roll, a fresh lash of rain crossed his left cheek. He had the feel of her now, he was beginning to enjoy himself, though she was a carthorse after *Marathon*, or even *Connaught*, which had handled like a cantankerous dowager rather than a thoroughbred.

'Midships. Steer two-four-seven.'

'Midships, sir. Wheel amidships. Course two-four-seven, sir.'

The last time he had sailed the Clyde was in *Marathon*, a long two years ago, under orders for the Mediterranean when her repairs from the *Seydlitz* action had been completed. Steer her a little to port again, the crosswind was trying to push her towards the line of buoys which marked the limits of the swept channel. Another salute, from an armed trawler over to starboard. Thurston was aware that Beveridge was watching him, sizing him up, and Vincent too, but in quite a different way. No doubt Vincent had read all the newspaper reports, and the VC citation which the more serious newspapers had printed in full, that *Marathon* had played cat-and-mouse with *Seydlitz* through the midnight twilight of the Denmark Strait in high summer, taken a direct hit on B turret which killed or seriously wounded nearly a fifth of her complement, that her Captain had remained in command despite having his jaw broken by a shell splinter and a hole in one shoulder which could take three fingers, writing his orders for the Officer of the Watch in pencil on the back of a signal pad. He rubbed with his index finger at the short horizontal scar left by the jaw wound, itchy still. It seemed now that all that had happened to a different man, part of a life that had finally ended a year ago.

'Secure from Leaving Harbour Stations. Mr Vincent, carry on.'

'Shall I dismiss the watch below to breakfast, sir?'

'Of course.'

Thurston allowed himself a smile. Beveridge could tell the wardroom, when he went below, that the new boy seemed fairly competent, on the initial showing, in that he hadn't actually run the ship aground or collided with anything.

'How do you find her, sir?'

'She handles a bit sluggishly, but otherwise it's like riding a push bike. Something one doesn't forget in a hurry.'

Beveridge grinned back, an acknowledgement that this was something he had heard before.

Sub-Lieutenant Michael Vincent was twenty but looked younger, with dark hair which insisted on flopping forward over his eyes however much he tried to comb it back tidily and hold it in place with hair oil.

He shivered inside his duffel coat and wished it was time to hand over the watch and go to the wardroom for breakfast. He could not decide whether to be relieved that the Captain and Navigator were there to take over if anything happened, or uncomfortable under their eyes.

Until a year ago Vincent had been a trainee tax inspector with the Inland Revenue in Oxford. He had won a scholarship to grammar school at the age of eleven, then passed his School Certificate in eight subjects five years later, and nurtured dreams of staying on at school to take Highers and reading languages at university. But his headmaster did not consider him to be quite scholarship material, and his parents could not afford the fees for higher education. His father, a senior clerk in the City Hall, got him the post with the Inland Revenue, assured him that this was as good a start in life as he was likely to get. He performed his duties in the tax office as required, and attended the necessary courses at night school two evenings a week, but he devoted equal energy to reading Balzac and Molière, took a French newspaper until the war made that impossible, attended a French conversation circle run by a master from his old school, and continued to dream that one day he would break free of the Inland Revenue and join the undergraduates whom he watched enviously in the city centre on Saturday afternoons.

The war began a month after Vincent started work, and might have provided an escape route, but for the first two years he was too young to be called up, and in any case the Inland Revenue constituted a reserved occupation. But as the war entered its third year, a cousin, newly returned from aircrew training in Canada, spent a couple of days of his leave in Oxford, and Vincent's mother sent them out for a drink one evening, Vincent slightly ashamed of his tax inspector's civilian suit alongside Andrew's brand-new sergeant's stripes and observer's half-wing. 'Don't you know? Once the war's over the government are going to pay ex-servicemen to go to university. In fact, the RAF are sending some chaps to university for six months when they call them up. Just get yourself out of the bloodsuckers.'

The same night he wrote a letter of resignation from the Inland Revenue, and left it on his superior's desk the next morning. But the Revenue, and the civil service in general, had had quite enough of trained and even half-trained personnel leaving by various means to join the services. 'You're far more valuable to the war effort here than as cannon fodder. It's not like the last war. You're just as much in it as you would be in uniform. You're in the Home Guard anyway. In

45

any case, the army will take one look at your qualifications and put you in the Pay Corps.'

For eight months he petitioned an increasingly testy superior each week, considered getting himself sacked, or simply disappearing and enlisting under an assumed name. The last idea he abandoned as it would cause too many upsets for his parents. Finally, when another trainee who had managed to enlist earlier in the war reappeared after being invalided out of the Royal Engineers with piles, the Revenue agreed to let him go. The RAF would take him as an aircrew cadet, but he would have to wait three months, the army told him he was ideal material for the Pay Corps, which was too similar to the job he had spent eight months getting out of. The naval recruiting officer mentioned that the Navy were now taking men with language qualifications with a view to training them as interpreters in Russian.

Since joining, however, Vincent had heard no more about his application for the Russian interpreters' course. Instead, the Navy had unexpectedly selected him as a potential officer during his basic training at a former holiday camp near Skegness; he spent three months in an old destroyer on east coast convoys before going on to *King Alfred* for his officer's training. His mother was embarrassingly proud when he went home on passing-out leave with his single wavy stripe, his rank qualified as much as it could be – Temporary Probationary Acting Sub-Lieutenant, Royal Naval Volunteer Reserve – forgetting now that she had pressed him to stay on with the Inland Revenue, especially after his cousin Andrew was posted missing on his third operation with Bomber Command.

'Alter course a point to starboard, Mr Vincent.'

'Aye aye, sir.' He bent to the voicepipe. 'Starboard twenty.'

'Starboard twenty, sir.'

The ship heeled obediently into the turn. At these moments he could feel a pride that a ten-thousand-ton carrier was responding to his commands alone.

'Midships. Steer two-six-oh.'

'Midships, sir. Wheel amidships. Course two-six-oh, sir.'

The Captain waited until he had completed the manoeuvre. 'Mr Vincent, for heaven's sake make your helm orders a bit more positively!'

Vincent's face, pale despite the wind, flushed suddenly scarlet. 'Sir,' he mumbled into his coat collar. The Navigator shot him a reassuring grin. Vincent stole a glance at his watch when the Captain was looking the other way. Only another twenty minutes.

Standing at the rear of the bridge, Ordinary Seaman Metcalfe heard the exchange and smiled to himself. For the last two days he had been Captain's messenger, *the* Captain's messenger, and he had written proudly to Dottie and then to his mam to say so. And he was chumming up with Spencer now, so he didn't need to hang round with Sutcliffe any more.

The sea was steepening, whipped up by the southerly wind funnelled through the entrance to the estuary. Sub-Lieutenant Vincent went below, relieved by Lieutenant Higgins. Thurston looked at his watch. The aircraft were due to land on off Arran, and *Crusader* was due to rendezvous with the escorts from Londonderry during the afternoon watch. Then it was back to the war.

6

'There they are!' Higgins called out.

Ten Seafires appearing out of the murk, eight in loose formation, the other two weaving behind and above them; a brief glimpse of elliptical wings as they passed overhead.

'Bring her into wind, Mr Higgins. Revolutions for seventeen knots.'

Crusader altered course to the north, the vibration increasing and the wind over her decks doubling in strength as she gradually worked up to her maximum speed.

'Wonder how long Chief can keep this up?' Higgins said to the Midshipman of the Watch, one of two midshipmen on board, confusingly named Young and Elder.

'Mr Higgins, I'll thank you to stop making clever remarks and to concentrate on the job in hand.'

'Sir.'

Thurston had the satisfaction of seeing Higgins set his teeth. With any other officer he would probably have let the remark go, but he had to admit that his first contact with Higgins had prejudiced him against him.

Commander (Flying) had arrived on the bridge, the batsman was in position on the port side of the flight deck. The arrester wires came up out of their slots in the wooden deck. The first Seafire began its approach, in a long graceful curve towards the ship's stern.

'He can't see over the aircraft's nose once it comes up, so he comes in in that sort of concave glide path so as to keep the ship in sight, and Bats of course, as long as he can,' Sterling explained.

With Higgins keeping the ship into the wind, Thurston was able to concentrate on the Seafire, now making small adjustments to port and then to starboard in response to the batsman's signals.

'Nice approach,' commented Sterling. 'Looks like Ken James. He usually gives the rest a lead.'

The Seafire was dropping gently towards the stern, making a final adjustment to its course before the long nose came up into the landing position. The batsman crossed his bats above his head. The Seafire's engine cut out, and the aircraft dropped onto the deck, bounced once before the arrester hook caught a wire which brought her up short.

'Very nice,' said Sterling.

Thurston saw that Lieutenant James was already out of his cockpit as the aircraft stopped moving, and the flight deck party were starting to move the Seafire over the lowered crash barrier and out of the way of the second aircraft, which had already peeled off from the formation to begin its approach.

The remaining nine Seafires each landed on without mishap, some as neatly as James, others more scrappily. One was sent round twice before Bats was satisfied.

'Simpson. He's never got the hang of landings,' Commander (Flying) said laconically.

Each time the flight deck party moved the new arrival out of the way, and finally one at a time onto the lift and below to the hangar. Then it was the turn of the Swordfish, which had arrived and orbited the carrier while the Seafires were landing on.

'The thing that slows us down, of course, is that we can only take them on one at a time, and that one has to be got out of the way before the next comes in, and then the lift only takes one. The limiting factor is the flight deck party, but as you see, sir, they're really not too bad.'

Thurston could see that this was the time when a carrier was at her most vulnerable, separated from the rest of the escorts and quite possibly steaming directly away from them, but committed to that course until all the aircraft were on board.

They ran into heavy weather almost before they cleared Malin Head after rendezvous with the escort group, weather which grew worse as they moved further west. *Crusader*, top-heavy with the extra weight of the flight deck and without the cargo she had been designed for, rolled her guts out, almost every man was seasick and a few were prostrated by it. Everything was wet through and nothing could be dried; there was only cold food because it was too dangerous to light the galley fires and in any case no pan would stay on the hob for more than a few seconds. Flying was impossible for a continuous period of eight days, and afterwards, when the weather moderated sufficiently to allow a Swordfish to take off – no one thought of launching the far less robust Seafires – it had to be called back ahead of time because a further worsening of the weather was forecast. Waves regularly broke over the flight deck, forty feet above the waterline, three Canadians were washed overboard from a Bofors position despite lifelines, and it was useless even to think of having one of the corvettes lower a boat for them.

After that the anti-aircraft crews were withdrawn, the sea was a far greater enemy than the Germans.

On the third night of the gale a Seafire in the deck park broke free from its lashings, and began to career back and forth as the ship pitched, being brought up short each time by the aircraft picketed around it. 'D'ye hear there? Flight deck party muster in the hangar. Flight deck party muster in the hangar.'

The night was so dark that even from the bridge, almost directly above, it was difficult to see the aircraft. What was more obvious was the noise of metal on metal as it fetched up against one of its neighbours, grinding sounds as the two were forced together, then the screech of rubber on the wooden deck as the rogue was carried away on locked wheels by the ship's motion.

'Get some lines on that thing,' the flight deck Chief Petty Officer ordered briefly.

But it was easier said than done. Two men got a hold on the starboard wingtip, but it was instantly wrenched out of their hands by a fresh roll, knocking a third man to the deck.

'Get up, Wells! Don't just lie there playing Hamlet!'

The man huddled on the wooden planking on his left side, one hand to his rib cage, face twisted in pain, swearing under his breath.

'Bust a rib? Well it's your own bloody fault, 'cos you shouldn't have been standing there like a spare prick at a wedding! Saville, take this stupid bugger below, and then come straight back here. I'm not having you sliding off as well.'

They threw a line over the fuselage in front of the tail, with men on either end trying to hold the aircraft steady, at least to slow down its crazy motion, so that the rest could attach lines to the undercarriage legs and the locking bolts which held the Seafire's folding wings open, ready to secure them to the deck rings. But the deck was treacherous with rain and spray, so that as the ship bucked and pitched the men were in danger of being swept into the water boiling forty feet below, the aircraft's momentum was too great, it continued to career wildly within the cage formed by the other aircraft, two of its propeller blades snapped off, unevenly like broken teeth, deep dents marking the underside of its nose. The two Seafires parked fore and aft had also suffered damage, one with an undercarriage leg collapsed, resting on one wingtip, which was sliding back and forth as far as the lashings would allow. The flight deck Chief Petty Officer told his men to break off, left them huddled against the base of the island, shielded from the worst of the wind, while he went up to the bridge.

50

'I'm sorry, sir.' The CPO had to shout above the wind. 'We're going to have to put her over the side. Get the rest out of the way and make enough space for her to run herself off. It means cutting one of the others loose – she would be the one right in the middle! So we'll likely lose her as well.'

'All right,' Thurston said briefly.

The flight deck Chief Petty Officer gathered his party up once more, had them check their lifelines and steered them out onto the open expanse of flight deck.

'Watts, Hall, Merritt, McEwan, come with me. The rest of you double up the lashings on the rest!'

After the brief respite the wind and motion seemed even worse, water found its way inexorably down the necks and up the sleeves of oilskins, and inside seaboots so that most of them found themselves walking on soggy sponges, flailing their arms to try to keep their balance against the ship's motion. One man ducked under each of the outside aircraft's wings, sawed with their knives at the sodden hemp cordage, stretched tight under the strain. It seemed to take many minutes before the knife blades made any impression, then the strands began to part, the remainder stretched even further, and then the final strands snapped, whipping upwards against the underside of the wing, sending fine spray over the faces of the men. Others got to work on the remaining lines, the task made more difficult now that the aircraft was beginning to shift, the rogue Seafire coming up against her each time the ship rolled to starboard. More men were at work on the remaining aircraft, struggling to pass the extra lengths of wet cordage through the deck rings which were already in use. The CPO began to cut the final lashing, now jerking taut, now slackening as the aircraft struggled to break free, his arms aching with the effort, the knife seeming to grow blunter with every stroke. Getting too old for this sort of caper, he thought to himself. The strands began to part at last, the ship rolled to starboard once more, the rogue Seafire butted into the aircraft's nose. Just a bit more, on the next starboard roll. The starboard side came up, throwing him against the fuselage, so that he lost his place on the line and had to fumble again in the darkness before he found it once more. The blade slid back and forth on the strands, seeming to make no impression on them. He swore, telling himself that someone was going to pay for not providing knives which held a proper edge. Almost there, the wet hemp gleaming faintly out of the darkness. The ship began to roll.

'Stand clear!' he shouted, waited a second for the rest to react, then

51

put his free arm up to protect his eyes, cut down blindly at the line. One of the cut ends lashed soggily across his face, he threw himself away to one side as the Seafire began to move, beneath the wing of one of the stationary aircraft. The brakes were still on, but the aircraft began to slide on locked wheels. One wingtip touched another aircraft, so that she changed her course a little, then she dropped over the edge, toppled over the catwalk below and into the sea. The CPO crawled beneath the fuselage of one of the tethered aircraft, reached up to the wing root and pulled himself upright. The ship was over on her port side once more, the rogue aircraft grinding against another. He wondered whether cutting one aircraft loose was going to be enough, then as the ship began to roll again, the rogue worked herself free with a further rending of metal, began to slide. The bows came up, the aircraft crashed against the one picketed astern, then came free, finally reached the deck edge. One of the wheels dropped down into the catwalk, the opposite wingtip rose up vertically, and then the aircraft was gone, the splash as it hit the water hardly noticed among the spray.

'Gawd, I hope we don't get any more of those,' someone said.

But for many men while the gale lasted there was the lurking fear that another aircraft would break free, either on deck or below in the hangar where damage and consequent petrol leaks could lead to an explosion, and the expedient of putting the aircraft over the side was not available.

The only consolation was that the weather kept the U-boats down. 'They'll be having a far worse time of it than us,' commented the Navigator cheerfully. 'It's true that they can stay submerged below the weather most of the time, but they've got to be surfaced for six hours in twenty-four to charge their batteries, with their hatches open, and they've got such a low freeboard that any decent-sized wave will go right over the conning tower and swamp them. Terrible for the rheumatism.'

'Is that why you left submarines?' asked Higgins.

Beveridge was silent.

Nobody spared much sympathy for the U-boats, or even for the smaller escort vessels. *Crusader*'s men were confined to their own heaving grey world, as they struggled westwards, bows on to the weather, hoping to find calmer weather beyond the gale. The Met Officer was apologetic, but he could not forecast any change.

'Time you got yourself a new piece of seaweed!'

During the gale Thurston rarely left the bridge, snatched only an occasional spell lashed into his bunk for the sake of maintaining his efficiency. He was learning the capabilities of the watchkeepers: that

Forrest was efficient enough despite his supercilious air, that Vincent was more competent than he believed himself to be, while Higgins, conversely, had a great deal more self-confidence than his ability warranted.

'Nothing much happening. *Thistle*'s having trouble keeping station. The Captain's been below about half an hour. He knows about it. Well, I'm off to make a few zeds.'

Forrest and his fellow watchkeepers disappeared below. Vincent checked the compass card, spoke briefly to the lookouts, the signalman and the quartermaster, satisfying himself that everyone had arrived for his watch and was where he should be. *Crusader* was pitching into a head sea, her engines running almost at maximum revolutions to maintain three or four knots of forward momentum. The gale came at them over the bridge screen, bringing rain and gouts of spray and a bitter chill which seeped through Vincent's layers of clothing.

'Dirty night, sir,' said the signalman.

'It is.'

'*I want to go home, I want to go home, I don't want to go to the war any more . . .*' one of the lookouts sang.

'Stop that, Jenkins.' Vincent had to search for the name.

'Sorry, sir.'

Vincent thought that Jenkins was laughing at him. He stamped his feet, looked out to port to see the corvette *Thistle* punching her way industriously into the waves.

'Bet you're glad you're not aboard her,' someone else said. 'Those things do everything but loop the loop.'

The ratings smiled. Vincent felt himself excluded by his single stripe. A wave broke over the flight deck; its spray hit the bridge, drained away through holes at the base of the bridge screen. Vincent felt the water run off his oilskins, but he was damp inside them now, and would remain so for the rest of the watch, even if there were no more seas like that one. Eighteen minutes after midnight and the best part of a four-hour watch still ahead. He looked down onto the flight deck, seeing the small huddle of aircraft picketed down next to the island, glistening with water. Up here on the bridge he didn't feel particularly queasy, but he knew that as soon as he went below at the end of his watch he would be sick again, and that his watch below would be a battle for sleep against seasickness and the pitching which threatened to throw him from his bunk. *Crusader*'s motion was irregular, the quartermaster having to work continuously to hold her on course and limit the wavering to either side which might, if unchecked, lead her eventually to broach to.

'Everything all right, Grinter?' Vincent called down the voicepipe.

'Yes, sir. Mind, I think my arms have grown six inches!'

Vincent shivered again, swung his arms across his narrow chest in an effort to work up his circulation. The portside lookouts were sharing a private joke.

'Watch your sectors.'

He was aware that he sounded like a querulous dowager. He wished that there was someone else here with him, but the Captain was in his sea cabin, and the Navigator turned in below. He rather liked Beveridge, who was prepared to take time to explain things to him, and didn't tease him the way that Forrest and some of the others did. There had been a night when Forrest had asked him to go ashore with them, they had said something about finding him a girl, had indeed picked one out in a pub who seemed nice enough, although his mother would have said she had too much make-up on, but when he walked her home she asked him for, 'Thirty bob, or three quid for all night.' His cheeks still burned at the memory and as far as possible he had kept clear of Forrest since. Forrest and the rest, of course, thought it all a huge joke.

Another sea broke over the deck. More water hit him, worked its way through the gaps in his outer clothing, into his seaboots and down his neck. He made up his mind, crossed the bridge, pressed the Captain's buzzer with his thumb.

The sound of the voicepipe cover being lifted, 'Captain.'

'Sir, I – I think the weather's getting worse.'

A weary, 'All right, I'm coming up,' movement, and the crackling of oilskins being pulled on.

The Captain reached the bridge a few minutes later. He stood in silence for a moment, legs straddled against the ship's motion, looking out over the sea, and then turned back towards the ladder.

'Carry on, Mr Vincent. If anything, it's moderated a bit.'

'Aye aye, sir.' Vincent tried not to betray his disappointment.

The Captain reached for the handrail. 'When you're relieved, organise some cocoa and bring it to my sea cabin.'

'Sir.' Vincent turned back dully to concentrate on his watch.

Thurston spent some time alternately dozing and trying to work out what he was going to say to Vincent, how he could strike the notoriously difficult balance between dissuading him from calling the Captain when it wasn't strictly necessary, and leaving him reluctant to call him when the need was genuine.

The knock on the door woke him from sleep. 'Come.'

Vincent stepped carefully over the coaming, nursing two mugs of cocoa as though his life depended on them. 'You told me to come and see you, sir.'

'Anything to report?'

'No, sir.'

'Put that fire on and get yourself dried off a bit. There's a towel under the basin.' Vincent handed over one of the mugs. 'Thank you. Managed to save most of it.'

Vincent smiled, then laboriously stripped off his oilskins and rubbed at his hair with the already sodden towel, looking about the cabin, the usual functional steel box furnished with bunk, table, chair, a shelf for books, a two-bar electric fire for warmth, a rack for binoculars and pegs for duffel coat and oilskins. Unusually, there was a second, smaller compartment attached, providing the Captain with a shower and lavatory, an example of American priorities in fitting-out of which Thurston thoroughly approved.

'Sit down.' Thurston indicated the end of the bunk, then seated himself astride the chair, which was bolted to the deck and could not be turned round. He proffered his cigarette case.

'No thank you, sir. I don't smoke.'

'Do you know why I've asked to see you?'

'To give me a pep talk, sir.' Vincent looked down at his cocoa, the mug held in both hands. He was shivering a little inside his damp battledress.

'That's about the size of it. And I've asked you to come now because what I have to say will not wait until we get into harbour.' He decided to come straight to the point. 'Mr Vincent, you called me during your watch on the grounds that the weather was worsening, when nothing of the sort was happening.'

'Yes, sir.' Vincent studied the cocoa more intently.

'Mr Vincent, I wouldn't be leaving you on the bridge by yourself if I didn't know you could cope.'

'No, sir,' Vincent said automatically, unconvinced.

'You've got to trust yourself a bit more. I'm not going to bawl you out for calling me unnecessarily, because then you'd think twice about calling me at the proper time, but it's a bit like crying wolf. One day I might not take sufficient notice when you've called me for a good reason. I took my time getting up to the bridge tonight, in a real emergency I'd need to be quicker off the mark. As I've just said, you're quite up to the job.' He looked straight at Vincent. Vincent looked past his shoulder. He looked very young, a tousle-headed schoolboy weighed down by the uniform and commission with only the bluish tinge of beard growth beneath his pallor to betray his true age. 'Mr Vincent, this is off the record.'

'Well, sir,' Vincent blushed and stared at the bulkhead, 'I'm sorry, sir. I'm just not used to this sort of thing. I mean . . . I've not done anything like this before.'

'The responsibility, you mean?'

'Yes, sir.' Vincent took a large pull at the cocoa.

'You weren't a prefect at school, or anything?'

'No, sir. I never got into the sixth form, and I wasn't a Boy Scout. And in my civilian job I was just a trainee so everything I did had to be checked.' He blushed more deeply. 'When I joined the Navy, I just wanted to be in the Navy . . . Well, I just wanted to be out of the tax office and doing something real. I never thought they'd make me an officer. I wish I'd just stayed an OD, sir.'

'That's the one thing you can't go back to. And since you've got what it takes to be an officer, it would have been a waste of resources if you'd stayed on the lower deck.' He sounded just like Campbell, the psychiatrist in Alexandria. 'How many of your squad at *Royal Arthur* were picked out as potential officers?'

'Four, I think, including me.'

'And how many were in the squad?'

'Thirty-one or two.'

'That's not exactly a high proportion. And to be picked out from a recruit squad is a damn sight more difficult than getting through a Dartmouth selection board you've been coached for. Then you got the recommendations from your ship, and then you passed *King Alfred*.'

'Yes, sir.'

'If you hadn't got what it takes, you'd never have got this far.'

'I suppose not, sir.' Vincent took a deep breath. 'But it doesn't seem like that.'

Thurston stuck out an arm to save himself as the ship pitched anew; his left arm, he noticed, it was only now that he was getting back into the habit of using it without having to think. He might have told Vincent that he was not the only man on board with doubts about his professional abilities, but the breakdown was still too recent. He listened for a moment to the gale howling through the ventilator, despite the old sock that was stuffed into it, felt the ship's bows drop once more into a fresh

56

void and fall until another sea brought them up once more. Some men found a gale and the awesome power of the sea in its anger exhilarating, others found it brought them nearer God, still others were simply terrified by it. Perhaps Vincent came into the last category.

'Excuse me, sir. I'm going to be sick.'

Thurston indicated the door at the foot end of the bunk. 'Through there.'

Vincent jumped up, hand to his mouth, returned a few minutes later. 'Sorry about that, sir.'

Thurston waited for a moment while Vincent sat down again and sipped at the remains of his cocoa. 'This sort of weather frightens you?'

Vincent took a long time to reply. 'Yes, sir.'

'I don't particularly enjoy it myself. Anybody who's never afraid is simply too stupid or too unimaginative to appreciate danger. Being frightened is just something you have to live with.' Vincent looked up in surprise, first at the red ribbon and then at him.

There was ordinary fear, which you could joke about afterwards ('I could hear your knees knocking just now, Number One'), but there was also twitch, which was something quite different. 'You do eventually get used to all this, strange as it may seem. You've got to learn to trust your own judgement, and you won't do that if there's always someone else on the bridge to take the responsibility.'

'No, sir.' Vincent drank the last of the cocoa.

Thurston glanced at his watch: 0440, and about time he went back to the bridge to see how Higgins was getting on. 'That's all there is to say. Now go and get your head down and make sure you're on time for your next watch.'

'Aye aye, sir.' Vincent stood up, came to attention. 'Thank you, sir.'

Thurston made a mental note to have the Commander amend the watch bill to put one of the midshipmen on watch with Vincent, so that he would have the dignity of his superior rank to maintain. He didn't know whether he had got through to Vincent; he had been through the motions, tried to bolster his self-confidence, come out with the usual platitudes, and a minor personal revelation to make Vincent think that he was not alone, but he had allowed Vincent to go on believing him to be the omnipotent and self-assured commander. He had sat in his father's study at Langdon one evening during his sick leave, looking for a long time at the photograph of himself on the desk, taken at Sullum Voe in the Shetlands just after *Connaught* returned from her second Denmark Strait patrol. The old man had written asking for a recent photograph, and there was the brand-new post-captain, standing on the teak planking of his quarterdeck, feet apart, telescope under his left arm, hands clasped in front to show off the gold lace, cap angled back and a little to one side, perhaps a little tired after nineteen days of blockade duty in foul weather, but smiling, confident. His father thought it a good likeness. The square-jawed young captain was a stranger, yet outwardly he was still the same man, though now there was grey in his hair, and the smile had gone a little crooked since his jaw wound. In a sense he was in the same position as Vincent: the Navy regarded him as competent, but unless and until he proved that to himself the private doubt would continue.

7

'Pretty godforsaken place,' said the Navigator.

'Rather reminiscent of Scapa, don't you think?' said Forrest, the Gunnery Officer, who had the watch.

'Acres and acres of nothing, with the odd bit marked out as a football pitch.'

'The wettest bit,' said the starboard lookout.

'Of course,' said Forrest.

'Will this place be full of Yanks, sir?' the same lookout asked.

'Unfortunately it will, Kelly. I believe Argentia is an American base.'

'Thought Newfoundland was British.'

'I'm afraid that when the Americans gave us those fifty clapped-out destroyers, we had to give them something in return. But you won't see John Wayne riding the range around here.'

'The Yanks are welcome to it,' said Beveridge.

Crusader was making her way into the harbour of Argentia, a shallow indentation of Placentia Bay on the southern coast of Newfoundland.

'Wasn't this where Churchill came to meet Roosevelt, sir?'

'I believe it was.'

'Wonder why they came here?'

'So's they wouldn't be bothered by the reporters,' said the Chief Yeoman.

It was a bright morning with only a few scudding clouds and a brisk wind blowing through the harbour entrance, which unfurled the American flag flying over the huddle of prefabricated buildings ashore. There was only one ship in harbour, another escort carrier, also flying the American flag.

'I say, it's our American cousin,' exclaimed Forrest.

'I thought that was a play,' said Thurston. He focused his binoculars on the stranger's bow. '*Fredericksburg.*'

'That's a German name, sir,' said Kelly.

'A lot of Americans have German names.'

'All the Americans I've met seem to have been called Schultz or Schmidt,' said Forrest.

Thurston swept the binoculars over the American's decks, taking in the scatter of men along the rails, one man taking the cigarette from his mouth, dropping it on the deck and crushing it with the heel of his boot. 'It seems we have an audience.'

'Must be their stand easy,' said Beveridge.

'I get the impression, Pilot, that our gallant Allies are on permanent stand easy,' said Forrest.

'Pearl Harbor.'

Everybody laughed.

Thurston looked astern; *Gosling*, the escort group commander's sloop, was following in *Crusader*'s wake, then two frigates, and finally the corvette, *Thistle*. Ashore a band struck up, but the sound was distorted by the wind, so that it was impossible to recognise the tune.

'Hard a-starboard.'

'Hard a-starboard, sir.'

Crusader came round into the final turn. Thurston felt the eyes of the Americans on him. The ship straightened up in response to his orders; he put the engines astern. She came to a halt, the anchor cable rumbled out through the hawse hole, the accommodation ladder was lowered, the boats swung out.

'Finished with engines.'

'Finished with engines, sir.'

'We're due to stay here for five or six days, that may change, of course, but send the Newfies on four days' leave.'

'We'll be lucky to see them again,' the Commander warned.

'But God only knows when they'll get the chance of home leave again.'

'That's what I mean, sir. Some of them haven't been home for four years. Newfoundland's a big place. Plenty of room for them to disappear.'

'It's a big place, but with a minute population and everybody knows everybody else for miles around. It's the big cities with plenty of people where deserters can go to ground easily. But make sure it's impressed on them that they will be recalled early if our orders change. And pipe a make-and-mend for this afternoon.'

'Of course, sir. Is there anything else?'

'Apparently the canteen ashore is dry. It's run by the Americans on their ground, and the strongest thing they serve is Coca-Cola. I'm going to clear lower deck in a few minutes, so I shall give the men the happy tidings then.'

'Is that necessary, sir? Captain Owen didn't do it very often.'

'In my experience the men like to know what's going on. I shall only keep them for a couple of minutes. Since we're going to be here for a few days, we'd better find them something to keep their minds off the beer shortage, so see if you can organise some football matches with the other ships.'

'I'll see what I can do, sir, but on past showings it won't achieve anything. This lot are quite happy to play football, or deck hockey for that matter, among themselves, but as soon as anyone suggests organising a team and playing other ships, or even organising a competition within the ship, they lose all interest. All they're concerned about is to get ashore, and as far away from the service as possible, and to fill their bellies with as much beer as they can stow.'

'Then something needs to be done about that.'

'Yes, sir,' the Commander said, his tone making it clear that he had heard all this before. 'Mind if I smoke?'

'Carry on.' Thurston waited while the Commander brought out his cigarette case and blew a large waft of smoke across the desk. This was the first opportunity he had had for a serious discussion with the Commander since leaving Greenock, and he had now been aboard *Crusader* long enough to see what was going on.

'The impression I'm getting, from what I've seen and what you're saying, is that the men don't believe they have any stake in the ship. Being in the ship, indeed being in the Navy, is simply something they have to put up with.'

'Conscripts, sir.'

'It doesn't have to be like that, Commander, conscripts or no. We had a good fifty per cent conscripts in my last ship and it didn't cause any particular problems, once they'd had time to shake down. No more sick grandmothers than usual.'

'I suppose not. But it only takes one bad apple to infect the rest, and we seem to have got the sweepings of the service.'

'Unfortunately, Commander, we're stuck with them for the foreseeable future.' Thurston was beginning to get impatient with the Commander. He reminded himself that the Commander was two years into the zone for promotion; he needed a successful tour as Commander of a large ship and a strong recommendation from Thurston himself. His appointment to an escort carrier must have come as a severe disappointment and, on their recent form, his disenchantment with the ship's company was not so surprising. Thurston could remember only too well his own departure from *Retribution* at the end of the commission, knowing that he had done all he was capable of, and had a glowing confidential report from Manning-Wilson to show for it, but that if he missed the fourth stripe this time the chance was unlikely to come again. 'Therefore, the officers will have to get to work and ginger the men up a bit. To begin with, the divisional officers must make themselves available to the men in their divisions and the men must be made aware of that.'

'Half of them are conscripts as well.'

'Then they should have a better idea what bugs them. Spell it out to them, that the men must come first, last and always.' He could see what the Commander was thinking – this bright boy with the chestful of medals sent to *Crusader* to sort everything out, who was telling him to wave a magic wand and deal in five minutes with problems which had proved intractable for eight months and had already brought about the removal of one captain. 'Secondly, as I said just now, the men usually like to know what's going on. Find out if there are any ex-newspapermen on board – there must be one or two – and get a news sheet started. If they put out some daily news – what the ship's doing, the latest news from the intelligence summaries, what films are showing at the pictures when we're in harbour, and something more once a week. We had one in *Marathon* and some of the men got very keen. We had a couple of regular columns – the padre did one – and someone else did a gossip column, and we had cartoons, jokes, crosswords, reviews of films, all that sort of thing.'

'Yes, sir. I'll look into it.'

Thurston had not intended to go on about *Marathon* – the Commander had probably heard quite enough about her from other sources – but at times the subject was difficult to avoid. 'See what you can do while we're here, Commander, and report back to me.'

'Aye aye, sir.' The Commander stubbed out his cigarette in the ashtray in front of him. 'But, if I may say so, I don't think you really appreciate how resistant this lot are. And that goes for the officers as well. Especially the engineers. I spoke to one of them about the rig he was wearing in the wardroom and he told me to my face that he had no desire to be an officer in the first place and would be much better off as an ERA. I've never heard anything like it.' He snorted. 'I have spoken to the Commander (E) more than once about their behaviour in the wardroom, but all he ever does is smile and say, "Ah, they're good lads." They may be good lads in that engine room of his, though I find that hard to believe at times, but their officer-like qualities leave a great deal to be desired. And the flyers are almost as bad. Because they don't have any shipboard duties all they do is sit around the ready room all day playing cards, when they're not actually flying.'

'Commander, I think you're forgetting that in essence this ship is nothing more than a floating airfield. The flyers are here to fly, the engineers are aboard to make sure we can actually get to where we're needed, and the measure of our efficiency is basically whether we can get the right number of aircraft to the right place at the right time, and whether the aircraft can then do what is required of them. Everybody on board has some part to play in that, whether he's a seaman, flyer, engineer, or he simply scrubs the galley floor.'

'Of course, sir, but even so, the engineers leave a great deal to be desired,' the Commander persisted. 'If you ask me, sir, Chief needs to get a grip on them. He's far too easy-going. He's really too old for the job, and he's had a sinking, of course.'

'So have I, Commander. Two in fact.'

'I apologise, sir,' the Commander said hastily. 'But it can't have been good for him at his age.'

'You make it sound as though the Chief is in his dotage. In any case, he wouldn't have lasted five minutes as a chief engineer in the Merchant Service if he didn't know what he was doing.'

'You've only just taken over, sir. You haven't seen this ship at her worst. Nor the men at theirs.'

'Thank you, Commander, for that piece of gratuitous advice. That's all for now. I'm going to clear lower deck.'

The Commander went out. Thurston rang for his messenger. 'Give the secretary my compliments and would he like to stretch his legs ashore in the dog watches?'

Ashore, a group of *Crusader*'s men were kicking a football around an open space, goalposts improvised with their greatcoats. The ship's seven Newfoundland ratings had already left, laden with kitbags containing four years' worth of presents for their families, to envious shouts of 'You lucky sods' from their fellows.

Argentia was emptiness, flat grey marsh stretching to the horizon on three sides, a huge expanse of pale blue sky above. If the men expected bright lights and girls on this side of the Atlantic they were due to be disappointed. There was only an artificial town of prefabricated huts, with a transitory population composed entirely of seamen of three nationalities, set up only because of the harbour, which took the over-flow of escort vessels from St Johns, the island's capital and main port.

'Worse than Scapa,' one of the old hands had remarked. 'At least Scapa's got hills.'

It was good to be ashore after three weeks at sea, free from confine-

63

ment to the bridge and his sea cabin, and the ladder and short length of passage between, to exchange his uniform for a sweater and an old pair of rugby shorts, to feel his legs, arms and back working to move him along, see his breath coming out as steam in the keen air. They passed a small group of American ratings in their short pea jackets and floppy pork pie caps.

'Not as smart as our chaps,' commented Scott.

Their gym shoes slipped on the tussocks, feet dropped into the shallow voids of muddy water between.

'Should have worn boots,' said Thurston.

'I'm not sure I'd have the energy to pick my feet up with boots on. I don't get enough exercise among my files.'

'I'd have thought you'd have plenty – picking them up!'

'Unfortunately I don't pick them up with my legs, sir.'

They circled back towards the camp, found themselves confronted by a high chainlink fence and followed it towards the harbour edge, trying to find a gate.

'Halt!' A sentry appeared out of a box. 'Your identification?'

Thurston's hand went to the pocket of his shorts, and found it empty. 'Have you got your identity card, Mr Scott?'

'No, sir.'

'Who are youse?' the sentry demanded.

'The Captain of HMS *Crusader*.'

The sentry shifted his chewing gum to the other side of his mouth. 'And I'm Fleet Admiral Ernest J. King.' He brought the rifle down from his shoulder. 'Jim!' he called.

Another American appeared, hastily buttoning his pea jacket and fastening the chinstrap of his steel helmet.

'I just stopped these two. They haven't got any identification. This one,' he jerked his head towards Thurston, 'says he's the Captain of that Limey flat top that just came in.'

'Who's the other one?'

'Paymaster Lieutenant Scott, Royal Navy,' supplied Scott.

Now he was still, Thurston was beginning to get cold. He decided that things had gone far enough. 'Take that gum out of your mouth, sentry!' The American looked surprised. 'Swallow it!' The American gulped. 'And don't you stand to attention in the presence of officers in the American Navy?'

The two Americans jumped to attention. 'Sure talks like an English captain,' the second man said doubtfully. He had a slow southern accent. 'Okay, let 'em carry on.' The sentry returned his rifle to his shoulder. 'But you can't go in there, Captain. That's the WAVE accommodation. You'll come to the main gate if you follow this fence another half mile. I'll call the main gate to say you're coming, but it'll save a lot of trouble if you carry your identification.'

There was an American-style salute with the fingers bent, and a forward flick of the hand on the downward stroke.

'Good thing they believed us, sir. If I may say so, you don't seem to have much luck with sentries.'

'D'ye think we'll get the chance to get into St Johns, Spence?' asked Metcalfe.

'Doubt it. Anyway, there's not much there, and the whole place stinks of rotting fish.'

'I want to get something for me mam. To show her I've been abroad.'

'You wouldn't get anything there. There's only things in the shops when they've got round to unpacking the lot which came with the last convoy. You see all these little notices in the shops, saying "Just landed", and "Just unpacked". And all the locals know that, so everything goes inside five minutes. Never mind, Charlie, we'll get ashore and try out the Coca-Cola, like. Might even meet some of the Yankee Wrens, WAVES they call them. Supposed to be some here.'

Metcalfe's first taste of foreign countries was proving a disappointment. He and Spencer reached the canteen soon after it opened, Spencer found a convenient corner, and left Metcalfe to occupy it while he went for drinks. He was away a long time, as the place was filling up, with both British and Americans. Metcalfe began to feel lonely and out of place.

'Hey, kid!'

Metcalfe turned and saw Sutcliffe, elbowing his way between a group of Americans.

'What you doing here, kid? Got fed up with the pigs?'

Sutcliffe seemed drunk, and Metcalfe wondered how he had managed it, then remembered that Sutcliffe bottled his tot. As if on cue, he produced the bottle, which had once contained brown sauce. 'Have a slug of that, kid.'

Spencer reappeared, a glass of Coca-Cola in either hand. 'Piss off, Sutcliffe.'

Sutcliffe swayed forward slightly, seeming to Metcalfe to become larger and more menacing. He turned towards Spencer. 'Whad'jer mean going off with my winger?'

'I never did,' said Spencer. 'Anyway, the kid's better off without you. Here, Charlie, look after these.' He passed the drinks to Metcalfe.

'Whad'jer mean, arse-licker?' Sutcliffe took another pull at the bottle, draining the last of its contents.

'Piss off!'

Sutcliffe looked at Spencer for another long moment. 'I need another fuckin' drink.' He lurched back towards the bar, fetched up against an American.

'Hey, feller, watch where you're going.'

'Shut up, Yank; who's winning the war for you?'

'What do you mean?'

Suddenly conversation around them stopped. Men, both British and American, turned towards them, waiting to see what would happen.

'Jus' that,' said Sutcliffe belligerently. 'Took your lot two fucking years to work up the guts to join in.'

'Why, you . . .' The American put up his fists. One of his friends pulled at him from behind. 'Steady, Jack.'

Someone else joined in. 'Where were you at Salerno, and when we were out on the oggin chasing U-boats?'

'How many U-boats have you sunk?'

'Ten!' said the Englishman off the top of his head.

An American prodded him in the chest with an index finger. 'If you've seen so much combat, where's your campaign ribbons and battle stars?'

The Englishman was not take aback. 'In the Royal Navy we don't get medals just for going somewhere. *We* have to earn them.'

'Royal Navy means Real Navy,' said another man in a stage whisper.

'Anyway, you haven't told us where you've been, and why you haven't got any of these fucking battle stars.'

'We haven't finished working up yet, but when we have . . . we just might turn our guns on the British instead of the Krauts.'

'*Our* skipper's a VC anyway.'

'A what?'

'Careful, Jack, that's like the Medal of Honour.'

Drinks had been put down on the scatter of small tables. Someone began to sing:

'From the halls of Montezuma, to the shores of Tripoli,
We're bloody fine hands in harbour, but oh my Christ, at sea . . .'

Jack picked up his glass once more, and very deliberately smashed it against one of the steel pillars supporting the roof.

'Sixteen men in the cells. Four in the sick bay, to say nothing of the ones the PMO sewed up before they went to the cells. And all that in a *dry* canteen, without a drop of beer in them, though I gather one or two had smuggled their tots ashore. Now do you see what I mean, sir?'

The messenger of the watch knocked on the bulkhead and entered the cabin. 'Captain, sir. The Captain of the *Fredericksburg* is coming aboard.'

'This could be interesting,' Thurston said to the Commander. He picked up his cap and telescope and was on the quarterdeck in time to see his opposite number reach the head of the accommodation ladder, give an American salute and ask, 'Permission to come aboard, sir,' of the Officer of the Watch.

Sub-Lieutenant Vincent was for a moment completely nonplussed. 'Er, yes of course, sir!'

Thurston stepped forward. Salutes and handshakes followed.

'Hello, I'm Dan Maloney.'

'Robert Thurston, how do you do.'

Thurston distinctly heard Vincent say to Midshipman Elder in amazed tones, 'He asked *me* for permission to come aboard!'

'It is rather early, but will you have a drink?'

'What do you have?' Maloney was a small man with an iron-grey crew cut, who managed to look as Irish as his name.

'Gin, whisky, sherry. Or coffee.'

'I think I'd better just have coffee.'

'Of course.' Thurston rang the pantry bell. 'Spencer, coffee.'

'Aye aye, sir.'

A ghost of a grin crossed Maloney's face at the sight of Spencer with one eye half closed and a strip of elastoplast covering a couple of stitches beneath the eyebrow. 'Looks as though you've been in a fight, sailor.'

'Yes, sir,' Spencer grinned back.

Maloney stirred sugar lumps into his coffee. 'I'm just here to apologise on behalf of my boys for what happened in the shore canteen last night.'

'It seems that my men were equally to blame,' Thurston said tactfully. 'My cells are full this morning.'

'So are mine, and I shall make sure they are all properly punished, as soon as I can hold a Captain's Mast. I'm really sorry, Captain, but when the guys get ashore they tend to let off steam. For most of them this is their first ship, and a lot of them never saw the sea before they were drafted. We're still working up. All of them were seasick, and I've never seen men so glad to get ashore. I'm surprised after all that they still had the energy to start a fight.'

'Somebody always will.'

They both laughed.

'Since we're going to be in the same harbour for the next few days, we had better try to live in some sort of harmony.'

'My boys don't seem to have much time for the British.'

'The feeling seems to be mutual. What we usually do when something starts between two ships is organise a football match or something similar, so they can work off their rivalry without beating each other up. But your people don't play our sort of football.'

'And you don't play ours. But it's worth trying. Just give me a moment to think. Is there any more of that coffee?'

Spencer, hovering, poured him another cup.

Maloney leaned back in his chair. 'There must be something, and it ought to be a team thing. Not boxing. Your people don't play baseball and it's not the season anyway . . . No, I've got it. Do your people row?'

'Pull? Yes, of course.'

'Then can we challenge you to a race?'

'Certainly. Two races. One for the officers and one for the ratings.'

'Sure.'

Thurston thought for a moment. 'If I remember correctly, the person challenged has the choice of weapons, and we have two six-oared cutters of the same pattern.'

'Just the thing. We don't have two boats the same, and only one of them has oars. At least we shouldn't have too much trouble getting an officers' crew together. Two of my ensigns rowed for Princeton, and I've another who was a cox at Yale. Tiny little guy, needs a cushion to see out of the cockpit. The enlisted men could be a bit different. When's it going to be?'

'Today's Wednesday. Let's say Saturday, at fifteen hundred.'

'Done! Well, Captain, I'd better get back to my ship and start finding me a couple of cutter's crews. We'll send you a formal challenge as soon as I can get it written.'

'And we'll send the cutter across.'

'My boys will have to get into training. And I would like to return your hospitality, so will you have dinner with me tonight?'

'Gladly.'

Thurston saw Maloney over the side, then told Spencer he would need his mess undress that night.

'Going to put one over the Yanks, sir?'

'Spencer, you know what's coming to you.'

'Sir.'

'*A cutter race?*' exclaimed Forrest as he stirred his coffee in the wardroom after lunch, and studied the notice board.

'We have been challenged by the Americans. Our officers against their officers, and our ratings against their ratings. We're supplying the boats,' explained Scott.

'Tell me, Scratch, has the Captain taken leave of his senses?'

'Not as far as I can see.'

'And we're expected to volunteer for this charade? Well, leave me out of it.'

'I don't know, Guns, it might do you good. You're starting to develop quite a middle-aged spread.'

'Very funny! You can't be leading a very healthy life when the only exercise you get is hitting the keys of the typewriter.'

'I've already been volunteered, thank you, and the Captain's volunteered himself.'

'I'm glad to hear that.'

'So we only need to find another four, plus someone to cox.'

'I'll cox, if you insist. I did some coxing at Dartmouth,' Forrest suggested.

'I think you've put on a bit of weight since then. You must weigh twelve stone if you weigh an ounce.'

'Eleven and a half, actually.'

'That's still about three stone too much, and surely the honour of Dartmouth demands that you, one of the few regular officers on board, as you keep reminding us . . .'

'That was below the belt,' Forrest protested. 'Oh very well. Who else can we find fool enough?'

Commander (Flying) offered to cox, 'since I'm going to be volunteered anyway.'

The Principal Medical Officer, Surgeon Lieutenant-Commander Barnard, was heard to say that he had rowed for St Mary's Hospital while a medical student, a pilot named Newell had rowed at school, and Sub-Lieutenant Vincent found himself roped in on the grounds that if he came from Oxford he must be able to row.

8

The officers' crew had their first practice that afternoon at 1600. It soon became clear that Thurston, Scott and Forrest had spent a fair amount of time in pulling boats over the years, but were all in varying degrees out of practice, that the PMO and Lieutenant Newell were much more used to racing eights than unwieldy naval cutters, the PMO declaring that he would in any case be much more usefully employed in treating the injuries of the rest than in actually taking part, and that Sub-Lieutenant Vincent knew no more of boatwork than he had been taught at *Royal Arthur* and *King Alfred*.

'Let's hope the Yanks are having just the same problems.'

'What, with all those chaps who rowed for Princeton?'

'As I've said before,' said Barnard, 'there's a world of difference between real rowing and doing it in one of these tubs.'

'Is that what you call real rowing?' said Forrest, looking out over the swell within the harbour. 'A racing eight wouldn't last long out here.'

'It wouldn't be expected to. The whole business is quite different.'

'Has anyone seen the Yanks out yet?' asked Newell.

'The Yanks never prepare for anything. Look what happened at Pearl Harbor.'

'Come on, gentlemen, we've time for another run before it gets too dark,' said the cox, bundled up in flying kit against the cold.

'With these blisters?' said Forrest. 'My lily-white hands are quite ruined.'

'Already? We've only just started,' said Scott unsympathetically.

'Salt water on them,' someone else suggested.

Forrest looked appealingly at the PMO, who said nothing. The cox exerted his authority. 'Let's get on. One more run now, and we'll have another try at 0700 tomorrow. Now, if Newell and the secretary can change places, we'll see if that works any better.'

'Ah, er, Metcalfe, we meet again. Where is the Captain?'

'In the shower, sir.'

'Then tell him I would like to see him as soon as he's finished.'

Metcalfe caught the tone of the Commander's voice and scurried away. He had appeared before the Commander as a defaulter that morning, been sentenced to fourteen days' stoppage of pay and leave, and been told that he was lucky to get away so lightly. Spencer, as a persistent offender, had been remanded to appear before the Captain the following day.

'Just a minute.'

Metcalfe heard the shower being turned off, and waited for the Captain to emerge a moment later wearing only his trousers.

'Captain, sir, the Commander's outside waiting to see you.'

'Ask him to wait while I get dressed.'

There was a muscled angular torso, in enviable contrast to his own narrow shoulders and staring ribs, and the scars exactly as Spencer had described them. An irregular crater beneath the collar bone on the left side, and when the Captain turned away from him a bluish-white area near the base of the shoulder blade, roughly in the shape of a four-pointed star, its longest arm pointing vertically downwards. And there was something else which Spencer had not mentioned, a faded ship's badge tattooed above his right elbow and, the edges becoming blurred with time, the words DARDANELLES 1915.

The Captain turned his head from the washbasin, chin half-lathered with shaving soap. 'Aren't you going to deliver that message, Metcalfe?'

The Commander was pacing about the day cabin, cap jammed beneath his left elbow, coming to a halt in front of the desk as Thurston sat down. The Commander (E) had also arrived and turned from contemplation of a sketch on one of the bulkheads to get his piece in first. 'Sir, Commander Canning has just put one of my fivers under close arrest.' He used the Merchant Navy term, from the title Fifth Engineer.

The Commander was more formal. 'Captain, sir, I have to report that I have just confined Sub-Lieutenant Shepherd to his cabin after he showed gross insubordination towards me.'

Shepherd? Shepherd? Thurston vaguely remembered the name, but nothing of its owner. He came to a decision. 'I would prefer to see you both separately, so if you could wait for five minutes, Chief, I'll hear your side next.'

'Aye aye, sir,' the Commander (E) said with some resignation, and went out with a sidelong glance at the Commander.

'You'd better tell me what this is about, Commander. Sit down.'

'There isn't much to tell, sir. I went into the wardroom about twenty minutes ago. It was 1824 to be exact. And I found Sub-Lieutenant Shepherd standing there in his overalls drinking a pint of beer. I

71

reminded him that this was contrary to standing orders at any time, and that the rig of the day in the wardroom after 1800 is Number Fives. The exact words he used, sir, were, "Go fuck yourself." I naturally asked him whether he would withdraw the remark. He refused. I asked him whether he knew what he was doing. He said that he did, and I had no option but to place him under close arrest.'

'He's confined to his cabin?'

'Yes, sir. I sent him there with another of the black gang as escort. Commander Hodgson arrived in the wardroom just afterwards, not in his overalls, I might add, and he went with them. Sir, there will have to be a court martial.'

'Don't tell me how to run my ship!'

'I apologise, sir,' the Commander said smoothly. 'But there were witnesses. Mostly Shepherd's cronies of course.'

'That's a bit of a sweeping statement.'

'There were several of the engineer subs present, to say nothing of the bar stewards.'

'You are aware, Commander, of what a court martial would mean?'

'Of course, sir, but there's no alternative. Shepherd was quite deliberately insubordinate. He knew exactly what he was doing; he may even have planned it. I wouldn't put it past him.'

'Commander, let's stick to the facts, not your surmises.'

'Sir. But this isn't the first occasion I've had to speak to him about his conduct in the wardroom. If he's allowed to get away with this, there'll be no hope of maintaining discipline and proper standards among these wretched engineers.'

'Commander, I don't think you do appreciate the full implications of a court martial.' Thurston stood up, and began to pace the carpet.

'Sir?'

'If there is a court martial, Shepherd will be found guilty and in all probability he'll be dismissed the ship. He won't be cashiered because, as insubordination goes, it's minor, and the service is short of engineers. More short of engineers than it is of commanders. He might get away with a severe reprimand if the court takes sufficient notice of the defence. But, as he's not a regular and he's unlikely to have any plans to stay on in the Navy after the war, even being dismissed the ship won't make much difference to his future in the service. But the defence case will be that he was provoked, that you drove him to it, and whoever defends him will make the most of anything he can dig up as evidence of your antipathy to engineer officers, which you've made plain to me

72

before tonight. The defence will dredge up a lot of mud, and because you're a regular officer some of that mud is going to stick.'

'I am prepared to take that risk, sir.'

'Noted. Nevertheless, Commander, there will be no court martial unless I am satisfied that there is no alternative, which from what I have heard so far is highly unlikely. I am going to see Commander Hodgson now, then I am going to see Shepherd himself and get his side of the story. Then I am going to sleep on all this. Whilst I am doing all that,' Thurston seated himself behind his desk once more, 'I would advise you to think very carefully about all the implications of a court martial, for you as well as for Shepherd.'

'Aye aye, sir. Is there anything else?'

'Not at the moment, thank you.'

The Commander (E) must have waited in the flat outside, as he came into the cabin as his opposite number was going out.

'I don't want the lad court-martialled, sir.'

'Neither do I, Chief, if it can be avoided, though not for the same reasons as yours.'

'Yes, sir. I told Arthur Canning I would deal with Shepherd, but he wouldn't listen to me.'

'I've already heard the Commander's side of things. What has Shepherd got to say for himself?'

Commander Hodgson waited a moment to organise his thoughts before beginning.

'According to Shepherd, he simply nipped into the wardroom for a quick beer after finishing a particularly thirsty job. We've been doing some work on the evaporator so that the water came back on a bit late tonight, and he couldn't clean up properly when he finished his watch. He never intended to stay more than a couple of minutes. Apparently the Commander spotted him when he came in, and started to lay into him. Shepherd says he tried to explain, but the Commander wouldn't let him. He is a bit hot-tempered, and I don't doubt he shouldn't have said what he did – he admits he said it – but Arthur Canning's constantly needling my lads, and Shepherd had just had enough of it.'

'Chief, the Commander was quite justified in rebuking Shepherd for going into the wardroom in overalls.'

'I know, sir. I've made that quite clear to Shepherd.'

'The Commander's story is that he reminded Shepherd of the standing orders, and Shepherd said what he said, with no attempt at explanation, which wouldn't justify his being in overalls in the wardroom anyway. He seems to want to make an example of Shepherd.'

'He would do.'

'He seems to find discipline among the engineers somewhat wanting.'

'I know, sir. I've heard all about it far too often. If I may say so, he's just not being fair to my lads. He seems to go out of his way to find fault with them.'

'Can we leave that for the time being, Chief, and concentrate on Shepherd?'

'Of course, sir, but this is all part of the Commander's conduct towards my lads. Obviously I'm not regular Navy, but I don't believe a court martial would accomplish anything.'

'I intend to deal with the matter on board.' The Commander (E) looked relieved. 'What do you think of Shepherd, Chief?'

'He's a good lad. Inexperienced, but he's learning all the time, and he never needs to be told anything twice.' The Chief smiled. With his near-white hair and wing collar he looked rather like an indulgent grandfather. At his age he probably was a grandfather. 'He's very bright, too, and a worker. He got his Ordinary National and Higher National Certificates before he finished his apprenticeship, which means three nights a week at Liverpool Tech for five years, and a lot of extra work on top, and passing every exam first time. I've only one other chap who managed that.'

'You're not just sticking up for him when he's in trouble, Chief?'

'No, sir, though I admit I'm fond of the lad. I know the family, in fact I've known young Shepherd all his life. His father and I were both apprenticed at the Coburg Dockyard in Liverpool and joined White Star as fifth engineers at the same time. Bill Shepherd's dead now, and I think that upset John a good deal. He went ashore when we were taken over by Cunard, and found himself a berth with another company when the war broke out. He'd started having some sort of heart trouble by then, but he must have kept it quiet. The ship was torpedoed early in '41, he didn't make it to a boat, and with a bad heart and going into the water from a hot engine room he wouldn't have lasted long. Then a couple of months later Shepherd's mother and sister were visiting an aunt in Woodhall Road one night. The mother left early for some reason, but his sister was caught in an air raid. She and the aunt were in the house when a land mine went off on the other side of the street. The house was virtually demolished, the aunt was killed and Shepherd's sister hasn't walked since. John was still in his apprenticeship then. He wanted to throw the whole thing up and join anything which would take him, but I happened to be on leave at the time and managed to talk him out of it. He's never said much about it, but he's got ideas about getting back at the enemy and he's been trying to get into submarines. The submariners have accepted him, but there's some problem with the paperwork because he's on T124X articles, and so he's still waiting to go. He is a bit short-fused, and his manners can be a bit rough and ready, but I've no complaints about his work, or about his attitude in the engine room.'

'So you would be prepared to deal with him yourself?'

'I would indeed. I certainly don't want to see his future in the Merchant Service blighted by a court martial. There are plenty of dirty jobs in awkward little spaces I can find for him if you want me to. It's about time we had a good look at the stern gland.'

Thurston laughed, rang for Metcalfe. 'Ask Sub-Lieutenant Shepherd to come and see me at once. If you can stay where you are, Chief.'

Shepherd had shifted out of the offending overalls and looked presentable enough, his hair still wet from the shower. He looked with some surprise at Thurston's mess undress and stiff shirt.

'Yes, sir, I did tell the Commander where to go. It probably was a stupid thing to do, but I'm not sorry.' Shepherd waited a second, then went on. 'Sir, the Commander does nothing but gripe at us. We're working like blacks all day and half the night, and of course we get covered in filth.' Shepherd gave a slight hesitation, as if he had changed his mind about which word to use. 'But we can't clean up when the water isn't on, which means we can't get so much as a cup of tea from the wardroom when we get off duty. The wardroom is supposed to be our mess as well as the deck officers', but we get treated as if we've just crawled out of the bilges.' Shepherd had a noticeable Liverpool accent when he was excited.

'John!' the chief warned.

'I'm sorry, sir, but that's how it is.' Shepherd was not to be deflected. 'The Chief gets treated like dirt as well.' He looked towards his superior for support.

'John, that's enough. You're not doing yourself any good at all.'

'I'm sorry, sir,' Shepherd said again, turned his head back towards Thurston and pulled himself more upright.

'All right, Mr Shepherd, I get the general idea. I asked to see you in order to hear your side of the story before I come to any decision. You are aware that the Commander wants you to be court-martialled?'

'He told me he'd have me court-martialled, sir.'

'In my ship, Mr Shepherd, *I* decide who is or is not court-martialled.'

'Yes, sir.'

'Have you anything more to say?'

Shepherd had come to a halt. 'No, sir.'

'All right, Mr Shepherd, you may go. You're under open arrest until I decide what I'm going to do with you.'

'He'll take what you give him, sir,' the Commander (E) said when Shepherd had gone. 'I'll have a quiet word in the morning when he's had time to simmer down.'

'Thanks, Chief.'

'I don't want to see him court-martialled unnecessarily. He's not a bad lad. He's just got a bit of an awkward streak.'

'I've got some idea how he feels, Chief. I hit a Sub when I was a midshipman.'

The Chief looked surprised, and grandfatherly at the same time. 'You must have had your reasons, sir.'

Yes, but even after all this time they were still too personal. Thurston scratched his broken nose. 'He hit me back and that's how I got this. There wasn't a court martial then, either. I had my leave stopped for three months and my backside beaten. The Sub was made to resign his commission, he was called up into the army as a private and was killed on the western front.'

The Chief's eyebrows were raised. Obviously he would like to have known more. 'I take it you'll deal with Shepherd in the morning, sir.'

'I will. Make sure you have got some dirty jobs for him.'

The Chief picked up his cap. 'This won't be an easy option, sir.'

Thurston went on deck, told the Officer of the Watch to call away his boat to take him across to *Fredericksburg*. His damaged wrist was swollen and aching, and he was beginning to stiffen from pulling an oar, so he began to walk up and down the flight deck while he was waiting. It had begun to rain, a thin drizzle coming out of a low blanket of cloud, so that the silhouettes of the other ships were blotted out and only their shaded stern lights left visible.

He had once been in the position which Shepherd occupied now, beleaguered, confused and yes, scared, and trying to cloak all that in a show of defiance. He had been seventeen and not twenty-two, and it had been he demanding the court martial, though his fate had been decided, as Shepherd's would be, by senior officers meeting in private, because far more was at stake than a mere sub-lieutenant or midshipman. The thing now was becoming a battle of wills between Captain and Commander, a battle which the Captain would win, because all

76

the big guns were on his side, but the result could easily be a hollow victory, leading to the departure of one of them, and that would be the Commander.

Until now there had been silence except for the wind and the faint shifting noises of the anchor cable, but out of the silence came the sound of bagpipes, the familiar swagger of 'Hielan Laddie'. Thurston's eyes were growing used to the darkness and he could now make out a small figure standing right in the bows, his back to him, the three drones spread in outline next to his head. Thurston stopped a few yards to the rear as the man turned to something else, a more private piece, all haunting melancholy beneath, which made Thurston feel he had intruded. The man must have become aware of his presence after a time, for his head flicked round, then the playing stopped abruptly, so that the air escaped from the bag with a sigh. He turned about and came jerkily to the salute.

'Sorry, sir. I was just finishing.'

'Don't stop. I was enjoying it.'

'Aye aye, sir.'

Thurston drew back a few paces. The man pushed his coat collar down and began again. But his concentration had been broken and the mood could not be recaptured.

'Ah'm sorry, sir. It's nae guid.'

'I'm putting you off.'

'Aye, sir, you are a bit.' He gathered the drones together, the tops rattling as they came into contact with each other.

'What's your name?'

'Stoker McCutcheon, sir.'

'Where did you learn the pipes?'

'In the Boys' Brigade at home, sir. The lads won't let me practise in the mess. They don't mind Best and his guitar, but they say I sound like a mob of cats with a bellyache. I know I'm no' very good, sir, but I still like to play.'

The Officer of the Watch came up, reported to Thurston that the boat was waiting.

'Goodnight, McCutcheon.'

'Goodnight, sir.'

As the boat moved clear of *Crusader*'s side the playing began again, another private piece, coming out of rocks and high moorland, spreading out across a night sea three thousand miles from home.

9

'There will be no court martial, Commander.'

The Commander took a moment to register this. 'May I ask the reason, sir?'

'Simply that a court martial would serve no useful purpose, and would not be in the interests of this ship.'

'It will hardly be in the interests of this ship if one of her officers is permitted to get away with an act of gross insubordination,' the Commander said stiffly.

'It was hardly *gross* insubordination, and Sub-Lieutenant Shepherd will not be allowed to get away with it. I'm not going to make a fool of myself by asking Flag Officer Clyde to convene a court martial over something like this, and I've no intention of prosecuting at such a court martial. As we all know, there's a war on, and Flag Officer Clyde would tell me to deal with it anyway. Shepherd's not holding out for a court martial, and the Commander (E) is prepared to deal with him.'

'I suppose Hodgson will pat him on the head and tell him to be a good boy in future. I suppose he knew his father.'

'He did, as it happens, and for that very reason he's likely to be hard on him. I don't doubt that Shepherd will find he's landed with the filthiest jobs going for the next month at least, and when he does get off duty he'll be so busy scrubbing all the muck off that he won't have time to go to the wardroom. That will be far more of a lesson to Shepherd than any sentence a court martial could impose, and he'll be dealt with a damn sight quicker, of course. Just remember how long it takes to convene a court martial, especially in wartime. And the buzz will soon get around the ship, and especially the wardroom, that he hasn't got away with it. I could log him, but I don't think it appropriate for something like this. He can furnish a written apology and reasons in writing, the Commander (E) will give him extra duties and that will be the end of the matter.' Thurston sat back in his chair, waiting for the Commander to reply. The scuttle behind his head was open and let in the ship's usual early morning noises, boots on the deck, the clank of buckets as they were carried empty. He wished he could do something with his hands to fill the impasse, but that would weaken his stature in the eyes of the Commander. His own eyes met Canning's, held them for a moment, one pair grey, one brown.

The Commander broke the silence. 'Aye aye, sir.' His voice was quite flat.

Thurston waited a moment. 'Shut the door.'

'Sir?' The Commander stood up and shut the cabin door.

'Commander, I don't want you to go away thinking that I've all of a sudden gone soft on discipline, or that I'm conspiring with the engineer branch in order to undermine your authority.'

'I didn't believe that you were.' The Commander was being very correct.

'I'm not doing this for Shepherd's sake. This is a very minor and rather stupid piece of insubordination which can be dealt with more than adequately on board. Shepherd answered you back, that's all.'

'Yes, sir. Is that all?'

'No, I've not finished.' Thurston had spent half an hour with the Commander's file after returning from dinner with Maloney the night before. There, once more, was a difficult balance to be struck, between ending any hope of co-operation from Canning in the future and allowing him to carry on in the same way as before. 'Commander, I appreciate that you've waited a long time for a seagoing job and that you've spent the last few years in training establishments which are pretty much a backwater, especially in wartime.'

'Yes, sir.'

'You're also in the zone for promotion and you're short on sea time. I could ask for a relief for you, and would not hesitate to do so if I believed it necessary, but I would prefer not to, mainly because this ship can do without a new commander at the same time as a new captain. But, if I find that you are not prepared to work *with* me to get this ship sorted out, I'll have no option but to get rid of you.'

'Yes, sir.' The agreement was automatic but the voice a little shaken.

'You're thirty-nine, you're well inside the zone, you haven't had a command yet and you've been stuck ashore for most of the war. And you're starting to get desperate. Am I right?'

The Commander did not answer, weighing the words up for a moment. 'You might put it that way, sir.'

Thurston fished a little. 'I suppose it must have been a bit galling to be posted to an escort carrier.'

'It was. When I came away from *Repulse* with my brass hat I thought I had the world at my feet. I had it all planned; I was going to do a tour at Whale Island, then I was going to be commander of one of the

King George V class battleships, and she was going to be the most efficient battleship there ever was, and I was going to get my fourth stripe at the first shot. Instead, I went to the Admiralty, and after that I went to *St George*, training snotty-nosed boy seamen. I did hope for a command when I got away from *St George*. After all, RNVR officers are getting ships now. Or at least I could be commander of a real warship. Instead, I got this thing. A couple of chaps from my term are commanding them, and wearing four stripes, but once again I'm Commander.'

'I can appreciate that, but you're not going to do much for your chances of a command if you keep riding the engineers and the flyers the way you've been doing. Of course discipline is essential, but you're overdoing it on the small things, the trimmings if you like. Shepherd was completely in the wrong on this occasion, but he's also expressing a general feeling among the engineers that you're determined to find fault with them, and that you seem to apply different standards to the seamen officers from the rest.' He stopped, The Commander said nothing. 'You want a command, and another stripe when you've got enough sea time in, and you're not going to get either unless you and I make this ship work.'

'No, sir.'

'And remember that carriers are becoming more and more important in this war. You were in *Repulse*, and you must know that she and *Prince of Wales* were sunk by aircraft without a Japanese ship within miles. The Americans sank the Jap carriers at Midway with aircraft alone, and I think I'm right in saying that the battleships didn't even sight each other, let alone come within range. It looks now as though big guns are becoming obsolete, and aircraft are going to take over from them. *Crusader* may be nothing more than a Woolworth carrier, but you are getting carrier experience, which will do your prospects no harm at all.' The Commander began to look more cheerful. 'But the most important thing is to make this ship work. To begin with, there's no point in trying to treat the men, or the officers for that matter, as though they were boy seamen at *St George*. Most of these chaps are civilians in uniform, with a civilian mentality; they didn't grow up with service discipline the way you and I did at Osborne and Dartmouth. They question things, and they're quite likely to jib at anything which can't be seen as a sensible way of getting things done. "That's the way it's always been done" isn't going to cut much ice with them. You have to lead them, not dragoon them – ride them with a light hand and set them an example to follow.' He had the Commander's attention now.

'Let me give you an illustration. When I was a boy my grandfather had a young mare he'd bought virtually for carcase value because she wouldn't have anyone on her back. Beautiful animal, iron grey, very striking, but very nervy, very excitable. The chap who'd had her before had tried to beat her into submission, which only made her worse. My grandfather was Indian cavalry and had dealt with some wrong 'uns in his time. He worked on her over a matter of months, took everything very slowly, and very gradually got her confidence. It took him about two years before she was happy to have him ride her, but in the end she would do anything for him; she used to follow him about the yard without a bridle, she even tried to come into the house with him, and he could take her up some quite steep steps, with very little space to turn in at the top, and she never turned a hair. That was discipline, and it was all based on trust. She wouldn't do it for anyone else. She would let me ride her – I'd helped my grandfather with her, so I suppose she accepted me – but she was always a very hot ride, and if she'd had enough she had no compunction about putting me off. Do you see what I'm driving at? You can get discipline – the best sort of discipline because it's a matter of trust and mutual respect – and efficiency without resorting to an iron fist. All too often the iron fist is counter-productive. The engineers do a difficult job and you're not going to get the best out of them if you set out to antagonise them and generally treat them, as Shepherd himself put it, as though they'd just crawled out of the bilges.'

'I suppose not, sir.'

'Have you been to the engine room recently?' The Commander was silent. 'Then it's time you showed your face down there. Get Chief to take you round, and see what goes on. And you can do the same for the flyers.'

'Very good, sir.' The Commander's tone was resigned.

'Now, the wardroom. I fully agree that proper standards must be maintained, including standards of turnout, but you're never going to get the manners of a vicarage tea party in there. You don't get them from regular officers in peacetime. The officers have got steam to let off, and better that they do it aboard where we can channel it than ashore in front of civilians. Obviously that doesn't mean they can slop around in overalls, or in flying gear either, but as long as they don't wreck the place, get into fights with each other, or bring tarts aboard and they don't drink at sea.' He gave the Commander a moment to digest all that he said. 'I'm going to have Shepherd in here now, and you and Chief can hear what I have to say to him.'

Shepherd had had a night to sweat, and no doubt the Commander (E) had made it clear that he was in serious trouble. He looked subdued, the defiance of last night evaporated as he stood before his Captain and the Commander and Commander Hodgson who were standing in grim-faced silence behind Thurston's desk.

'You went into the wardroom in your overalls and working filth, in defiance of standing orders as well as all the normal rules of conduct, and the Commander was more than justified in rebuking you. Your language when rebuked would have been insulting at the best of times, the more so when used towards an officer considerably your senior in rank and experience. Not only that, your conduct was witnessed by several of your brother officers and by the bar stewards, to whom you set an extremely bad example. Commander Hodgson thinks very highly of you, Mr Shepherd, and for good reasons. You've let him down, and you've also let down your profession. We all know that engineer officers are supposed to be ill-mannered louts in greasy overalls, and you seem to have done your level best to live up to that not-very-flattering and generally inaccurate stereotype.'

Shepherd's face had begun to redden. He was wearing what was clearly his best uniform, the single stripe very bright and new.

'If there were any purpose to be served in having you court-martialled, I would not hesitate.' Relief began to spread across Shepherd's face. 'But my deciding against a court martial does not mean that I do not take a most serious view of this matter. In my ship I will have discipline and I will have proper respect for senior officers, Mr Shepherd, whatever your private opinion of them.'

Shepherd shot a glance at the Commander. 'Yes, sir.'

'Very well. You will furnish the Commander with a written apology by 1800 today. You will also provide reasons in writing for being in the wardroom in overalls in the first place, again by 1800, and you will carry out whatever extra duties the Commander (E) sees fit to give you. Do you understand?'

'Yes, sir.'

'You may consider yourself fortunate.'

'Yes, sir.'

'I don't wish to hear your name again, Mr Shepherd. You may go.'

The Commander and Commander (E) remained standing after Shepherd had gone.

'I'll see you get that apology, Arthur, and the reasons in writing.'

'Thank you, Chief, but I hope you're going to make that little blighter *work*.'

'I shall keep his nose firmly to the grindstone, never fear.'

'One thing before you go, Chief,' Thurston broke in. 'Can you spare Stoker McCutcheon from the boiler room when we leave here?'

'Ah, you've heard him with his bagpipes. I daresay we can.'

'Bagpipes?' the Commander said in a faint voice.

'Bagpipes are one thing the Yanks won't have.'

'I see, sir.'

'It will be in the open air,' Thurston reassured. 'If it works out, we can make a permanent thing of it, provided McCutcheon's willing and the engine room can spare him.'

'He'll be willing, sir,' the Chief said, smiling.

'Double march, double mark time. Pick those knees up! Halt! Off cap. Able Seaman Spencer, sir.'

'Read the charge, Master.'

Captain's Defaulters proceeded in its proper manner.

'Able Seaman Harold Thomas Spencer, sir, Official Number P/JX 137421. Fighting contrary to Article XVIII of the Articles of War in that he did, without reasonable excuse, fight with members of the United States Navy at Argentia, Newfoundland, on 7th November 1943. Witness, RPO Slingsby, sir.'

'Sir, I was in charge of the shore patrol on the 7th November 1943 and was called to investigate a disturbance at the shore canteen at approximately 1950. I arrived at the canteen with the patrol at approximately 1956 and found the Accused in the act of grappling with a member of the United States Navy whose identity I was unable to ascertain. I separated them and arrested the Accused, who appeared to be sober at the time. On arrival on board the Accused was placed under open arrest to appear on Commander's Report.'

'Do you wish to ask any questions of this witness, Spencer?'

Spencer knew the form. 'No, sir.'

'Thank you, Slingsby.'

Regulating Petty Officer Slingsby departed with a quivering salute and a crash of highly polished boots.

'Do you wish to call any witnesses on your behalf?'

'No, sir.'

'Have you anything to say?'

'No, sir.'

'Will you accept my award or do you elect trial by court martial?'

Spencer said nothing. His black eye had faded a little since yesterday, and his face was quite expressionless.

83

'May I see this man's documents, Mr Scott.'

Scott brought out Spencer's service certificate. Thurston rifled through it, for effect since both he and Spencer knew quite well what was in it. He put the document down on the green baize covering the table and waited a moment before beginning to speak.

'Spencer, you are a bloody fool! You have left a trail of similar offences extending back before some of your present shipmates were even born!' He picked up the parchment, and slammed it down again for emphasis. 'You've been disrated for fighting, you've done time in the cells for fighting, and more 10A than I can be bothered to count, and none of that has made the slightest impression on you. This time you don't even have the spurious excuse of being drunk! Spencer, the Americans, strange as it may seem, are on our side, and you can't go round trying conclusions with our allies. Do you understand?'

'Sir.' Spencer's expression had not changed. He had heard all this before, and would also have heard the usual stuff about letting himself down and letting the ship down.

'Spencer, this time I'm going to hit you where it'll hurt you. Someone of your age and length of service should be setting an example to the younger ratings, so I'm going to make an example of you. Three *good conduct* badges hardly square with your recent conduct, and so I am going to take them off you. Remanded, open arrest.'

Spencer's facade had collapsed. He would have expected to lose one badge, in conjunction with loss of pay and leave, but not all three.

'Remanded. Open arrest,' repeated the Master-At-Arms in ringing tones. 'On cap, salute the Captain. That's a sloppy salute, Spencer, you're not an American! Do it again! About turn! Double march! Pick those feet up, Spencer, move it!'

The defaulters had appeared in alphabetical order, and the last one was Stoker First Class James Watson, Official Number P/KX 311627, who grinned defiance across the table as he was convicted, subjected to the requisite bawling-out and sentenced to lose fourteen days' pay and leave. RPO Slingsby appeared as a witness once more, the Master-At-Arms announced for the seventh time that morning that his was a sloppy salute and to do it again. Thurston returned to his cabin, where an uncharacteristically silent Spencer produced a cup of coffee and a plate of chocolate biscuits.

'Every person subject to this Act who shall quarrel or fight with any other person, whether such other person be or be not subject to this Act, or shall use reproachful or provoking Speeches or Gestures tending to make any Quarrel

or Disturbance, shall suffer Imprisonment or such other punishment as is hereinafter mentioned.'

'On caps. Accused stand fast.'

The lower deck had been cleared, Spencer marched in under escort, and the relevant Article of War read.

The Commander cleared his throat anew and opened the punishment warrant with a dry crackling of paper. *'This is a warrant by Captain Robert Henry Maitland Thurston VC DSO Royal Navy, of His Majesty's Ship* Crusader, *dated this ninth day of November 1943. "Whereas it has been represented to me by Commander Arthur Templeton Canning, Royal Navy, that Harold Thomas Spencer, P/JX 137421, Able Seaman, did fight with members of the United States Navy while ashore at Argentia, Newfoundland, on the seventh day of November 1943.*

' *"I did on the ninth day of November 1943 summarily try the Accused.*

' *"Having heard the evidence of the following witnesses, namely Richard George Slingsby, P/JX 152684, Regulating Petty Officer . . ." '*

The back of Metcalfe's neck had begun to itch. He wished he could move to scratch it, wished the whole business was over. Spencer had already cut the badges off all his suits except the one he was wearing now. Metcalfe had told him he was sorry about it all, but Spencer just grunted and told him to go away.

'And the Accused having called no one on his behalf, I find the charge proved and I hereby sentence the said Harold Thomas Spencer to be deprived of three Good Conduct badges.

'Signed R. H. M. Thurston, Captain RN.'

'Accused and escort, march out! Remainder, dismiss!'

10

'Couldn't we just sabotage the Yank boat? Pull the bung out or something?' suggested Forrest.

'That's hardly sporting, Guns, I'm surprised at you. But if you want to swim under the Yank boat and drill a hole from below I won't try to stop you,' said Scott.

'We'd better just pray that God is on our side,' said Newell.

'This bloody boat isn't,' declared the PMO, 'I've never known anything like it.'

Thurston sat in his place and listened to the banter. It was another bright day with a cutting northerly wind, and while the boat was still he rather envied the cox his warm clothing. He flexed the fingers of his left hand. Spencer had produced some ice after the previous practice, and had insisted on strapping the wrist, but the arm seemed already to be swelling inside the bandages.

'Two minutes.'

The ratings' race had already been run, and won by the Americans by half a length. The Americans were expecting another victory from their officers, who were getting into their boat on the other side of the buoy.

'Look pretty impressive, don't they?' someone said.

The six Americans seemed, to a man, to be tall and tanned to the same degree, dressed in the same light blue tracksuits, which contrasted with a rich British assortment of football and rugby shirts, shorts and old grey flannels, weather-reddened faces and pale arms and legs.

'Off with that flying jacket, Wings. It must add two stone at least.'

Commander (Flying) stood up, shrugged out of the heavy sheepskin garment, and passed it to the Commander, who was standing in *Crusader*'s motor cutter with his American opposite number, ready to start the race.

'Good luck. I don't want to lose another fiver.'

Fredericksburg's Commander was saying much the same thing to his own crew. Thurston turned his head, saw Vincent's white knees protruding from long socks one place behind on the starboard side of the boat, hands gripping his oar. He grinned at Vincent, Vincent grinned back, flushed slightly. The Commander was giving last-minute instructions.

'Gentlemen,' the motor cutter rocked so that he had to straddle his legs to stay upright, 'this race is of one mile. You will go out to the buoy, turn round it to starboard. There is a judge there and any boat which fails to do this or which touches the buoy will be disqualified. You will then come back to the finishing line here.'

Maloney was in his own boat moored astern of the motor cutter, binoculars in his hand.

'Gentlemen, to your marks.' The Commander raised his starting pistol. The shot seemed to take a long time to come, and when it did it was unexpected, so that Crusader's crew took a moment to react and the Americans were already away and beginning to pull clear when they found their rhythm.

'Pull! Let's get it together.'

Maloney's boat had left the buoy and was following, sufficiently far away for the bow wave not to reach them. Crusader's cutter met a wave badly, so that part of it broke over the gunwale and the crew suddenly found a couple of inches of water around their feet. Commander (Flying) produced a bailer and got to work with one hand, using the other to steer the boat. Thurston sneaked a quick look ahead. The Americans had half a length's lead, but the gap was remaining constant.

'Pull! Lengthen your stroke a bit, PMO!'

Further out in the bay the water was rougher, and both coxes were having to bail continuously. American shouts were coming from their cox, and from Maloney's boat. Much further off, men were clustered along the rails of the warships, shouting encouragement, but the words were too far away to hear. Behind them was the grey-green marshland, extending featureless to the horizon.

'Buoy's coming up. Ready.'

The Americans went round the buoy still ahead, but took it fairly wide, keeping the starboard oars well clear. Commander (Flying) saw his chance.

'Right, we're going in close. Starboard side, stop pulling, toss your oars.' The buoy seemed to pass less than a foot away, a dull metal sphere, the paint worn away in places. Thurston looked up, to see the two ships' First Lieutenants watching in surprise, the American opening his mouth to protest.

'Everybody, pull!'

All six oars pulling again, Crusader's cutter shot away from the buoy, suddenly level with the Americans, only a few feet between the blades of the oars.

'Come on, lads, we've got them now.'

Thurston saw the American level with him, knuckles whitening on his oar, breath coming out as steam, upper body working back and forth in machine-like rhythm. His wrist had begun to hurt, a constant aching, with a sharp tugging up the inner side as his arms extended with each stroke.

'Come on, pull! Keep it going!'

There was the American's back, sweat darkening the light blue tracksuit. But the Americans were coming back, contesting every foot of advantage. Commander (Flying) was yelling himself hoarse, out-shouting the American cox. They were passing alongside the frigates now, and there was more yelling. '*Crusader, Crusader,* come on!'

There was a flash of foam at the end of a blade as an American caught a crab.

'Now's our chance! Speed it up!'

In the time it took the Americans to recover and regain their rhythm, the British had pulled half a length clear.

'Come on! One more effort!'

The Americans were coming back again, wearing away the lead by slow inches. But it was too late. *Crusader*'s boat crossed the finishing line with her bows still ahead, the crew dragging in each breath like drowning men and Thurston's weakened wrist hurting like hell, tossed oars a little untidily, and came to rest. They bent over their oars, for a moment caring about nothing but getting their breath. The Commander appeared, speaking congratulations and shaking hands, then the American commander, then Maloney himself.

'That was some race. One each. Or do you want a run-off against our enlisted men?'

Thurston stood up, stretched himself. 'Honours are even. Shall we leave it there?'

'Fine, but just you wait until next time!'

Someone produced a bottle of champagne, and persuaded the Americans that aboard *Crusader*'s boats they were on British soil and the rules of their own Navy did not apply. For a few minutes everybody was talking at the same time, re-running the race, arguing over *Crusader*'s turn at the buoy ('All the rules said was that we couldn't touch. Nobody said anything about all oars pulling!'), issuing invitations aboard their respective ships that evening. The Americans picked up their cox and threw him into the water; he was hauled aboard the motor cutter, dripping, by one of its crew.

Dinner had been cleared away and Thurston and Maloney were sitting in Thurston's cabin, each nursing a glass of brandy. Maloney had taken out a cigar and its aromatic smoke rose gently towards the deckhead.

'Well, it was quite an afternoon. I never thought you would get past us after that start of yours.'

'It's said that the British always fight best with their backs to the wall.'

'Yes, and you've kept on showing that right through this war. When I think of all the bombing you've had, and all the defeats, and you people just come back for more.'

'We haven't had much alternative.'

'Perhaps not, but it's pretty impressive all the same, when you look at the French, or the Belgians.'

Thurston was silent. He was comfortably full of wine and food – soup, roast lamb with all the trimmings, followed by the apple pie for which the wardroom chief cook had a justified reputation – and slipping into half-sleepy contentment.

Maloney was going on. 'I think it's been good for my boys to see how you people operate. Most of them get their ideas about the British from the movies. They think you all live in big houses in the country with rooms full of portraits and lots of maidservants or slums with outside sanitation.'

'Some of our chaps do, but not all of them by any means. More of them from the slums than the grand houses.'

'Where do you come from, Bob?'

'Northumberland. Up near the Scottish border, a very small place called Langdon, where my father was parson until he retired.'

'Sounds nice.'

'It can also be very bleak. The wind comes straight off the Cheviots, and the locals call it a lazy wind, because it can't be bothered to go round you, it goes right through you!'

Maloney laughed, topped up his glass from the decanter at his elbow. Spencer was hovering, an unfaded patch showing on one sleeve where his good conduct badges had been. He had been unnaturally quiet over the last few days, without his usual bounce and inconsequential chatter, though he had continued to carry out his duties as efficiently as ever.

There was a knock on the bulkhead, and the Commander's messenger came in.

'Captain, sir, the Commander sends his compliments and asks whether you and Captain Maloney will come to the wardroom.'

'Tell the Commander that we will be glad to.'

The wardroom was crowded and noisy, a mixture of English, Scottish and American accents rising above the general hubbub.

The Commander was waiting for them near the door, a steward nearby.

'Would you like a drink, sir?'

'Thank you, a small whisky.'

'I think I'd like to try your pink gin which I've heard so much about.'

The Commander said something to the steward, who glided away through the throng. Some of the pilots were noisily comparing the flying characteristics of the Seafire and the Hellcat, with which the Americans were equipped, Commander Hodgson and *Fredericksburg*'s Chief Engineer were deep in abstruse technical conversation about fuel systems, the cutter's crews were still arguing over *Crusader*'s turn.

'I'm afraid they're all talking shop,' the Commander apologised.

'At least it's friendly shop.'

'No reports of any trouble ashore,' said the Commander. 'Yet.'

'Seems we've buried the hatchet,' said Maloney.

'For the time being.'

Perhaps one more hatchet was about to be buried. Scott had told Thurston earlier that the wardroom was fairly buzzing with the news that the Commander had been seen in the engine room. Scott's informant, the Senior Engineer, declared that he had never expected to see anything like it, the Commander had even borrowed a pair of the Chief's overalls in order to go into some of the smaller spaces.

11

Crusader sailed from Argentia with the four ships of the escort group the following forenoon, with among the ship's company a definite air of having 'put one over the Yanks' – everyone seemed to have forgotten that the ratings' crew had been beaten by the Americans. The seven Newfoundlanders had returned from leave on time, despite the Commander's dire prognostications. A telegraphist who had once belonged to a Sea Cadet drum and bugle band had come forward in response to a notice Paymaster Lieutenant Scott placed in the first issue of the news sheet: 'Smart bugler wanted. Apply to Regulating Office' and was in his place ready to deal with salutes. The small figure of Stoker McCutcheon was standing in the bows playing 'The Black Bear' with gusto and considerable volume.

'One in the eye for the Yanks I'm sure,' commented Forrest, 'but did it have to be a *bagpiper*?'

Crusader had cast off her moorings and moved away from her berth, the whole operation proceeding exactly as it should up to that point.

'Port twenty.'

'Port twenty, sir.' A pause, then the Chief Quartermaster said in the same voice as before, 'Ship not answering helm, sir.'

The automatic response, 'Change to emergency steering. Hoist not-under-command signals.'

Fredericksburg's port bow was ahead, and getting close. The turn to port would have taken *Crusader* well clear, but she was still going ahead, closing the American ship at ten knots.

'Full astern.'

'Full astern, sir.'

The telegraph clanged, but it would take a moment for the engine to be put astern, and longer for the way to fall off, and *Fredericksburg* lay peacefully at anchor. Behind Thurston the Chief Yeoman had pushed through to the signal locker, with a brisk 'Gangway, sir!' to Forrest who had been standing in his path, and the two black balls were rising gently towards the yardarm.

'Cutting it fine,' someone muttered.

Thurston's lips were dry. *Marathon*'s helm had jammed hard over a month before that final convoy; she had come close to ramming the

91

flagship, and she was a quadruple-screw ship which could be steered with engines.

There was a change in the motion, and *Crusader* began perceptibly to slow.

'Just going to make it,' Forrest breathed.

The Chief Quartermaster's steady voice. 'Steering ready in emergency, sir.' *Crusader* came to a momentary stop, then began to go astern.

'Very good. Steer in emergency. Report ship's head.'

'Report ship's head, sir. Ship's head two-five-niner, sir.'

Thurston took a moment to weigh up the next order, looked briefly around him. Apart from *Fredericksburg* the other ships were well clear. The prudent course would be to keep on making stern way and create more room, but there was the familiar thrill of taking a risk, and the Americans were watching.

'Slow ahead. Hard a port.'

'Hard a port, sir.'

The engine room telegraph clanged. *Crusader* began to move forward, dipped her port side into the turn as eight stokers wrestled the helm over by hand. *Fredericksburg* was very close. Thurston found himself looking down onto her flight deck and at surprised upturned faces.

'Midships. Steer two-two-four.'

The ship settled to her new course. Just a turn to starboard and then a straight course out of the harbour. Forrest's breath came out in a long whistle. 'Never happens when we've got plenty of sea room and it doesn't matter,' said Beveridge.

'We made the Yanks shake a bit. Did you see them scatter?' said Forrest.

'Might be one or two pairs of dirty underpants among them.'

'What about dirty underpants here? That was a sight too close for my tastes.'

'It's phlegm you lack. Look at McCutcheon. He didn't notice anything, not even when the Yank's shadow fell across him!'

For a moment all was jokes and laughter, a sudden release of tension; for Thurston a glorious sense of relief that in an emergency the training had simply taken over, one half of his brain had reacted precisely as it should, his voice had issued the necessary commands without a change in tone, whatever the peaks of excitement and tension the rest of his brain found. He was aware that he was grinning rather foolishly as he stood there, conning *Crusader* through the final turn which would take her out of the harbour. In a minor emergency everything had worked: the engine room had been quick to put the engine astern, it had taken

92

only a couple of minutes to connect up the emergency steering, and a messenger had just arrived to state that Commander Hodgson had a party at work to find the fault. And down on the flight deck the men lining the rails had stood fast, and Stoker McCutcheon had continued to play, with no perceptible hesitation.

The improvement in morale might have lasted had things continued to go well, but six days out from Argentia they began to go wrong. The weather was good enough to allow a full flying programme, so that two Seafires were airborne over the convoy throughout the daylight hours, and a Swordfish patrolled at each quarter of the compass.

During the afternoon watch, just as the watchkeepers were beginning to think of getting below to tea, one of the Seafires smashed its undercarriage on landing. It was nobody's fault, the ship's stern suddenly dropped a few feet into a trough just at the point when the pilot had committed himself to a landing. The aircraft missed the wires, bounced heavily between them so that the fragile undercarriage collapsed outwards, and slewed round to port, looking for a moment as though it was going to run over the side, but coming to rest on a bent propeller with the port wheel hanging down into the catwalk below deck level and the wingtip over the edge. The pilot pushed back his canopy, climbed out rather gingerly and walked away, the flight deck party rushed up and got to work to move the aircraft clear of the landing area, but it would not budge.

'We'll have to shift her,' fumed Commander (Flying). 'She's blocking half the bloody flight deck.'

The second Seafire came up on the radio and announced that he only had five minutes' fuel left. The flight deck party, watched now by various men who were off watch and had been alerted by various means to come and see the fun, redoubled their efforts, tried to shift the Seafire forward, then aft, had men pushing the port wing up from below, while others sat on the starboard wingtip to weigh it down and act as a lever, even jumped up and down so that there was a loud metallic ringing and dents appeared in the surface.

'Put it over the side,' Thurston said finally.

But still the Seafire would not move far enough.

'We can't seem to get a proper purchase on it,' apologised Commander (Flying).

'He's down to two minutes' fuel,' someone reported.

'Tell him to ditch alongside one of the frigates.'

93

Commander (Flying) spoke into his radio handset. 'He wants to try a landing, sir. Think he's got just enough room.'

'All right, if he thinks he can make it.'

They watched as the Seafire began its approach, Commander (Flying) muttering under his breath, 'He should have just enough juice. There's always some sloshing about the bottom of the tank below the fuel gauge . . . Oh hell, he's off to starboard. Straighten up, for heaven's sake.'

The batsman waved the aircraft off.

'He'll have to ditch now . . . No, what the hell's he doing?' Commander (Flying) almost shouted into the handset. '. . . he wants to be a hero. He's not bloody well answering.'

The Seafire went round a much shortened circuit, and made a second approach.

'Who is it?'

'Newell. Just wait until I get my hands on him!'

All was suddenly very quiet, all eyes on the Seafire. The arrester hook picked up a wire, and for an instant it seemed that the aircraft was going to come down safely, but as the wheels were still above the desk, the port wingtip brushed the wingtip of the crashed aircraft. The Seafire swung violently to starboard, the pilot tried to recover, but the aircraft bounced as it hit the deck, one leg of the undercarriage collapsed, the swing to starboard continued, the still spinning propeller gouged a deep furrow in the wooden deck, and the Seafire finally fetched up against the base of the island.

Because the fuel tanks were empty there was no fire, but still the pilot made no move to get out. The flight deck party rushed up, hoses unravelling behind them. A man jumped up on either wing, they got the canopy open, dragged Newell out, his face streaming blood, deposited him on a stretcher and rushed him below. The remainder got the Seafire onto a trolley and trundled it over the barrier out of the way.

Commander (Flying) returned from the flight deck. 'Silly bugger didn't have his straps tight enough. Bashed his face on the gunsight. He's going to look lovely tomorrow. Still, the aircraft can be patched up, so we haven't lost it. Don't blame him for wanting to try a landing. The Seafire's a pig to ditch. She's nose-heavy to start with, and the radiator scoop in the nose just takes in water so she's likely to go straight down. You're better taking her up to two thousand and jumping, if it's at all possible.'

Thurston brought Commander (Flying) back to specifics. 'How long before the Swordfish are due back?'

'Twenty minutes.'

'Then your flight deck party has twenty minutes to get that Seafire out of the catwalk! And from what I've seen of them this afternoon they're not very good at getting aircraft out of the awkward spots they're likely to end up in, so instead of putting it over the side, they can use it to practise with until they *do* know how to do it!'

The following day the weather changed. A fierce headwind sprang up which brought flurries of snow and caused all the aircraft already airborne to be recalled. Two Seafires and three Swordfish landed safely, the fourth, patrolling astern, remained a distant blip on the radar screen.

'He's going to have a job getting back. The wind's up to fifty knots already.'

'How much fuel has she got?'

'Another half-hour, sir.'

'Keep me informed.'

The blip moved gradually closer, until the aircraft would have been visible, but for the snow.

'Twenty minutes' fuel, sir.'

'Thank you.'

On deck the flight deck party were striking the other aircraft below, the after lift yawning open. Double lashings were being put on the aircraft which would remain on deck.

Commander (Flying) appeared from the Air Plot. 'Sir, could we slow down? They're not going to make it if we keep up this speed.'

But they couldn't slow down. *Crusader*'s job was to stay with the convoy. And she was vulnerable herself, a tempting target for any U-boat which could get within range, and U-boat captains were becoming aware of the danger posed by escort carriers and their aircraft. Built on a merchant ship's unarmed and poorly compartmentalised hull, *Crusader* would be easy pickings away from the escort screen.

'No.'

Thurston went into the Air Plot. The blip was still there on the screen, keeping pace with the ship but moving no closer. The wind was still rising, the cups of the bridge anemometer spinning faster, it seemed, with every minute.

Commander (Flying) had followed him and went back onto the bridge with him. 'Sir, we'll have to turn back, or at least slow down,' he said in an urgent voice, though pitched low enough that only Thurston could hear.

There were three men aboard the Swordfish, but there were six hundred more aboard *Crusader*, to say nothing of the hundreds more aboard the merchant ships and the cargoes the merchant ships carried, who would be left without a carrier's protection for the time it took to slow down, for the Swordfish to land on, and then for the ship to catch up with the convoy.

'No.'

Commander (Flying) was about to say something, but Thurston cut him short. 'I can't turn the ship round, and you know damn well why.'

Commander (Flying) straightened up, 'Aye aye, sir,' and turned away.

One of the smaller escorts could be detached to pick up the Swordfish crew, if the escort commander could spare one. The snow cleared, and the sun came out, so that the Swordfish was just visible above the horizon.

'Ten minutes' fuel, sir.'

Even if they did not turn round now, the aircraft would no longer be flying when they reached her, and more precious minutes would be taken up while *Crusader* turned once more into wind to allow a landing. The men on deck were all silent now, mesmerised by the speck on the horizon, those in the Air Plot watching the blip on their radar displays.

The Officer of the Watch – Higgins – broke the silence by picking up the TBS handset. 'Captain, sir, *Thistle* reports an asdic contact.'

The corvette *Thistle* turned away from her position in the screen, to be followed by one of the frigates in response to the group commander's orders. Eyes on *Crusader*'s bridge flickered back and forth, torn between the Swordfish and the excitement of the hunt for a U-boat in which they could not participate. The minutes went by. The Swordfish was still airborne. *Thistle*'s first pattern of depth charges exploded, throwing up columns of yellowish water.

The ten minutes had passed, and the Swordfish was still in sight, just close enough for her biplane's double wings to be visible. *Thistle* and *Cothi* were a few cables apart on the port beam of the convoy, waiting the frustrating fifteen minutes while the disturbance caused by the depth charges calmed enough to allow their asdics to operate. The late afternoon sun was blotted out by cloud, more snow began to fall. Higgins picked up the TBS handset, spoke into it briefly, then replaced it on its bracket.

'*Thistle* reports contact lost, sir.'

The hunt was off, but they all knew there was no chance of an escort

96

being detached to search for a ditched aircrew while there was a possibility of a U-boat close to the convoy.

'Air Plot . . . Bridge.'

'Bridge.'

'Radar contact lost, sir.'

'Thank you.'

Thurston pulled himself up onto his bridge chair, settled the skirts of his duffel coat over his knees. No one spoke. They all avoided his eyes: Wings, Higgins and the rest. The sea was rising and the weather was cold. The snow settled on his knees in separate crystals which took a moment to turn transparent and collapse into droplets of water which disappeared into the heavy cloth. But the Swordfish crew were healthy young men and if they managed to get into their dinghy they might live for several days, growing weaker, first gradually and then more rapidly, but a rubber dinghy would not show up on radar and was unlikely to be sighted in the dark, and then when the last of their will to live had gone they would die.

His last clear memory of his own time on *Connaught*'s raft was of a grey pre-dawn, the fourth dawn after the sinking, holding a dead Royal Marine bandsman against his chest for a long time, filled with cold rage against the sea, and against Band Corporal Jeffries and all the other men who had died before him, until another man took Jeffries from him, quite gently and without speaking, and put him over the side. There had been dull stupor after that, broken from time to time when he would rouse himself to ask, as he had been doing ever since the sinking, 'Are you all right, West? Are you all right, Townsend? Are you all right, Petherick?' round all the other fuel-blackened wraiths who lived on, huddled together for a semblance of warmth and the primitive comfort of bodily contact. 'Are you all right, Macrae?' 'Are you all right, Cartwright?' A brief stir once when someone politely asked after he had completed the circuit, 'Captain, sir, 'are *you* all right?' He had known somehow that when all the rest were gone he would live on a little longer, surrounded by the bodies of his dead comrades which he no longer had the strength to put over the side. Thurston shuddered involuntarily, shook his head in an effort to clear the memory, and stood up.

'I'll be in my sea cabin.' A corvette had sighted *Connaught*'s raft on the evening of that day, and picked up twenty-one men who still lived, of whom three died later, so that eighteen survived of *Connaught*'s four hundred.

Commander (Flying) came to the sea cabin, and brought Bernard Mann, the squadron commander.

'Sir, I am not going to allow my Swordfish crews to patrol astern of the ship in severe headwinds again.' Mann was still wearing his flying kit and yellow Mae West, and was both angry and upset.

'Commander Sterling, do you concur with this?'

Commander (Flying) waited before replying. 'No, sir. I've made my views plain to Bernard, but he insisted on seeing you.'

'You can put me in irons if you like, sir, but I'm not going to do it.' Mann's jaw was set, his fingers clenched over the battered old cap he only wore at sea.

Thurston got up from the bunk he was sitting on. He was comfortably taller than either Commander (Flying) or Bernard Mann and seemed to fill the narrow space in front of them. 'Mr Mann, I'll make myself quite plain. Your aircraft and their crews are here to protect the merchant ships, and that is what they will do. If that requires them to do stern patrols in headwinds, then so be it. And you will ensure that they do it.' He did not trust himself to say more, to try to justify his stance.

Bernard Mann seemed about to say something, then he was cut off by a glance from Commander (Flying). There was a long silence, a meeting of eyes, as there had been with the Commander.

'Aye aye, sir. But I wish my protest to be on record.'

'Very well. Return to your duties.'

Commander (Flying) ushered Bernard Mann out, talking to him at a soothing pitch, '... Nothing else to do, Bernard ...'

The escort group commander sent *Thistle* back to search for the Swordfish crew, under wireless silence so that it was not until she returned hours later that they knew that all she had found was the dinghy, empty and overturned. *Thistle* had not lingered; she also was vulnerable to U-boats, and in any case no one could have lasted that long in the water.

Thurston left the bridge and went into the Air Plot, where the FDO was rubbing a blank space on the state boards with a damp rag, so that a glossy black area was left in the chalked surface.

'What were their names?'

'Sub-Lieutenant Curtis, Petty Officer Crane and Leading Airman Mason.'

Three names, to which he could not put faces, and he had killed them, just as surely as if he had taken a machine gun and shot down their Swordfish himself. He went to his sea cabin, pulled off his seaboots and duffel, sat on the bunk for a long time watching the opposite bulkhead. It had been the right decision, there had been nothing else to do, as with so many other things in this bloody war, the lives of a few men against those of hundreds.

There was a knock and Metcalfe came in. 'Brought you some tea, sir.'

'Thank you. Put it on the table.'

'Would you like anything to eat, sir?'

'Not now, Metcalfe. Perhaps later.'

'Are you sure, sir? You haven't had anything since dinnertime.'

'Metcalfe, I said no!'

Metcalfe seemed to jump back a pace, waiting to be dismissed. Thurston rubbed one eyebrow. 'Sorry, Metcalfe, that was uncalled for.'

'Spencer said you'd want to be by yourself, sir.'

'He did, did he?' Thurston stretched a hand out to the table, lifted the mug and drank some of the tea. 'And what brought you here against Spencer's advice?'

Metcalfe blushed a little. In his oversize duffel coat and sailor's cap he looked ridiculously young. 'I thought you could do with some tea, sir, and . . .' he continued awkwardly, the Geordie accent very noticeable '. . . well, that someone ought to make sure you were all right.' He hesitated again. 'It was an awful thing to have to do, sir.'

Thurston drank some more tea, turned his head back towards Metcalfe. 'I know. More than you know. More than Spencer knows.'

'Spencer said you'd had a sinking, sir.' Metcalfe seemed unable to decide what to do with his hands, finally contented himself with letting them hang loosely at his sides. 'But you ought to have some food, sir.'

'All right, since you're determined.' Thurston stretched his arms above his head, realised that he was indeed hungry, that the emptiness inside needed to be filled somehow. 'Tell Spencer that if he cares to do me one, I'll have one of his steak and kidney pies.'

'Aye aye, sir.' Metcalfe went out.

Thurston got up and went back to the bridge. It was still snowing, settling now on the wireless and radar aerials and as a white rime on the flight deck now that the wind had dropped once more. Perhaps it had not lasted long, the three men would not have known much about their end, though there would have been the drawn-out interval when it became clear that *Crusader* was not going to turn back for them, and the minutes or seconds of cold and terror in the sea itself. The convoy was spread out on four sides, each ship marked out by a light tracing of snow on her horizontal surfaces, a peaceful scene, but one which could be broken in a split instant of time, and then there would be pain and suffering and death by fire and drowning in the black water.

12

'Captain, sir. Commander (E) on the line.'

This, too, had become a frequent happening in the last few days. Commander Hodgson had already declared that he could not promise more than twelve knots because of contamination of the boiler fuel oil with salt water, and had more than once insisted on a further reduction in speed for brief periods while he dealt with a specific fault.

'Yes, Chief, what is it this time?'

Hodgson's voice was heavy and distorted by the telephone. 'We've had an accident in the boiler room, sir.'

'How serious?'

'Quite serious enough. A blowback. Two of my stokers were in the way. And my Senior Engineer's burnt as well. We're just clearing up. Can I give you a full report when that is done?'

Stokers Murray and Watson had been changing the burner bars in the furnaces, a routine task when the watches changed, a few minutes after 2000. They were well practised, and worked together in a series of co-ordinated movements, Murray turning off the fuel supply to each bar in turn, closing off the air inlet and unscrewing the clamps, while Watson deftly pulled out the bar and replaced it with one which had been cleaned during the previous watch; Murray clamped it into place and turned the fuel and air supply back on, so that the bar once again carried ignitable fuel-air mixture into the furnace. Murray and Watson had dealt with one furnace, and most of the bars in the second. The Senior Engineer, who had the watch and was making his habitual initial tour of the engine and boiler rooms, was keeping an eye on them, when suddenly there was a roaring noise, and a bright rush of flaming gases shot out of the front of the furnace. Watson had got the bar out, and was leaning forward to slide the fresh one into place, and suddenly he was screaming, his overalls on fire above the asbestos gloves he was wearing, the fire feeding itself on the old oil and grease splashes down the front. He turned and ran blindly away from the furnace opening. Murray had been off to one side and jumped clear, thumping his burning sleeve and leg with his gloves.

The Senior Engineer was rooted to the spot on which he was standing for a second, then he recovered, rushed forward in a few long strides.

He almost cannoned into Watson, then grabbed him by the shoulders, turned him round and pushed him down onto the deck, rolling him over and over. The junior engineer of the watch had realised what was happening a moment after him and came running up.

'Don't just stand there gawping! Get the fucking extinguisher!'

The Sub-Lieutenant wrenched the fire extinguisher off the bulkhead, struggled to turn it on. 'Bloody thing's jammed!' He cursed and struggled a little longer, then turned, saw a wheel spanner lying nearby and dealt the top of the extinguisher a heavy blow. Foam spurted out, the Sub wrestled to hold the thing steady.

'Point it this way, you idiot! Oh turn it off, it's doing nae good now.'

Stoker Watson lay face up on the deck plates, no longer screaming but only moaning, sucking in air through the gaping red hole where his mouth had been. His features seemed to have dissolved, swelling even as the Senior Engineer looked down on them in appalled fascination. The front of his overalls had been burnt away as far as the knees, leaving a few charred shreds which would flake away at a touch. The flesh beneath was charred, and blackened in places like the face, and gave off a strong aroma of roasted beef. The Sub-Lieutenant had turned aside and was being sick.

'Turn that bloody extinguisher off, you fool!'

Watson screamed again. 'I can't see!' The Senior Engineer tried to reassure him. 'Sir, I can't see!!'

Murray was standing with his back to the bulkhead, looking stunned, burnt all down one side, the right half of his face, right arm and right leg.

The Senior Enginee looked up from Watson, turned to the Sub, who was leaning white-faced against the nearest ladder. 'Get a stretcher, and the PMO, and get hold of Chief. Tell him we've had a blowback . . .' His voice trailed off. The Sub did not move. 'Get on with it, boy! Or I'll throw *you* in the bloody furnace!' The Sub began to talk into the telephone. The Senior Engineer tried once more to quiet Watson, aware only of a great helplessness in the face of all this. He was a tall stringy Aberdeenshire Scot, named William Duff and known variously as Huff or Figgy Duff, both of which he disliked.

When the PMO arrived with the stretcher party Duff moved away, propped himself half-sitting on the ladder, took little notice of what was going on, found himself shivering although the boiler room was as hot as it normally was.

'You'd better come with us as well,' the PMO said briskly. 'Get those hands fixed up.'

Duff looked down at his hands, became aware for the first time that the palms were scorched richly red and rising in blisters. He was silent for a time, holding his hands in front of him, hardly noticing the Chief, whose arrival he had not taken in, telling him that he would take over for the rest of the watch. The Chief was telling him to go with the doctor, laying a hand on his shoulder. He began to whimper, and then someone took him by the arm and led him away.

Stoker Watson died five hours later. Surgeon Lieutenant-Commander Barnard rang the bridge, reporting the death to the Officer of the Watch.

'You'll have to come up,' Forrest told him.

'What for?' Barnard was tired, and a little irritated.

'When there is a death on board, sir, the medical officer reports it directly to the Officer of the Watch.'

'Oh, very well, if you insist, but since I've already told you once I can't see what difference it will make.'

Barnard came up to the bridge, made his report anew. Forrest moved to the Captain's voicepipe.

'You can't wake the Captain *now*. It's after one a.m.'

'Of course I can. This is the way it's always done,' Forrest said with his usual air of condescension towards non-regular officers. 'Captain, sir. The PMO's here.'

'All right, I'm coming up.'

This is so bloody pointless, and unnecessary, Barnard thought as the Captain arrived on the bridge and Forrest made the formal report. 'Sir, Stoker Watson died at 0119.'

'Put it in the log.'

'Aye aye, sir.'

Thurston turned to Barnard, waiting for him to say something.

'It was no go from the start, sir. Forty per cent burns. He never had a chance.' In civilian life Barnard was a paediatric registrar in a large hospital in Manchester. He was learning now that the age of a patient made little difference to the sense of loss at his death.

'What about the other two?'

'They'll be all right. Senior's burns are fairly superficial, but he's very shaken – hardly surprisingly – and so I'm going to keep him in the sick bay for a couple of days. Murray will probably need some skin grafts.'

'Tell the sailmaker to go to my cabin when he's finished and get a glass of brandy from my steward.'

They buried Watson from the flight deck at dawn, sewn up by the sailmaker in a length of canvas, with the traditional last stitch through what remained of his nose as a final proof that he was dead. *Crusader* carried no chaplain so Thurston read the service, Stoker McCutcheon played a pibroch, and the telegraphist who had been a bugler in the Sea Cadets sounded the Last Post and Reveille for him, for the Swordfish crew and for all the other young men who would never have the chance to grow old.

'Don't suppose we'll see much of Sails today,' Spencer confided to Thurston at breakfast. 'He was telling me when he knocked me up for his brandy that he had to go to the wardroom to get a whisky on the Chief's bill and another on the doctor's, and Watson's mess are going to give him gulpers at tot time.'

Crusader came into the Clyde two days later, her men much subdued. Several times a Swordfish had come back early with the crew complaining of falling oil pressure or some other defect which the engineers could not afterwards locate, the stokers had shown a marked reluctance to do any job involving the furnaces, a situation which only improved after the Commander (E) and the Chief Stoker summoned them all to the engine room and bade them watch while they changed the burner bars themselves.

The ship was still under way when a motor cutter crewed by Wrens came alongside, kept pace with her while a young Wren officer climbed the Jacob's ladder to the quarterdeck, hand to her tricorn hat.

'Orders, sir.'

Thurston signed the proffered clipboard, took the sealed envelope.

'You're to go straight to the oiler, which is ready for you, and the petrol barge.'

'We're going out again?'

'Yes, sir. It's all in the orders.'

The men must have realised what was going on, for there were no wolf whistles this time, and only the merest suggestion of banter towards the Wren coxswain who was fending her vessel off with a boathook.

'D'ye hear there? Captain speaking. Our orders have just arrived. We are going to refuel and sail at 1800 hours to join the escort for another convoy. This means that there will be no shore leave on this occasion. That is all.'

'The men aren't going to like this,' someone said.

'Unfortunately, the men are going to have to put up with it.'

'Boat ahoy?'

104

'Flag *Spartiate*!'

'Barge approaching, sir.'

Rear Admiral Manning-Wilson came aboard as soon as *Crusader* was secured to the oiler and fuel had begun to flow into her tanks.

'Nothing for me, Bob. I shan't stay long, but I wanted to see you before you go out again. I must say I'm very taken with your piper. Even Johnnie Walker makes do with gramophone records.'

'I'm afraid it's not original, sir. *Scylla*'s had pipers for a long time and I don't suppose she's the only one.'

'Nevertheless, it adds an interesting touch. How did you get on? Are you getting to grips with my problem child?'

'It's all in the report, sir.' Thurston was tired, and the damp had crept into the old wound in his shoulder, making him more irritable still. He found he was saying much more than he intended. 'We lost eight men, all without even a sniff of the enemy. A pom-pom crew went overboard on the way out. Then we lost a Swordfish because I didn't turn back for them and they ran out of fuel. I had my squadron commander in afterwards to tell me that he wouldn't have his chaps patrolling astern in high winds again, and I had to tell him that he would do his duty and they would do theirs, and that was whatever was required of them.' He had got up from his chair and was beginning to pace the carpet, hands thrust into his side pockets, pain stabbing between his shoulder blades. 'In his place I'd probably have done the same . . . And when you've gone I've got to sit down and write to their mothers, wives or whatever and tell them that they died doing their duty and all the usual hogwash . . . I shouldn't be talking like this, I know, sir . . . And there was a stoker, in the boiler room . . . I shouldn't be talking like this,' he said again.

'It doesn't matter, Bob. Better to get it off your chest if you need to. We've lost far too many ships from swanning off by themselves without orders, whether it's to pick up survivors or anything else, and far too many men with them. You did the right thing, but it's not the easy thing.'

'It's all in the report anyway. It's being typed up at the moment.' Thurston sat down again, found he was avoiding the Admiral's eyes.

'I think I'd better have that drink.'

Thurston rang for Spencer, who busied himself with glasses.

'Just ginger ale for me, Spencer.'

'Aye aye, sir.'

'And don't think I don't know,' Manning-Wilson said when Spencer had gone out, 'I sit behind my desk facing far less danger from the enemy than there is in crossing the street in the blackout, sending ships and men out, and all too often they don't come back, and I wish to God I could just be out there with them. Don't blame yourself. It's the war. Have yourself a brandy and get your head down while the oiling's going on.'

'Not when we're sailing, sir.'

'Ah, yes, of course. You still don't drink at sea. Get the doctor to fix you up if you need it.'

'I'll be all right, sir.'

'Good man. I won't detain you any longer, but we'll have that dinner when you get back. It's about time.'

The next caller was the Commander (E).

'I'm just writing to Watson's mother, before the mail goes ashore.'

'That's what I've come about. One of his messmates found these when he was going through Watson's effects.' The Chief deposited a photograph and several letters on Thurston's desk. 'It seems that Watson had a girlfriend ashore and a child by her, whom I didn't know about.' Watson looked out of the creased snapshot with the same cocky grin he had shown on Defaulters, a clean-scrubbed young sailor with his arm around his girl, the baby on his knee. 'Obviously the girl won't get the telegram because she's not his next-of-kin, and we've no idea whether Watson's family know about her. I think the best course is to send her these, and I'll write to her, but I thought I should clear it with you first.'

'By all means, Chief. I'd better write to her as well.' That made another to add to the letters waiting to be done. 'Any news of Senior and Murray?'

'Murray's gone to hospital ashore. Wullie Duff came to me just now and said he wanted to go back on duty. He can't use his hands much but he's had his fill of the PMO fussing around him. But he's still a bit shaken up, so I'm going to keep an eye on him.' The Chief looked weary, and older even than his years. He was still talking, almost to himself. 'The doctor doesn't think he suffered much. Not after it happened at any rate. He says that he was so badly burned all the nerve endings were gone.'

'It wasn't your fault, Chief.'

'I know, sir. I'd like to tell whoever designed these American fuel systems just what I think of his work, and I'd have liked him to see what they did to Watson. He was a cocky little devil, and he could be

106

awkward with it, but he was one of my men, and it happened in my boiler room.'

'And in my ship, Chief.'

'Yes, sir,' the Chief said simply.

The mail had arrived and Thurston would have liked to settle down with six weeks' worth of letters from Kate, but there were the condolence letters to be finished, a session with Scott and the most urgent paperwork, and the ship to be manoeuvred from the oiler to the petrol barge to top up her tanks with aviation spirit, before he could get into the bathroom and start to clean off the traces of three weeks at sea. But this time there would be no chance of indulging himself in a long hot bath and an early night between clean sheets – in any case the Americans had only provided showers.

'Want me to rub your back when you're finished, sir?' Spencer called out.

'How do you know?'

'You're walking a bit funny, sir. I always know.'

'Spencer, sometimes you know too much.'

He washed his hair twice, stood under the hot water for several minutes, then turned on the cold for a few seconds. He put his trousers back on and padded barefoot into the sleeping cabin, to stretch out on his bunk with his face on his forearms and submit himself to Spencer's ministrations. Spencer upturned the bottle of brownish liniment, shook some onto his hands, sent up a pungent smell as he rubbed them together.

'Did you get any mail from Rosie, Spencer?'

'Yes, sir. Quite a pile. She's got the cake made, and put it away to mature a bit. But,' his voice became gloomy, 'I dunno what's going to happen now. I haven't told her about losing me badges yet. I don't know what she's going to think. It was bad enough when I lost me hook last time. I'm just thinking, sir, maybe I should just leave it until I get them back, and then she won't know.' Thurston considered for a moment. 'It might be better to tell her. You're likely to get leave between now and then and she might find it a bit strange if you turn up to see her without them.'

'That's true, sir. Or I could just not go on leave.'

'She might find that a bit strange too.'

'Yes, sir. That's the problem. And I don't want to be left hanging round the ship when I could be with Rosie. Got to make sure the Yanks keep off her.'

107

'Guarding her jealously, are you?'

'Yes, sir. I don't think she'd go off with a Yank. She's not that kind of girl,' he added determinedly. 'But I can't take a chance. Rosie's my girl, and that's how it's going to stay.' Spencer ceased his rubbing for a moment and pushed back the sleeve of his jumper to reveal a fresh tattoo depicting a rose and a heart entwined, with *Mine Forever* spelt out beneath.

'Spencer, you'll get your badges back in six months – five and a half now – if you can keep your nose clean that long, and you'll get your hook back six months after that . . . But it's about time you grew up a bit and stopped getting into fights like some sprog OD on his first shore leave and full of swank, trying to prove himself a hard case.' Thurston winced as Spencer found a tender spot, and again as Spencer turned his hand over and began to knead with the knuckles.

'That's all in knots, sir. Every time I think that's going to be the last, but it just seems to happen again. I'm not bothered about the hook meself, it's Rosie who thinks it's important. But the badges are special.'

'That's why I took them off you. Only thing that was going to make any impression.'

'I know. You told me last time you'd have them off me if I did it again.'

'Spencer, it sounds as though she's worth a bit of effort on your part. Worth keeping out of trouble for. You write to her. Tell her that the honour of the Royal Navy needed defending against the Yanks, or you were trying to protect Metcalfe or something – you're pretty good at dressing things up. Ow!' Spencer's knuckles had begun to drive into the corrugated muscles between his shoulder blades.

'If it hurts it must be doin' some good, sir.'

'And simply beg her forgiveness.'

'Do you think it'll work, sir?'

'I don't know, Spencer. I don't know the lady. But if she's refusing to marry you until you get your hook back, it may be that she's waiting for you to prove to her that you're a responsible fellow, and losing your badges is hardly in keeping with that.'

'Yes, sir. She's been telling me that it's not just her I'm taking on, but the girls as well.' Spencer thought for a moment, probed with his fingers and started work on another tender spot. 'Maybe if I put some nylons in with the letter. I got her some at Argentia.'

'How did you manage that?'

'Ah, wouldn't you like to know, sir.' Spencer flashed his wide con-spiratorial grin. 'I was keeping them for when I go on leave, but maybe this time . . .' Spencer stopped speaking again for a time, working at Thurston's back with both hands. 'Sir, could you have a look at the letter when I've done it? See if it's all right?'

'Spencer, I'm not here to sort out your private life, and the thing will sound a bit artificial if I draft it for you. Just do the best you can. I'll check the spelling if you want me to, but that's all. And you'd better get started if you're going to catch the mail.'

'Aye aye, sir. Just about finished this now. That any better?'

Thurston lifted his chest off the bunk, stretched his arms out sideways. 'Much, thanks.' Warmth and looseness had begun to spread through his back, the heat from the liniment and the rubbing doing their work.

'There you are, sir.' Spencer sniffed the air. 'You're going to smell lovely on the bridge.'

He glanced through his letters; the proper reading would have to wait. George had damaged an accommodation ladder with one of *Duke of York*'s boats, and been given a week's masthead watches in consequence – *better than getting my leave stopped though it is a bit of a bore.* Kate had stopped being sick. *I woke up yesterday morning feeling fine. I got up still feeling fine, and I've been fighting fit ever since, so it looks as though it's finally stopped, thank heavens.* Langdon was enjoying a spell of fine weather and his father had gone out with the hunt for the opening meet of the season, *though it proved a blank day and I brought Omega home early.* The old man had been advised by his doctor years ago to give up hunting, but he continued to declare that he had no intention of doing so and that he was not ready to restrict himself to idling about the lanes yet. Scott brought some letters for signing; Thurston added a few more lines to the pile in the envelope addressed to Kate. Spencer brought a scribbled and much crossed-out epistle for scrutiny, and Thurston, somewhat against his better judgement, lent him a pen with which to write it out properly.

Commander Canning arrived to report the ship ready for sea. 'We've one man adrift, sir. Able Seaman Dennis failed to report for his watch. We checked with his messmates and he hasn't been seen since we got in earlier, except that one of the sentries noticed someone hanging round the fuelling hose whom he thinks could have been Dennis. It was getting dark by then and he didn't get a proper look at his face. If it was Dennis he could quite easily have got himself to the petrol barge and then ashore from her. Someone from Dennis's mess said that

Dennis had been saying that "they" wouldn't get him to sail with this – I'm sorry, sir – this "hoodoo ship" again.'

'Who is Dennis?' Thurston cursed his incomplete knowledge of *Crusader*'s men.

'He's another T124X. Fancies himself as a hard man, and he certainly looks a bruiser. He's gone absent before, from one of the *Archer* class, which one escapes me at the moment.'

'We haven't time to send a patrol out for him before we sail, and he could be well away by now. Get a signal off to *Spartiate*. Where does Dennis come from?'

'London, sir. Somewhere in the East End, I think.'

'Then he'll presumably head for Glasgow to begin with. A Londoner's hardly going to hole up in the Highlands at this time of year. Could you alert all the railway stations in Glasgow? If he's on his way there now he may just step off the train into the hands of the Military Police.'

'I've already done that, sir.'

'Excellent. Let's get this ship to sea.'

It was quite dark now, and raining out of a leaden sky, a sense of weariness hanging over everything as *Crusader* manoeuvred herself clear of the petrol barge and set course seawards.

13

'When is it that our ASV Swordfish can find U-boats? When the U-boats are on the surface. And when are the U-boats most likely to be on the surface? At night. And it is at night that they are most likely to attack the convoy. Then why, gentlemen, do we not have our aircraft flying patrols at night?'

Bernard Mann shifted uncomfortably on his chair. 'My chaps haven't had much training in night flying,' he said rather lamely.

Commander (Flying) came to his rescue. 'The problem is landing at night, sir. We've a radio beacon to guide them back to the ship, and the Swordfish can find us by ASV of course, but we've still got to get them down safely. And if you turn on all the lights so they can land on, we become a beautiful brightly lit target for any passing Hun.'

Thurston, Commander (Flying) and Bernard Mann were sitting in the Fighter Direction Room, otherwise empty now that flying had finished for the day, cups of coffee in front of them and the air, stale already from its normal occupants, growing heavy with cigarette smoke.

'Could the lights not be shielded so they can only be seen from directly above and a few degrees on either side?'

'What about the batsman's signals?' asked Bernard Mann.

'Put lights on his bats. The deck lights would need to be visible from well astern for landing, but they wouldn't need to be all that bright, just enough to show where the deck is. The chaps should be able to fly themselves back to within visual touch of the ship by the beacon and ASV. They'll only need the lights for the landing.' Commander (Flying) was warming to the idea, swinging his legs over the side of the desk he was sitting on. 'After all, there's nothing new about night flying from a carrier. What about Taranto? And the *Bismarck* chase?'

'Of course it's been done,' said Bernard Mann. 'But this thing's only got about a quarter of the landing space of *Illustrious* or *Victorious*.'

'You don't need that much space to put a Swordfish down. I wouldn't fancy it with a Seafire, but a Stringbag'll do anything. Someone I know flew from Malta to Algeria with a push bike lashed to the fuselage. He landed up in a marsh but that was duff intelligence, nothing to do with the aircraft. Come on, Bernard, where's your sense of adventure?'

'I don't think it's a matter of a sense of adventure. I mean to survive this war and I would like as many as possible of my chaps to survive it as well. We have quite enough accidents landing in daylight. Captain, sir,' he turned to face Thurston, 'with the greatest respect, you're not a flyer and you can't therefore be fully aware of the problems involved, and I don't know whether Commander Sterling's done any night landings aboard an escort carrier.'

'Nevertheless, at this time of year we're losing about fifteen hours in twenty-four by not flying between dusk at 1700 and dawn at 0800, and those fifteen hours are precisely the time when we're most likely to be able to find U-boats.'

'Of course, sir,' said Mann. 'But I don't think the loss rate would justify it. We'd find ourselves running out of aircraft, or worse, crews, inside a week.'

'You don't seem to have much faith in your pilots, Bernard.'

'Most of them are on their first operational squadron, they've been rushed through training and it's only now that they're getting the hang of deck landing in daylight, let alone at night. It's not like peacetime, when they had time to learn, and make a few mistakes in the process.'

'I think you underestimate them.' Commander (Flying) was doing the talking for Thurston. 'They learn far quicker in wartime than in years of peacetime flying. I think we should get the engineers to look at the flight deck lights, wait for a fine night and simply have the chaps go through some circuits and bumps. We can start with the most experienced, and if they can do it all right, the rest can have a try. In point of fact, I need to fit in a few more hours before the end of the year to keep my flying pay, and this seems as good a way as any of doing it.'

Bernard Mann found himself overruled and, reluctantly, agreed to the experiment.

'I'm a bit worried about him, sir,' Commander (Flying) admitted. 'I think he may just be starting the twitch. He didn't used to be as defeatist as this. That business when Curtis's crew ditched did shake him up pretty badly. I've never seen him like that either.'

'Is it affecting his flying?'

'Not so's you'd notice. As far as flying's concerned he's as safe as he ever was.'

Thurston knew well enough from his own experience that if a man obviously cracked, so that his judgement had gone and he could no longer do his job, the service would step in and get him ashore and out of harm's way. But if he maintained his professional efficiency, even

112

though he might be falling to pieces inside and those around him knew it, it was up to him to go to his superior, or to the doctors, and have himself put ashore, and take the guilt that was engendered by a sense of deserting his post and failing to meet his responsibilities.

'How long has he been flying?'

'He was on either the first or the second RNVR pilots' course in '39, so it's about four years in all, though not operational flying all through.'

'And this is his first squadron command?'

'Yes. He's had the squadron about four or five months. He was Senior P while they were working up and for the first couple of months aboard, and got his half-stripe and took over when the last chap pranged about June–July time.'

'Keep an eye on him, if you could, Wings, and push him towards the doctor if you think he needs it.'

'Aye aye, sir.' Sterling got up to leave.

'Don't go yet, Wings. There's one more thing. Bernard Mann's quite right about one thing. It's a distinct disadvantage in this job, not being a flyer, and it might give me a better idea if I had some first-hand knowledge. I know the Yanks insist that any officer posted to a carrier qualifies as a pilot or observer if he isn't already. Would it be possible for me to learn to fly?'

'Not in a Swordfish, sir, and certainly not from a carrier at sea.' Commander (Flying) paused while he lit another cigarette. 'Getting you airborne is no problem, but actually teaching you to fly is another matter. We haven't a suitable aircraft on the squadron, and I'm not a QFI so I couldn't teach you, but... Let me think.' He blew some smoke out through his nostrils. 'There's a chap I trained with in the RAF; he stayed with them when I transferred and he's doing some sort of liaison job at Abbotsinch at the moment. Nobody seems to have worked out what he's supposed to be doing and he's bored stiff. They've also got a Tiger Moth at Abbotsinch which he can get his hands on. He is a QFI – he was instructing on Magisters at Luton until a few months ago – and he might be glad of a chance to keep his hand in. I'll have a word with him when we get in. Of course, you appreciate that it would be highly illegal and we'd have to keep it all very quiet. And you are a bit on the old side to start flying from scratch. How old are you exactly, sir?'

'Forty-four.'

'It's a good deal easier to learn when you're nineteen or twenty. Your reactions are a bit quicker and you don't have so many inhibitions –

113

you're not worried about making a fool of yourself. However, that doesn't mean it hasn't been done. The Yanks make a big thing about Halsey getting his wings at over fifty, though there may be a bit of a fiddle involved there, and I do know that the Commander at Machrihanish, who must be at least your age since he was in the last war, got someone to teach him and now he goes up in anything he can get his hands on, even Barracudas, which certainly shows some want of grey matter. They're absolute pigs. Do you ride, sir?'

'Yes, of course.' He smiled. 'I was practically brought up on horseback.'

'They do say that if you can ride a horse you can fly a plane. Not a hundred per cent true, but it does mean that you're unlikely to be heavy-handed. I'll have a word with this chap. It'll be up to him whether he does it or not, and I don't know how far he'll be prepared to take you – whether he'll be prepared to try to get you solo – but I think I could persuade him to give it a go.'

'Any prospect of a calm night tonight, Met?'

The Meteorological Officer, an Instructor-Lieutenant RNVR who had once considered entering the Church and had in peacetime taught history and divinity at a minor public school, blinked behind his spectacles, and bent towards his chart. 'Sir, this area of low pressure here,' he indicated with a pencil, 'is gradually moving away and filling. This means that the present Force Five winds should gradually moderate during the afternoon.'

'How far?'

'Possibly as far as Force Three, sir, but certainly below fifteen knots. And broken cloud, between five and seven-tenths, with the cloud base above two thousand feet. Unfortunately, sir, I cannot be any more precise.'

Commander (Flying), standing on the other side of the Met Officer, listened and nodded. 'Then it's on for tonight. If you could ask the SO Escort to position a frigate as a safety boat in case someone goes in, assuming he can spare one, of course. I'll arrange a late supper for the Swordfish crews and we can start as soon as it's dark. With any luck the U-boats will just be getting some fresh air down their throats and will leave us all in peace for a couple of hours – Touch wood!' Commander (Flying) tapped the side of his head.

It was very quiet on the bridge. The wind had dropped as promised and the single Swordfish which had been brought up from below was silhouetted against a sky of ragged cloud and the first pale stars. From the bridge small points of light were visible at regular intervals along the margins of the flight deck, red to port, green to starboard. For two days there had been earnest discussions between the Commander (E), the Air Engineer Officer and the Swordfish pilots as to the extent to which the lights had to be visible from above; the workshops had produced movable steel shades for all the flight deck lights and several hours had been spent in adjustments until the other escorts could confirm that nothing was visible from the sea. Commander (Flying) made a brief appearance on the bridge in flying kit and Mae West, helmet and goggles in hand. 'Time I did something to earn my flying pay.'

The first Swordfish was in position for take-off, her guns loaded, but with no depth charges in the racks, and only a moderate fuel load. Thurston turned *Crusader* into wind. Commander (Flying), the observer and telegraphist air gunner climbed aboard. Two men inserted an outsize starting handle into the aircraft's nose and began to crank it. At the third turn the engine coughed and a second later fired, gradually settling into even running. The batsman held up a green-shaded torch and the Swordfish began to move forward, her engine note rising as she reached maximum revs. She reached the end of the flight deck, dropped out of sight below the bows momentarily and then began to climb away. Commander (Flying) made a circuit to port, flew over the ship, then began a second. Someone appeared from the Air Plot.

'He's asking for the lights to be adjusted. Says he can't see enough astern.' There was silence for ten minutes as the Swordfish orbited the ship, and a party went round the flight deck moving the shades.

The TBS crackled into life. Sub-Lieutenant Vincent picked up the handset. 'Sir, *Deveron* says we're all lit up astern.'

'Signal from *Gannet*, sir. *I do like your fairy lights.*'

'Signal from *Mawddach*, sir. *You look like a Brock's benefit.*'

Again the flight deck party had to reposition the shades, until the humorists were satisfied.

'Put the speaker on.'

The loudspeaker at the rear of the bridge crackled on. 'Ah, that's better,' said Commander (Flying)'s voice. 'Here we go.'

The Swordfish came round to *Crusader*'s stern. 'That's lovely. You're nicely in sight now and . . . just a moment, I lose you if I drop too low. And there's Bats now. Coming in.'

Crusader ploughed on serenely, pitching fore and aft in a moderate

115

sea. Commander (Flying) came in, the batsman indicated frantically to starboard and then waved him off.

'A bit off to port. I think we could do with a couple of lights down the middle of the runway. Right, let's try it again.'

This time there was no mistake. The Swordfish approached, fishtailing to lose height, and landed neatly up the centre of the flight deck.

'Basically,' Commander (Flying) said when he came up to the bridge, grinning triumphantly, 'the lights are fine as they are. There are probably some fine adjustments we can make, but all we really need now is a couple of lights up the middle of the landing run. And once we've got that sorted out, we'll only need to switch everything on when someone's actually about to land. But I had to be quite close to the ship before I saw anything, especially ahead, and nothing at all when I got near the water.'

There was another hiatus while a couple of white lights were brought up from below and rigged at either end of the landing run, then Commander (Flying) took off once more, made two more landings and handed over to Bernard Mann. One by one the pilots took off, and made their circuits and landings, without mishap, beyond one who had to be waved off twice.

'Satisfied?' Commander (Flying) asked of Bernard Mann.

'All right, it works. But this is a quiet night and the aircraft's not fully loaded.'

'We've got to start somewhere. And you needn't bring up Hope. He does that often enough in daylight. Anyway, with any luck you won't have too many landings with depth charges aboard – you'll have used them on some poor unsuspecting U-boat!'

Later that night two fully laden Swordfish took off, patrolled in the vicinity of the convoy for their allotted span, and returned safely to the ship to report a completely blank patrol.

14

Over the next few days the aircrews gradually settled into a new routine, the Seafires patrolling by day and releasing the radar-equipped Swordfish for work at night. A Canadian escort group from Halifax took over the westbound convoy and *Crusader* and the British escorts turned southwards to meet a second convoy homeward bound.

The Commander came up to the bridge soon after 2300. 'I've had a report of a strong smell of petrol in the wardroom bedding store. Higgins came to see me just now to say that he noticed it when he went to get an extra blanket. He got halfway down the ladder, then decided to put up with cold feet. Commander (E) thinks there must be a leak in the vent pipe from one of the petrol tanks and he's sent a party to check.'

The Commander went back to his cabin, took off his seaboots, took out a cigarette and then thought the better of it. Ten minutes later the telephone buzzed.

'Commander.'

'Sir, can you come? Mr Milburn's down in the bedding store and he hasn't come out.' The voice was high and excited.

'Who's that?'

'Stoker Brooking, sir. Can you hurry up, please, sir? There's two of them in there!' The man had begun to gabble.

'Brooking,' the Commander said sharply. 'Calm down and tell me exactly what has happened.'

'Aye aye, sir.'

'Where are you speaking from?'

'Passage above the bedding store, sir. Mr Milburn told Hobbs and Boddington to go in and check. Hobbsy came out by himself. He looks terrible. You can probably hear him, sir.' There were gargling noises in the background when Brooking moved the telephone handset away from his mouth. 'He looks terrible, sir. Said Boddy started laughing and swaying like he was drunk, and then he just fell over. Then Mr Milburn went in to get Boddy out . . .'

'Who?'

'Mr Milburn, sir! Oh, Stoker Boddington, you mean. And they

117

haven't come out yet! I can hear Mr Milburn, sir. He sounds like he's down the rum store, not the bedding store.'

The Commander put the telephone back on its bracket and picked it up again, rang the bridge and told the Captain in a few sentences what had happened. Almost as an afterthought he took his respirator from its peg and put the strap of the haversack over his shoulder, pushed a torch into his pocket. The loudspeaker in the flat outside clicked on.

'D'ye hear there? Damage control party muster muster in the officers' cabin flat. Damage control party muster in the officers' cabin flat.'

The Commander arrived in the passage to find two men in overalls staring at a raised hatch cover and the opening beyond, one of them flushed and sweating, propped against the bulkhead. The air was heavy with petrol fumes.

The man sitting against the bulkhead pulled himself more upright. 'Mr Milburn told me and Boddington to go in and do a quick check for fumes before he started to look for the leak. Place is full of the stuff, sir. I tried to get him out, but he was too heavy to get up the ladder, and the fumes were getting to me, so if I'd stayed any longer they'd have got me too.' Hobbs leant to one side and was sick onto the deck.

The Commander went to the opening, looked down and saw nothing but darkness. He flashed the torch on, praying that it would not make a spark, but saw only the bottom of the ladder. He leant over further, 'Milburn, are you there?' got a lungful of petrol vapour, so that he nearly overbalanced.

'He's gone a bit quiet, sir,' Brooking said.

No answer. He thought he saw something at the very limit of the torch beam. He pulled himself upright, light-headed from the fumes, remembering that the author of one of the damage control manuals had likened the effect of a dose of petrol vapour to half a bottle of whisky. 'Get me a line, Brooking. Hurry it up, man! And take your boots off before you go!'

The Commander took off his boots, laid them down carefully on their sides, emptied his pockets of keys and loose change.

Someone appeared at the bottom of the ladder. The Commander recognised Shepherd, thought with a little bitterness that it would have to be *him*. 'What the blazes are *you* doing here?'

'I heard the pipe, sir. I knew there was a party here – I've just been in the engine room finishing something off.'

Brooking reappeared with a coil of lifeline. The Commander wrapped a couple of turns round his waist, knotted it with hands which trembled slightly.

'Sir, I'll go.'

'No you won't.'

'Sir, I bunk with Milburn. He's my mate.'

The Commander turned to Brooking. 'Take Hobbs up on deck and get him into some fresh air.' He turned back to Shepherd. 'You're not going down there, because you've got no respirator and no sense. If you waste any more time trying to argue with me, you won't be bunking with Milburn any longer. I need someone reliable here, and in the absence of anyone else I'll have to make do with you.'

'Sir.' Shepherd sounded shaken.

'Tell the PMO to get down here with a stretcher party at the double. Two men asphyxiated. Tell him no boots.'

'Aye aye, sir.'

'If I give two tugs on the line, haul me up fast. And if you even think of following me I'll make sure you really are court-martialled this time!'

Someone else came down the ladder, wearing a dressing gown, scratching his head with one hand. 'What's going on?'

'Never you mind,' the Commander snapped. He saw a lighted cigarette in the man's hand. 'And put that bloody thing out!'

The young officer, shaken, obeyed.

'Now you're here, you can station yourself at the top of that ladder and make sure we don't get any more sightseers down here.'

Shepherd finished talking into the telephone. The Commander put on the respirator. It would not be proof against petrol fumes but it might give him vital extra time. His feet slipped on the rounded steel rungs of the ladder.

Once inside the fumes were much worse. He didn't have much time. He flashed the torch around, saw only wooden shelves piled high with bedding, his socks slipping again as he reached the bottom. He remembered that petrol vapour is heavier than air and that he must stay on his feet. He put his hand on a shelf, began to follow it, the other hand moving the torch methodically back and forth, trying to fix in his mind the position of the ladder, trying to breathe as little as possible, resisting the urge to shout for Milburn.

He turned the corner at the top end of the store, began to follow the shelf back towards the ladder. There was something there, visible through the swirling fog in his brain, a man leaning against the shelving with his back to him, holding onto something else which was sprawled on the deck. The Commander moved slowly towards them. The standing man began to move again, away from him, dragging the other with him, as fast as the Commander could move towards them. The Commander followed, almost despairing, wanting nothing more than to cease this struggle and drop gently onto the deck to go to sleep. The other man hit the shelving, came to a halt and subsided quite gently. The Commander reached him and tugged at his overalls.

'Milburn!' The sound was muffled by the respirator.

'Go 'way. Wan' to sleep.' Milburn must have seen his rank badges. 'You can't start on me, Commander, sir. This isn't the sodding wardroom.'

The Commander shook him. 'You'll do as you're bloody well told!' He had no idea whether Milburn heard him, but got one hand onto Boddington's belt, the other round Milburn's shoulders. 'Come on. Move!' They began to move, very slowly, dragging Boddington between them, his face turned upwards, bluish in the torchlight.

Where was the ladder? Because of the lifeline they had to go back the way the Commander had come, back to the top end of the store and around the shelving which ran down the centre. The line went slack, and then tautened again as Shepherd began to haul it in. They turned the corner, almost by feel, began the long haul down to the ladder at the far end. Where was the ladder? The grip of the Commander's hands was weakening and he dropped the torch, so that it rolled away, casting a small beam of yellow light under the shelving. He was weakening, so that his brain was working more and more fuzzily, so that the vapour was going to get him in a moment. Dully, he remembered the signal, gave the two jerks, weak and spaced far apart. He felt the tugging at his waist as the line was hauled in, rapidly now, struggled to keep his grip on Milburn and Boddington, feet slipping anew so that he was dragged towards the ladder on his side, almost unconscious now. His shoulder struck something solid, pain came through the fog. He looked up, saw the lighted square of the hatchway above, then felt despair as something blotted it out. There were feet slipping on the rungs, someone taking hold of Boddington, putting another line round him and signalling someone to haul him up the ladder. All he could see of the rescuer were his eyes, the whites unnaturally bright inside the respirator. Milburn too disappeared upwards, arms outstretched, upper body bumping against the ladder. Then he himself was being hauled up, being shoved from below, more pain as his face hit the rungs, once and then twice, and then hands were under his arms, hauling him out through the hatchway. Someone pulled his respirator off and dragged him clear on his back. He looked

120

up and saw that it was Shepherd. There were other faces: the PMO, astride Boddington's prone body giving him artificial respiration, the Commander (E), bending over him and asking in anxious paternal tones, 'Arthur, are you all right?'

Shepherd wrenched the Commander's tie off and unfastened his shirt collar, pushed him into a sitting position against the bulkhead. Someone else shut the hatch. The Commander (E) was asking the PMO whether they were going to be all right.

'Gangway!' someone shouted, and a stretcher disappeared with Boddington on it.

'Is he going to be all right?' the Commander found himself asking the PMO.

'Can't say yet. He'd stopped breathing. But you worry about yourself for the time being.'

The Commander leant over dizzily and vomited into his lap. 'I'll be all right in a minute,' he insisted. The PMO dropped to his knees, and pushed the heel of his hand into the Commander's stomach several times. 'What are you doing that for?'

'Push some of that rubbish out of your lungs.'

Milburn was propped against the bulkhead opposite, someone else doing the same to him. The Commander managed a shaky grin at Milburn, who took a moment while it registered, and grinned back. The Commander (E) squatted down next to Milburn, and started telling him that he shouldn't have gone down without making sure of his own safety.

'Right, let's get these two out into the fresh air.'

Two men pulled him to his feet and half-led, half-carried him up several ladders to the flight deck. Cold rain was falling again. The PMO pushed a mug in front of his face. 'Drink this,' he commanded.

'What's that?'

'Milk.'

'What on earth for?'

'It absorbs hydrocarbons.' The PMO had obviously been summoned from his bunk, the collar and lapels of a pair of striped pyjamas protruding out of his uniform jacket.

The milk and the sudden exposure to fresh air made him sick again. He and Milburn seemed to sit against the base of the island in the rain for a long time before the doctor was satisfied and allowed them to be taken below, Milburn to the sick bay, the Commander to his own cabin.

Much later the Captain came to see him.

121

'Boddington hasn't come to yet, but Barnard thinks he's going to pull through. Barnard wants to keep Milburn in the sick bay for a couple of days, but Milburn's giving him a hard time already. He knows he was a bloody fool going down there without thinking – I've already made that clear to him, and so has Chief.'

'I suppose I was a bloody fool too, sir,' the Commander said after a pause. 'Should have waited for the damage control party to turn up.'

'You probably were a bit of a fool, but we'd have lost them both if you hadn't been. How are you feeling yourself?'

'I think I've slept off the worst now.' The Commander's seaman servant had pushed him under the shower and washed him like a huge baby, then put him to bed, where he had gone out like a light for twelve hours. 'But I've got a hell of a head.'

'I'm not surprised.'

'And I hope I'm not going to get pneumonia from hanging about on deck in the rain last night. Barnard's got some peculiar ideas. He keeps telling me to drink milk. I don't like the stuff when it's fresh, let alone when it comes out of a tin.' He shifted his head on the pillow.'What's happening about the leak? Have they found it yet?'

'Not yet. The Chief says he's got to get rid of the fumes before he sends anyone into the bedding store to find it, and especially before they try to weld anything over it.'

'Obviously.'

'He's pumped out all the petrol that was still in the tank, and he's going to fill it with water and pump it out a couple more times to get rid of anything that's left. And we've got all the fans going and every scuttle open to get rid of the vapour. The repair's going to be a very ticklish job. The Chief's called for volunteers to do it, not that it will make much of a difference if they make a mess of it, since we'll all be blown to glory.'

'*Dasher*,' the Commander said.

Another escort carrier had blown up in the Firth of Clyde that spring with the loss of most of her crew, many of whom had been able to jump overboard, only to be roasted alive as the spread of burning petrol overtook them. It was surmised that a carelessly dropped cigarette end had ignited petrol vapour somewhere on board.

'I've signalled everyone else to keep well clear, and there'll be no smoking anywhere aboard until the leak's dealt with.'

'That's another thing the PMO warned me off,' the Commander grumbled.

'One thing which may interest you. You seem to have won yourself an admirer. According to Chief, your *bête noire* Shepherd is busy singing your praises around the engine room.'

'He did a good job, sir.' The Commander had paused before replying. 'He was stroppy to begin with, but he did exactly what I asked of him. He's still a bolshy little so-and-so but he's got the right kind of guts.' He stretched himself within the confines of his bunk. 'I'm going to get up later on, whatever Barnard says. He's a real old woman.'

Thurston picked up his cap. 'I'd better get back to the bridge. We're going to need you fit, Arthur, so stay where you are and drink your milk.'

The Commander (E) came up to the bridge two hours later. 'We've found it, and we're just about to start patching it.'

'Did you have any trouble getting your volunteers?'

The Chief drew himself up a little straighter. '*All* my junior engineers volunteered. Wullie Duff's going to do it. He picked out young Knowles and young Shepherd pleaded so hard I had to let him go as well.'

'Chief, I'm impressed.'

'It's what I'd expect of my lads, sir. John Shepherd said he was going to do it because *he* does all the rotten jobs, and there's no better man in an awkward corner than Wullie Duff.'

Lieutenant Duff and Sub-Lieutenants Knowles and Shepherd had found the leak after a long search, measured it up, and withdrawn to make a patch to size.

'How do we know when the vapour's down far enough?' Knowles asked when they went back to the bedding store.

'We'll send you down into the tank, and if you're still alive when you come out, we get started on the welding.' Knowles began to look worried. 'No, we'll use the miner's lamp.'

They opened the hatch set into the steel deck, lowered the lamp into the tank on the end of a line and waited.

'That seems all right,' Duff said at last. 'Now then, Knowles, down you go and check in all the corners. If the lamp goes out, come up fast and Chief will just have to pump the tank out again.'

Gingerly, Knowles descended the ladder into the tank, thinking of Boddington, still unconscious in the sick bay. Duff and Shepherd waited tensely for several minutes, listening to the hollow echo of his footsteps on the bottom. Knowles came back at last. 'Seems all right.'

'Sure? Did ye check every corner?'

'Yes, sir.'

123

Duff pulled the field telephone they had brought with them towards him, lifted the handset. 'Come on,' he urged the switchboard. Someone answered. 'Get me the engine room . . . Chief Engineer, sir, this is Duff. We're ready to start . . . Aye, thank you.' He put the telephone down. 'Guid luck, Wullie.' He turned to Knowles. 'Go and make us some tea.'

Knowles opened his mouth to protest.

'You've done your job, and it's Shepherd here who does all the dirty work. You'll only get in the way.'

Knowles gulped and crawled away as ordered. The leak was at the end of the bedding store furthest from the ladder, beneath shelving which went down to within eighteen inches of the deck. Duff got down flat on the deck, his legs and backside sticking out from under the shelving, Shepherd crouching behind him. He poked his head out, fished for his torch and took a final look at the leak, a two-inch split where the pipe had bent and fractured, yawning too wide to be simply welded over.

'All right, let's get started.' Shepherd put the welding torch in his hand, helped him on with the mask. 'Well, here goes.'

Shepherd turned the switch, mesmerised as the flame came out, but forcing his eyes away, unable to watch. Duff was holding the patch in place with long metal tongs, the flame creeping far too slowly round its edge. Shepherd found himself silently praying.

At last Duff eased himself out from under the shelving, feet first. His face streamed sweat as he lifted the mask. 'Man, I don't want to do that again in a hurry.' He sat on the deck, pulled the field telephone towards him anew. '. . . Chief Engineer, sir. This is Duff. We've finished . . . Aye . . . And you can get us all a whisky, gey big eens . . . Aye, I don't care that we are at sea.'

'It's done, sir,' the Commander (E) said simply.

Thurston felt the tension of the last hours fall away from him almost palpably. 'Any particular problems?'

'No, sir. However, when we get in we should make a thorough inspection of the whole system. A leak like that didn't happen out of the blue, and there could be others starting.'

'I'm going to make sure we stay in harbour long enough to do it this time. And I think we could forget about the rest of Shepherd's extra duties.'

'I'm glad, sir,' the Chief said after a pause.

'. . . with assistance from Sub-Lieutenant (E) Milburn, who was not as severely affected by the vapour. But for this prompt action by Commander Canning, the lives of both Stoker Boddington and Sub-Lieutenant (E) Milburn would certainly – better make that almost certainly, Scratch, to allow for the works of the Almighty.' Scott nodded.'. . . would almost certainly have been lost. We'll see if that makes Their Lordships sit up.' Scott looked up from his shorthand pad. 'New paragraph. I wish also to commend my Commander (E), George Hodgson RNR, and all engine room personnel for their promptness and efficiency in dealing with the damage to the vent pipe, in particular my Senior Engineer, Lieutenant (E) William Duff RNR, and . . .' Thurston glanced down at his notes, 'Sub-Lieutenants (E) Anthony Richard Knowles RNR and John William Shepherd RNR, who located the leak and carried out the repair under difficult conditions and at considerable risk to themselves. That ought to do. Usual endings, and put it with the report of proceedings.'

15

The last Swordfish of the night took off two hours before dawn, flown by Sub-Lieutenant Wallace, with Petty Officer Kornilov as observer and Leading Airman Powell as gunner. They climbed to five thousand feet, Kornilov tuned his radar set, Powell fired a burst with his gun once they were clear of the convoy, and they settled down to the monotony of patrolling. Ahead of the convoy and at right angles to it, back and forth, as far as the limits of their patrol square, turn and back again. Somewhere astern of the convoy a second Swordfish was doing the same. At one end of the square the convoy was in sight, small blips on the radar set, some ships visible from stray points of light on deck or occasional sparks from their funnels, all approximately in their allotted stations, six columns of eleven ships each, the smaller escorts disposed around the margins, and *Crusader* in her 'box' towards the rear, taking up the space of two columns in one direction and three ships in the other, so that she had room to turn into wind when necessary; the merchant ships around her, too, would act as a shield against torpedoes.

Kornilov banged his hands on his knees, pulled off his leather outer gloves, and delicately manoeuvred the tuning knobs of the radar set, stopping every few seconds to warm up his hands anew. A Swordfish's open cockpit was never warm, and at five thousand feet on a December night the cold soon worked its way through even the thickest clothing.

'How's the set, Korny?'

'Same as usual. Just wandering off tune when it feels like it.'

'Just plain fickle,' contributed Powell from the rear.

'Like a woman.'

'Your bint stood you up again? What do you expect of a Wren?' Kornilov teased. 'All they're after is gold lace. Perhaps you should introduce her to the skipper.'

'I don't need you two as matchmakers,' Wallace retorted. He brought his Thermos flask out of its stowage, jammed the stick between his knees and used both hands to get the lid off and pour himself a cup of coffee.

'Don't drink too much of that stuff,' Kornilov counselled. 'I don't want you peeing on the wave guide and shorting the set out again.'

'What do you think I carry a can for?'

126

Another half-hour passed. Kornilov continued to make minute adjustments to the radar, Powell ate some barley sugars, Wallace treated the empty air to a noisy rendering of 'Sweet Lass of Richmond Hill' – he had sung in a choir at school until leaving a couple of years earlier.

'That was bloody awful,' said Kornilov, who had caught some of it when Wallace pressed the intercom button accidentally.

'What would you rather have, "The Volga Boatmen"?' Kornilov's father had left Russia as a result of the Revolution and, after a lengthy odyssey, had finally settled in Liverpool as a general practitioner.

The time crawled on, in the monotony of back and forth, the convoy visible on the radar in one-third of the square, and they were starting to look forward to the landing, hot drinks and breakfast when Kornilov jerked himself out of the stupor of boredom.

'Bill! I've got something!'

'Sure it isn't gremlins in the set?'

Kornilov fiddled with his knobs. The blip stayed solid. 'Looks pretty good.'

'Ship gone out of station?' Wallace prodded.

'No, it's too far away. Must be thirty miles from the convoy, right over to port. And it's a bit small anyway.'

'Well, let's go and find out. Call the ship up, Taff, and tell them what we're doing.'

Boredom had gone, replaced by rushing excitement.

'Might not be a U-boat all the same. Could be a life raft or something,' said Kornilov cautiously.

'At least we can get them picked up,' said Powell.

'If it is a U-boat I hope that gun of yours is going to work.'

The aircraft had turned to port and was following a straight course towards the contact.

'Hope she doesn't dive before we get there. Did you get anything from the ship?'

'SOE's sending a couple of escorts. Pity this crate won't go any faster.'

'Don't you refer to my aircraft as "this crate", *Leading Airman* Powell.'

'Listen to who's getting high and mighty all of a sudden. You're just the cab driver while Korny and me do all the work.'

'Pipe down and let's concentrate on this U-boat,' said Kornilov in a muffled voice, his face pressed into the rubber eyepiece of his radar set.

'If it is a U-boat.'

'Whatever it is.'

Kornilov had turned the gain on the radar display as far down as it would go, so that the blips were visible as faint spots of lighter colour amid the darkness. As the range decreased he switched from plan position indicator to left-right scan, so that suddenly there was only the one blip visible.

'He's still there, Bill. About ten miles ahead and a couple of degrees off to port.' Wallace made slight movements with stick and rudder. 'That's it. Right down his throat.'

'I hope you don't mean that literally! Depth charges ready?'

Unnoticed, the firs pinkish trace of dawn had begun to colour the eastern horizon, but at their altitude it was still quite dark.

'Ten miles now, and heading straight for the convoy. Little does he know.'

'Can you take me round astern of him, Korny?'

'There he is!' Powell suddenly shouted through the intercom.

There was the U-boat, a long lean shape low down on the water, the sea a little silvery in the early light.

'Here we go.'

Wallace put the aircraft into a shallow dive. Powell tightened his grip on the Lewis gun. For Kornilov there was now nothing to do but watch and wait, as the U-boat came gradually closer.

He hasn't seen us. He hasn't seen us!

Kornilov found himself wondering coldly whether the U-boat's Metox radar detector was working. Wallace, concentrating on aiming the aircraft at the U-boat, was muttering to himself through clenched teeth, *Not before we get there. Don't dive before we get there.* Blobs of colour came hosing up from the U-boat.

'Tracer, he's seen us!' Powell shouted unnecessarily. Something went through the fabric of the upper wing. Closer, closer. The U-boat was starting to fill the sight, men clearly visible at the guns which were hurling cannon shells towards the unarmoured Swordfish. Wallace's thumb pressed in the trigger, the aircraft leapt upwards as the two 250-pound depth charges fell away.

Kornilov, hanging half out of the cockpit, shouted 'Straddle!' as foam creamed up on cither side of the U-boat. A moment later there was an explosion, but only one.

'Other fucker hasn't gone off!'

Powell was firing his puny .303 gun at the U-boat's decks, but the gun's crew were already disappearing below, slamming hatches shut as the bows dipped downwards and white water covered her.

Reaction struck them. Powell called up the ship on the radio and reported that they had attacked the U-boat, but one of the depth charges had malfunctioned and she had been able to get away.

'How much juice have we got? They want us to orbit this spot until someone else comes and takes over. Two of the frigates are on their way here.'

'If that bloody can had just gone off...' Kornilov cursed.

They waited another half-hour, circling over the place where the U-boat had dived, growing cold again and cursing whoever had manufactured the depth charges, until the second Swordfish arrived to relieve them.

'Well, let's hope the cooks have got something worth eating when we get there.'

It was almost full daylight now, though the sun was still below the horizon at sea level, the port column of the convoy visible in the distance, a pall of smoke from the coal burners discolouring the horizon.

'Look!' Powell suddenly shouted, gesturing over the side. 'Oil! He's sprung a leak. We hit him, fellers!'

There it was, a spreading dark streak on the silvered water, running parallel with the convoy's course and very slowly lengthening.

Two hours later the frigates *Deveron* and *Mawddach* picked up the U-boat's asdic trail, guided from above by *Crusader*'s Swordfish, at first at their maximum eighteen knots to close the gap, then slowing to give their asdics the best possible conditions for picking up the U-boat.

Thurston had been on *Crusader*'s bridge since Wallace's Swordfish had first reported the U-boat contact. Reports of the hunt came from the frigates over TBS and from the Swordfish circling above. *Deveron* picked up a contact, began to guide her sister ship in a creeping attack, *Mawddach* approaching slowly, with her own asdic turned off, and her approach concealed from hydrophones by the U-boat's own propeller noises. The U-boat, manoeuvring to keep clear of *Deveron* would, with luck and good judgement, have no inkling of the presence of a second ship.

'Put the TBS speaker on.'

Deveron: 'Echo bearing two-five-oh degrees. Range twelve hundred yards.'

129

Mawddach: 'Steering two-five-oh. Attacking with Hedgehog. Speed six knots.'

Deveron: 'Target bearing two-seven-six degrees. Range seven hundred.'

Mawddach: 'Steering two-seven-six. What's he doing now?'

Deveron: 'Still on two-seven-six. Range four hundred.'

Spencer appeared from below. 'Coffee, sir.'

'Thank you.'

Spencer went back below with the tray which had contained Thurston's breakfast. The range of Hedgehog, which fired mortar bombs forward, unlike conventional depth charges, which were fired over the stern when directly above the target, was two hundred and fifty yards, but the disadvar ge was that Hedgehog bombs only exploded on contact, though one explosion would set the whole pattern of twenty-four off.

Deveron: 'Within range now.'

Two thousand feet above the frigates, the orbiting Swordfish saw the Hedgehog pattern create columns of water ahead of *Mawddach*, waited tensely for an explosion. Thirty seconds, a minute.

'Must've gone deep,' the pilot, Lieutenant Thwaites, said laconically.

Suddenly there was a spreading area of white on the surface, and then the sea began to boil.

'Got 'im!' shouted Midshipman Roberts in the observer's seat.

The U-boat broke surface a couple of cables to port of *Mawddach* which had already turned to begin a second attack.

'Right, we're going in.'

Thwaites pushed the stick forward. Men had appeared on the gun platform aft of the U-boat's conning tower, bringing the guns into action. Splashes around the U-boat showed that *Mawddach* and *Deveron* were finding the range with their four-inch guns.

'Hope they realise we're on their side,' muttered Roberts.

The Swordfish came in, dropped its depth charges on the port side of the U-boat, began to climb away, Leading Airman Prentice spraying the decks with his gun as soon as he could bring it to bear.

'Cans didn't go off!' someone shouted.

'Shit!'

'She's going!'

Men were dropping into the water from the U-boat's conning tower and gun platform. The frigates had stopped firing. The U-boat's bows reared up and she began to slide away stern first, at an angle which

130

increased towards the vertical. A moment later there was nothing left of her but a few bobbing heads and some odd scraps of wreckage amid a widening circle of oil.

'Poor sods,' said Prentice.

'What about the poor sods they've sunk?' said Thwaites, who had been torpedoed himself in the carrier *Eagle* sixteen months earlier.

Deveron manoeuvred into the oil and began to pick up the U-boat's survivors. The Swordfish set course back to *Crusader*.

Aboard *Crusader* there was jubilation, mingled with frustration.

'Wouldn't have needed the frigates if the bloody depth charges had worked!'

Commander (Flying) grasped Bernard Mann by the shoulders and pulled himself up on tiptoe to yell in his ear, 'Now does that convince you about night flying?'

Stoker McCutcheon, off watch, rushed up from below with his pipes and played 'Cock of the North' very loudly until the flight deck Chief Petty Officer warned him firmly to desist. The two former provincial journalists who wrote the ship's news sheet, and who had obviously been waiting impatiently for a story worthy of their talents, rushed into action, interviewing Wallace, Kornilov and Powell, and Thwaites, Roberts and Prentice and producing an artist's impression of a Swordfish attacking a U-boat. Thurston was approached for a comment, he reeled off something he hoped was apposite and found himself quoted the next day as saying that this was an example of successful teamwork between the two Swordfish, one of which had found and damaged the U-boat in the first place and the other which had guided the frigates into attack, and *Deveron* and *Mawddach* which had finally sunk her, and that he hoped this was to be the first of many successes. The armaments officers began enquiries into the cause of the depth charge failures.

'What we forgot about in all the excitement is finding some means of illuminating the target when we attack. We were lucky this morning in that it was just getting light when Wallace's crew found her. I haven't yet worked out how we're going to do it.'

'How do Coastal Command do it?' Thurston asked.

'They've got big searchlights in the aircraft – fifteen-inch lamps I think. They call them Leigh Lights after the chap who thought of the idea. But they're using four-engined aircraft, Liberators and the like, with the space and the load-carrying capacity. Our Swordfish are just about on their weight limits already. I'm going to get together with the

AEO and see if we can work something out. Still,' Commander (Flying) pointed out, 'even if we aren't yet managing to sink them at night, by being airborne we're persuading them to keep their heads down. Now they've got Metox they usually submerge as soon as they pick up an aircraft's radar – presumably today's U-boat didn't have his working.'

'I'm glad we're not the only ones with technical failures.'

'The thing about Metox is that doesn't distinguish between types of aircraft or give a range. All it does is tell the U-boat captain that there's an ASV aircraft somewhere – it may be half a mile away or fifty. Some will stay surfaced if they don't see anything with the Mark One eyeball, but a lot of them will just slam down the hatches and go deep. Of course, while they're submerged they're draining their batteries and not doing more than eight or nine knots. And, of course, they're not attacking the convoy. Anyway, sir, the AEO and I will get our heads together and see if we can't sort out this target illumination.'

16

'Kate? It's me. We've just got in.'

'How are you?'

'Fine. We got a U-boat, or half a U-boat at any rate. How are you? And how's young Thomas?'

'Or Charlotte!' They both laughed. 'Moving! In fact he – or she – is starting to get quite active. Are you going to get any leave this time?'

'Doesn't look like it. But we're going to be here for a few days. Long enough to be worth your coming up, if you're fit enough.'

'Bob, I'm having a baby, not training to climb the Matterhorn. I think so. If the Glovers would keep an eye on Helen and Jim.' Jim was the dog. 'Term doesn't finish until the end of next week and she can't miss any more school.'

'Has she been off?'

'Flu, that's all, but she was off for most of last week with it. I haven't got it, touch wood.'

It came as a surprise that it was the middle of December, with school terms ending and less than a fortnight to Christmas, when *Crusader* had spent only a few hours in harbour in six weeks, and except for those few hours' oiling, had been away from her home port for more than two months.

'I'll book you a room. I'll have to be on board, of course.'

'I hope I'm not going to be left by myself after coming all that way.'

'You shameless hussy,' Thurston said in mock horror. 'And in your condition.'

'Who got me into this condition?'

'You're not going to let me forget that.'

'Of course not.'

'If you can get here for tomorrow night, the wardroom are throwing a party for the U-boat.'

'I'll do what I can.'

'Ring me when you get to Glasgow and I'll meet you this end.'

As soon as *Crusader* had got in, Thurston had gone to the Captain of the Dockyard, taking the Commander (E) with him, and insisted on a thorough inspection and overhaul of the ship's petrol system. With that, and some other engine room defects to be dealt with, there would be at least a week in harbour, and the summons was already going out to wives and girlfriends. Rear Admiral Manning-Wilson had come aboard, issued congratulations on *Crusader*'s share in the U-boat and accepted an invitation to the party. An escort was sent to London for Able Seaman Dennis, who had been picked up by the Metropolitan Police as drunk and disorderly three days earlier and found to be lacking in the documents carried by those servicemen legitimately on leave. His plea of having had his pocket picked fell on deaf ears.

As Thurston put the telephone down, Commander (Flying) came in.

'Can I ask what size you take in shoes, sir?' Thurston looked surprised. 'You're going to need some flying kit, and mine isn't going to come anywhere near you. I've just been on to my pal at Abbotsinch, and he's prepared to give it a go, on the strict understanding that if he finds you don't have sufficient aptitude for flying, the whole thing stops there. He says he can get hold of the Tiger tomorrow morning. If you're free then, of course.'

Thurston thought rapidly for a moment. A bit of rescheduling . . . 'Yes, I should think so.'

'It's not going to be light enough until getting on for ten – pity about the time of year – so he'll send some transport for 0900 and draw a set of flying kit for you. I'll come out with you this time to do the introductions, but, provided you agree, sir, I'd prefer to leave things to Reynolds from then on.'

Thurston assented.

'I'd better just warn you, sir. Reynolds made it clear that he's doing this as a favour to me. He's pretty brassed off with this liaison job of his, and he doesn't have a very high opinion of the Navy at the moment.'

A letter had come for Spencer in the mail, reproaching him for his lack of a sense of responsibility, but giving him, it seemed, one more chance.

'It worked, sir!' 'She doesn't want to waste the cake. Or lose her source of nylons!' so that Spencer had retired to his pantry where he was sucking his pencil over a lengthy reply.

'This, sir, is a Tiger Moth.'

The promised transport had met Thurston and Commander (Flying) on the dockside at 0900 and the Wren driver, who seemed to find difficulty in seeing over the bonnet, drove in a rather diffident fashion out to the airfield and deposited them alongside a hangar, where two strange senior officers seemed to provide a focus of mild interest for passing ratings. Squadron Leader Reynolds arrived at last. 'Sorry to be late, sir. Couldn't get off the telephone.' He was an untidy-looking man with a boxer's nose and uneven front teeth, the physical antithesis of Commander (Flying), who made brief introductions and then withdrew.

Reynolds tapped the biplane's fabric-covered fuselage and twanged one of the rigging wires. 'Now, we don't start by leaping aboard and starting the engine. As with most other things there are checks to be done before we do anything else. The groundcrew will have done a full DI – daily inspection – before we arrived, so what we do is to walk around the aircraft and look for obvious signs of damage. So if you'll follow me round, sir.'

Thurston followed him, feeling vaguely uncomfortable and conspicuous in flying kit which was straight from the stores – a suit of grey overalls with many pockets, sheepskin Irvin jacket, and flying boots which were also sheepskin lined and would not do for walking far – watching as Reynolds inspected the fabric for tears, kicked each of the tyres, and twanged more wires. 'When the aircraft's correctly rigged, the wires are all supposed to make the same note, but I can never remember what note it's supposed to be, and anyway I'm tone deaf, so I have to go by the feel.'

Satisfied, Reynolds bade Thurston climb aboard. 'This thing is normally flown from the back seat, where the view's better, because the upper wing doesn't get in the way, so for the first couple of trips you sit in front. When you start to do most of the flying, we change over. The controls are quite straightforward – stick, rudder bar, throttle, mixture control and a trimmer, which you can adjust to take the load off the stick in the attitude you want to fly in – nose up, nose down, or level. The instruments are also very simple: altimeter to show how high you are, air speed indicator, turn and bank – you'll see what that does once you start doing turns – and a compass. You also have an RPM gauge and an oil pressure gauge. Before we try to do anything else, we must do the cockpit check, which is FMHIICST. That is to start with, fuel; check the gauge. It's quite surprising the number of people who've tried to take off with no juice at all, or they've had just enough to get off the ground and then pranged. M – magneto switches off. H – harness; make sure your straps are tight or you could end up with a nose like mine. I – intercom working; in other words, you've got your Gosport tubes plugged in and you can hear me. I – instruments; altimeter set to zero, compass grid ring rotating freely. C – controls; full and free movement on both stick and rudder. S – unlock slats. T

135

– trim, which needs to be set right back for taxiing. Confusing, sir? You'll be doing it in your sleep in a couple of days. John Sterling tells me you've been up in a Swordfish, so you've got some idea about what it's like in open cockpits, but all we'll do for today is fly a couple of circuits of the airfield to remind you, and I'll point out the major landmarks around the airfield.'

Reynolds signalled with his hand and a rating came running up, took hold of the propellor blade with both hands.

'Switches off.'

'Switches off, sir.'

'Suck in.'

'Suck in, sir.'

'Switches on. Contact.'

'Switches on, sir. Contact.'

The rating swung the propeller, the engine fired and Reynolds waited for it to warm up.

'That's about right,' he said eventually. 'She takes about five minutes to warm up from cold. Now we can open the throttle and check the magnetos and the oil pressure. When I switch off each magneto in turn, thus, the revs shouldn't drop by more than fifty – that looks all right – then I switch them back on again, and open the throttle fully, the oil pressure should be around forty psi and in any event not below thirty. Just about ready. This is a grass field so we can take off and land straight into wind. Look across to the windsock and see where the wind is. On the ground we use the rudder to turn and we need to keep the stick well back so that the tail stays on the ground, which is why the trimmer is wound fully back for taxiing.'

The Tiger Moth bumped slowly over the grass, the nose swinging back and forth in time with movements of the rudder bar. 'Notice that the nose blocks off your forward view when we're on the ground. Therefore we have to zig-zag when taxiing in order to see where we're going.'

A final movement of the rudder brought the aircraft into wind. 'Now we set the trim forwards, which means that if you lose your engine on take-off the nose will go down and you won't get into a stall. Stalling is lesson five – if you last that long. Mixture to rich, check the oil pressure once more. Ready, sir?'

The engine note changed as the throttle was opened. The aircraft speeded up, then suddenly the bumps smoothed out, she came clear of the ground and began to climb away. The altimeter needle crept up, then settled at five hundred feet. Reynolds turned the aircraft smoothly round to port and continued climbing.

'Now we're in straight and level flight,' came Reynolds' voice through the Gosport tube, 'at one thousand feet which is the correct height at this stage in the circuit. Have a look round and get your bearings, because this is the only chance you'll get for sightseeing from this point on.' Reynolds must have decided to treat him as just another pupil.

Below there was a patchwork of greens and browns; to the east, sprawling Glasgow and its industrial haze, a low red sun breaking through grey cloud. Westward, in the distance, was the Firth of Clyde, silvered a little by the low light. The airfield's hangars had shrunk to a fraction of their normal size; a military convoy, camouflaged in dark green paint, followed the ribbon of road, darkened by the night's rain, around the edge of the airfield. Directly ahead was a cat's cradle of rigging wires, two sets of struts to hold the upper wing clear of the engine, and a hazy line of horizon, a whiff of hot oil, a slight rippling of the air where the propeller rotated.

Reynolds made two circuits of the airfield, landed the Tiger Moth neatly beside the hangar. 'That's today's effort, sir. If that hasn't put you off, come back tomorrow and we can get started in earnest.'

That afternoon Thurston was waiting at the railway station, checking his watch every few minutes. Spencer stood behind him, idly watching the streams of people who moved apparently aimlessly back and forth. Drab-looking civilian men, women in headscarves, younger women with raffish hats and over-made-up faces. There were servicemen of three services and many nationalities: the inevitable Americans, four kilted Seaforth Highlanders, a spruce Polish major in a square-topped cap, a couple of men in civilian clothes with weathered seamen's faces and small Merchant Navy badges in their lapels. Spencer eyed up a trio of ATS girls and grunted appreciatively.

The train came in, late, sending steam and soot upwards to further colour the curved glass roof above, and began to disgorge its cargo. A baby began to scream, a small girl, dragged along by one hand, was scolded by her mother. Two soldiers in glengarries hefted kitbags onto their shoulders and walked towards the Military Policemen who waited at the barrier. And there was Kate, in a dark woollen coat and carrying a small suitcase. She came through the barrier, pushed her ticket into the coat pocket. Thurston put his arm round her briefly, planted a quick kiss on one cheek. Spencer took her bag and followed them a couple of paces behind.

137

'Good journey?'

'It wasn't too bad. All the same I'm glad I've got to the end of it.'

'Do you want to drop your things off at the hotel and then come straight out to the ship? Spencer's itching to organise some tea.'

Kate turned to Spencer with a wide smile. 'Not with some of your wonderful hot buttered toast?'

''Course, ma'am. And I've got a cake made as well.'

'Then how could I refuse? Spencer, I haven't seen you for far too long. How are you?'

In the taxi to the docks Spencer sat on the jump seat opposite and told Kate enthusiastically about Rosie, brought out Rosie's photograph to show her and agreed that he was certainly not going to take her for granted once they were married. Thurston felt slightly excluded, he was impatient to have Kate to himself, but she would want to see the ship, and he wanted Kate to see *Crusader*.

The Captain's boat was lying at the pier, smart in her blue paint with white upperworks. Petty Officer Pym ran the pennant up the miniature mast to show that the Captain himself was on board.

'Bear off, for'ard. Bear off aft. Slow ahead.'

Crusader lay half a mile out, moored to buoys at bow and stern, an ugly flattopped outsider among the cruisers and destroyers, lacking in their thoroughbred grace, but impressive still in her own way. The Still sounded from one of the destroyers as *Crusader*'s boat passed along her port side. Thurston, standing by himself in the stern sheets, returned the salute. Kate was peering out of the cabin door, taking in the scene with bright eyes. The boat came round to port, passed close under the destroyer's stern.

'Boat ahoy?'

'*Crusader*!'

The boat crossed the short stretch of open water between the two ships, coming from sunlight into shadow beneath *Crusader*'s high side and the overhang of her flight deck. Pym put the engines astern and the boat came neatly to a standstill alongside the gangway. Thurston judged his moment to make the step across, doubled up the ladder with the briefest glance behind to see that Pym was handing Kate onto the slippery-wet wooden platform. The pipe shrilled, he brought his right hand up to his cap. Bruce, the Officer of the Watch, and Scott came forward to greet him. Kate reached the head of the ladder, Spencer bustling up close behind her, realising with evident surprise that the accommodation ladder terminated in a dark space beneath the flight deck, instead of in the open air as in a conventional warship.

138

Below, Spencer busied himself with making tea, and Kate prowled round the Captain's day cabin, taking in the familiar features – the standard portrait photograph of the King as an Admiral of the Fleet, the standard Admiralty-pattern furnishings, provided on the scale allowed to post-captains in command, and a scatter of more personal items which had been added, a sketch of the church at Langdon, another of a destroyer punching into a head sea, which Thurston had done from *Marathon*'s bridge in the early days before the *Seydlitz* action.

'The bathroom's through there if you want to do your face or something. The water should be back on by now.'

Thurston sat on his bunk and waited for Kate to finish in the bathroom. It was less than three months since he had last seen her, hardly a long separation by their standards, but there was still the initial strangeness at having her with him again, the slightly uncomfortable sensation of having his wife intrude on his ordered professional life, and a vague puritan's sense of guilt at being aboard his ship and on duty, while contact with his wife and his responsibilities ashore distracted him from that duty. Kate reappeared, her eyes taking in more Admiralty-pattern furnishings in the sleeping cabin, a line of boots and shoes arranged in order of type on the deck, all kept polished to mirror brightness by Spencer, the greatcoat with its four gold lace bars on the shoulder straps hanging on the back of the door, telescope on a couple of leather loops alongside. She had once said that she found his cabins a little depressing in their sameness, their orderliness and austere masculinity, a place, like the ships themselves, from which she and any other feminine influences were excluded.

Thurston got up off the bunk and stood in silence for a moment, looking at Kate. Her pregnancy was showing now, a rounded swelling above and below the waist. She looked healthy, a little plump, and infinitely desirable.

'You look lovely.'

'Do you think so? I thought you liked me slim, and I'm definitely starting to look like a Rubens.'

'I do. But this is different.' It came out a little lamely.

Kate laughed. 'Will you be saying the same in a few months' time when I'm bearing a remarkable resemblance to those revolting mother goddess statues in the Maltese temples?'

He did not answer but moved towards her, rested his hands on her shoulders and drew her close. She took his hand, and there was a faint fluttering movement beneath the palm when she moved it to her belly. Her tongue was exploring his mouth, there was the swell of her breasts against his lower ribs and the brass buttons of his uniform, a surge of desire for her.

'Oh, darling, I've missed you,' she was whispering. She had chided him gently for years that he never said he loved her ('I know you do, but it would be nice if you would tell me sometimes.'); now the words were sounding in his ears but still they could not be said. The desire for her was becoming insistent; if they had been anywhere else he would have gone on, but . . . He squeezed her against his chest, released her and stepped back a pace. 'Have to wait until we get ashore. Any minute now Spencer's going to come banging on the bulkhead and saying, "Sir, yer toast's ready and yer tea's stewing." '

'Anxious to protect your virtue.'

'I'd have thought it was your virtue he was worried about.'

'It's a bit late for that, and he does have some curious ideas. He thinks you need protecting from this floozie who's come to lure you away from the path of duty.'

As if on cue, there was a discreet cough outside.

'I must have a bath before I do anything else. How long have we got before this celebration party?'

'It's due to start at eight, but we needn't be there straight away. If I know the Admiral he won't arrive until after nine, and as long as we're there before him. Do you want to have something to eat before we go?'

'After all Spencer's toast and fruitcake? And I'm absolutely awash with tea. Spencer's very sweet, but his hospitality can be a bit overpowering. I do hope it all works out with this Rosie. She should be good for him.' Kate was rummaging in her suitcase. 'I always manage to forget something vital when I go anywhere, and this time it's my dressing gown.'

Thurston passed her his greatcoat.

He went to the bathroom with her, and sat on a rickety wooden stool while telling her about the ship and about learning to fly. It was easier now that he was away from the competing call of the ship, with no Spencer or Scott with his files to distract or remind him.

'This place has seen better days,' Kate said from the bath.

The bathroom had clearly been partitioned from a larger room at some time; its proportions were wrong, and the ceiling was bordered in white on three sides only. Marks of war were evident in the cracks in the linoleum around the legs of the bath; the bath itself had a black line painted around the inside, four inches from the bottom.

Kate passed him the soap. 'Wash my back, darling.'

He got down on one knee, a little water which had splashed onto the floor working its way through his trouser leg. He dipped the soap into the hot water and began with slow strokes, sweeping across the smooth taut skin of her back, working up as far as the feathery wisps of hair at her neck, absorbed in the task and content to take his time. He put the soap down, splashed some more water on, washed the suds away downwards.

'Finished?'

She nodded. He hoisted her to her feet, holding her closely in case her feet slipped on the bottom of the bath. 'You'll get yourself all wet.' He put his hands on her breasts, veined now with faint blue lines and a little larger than he remembered, the nipples growing hard beneath his fingers. He kissed the back of her neck, smelling the clean scent of soap and hot water.

She turned towards him within his arms. 'Not here.'

Kate stepped down from the bath; he draped the greatcoat around her shoulders. She thrust her feet into her slippers, 'I did remember these,' shuffled three doors back to the bedroom. He kissed her again, she moved her arms backwards so that the greatcoat fell to the floor. He moved to pick it up. 'No.' Underneath she was still a little damp from the bath, a few small droplets surviving on her warm naked flesh. She was unfastening his buttons, running the flat of her hand over his chest and then inside his shirt. He stood still, kissing her mouth and stroking her hair while she eased away his jacket and shirt. Time seemed to have stopped as he bent to kiss her breasts, moved his hand to feel again the movements of his child inside her womb. Her fingers teased at his trouser buttons, moved inside to cradle his balls and fondle him. He pressed himself against her, hard against the dome of her belly, then drew away a little while he stood first on one foot and then the other to get his shoes off. His arms went round her again; his mouth found hers as she pushed the last of his clothes clear of his hips and he stepped out of them. He moved backwards to the bed, pulled her down on top of him. He whispered a command; she straddled him and then mounted him with a swift movement. He was smiling as he watched her at work astride him, reached up to take her breasts in his hands and caress the nipples with his thumbs. She began to moan, swaying, eyes half-closed. He pulled her down to his chest and rolled her over, still joined, to take his weight on his hands for the final thrusts towards his own climax.

*

141

She was lying in his arms, running the tips of her fingers through his chest hair.

'Do we have to go to this party?'

'I have to. You could stay here if you don't feel up to it.'

'It's not that. It seems all wrong somehow, to be celebrating something like that. How many of the U-boat crew were picked up?'

'*Deveron* picked up thirty-one. More than half of them. They were lucky. Most U-boat crews don't get out.'

'I often wonder about them, the Germans. Do they really believe all that propaganda?'

'Some of them must do. The average matelot, perhaps not. At any rate ours don't take much notice of politics.'

'Did the U-boat crew who sank *Connaught* have a party to celebrate?'

'I expect so. We would just have been a target to them.' Kate sat up a little, moving from half-sleepy languor to wakeful interest. He wondered whether to continue. 'After all, I don't suppose they ever saw any of us. There have been plenty of cases where the U-boat has gone in close afterwards and the Captain or someone who speaks English has actually spoken to the chaps in the boats. Usually they're just trying to get the name of the ship and the type of cargo, and where the ship was making for, but they sometimes give them a course to the nearest land, food and so on. Not so often as they used to. But no one came near us, and we never saw what hit us. At the time you're just firing at a target. You don't normally see any of the men on board, they're too far away, and you've other things to think about. It's only if you see the survivors or the wreckage afterwards that it comes home. And that doesn't happen all that often.

'All the same, I'd like to know who it was who sank us and what's happened to him, whether he's still alive. Just a bit curious, nothing more.'

She fingered his identity discs, suspended from his neck on a leather bootlace. 'And they put your religion on these so they know which burial service to give you. It's rather horrible.' She shuddered. 'You will be careful.'

'I'll be all right. I'm a professional survivor,' he said lightly.

It did not pay to think about that too deeply. There had been a very short, very correct letter from Watson's girlfriend – 'Dear Sir . . . Yours Faithfully' – among his mail when *Crusader* got in, and he supposed Chief had had a similar one. He rolled over, kissed Kate again, felt the rising tide of desire once more, guided her hand down to meet his stiffening flesh, slippery now from the first time.

'We've just got time.'

'You will be careful? Not take any more stupid chances?'

His mouth went down on hers again. Danger, like responsibility, was a part of that professional world from which Kate was excluded. There were dangers which could be avoided, or minimised, but far more which could not, and in the end, when a ship sank, every man aboard, be he Admiral of the Fleet or boy seaman, faced the same and equal odds.

17

The party was adjudged a success. There were a dozen or so guests: the Admiral, his flag lieutenant and a couple of staff officers, Kate, the Commander's wife, two or three Wren officers, one of whom seemed to be attached to Scott, the Captains of *Deveron* and *Mawddach* and the Captain of the Dockyard. At first it was a decorous affair. Kate chatted with the Admiral, and was introduced to the younger officers by a bashful Sub-Lieutenant Vincent, one of the Wren officers was heard to describe the Commander (E) as an 'old sweetie' after talking to him for twenty minutes; stewards circulated with drinks and plates of sandwiches and miniature sausage rolls. About midnight, when the ladies had gone ashore, the Admiral rubbed his hands together and announced that things needed livening up.

'With your permission, Bob.' He emptied his glass and bellowed, 'Dogs of War on the Commander!' then dived at the Commander's legs to bring him down in an enthusiastic rugby tackle. Several others joined in and there was a tangle of arms and legs and much shouting as the Commander was manhandled through the door and deposited in the flat outside.

He came back in, tie at half-mast and most of his buttons undone. 'Dogs of War on the Admiral!' The Admiral, struggling manfully, was dragged out in the same fashion, and from then on it was no holds barred, with all the senior officers being forcibly ejected in succession, with varying degrees of struggle, all except the Commander (E), spared on the grounds of his advanced age, and the PMO, who declared the whole business to be completely childish, refused to put up any resistance and so was not thought to be worth the effort.

There was a brief interlude, while everyone got their breath back and slaked their thirsts. The Commander (E) declared that, contrary to popular opinion, he was not ready for a bath chair yet, and claimed an ability to drink a pint of beer while standing on his head which he was easily persuaded to demonstrate, to loud cheers when he deposited the empty glass on the carpet. Someone held up a cushion from one of the chairs, all the furniture which could be moved was pushed into the sides, there was a general jettisoning of jackets, ties and false teeth.

'Right then, Lieutenant-Commanders and above against the rest!'

'Won't the numbers be a bit uneven?'

The senior officers pulled rank and co-opted a dozen of the junior engineers, someone blew a whistle, the cushion was thrown into the air and the battle began. The cushion never moved very far, as anyone who got hold of it was wrestled to the ground by three or four others, and nobody had worked out where the goalposts were to be. For Thurston it was a rare occasion when he could throw off the trappings of rank in a service setting, and become just another individual with his blood up in the centre of the crush.

At length the mêlée collapsed from exhaustion. One of the staff officers had neglected to take off his spectacles and started to crawl round the edge of the pile trying to find them. A junior engineer emerged white-faced and holding his wrist and was hustled away by the PMO. Thurston, one side of his collar adrift and most of his shirt buttons missing, grinned at the Commander (Flying), who was running his tongue around his teeth to make sure they were all still there. The staff officer found the twisted remnants of his spectacles, tried to straighten them up and decided it was not worth the trouble. The Admiral, one trouser leg ripped open to the thigh, called for a very large brandy and declared that he hadn't enjoyed himself so much in years.

'Give the Commander my compliments and ask him if he'll have breakfast with me. If he's already had breakfast, ask him to come and see me in fifteen minutes.'

'How's your head this morning?'

'I swore I would never complain about a hangover after a dose of petrol fumes,' the Commander said ruefully, 'but . . . Though I think it's the effect of somebody's size eleven boot in my ear as much as the gin.'

Thurston chuckled. 'I can offer you something for it. Spencer's got hold of some real eggs.'

'I don't think we need go that far, sir. It would be a terrible waste.'

Spencer, standing in the background, grinned. 'Double fried then, sir?'

Thurston hesitated momentarily. 'Better make it poached, Spencer.'

'We've got Able Seaman Dennis back on board. The question is, what do we do with him?'

'You mean, what do we charge him with, sir?'

'Of course we could charge him with everything and if we can't prove desertion then we can make breaking out of the ship and being absent

145

without leave stick. But . . . There seems to have been a lot of this in this ship before I arrived, and the usual sanctions don't seem to have had much effect.'

'Yes, sir. There's been far too much of it. Again, it's these T124X men. Whether they get caught or not, they get away from the ship and that's what they want. If they don't get caught, they're clean away. We've several who've been on the run virtually since commissioning. A whole drove disappeared after our first convoy and a good half of them haven't been seen since. Obviously, sir, you've read the files and you know all this.'

'Yes, but carry on.'

Spencer arrived with the eggs, poured them each a cup of coffee and retired to the pantry.

'If they do get caught, sir, they still get out of the ship, because if they get more than fourteen days they have to be put ashore, and because they're T124X they go back into the pool at Liverpool instead of coming back to the ship.'

'And no doubt some of them manage to swing a permanent job ashore. So they think it's worth risking a long stretch in chokey. That's exactly my thinking, Arthur. If we charge Dennis with desertion and we make it stick – prove that he never intended to return – I'll have to give him ninety days and he leaves the ship rejoicing. That sets another precedent for the rest. Therefore, I intend to charge him only with breaking out of the ship and being absent, which we'll have no difficulty in proving. Then I can put him in Second Class for Conduct and leave him there for as long as I'm allowed to, and that way he stays aboard. With any luck that may encourage some of the others to think again.'

'Yes, sir.'

Thurston grinned. 'I thought I'd have more of a job to convince you.'

The Commander put a piece of poached egg into his mouth and chewed it thoroughly before he answered. 'I had time to do a bit of thinking when I was laid up, sir. If the big stick doesn't seem to be working, it may be worth trying something else.'

'Good. Today's Thursday, so Dennis won't be cluttering up the cells for very long. He can come up before you at ten and before me at eleven if we move fast.'

The defaulters list was a long one. Some of *Crusader*'s men had celebrated the sinking of the U-boat rather too enthusiastically on the first night in harbour, and put Inspector Mackay on the warpath again.

There were several men charged with fighting, a couple with resisting arrest in addition.

'What can you tell me about Dennis, Scratch?'

Thurston had seen Dennis's documents, knew what was recorded there in terse service prose, but there was background information beyond that which would be known to the secretary.

'It's rather surprising that he hasn't been up before you until now, sir. He's something of a bully boy. He fancies himself as a hard man and his mess is very much under his thumb. Unfortunately, we've never managed to pin anything on him for that. He ran from *Dasher*, was picked up after five weeks and got ninety days for going absent.'

Thurston looked again at the back of Dennis's service certificate. 'So he was in detention barracks when she blew up. No doubt he thinks that was worth ninety days. Anything I should know about this time?'

'He's claiming he went off because he had a letter from his mother to say that his father had pneumonia.'

'Can you get it checked?'

'I'm already working on it, sir. I rang the welfare people in London and they've sent someone round to the address on his next-of-kin card. I'm waiting for them to ring back.'

'Good.' Thurston got up from his desk. 'If that's everything, I'm going ashore now and I will be back aboard for 1100.'

Scott looked surprised. Thurston had called Scott in to go through the defaulters list earlier than usual, and it was uncharacteristic, to say the least, for the Captain to disappear ashore at this time in the morning, let alone two mornings in succession, and without saying where he was going.

Reynolds ran through the instruments and all the checks once more, 'to see how much you've forgotten since yesterday.' The same rating came up to swing the propeller, the engine started.

'Now, if you'll put your feet on the rudder bar and hold the stick lightly in your right hand, we'll make a start.'

Reynolds was more purposeful this morning, firing pieces of information at him as he manoeuvred the aircraft into position for take-off. 'Notice that I have to open the throttle each time I use the rudder to zig-zag, but don't forget to close it again. This aircraft tends to swing to the right on take-off – because of engine torque – and you need a touch of left rudder as you open the throttle to counter it. Take-off speed about sixty-five, and the same on your landing approach.'

'Now we're in the proper straight and level flying attitude, at a thousand feet. This is a fairly busy airfield so you need to keep your eyes skinned, but you'll find that other aircraft only come into the circuit on take-off and landing, so they won't be too much of a problem, whereas at a flying school you'd have several in the circuit at once and you have to be very careful. It's a good habit to get into, so always keep looking out of the cockpit. Only look at your instruments when you actually need them. Look round and see where the nose is in relation to the horizon. Found it, sir? All right, if I push the stick forward, the nose goes down. If I move it back gently the nose comes back up.' The stick moved in Thurston's hand as Reynolds demonstrated. 'I move the stick to the left – or port as you fishheads insist on calling it – the left wing goes down but the nose stays where it is.' The port wing dropped, there was suddenly a clearer view of the grey metal hangar a thousand feet below. 'I move the stick to the right, the right wing goes down.' The aircraft came level, then the starboard wing dropped; Thurston noticed a small winding stream dividing two fields. 'I push the rudder bar forward with my left foot, and the nose yaws to the left.' The wings level once more, the rudder bar moved, the nose skidded round to port. 'The same if I move it forward with my right foot.' Reynolds demonstrated, then straightened the aircraft up.

'Those are the primary effects of controls. All right, now that you've seen the effects of controls and the aircraft is flying straight and level, you can try them for yourself. You have control. Move the stick forward. Gently, the wing and a prayer stuff comes later. Now ease it back. Stick to the left. Straighten up. Stick to the right. It's quite simple, the aircraft moves in the same direction as the stick, and the same direction as the rudder. Move your left foot forward. Centralise the rudder. Now your right foot. Before we start to think about landing, let's see if you can keep the horizon in the same place.'

Reynolds had made it all seem quite easy, but the Tiger Moth felt fickle and unstable without his sure touch on the controls. The aircraft bumped immediately, the nose dropped. Thurston tried to bring it back up, over-corrected so that the horizon disappeared, pushed the stick forward again. Then another bump, the left wing dropped. The stick seemed very light, he couldn't hold the horizon in one place for more than a second.

Then Reynolds' voice: 'All right. I have control,' and relief. Thurston remembered the briefing on the ground, took his feet off, raised his hands above his head. Reynolds made some deft movements with the controls and once more the Tiger Moth was flying sedately along.

'It comes with practice, sir. Everyone starts by doing either too much or too little, usually too much. She'll actually fly quite happily hands off, so you don't need to heave the stick around or put on a bootful of rudder the way they do in American films. If you put your hands and feet back on and follow me through, we'll start to think about the landing.'

It was twenty past ten when they landed, and cutting it fine for getting back aboard *Crusader* for Captain's Requestmen and Defaulters at eleven. The Wren driver was waiting outside the hangar, mirror propped on the dashboard, peacefully attending to her nails.

'Out you get. I'll drive.'

The Wren had obviously been trained not to argue with post-captains. She gathered up her make-up and jumped out with considerable speed. Thurston rapidly divested himself of his flying kit, pushed his feet back into his shoes without bothering to fasten the laces, and took the Wren's place, finding that the driving seat refused to be pushed back and his knees were jammed up against the underside of the steering wheel. He covered the fifteen miles from Abbotsinch to Greenock at seventy all the way, foot hard down, sounding the horn on every corner, thinking that it would be ironic if he was stopped for speeding when on his way to deal with defaulters. Fortunately, the only traffic, apart from an American convoy heading the other way, was an elderly farm tractor whose driver raised a fist as if to say, 'Bloody Navy – haven't they got enough sea to mess around in?' He looked round once at the Wren, found that she had lowered her head beneath the dashboard and was determinedly concentrating on her nails. He came to the dock gates, flashed his identity card at a surprised sentry, then manoeuvred rather more sedately along the narrower and busier road towards the quay, brought the staff car to a halt abreast *Crusader*'s boat. The Wren got out, and raised her eyebrows towards Petty Officer Pym to enquire, 'Is he like that with the ship?'

Scott was waiting anxiously on the quarterdeck with the Officer of the Watch.

'Have you had an answer from the welfare people?'

'Yes, sir.' Scott was having difficulty keeping up as they walked towards the flat outside the Captain's cabin where the defaulters' table was set up. 'They rang back about ten minutes ago. Dennis's father did have pneumonia, but,' Scott was grinning, 'that was five years ago, and he died of it.'

149

'Able Seaman Robert Charles Dennis, sir, Official Number P/JX 321860. Breaking out of the ship contrary to Article XXII of the Articles of War, in that he did improperly leave His Majesty's Ship *Crusader* at 1530 on 25th November 1943, being apprehended by the Metropolitan Police in London at 2250 on 7 December 1943, thereby absenting himself without leave two hundred and ninety-five hours and twenty minutes, sir, an aggravated offence, the ship being under sailing orders, sir.'

Dennis was a short thick-set man with a blow-flattened nose and cauliflower ear, glowering belligerence across the table. There was evidence in a written report from the Metropolitan Police, from the petty officer to whom Dennis had failed to report for his watch at 1600 on 25th November. Sub-Lieutenant Vincent, who was Dennis's divisional officer, appeared haltingly as a character witness.

'So you think you're a hard man, Dennis.' Thurston paused, fists resting on the table. 'But you've just proved that you're like most hard men, underneath there's no backbone. There are six hundred and forty-six men aboard this ship, six hundred and forty-five of them heard this buzz about a hoodoo ship and took no notice. The one exception was Able Seaman Dennis, self-styled hard man.'

Dennis was rigidly at attention, continuing to glower.

'And when you were picked up by the civil police and brought back here, you tried to lie your way out with a sick grandmother story. You know damn well what you should do if you have got trouble at home. You go to your divisional officer; Mr Vincent in your case,' Vincent looked down at the corticine, 'and if the grounds are there you'll get compassionate leave. The one thing you don't do is break out of the ship, or break your leave. Now you think I'm going to give you ninety days so that you can go back into the pool at the end of it and slide into some safe berth ashore, well away from this so-called hoodoo ship, so that the greatest threat to your miserable life will be a dose of the clap. But I'm not going to let you wriggle away that easily, Dennis, you're staying aboard, because I'm going to reduce you to the Second Class for Conduct.'

Dennis reacted for the first time. 'I want a court martial.'

'Sir, I request a court martial,' intoned the Master-At-Arms.

'Sir, I request a court martial,' Dennis repeated sullenly.

'Not approved.'

For a moment Dennis remained standing at attention, then he lunged forward towards the table, fists raised, shouting obscenities, until RPO Slingsby seized him from behind and twisted one arm upwards behind his back in a practised fashion, and he subsided, mouthing further curses.

'Thank you, Slingsby.' Thurston had not even needed to step backwards; with the full width of the heavy oak table in front of him he was well out of Dennis's range. 'You're quite determined to get ninety days, Dennis, but I'm not going to indulge you. Get him out of my sight, Master-At-Arms. Remanded. Close arrest.'

'Remanded. Close arrest. It's going to be a real pleasure having you under my eye for the next six months, you mangy little coward, because by the time I've finished with you, you're going to wish you'd never been born! On cap, salute the Captain! Salute, don't wave your hands about like you were the Queen! About turn! Double march! Pick your knees up, Dennis, we're going to start as we mean to go on!'

Dennis was frogmarched out, with RPO Slingsby shouting in his ear. Second Class for Conduct subjected a man to a tedious regime of restricted pay, leave only at the Captain's discretion, extra work and drill, and inspections of himself and his kit, again at the Captain's discretion.

There was a few minutes' delay while RPO Slingsby brought the next defaulter up from the cells. Thurston walked across the flat, stared for a moment at the notice board screwed to one of the bulkheads, bearing the naval crown and the ship's name carved into its surface, half-listening to an exchange between Scott and the Master-At-Arms. Dennis had broken out of the ship and gone absent without leave, and he, Thurston, had stood in judgement over him and punished him for it, but were he and Dennis any different? He had cracked because he was afraid, and because the effort of holding down the fear had become too much, but a post-captain of the Royal Navy could not be a coward; if he could not take it he must be sick. They had put him in hospital and talked of 'combat fatigue'. Dennis too had been afraid, and unable to take the fear any longer, but he must be treated as a defaulter and punished for it,

Thurston looked down at the red ribbon with its miniature bronze cross. One night in *Marathon*, drinking to forget, he had taken the medal out of its box intending to go up on deck and throw it into the sea, but while he was still sitting and looking at it, with the half-empty whisky bottle at his elbow, Spencer had come back from shore leave, taken the cross from him and put him to bed. He found himself, unwillingly, thinking of *Connaught* again. They had done a muster the day before leaving Gibraltar, and the men had filed past him in a long line, four hundred and seven of them, each one shouting his name and rate as he came abreast, 'John Cole, AB, sir!', 'Andrew Melville, Stoker First Class, sir!', 'Henry Hobson, AB, sir!' Ten days later three hundred and eighty-six of them were dead, and the few still alive huddled together on a Carley float seven hundred miles south-west of Bantry Bay. No matter that the Board of Enquiry had absolved him of all blame, the final responsibility was still his. He found himself shivering, clenched his jaw, wondered whether he had been right to insist on coming back, whether it was right to put a ship and her men at risk from his incompetence.

Scott's footsteps sounded on the corticine behind him. He turned his head over his shoulder. 'Are you ready, sir? The next one's outside.'

18

The inspection of the petrol system was completed, but *Crusader* had missed one convoy sailing and remained in harbour while another convoy assembled. The Commander (E) made use of the time in another attempt to trace the condenser leak which was causing contamination of the boiler feed water with salt and consequent corrosion of the turbine blades. Sub-Lieutenant Vincent put in another application for the Russian interpreter's course and waded through a volume of French poetry culled from the local library. Kate made friends with the Commander (E)'s wife who was also visiting her husband and staying at the same hotel. Spencer wrote daily letters to Rosie and anxiously awaited the arrival of the mail each morning.

Thurston was at Abbotsinch for first light each day, found that he got the feel of handling the Tiger Moth's controls and made steady if unspectacular progress through turns, straight and level flying, stalling and circuit procedure. The landing was another matter. Reynolds' landings were smooth balanced affairs with the wheels and tail skid meeting the ground at the same moment, the only bumps being caused by the uneven surface of the field. His own were a series of teeth-rattling thumps, preceded by a sudden alarming drop onto the ground, and Reynolds' voice through the Gosport tubes. 'Hold her there. Your left wing's starting to drop – keep the wings level. No, no,' and occasionally a shaming, 'I have control.'

Reynolds told him to climb out, waited until they were well clear of the aircraft and lit a cigarette.

'You're holding off too high. In other words you're trying to land on thin air instead of on the ground. So when she loses flying speed and has to land she drops about four feet instead of six inches. You're also tending to keep the tail up so you come down on the main wheels only which makes her bump even more. You can see how the aircraft sits when she's on the ground. That's the attitude you need to get into for a proper three-point landing. Get yourself into a nice straight glide with plenty of speed on, then when you're close enough to see the individual blades of grass, just ease the stick back far enough to get the tail down and she'll land herself. Let's get back in and do a couple more before we finish for today.'

Circuits and bumps. Take off straight into wind, climb to five hundred feet and turn crosswind to port. Continue climbing to a thousand feet and turn downwind. At the first line of fencing beyond the airfield boundary, turn crosswind once more and descend gradually to five hundred, turn into wind, close the throttle and glide in to another thumping landing, open the throttle and go round the circuit again.

'Apart from landing,' Reynolds said as they walked back to the hangar, 'there's nothing basically wrong with your flying. You've got good hands – chaps who ride usually have – and you've got the hang of co-ordinating the stick and rudder in turns instead of trying to do it all on a bootful of rudder. But having got airborne you've got to get down again. It's actually a very common problem, about the most common after plain ham-fistedness. Practice, sir, that's the only answer, and ten to one you'll suddenly get it – like rising to the trot.'

'Just for a change,' Reynolds said the next morning, 'and because I could do with a break from your landings, we're going to do spinning today. To start with, how do we get into a spin in the first place?'

'By stalling with the aircraft yawing.'

'Correct. You get into a stall when the speed falls too low to maintain the airflow over the wings with the aircraft in that attitude. You're flying along, minding your own business, you let the nose go up and the speed fall off, and suddenly you fall out of the sky, which will happen at about forty-five in this particular aircraft. Remind me how you recover from a stall.'

'Move the stick forward to increase the speed, then open the throttle. When you've reached normal flying speed ease the stick back into straight and level flight.'

'Correct. You can't spin without stalling and therefore if you keep the aircraft flying at above the stalling speed you will never spin. But people still do it, and the classic time it happens is when you're making your final turn into your landing approach, when you don't have room to recover. We're going to need plenty of space for this, so take her up to five thousand. The Douglas Baders of this world might do rolls at nought feet and end up legless in the process, but standing orders prohibit aerobatics below three thousand and if you've any sense at all you stick by that.'

At five thousand feet the airfield and its hangars were much smaller and further away, a green splash amid the farmland, marked with grey rectangles at one side. It had grown noticeably colder.

'I'll do one to show you how it's done and then you can do a couple. Do you get seasick, sir?'

'Only after a long time ashore.'

'You may find this a rough ride. Straps tight, sir.'

Thurston pulled out the safety pin of his Sutton harness and pulled each of the straps a hole tighter. The throttle lever closed. The stick moved back in his hand. It was suddenly very quiet. The horizon disappeared. He could hear Reynolds' breathing through the Gosport tubes. Reynolds suddenly applied full left rudder, the stick still hard back. The aircraft suddenly lurched and cartwheeled to the left. The ground began to rotate, coming dizzingly closer; at one second a crushing against the seat, the next being hurled against suddenly rigid straps, slack having appeared in them from nowhere.

Reynolds' voice sounded in his ear: 'One, two, three, four turns. Recovering now. Stick forward. You'll find it feels quite loose and moving it in any other direction won't have the slightest effect on the spin. Pause. Full opposite rudder.' The cartwheeling stopped, but the ground was still coming up fast. 'Centralise the rudder as soon as the rotation stops, or you'll just start to spin the other way. Open the throttle and then gradually ease the stick back into straight and level flight.'

The Tiger Moth obediently levelled out, a thousand feet lower than they had started.

'Okay, sir, take her back up. We'll do a couple of incipient spins to make sure you've got the idea, then the real thing.'

Reynolds closed the throttle, pulled the stick back and put on right rudder. There was the silence, the brief interval in which to react. Stick forward. Pause. Full left rudder. Centralise the rudder once the rotation stops, open the throttle and then ease out of the ensuing dive.

'You seem to have got the hang of that, sir. Let's just make sure.'

Thurston checked his straps again.

'Ready?'

'Ready.'

The silence, a dry mouth, Reynolds holding the stick back and full rudder on, so that Thurston could not take any action to prevent the spin. The aircraft hanging in the air. Then the lurch, the stomach dropping away, and the cartwheeling, this time on the starboard wing, the impact against the straps, then gravity crushing him into the seat. Four turns, and then a calm voice through the tube: 'You have control.'

The stick moved slackly in his hand. There was the instinctive urge to pull it back, which must be resisted, because this, like so many things aboard ship, was an action diametrically opposed to instinct, a drill which had itself to become instinct. The stick, weightless, moved for-

155

ward. Full opposite rudder, left foot forward as far as the rudder bar would go. Centralise the rudder once the rotation stops, open the throttle, ease the stick back. Reynolds turned his head to look back at him. He seemed to be grinning, though little of his face could be seen.

'That wasn't too bad, sir. Take her back up and do another one, then we'd better do a few landings to finish off.'

Thurston spent fifteen minutes on the telephone pointing out to a bored functionary several hundred miles away that Sub-Lieutenant (E) J. W. Shepherd RNR had been accepted for service in submarines five months ago, and agreed to relinquish T124X status, which only required him to serve in requisitioned merchant ships, at that time, but had still not been permitted to go on the necessary course, because the Second Sea Lord's branch had not apparently woken up to Sub-Lieutenant Shepherd's change in status, and would the functionary ensure that the matter was dealt with immediately. The Admiral's flag lieutenant rang to enquire whether Thurston was able to dine with the Admiral on the following night. It was an order, not an invitation.

'Very good, sir. There'll be a car to pick you up at 1830.'

Kate, when he told her about the invitation that night, was angry and disappointed. 'Can't you put him off? I got us tickets for a Leon Goossens recital tomorrow night.'

'No, I can't.'

'I know,' Kate sighed. 'When the Admiral says jump, you jump. It's always the same. He knows I'm here. Couldn't you have reminded him?'

'I couldn't have taken you anyway. You know perfectly well he only wants to see me to talk shop. You'd be bored to death.'

'Surely you and he can talk shop in the daytime? You spend enough time aboard your wretched ship.'

The grievance was beginning to move from the particular to the general.

'I've got to go.' It was late; Petty Officer Pym would be waiting at the pier with the boat.

This seemed to inflame Kate. 'I don't know why you insist on sleeping on board anyway. Most men whose wives come five hundred miles to see them try to spend at least some time with them. All you can be bothered to do is fit me in for a couple of hours in the evening. I've played second fiddle to the Navy ever since we got married; now I seem to come behind your flying lessons in your scale of priorities as well!'

156

'Kate, I've got to be available if anything happens, and I've got an example to set.'

'Oh, don't strike attitudes, Bob. The ship won't fall to pieces just because the Captain spends a few nights ashore. I suppose the next thing is that you won't come on leave because you can't leave your precious ship.'

'And as for the flying,' he continued, 'if I'm going to do this job properly, I've got to have some experience of flying. I don't want to have Wings holding my hand for ever. The chance just happened to come up now.'

They had been to the cinema, then gone back to the hotel and made love. He was standing on the worn carpet in his socks, half his buttons undone because he had been interrupted in fastening them. Kate was still in bed, sitting up, face flushed, hair dishevelled.

'You're prepared to make time to learn to fly, but not to be with me. All you care about is your blessed ship. I'm not surprised that Jennifer Manning-Wilson left the Admiral, if he treated her anything like the way you treat me. You make love to me, you make me *pregnant*, blast you, and then you go swanning off back to your beloved ship until you feel you can be bothered with me again.'

'Kate, it's not like that!'

'Then I'd like to know what it is like.'

He took a deep breath, counted to ten. 'Kate, I'm sorry if that's what you think about me, but you knew what it was going to be like when you agreed to marry me. Dammit, your father was in the army. You must have known.'

'Yes, my father was in the army, and yes he was away a lot, but he paid some attention to his family as well as his regiment! And I suppose you think I'm acting like a silly little girl, and it's all because I'm having a baby. *Your* baby, since you seem to have forgotten. You're not taking the slightest interest.'

'What do you expect me to do? It's not me that's having it.' He found himself out of his depth with these matters.

'No,' Kate sighed. 'All you have to do is go round thinking how clever you are to put me in the club.'

'It's not like that. I'm sorry if you've got the wrong idea. Of course I'm interested. I couldn't not be. There's just not much I can do.'

'Certainly not when you spend all your time with your toy boat!'

Someone in the next room banged on the wall. The argument was going nowhere. He had a sudden urge to grab her, shake her, shout, 'Dammit, woman, can't you see!' at her. But he fastened the rest of his buttons, found his shoes under the bed and put them on. 'I've got to go.'

'Can't keep your coxswain waiting.'

'I'll see you tomorrow before I go.'

'If I'm still here. Go back to your toy boat, sailor boy.'

He slammed the door behind him, strode away down the landing, almost cannoning into a Wren officer on the arm of a naval lieutenant.

'Can't you look where you're going, woman?'

The girl coloured, then turned to her companion, waited until Thurston was halfway down the stairs. 'I don't want you to be a Captain if that's what they're all like.'

Spencer knew the signs and was adept in avoiding trouble. He kept his distance and, unusually for him, spoke only when spoken to, and ensured that everything was done exactly as it should be. But Metcalfe was snarled at, and Scott found the Captain more than usually taciturn, even abrupt. At Abbotsinch it was difficult to concentrate on flying. Reynolds had continued to treat him as if he were any student pilot, apart from a salute at the beginning and end of the instruction period, and the interjection of an occasional 'sir', so when Thurston brought the Tiger Moth to a halt after the heaviest landing yet, there was a blasting.

'I don't think you've been listening to a word I've said all morning, sir.' They were out of the aircraft and standing on the grass beside it. 'If you could see separate blades of grass from that height you must have telescopes instead of eyes. I agreed to take you on as a favour to John Sterling but if you're not going to meet your side of the bargain that's the end of it.' Reynolds, hair unruly now that he had taken off his flying helmet, began to walk away.

'Mr Reynolds.' Reynolds stopped and turned his head back. 'I don't know what standards of discipline the Royal Air Force has, but if *you* were one of *my* officers . . .'

Reynolds turned round to face him, silent for a moment, hair blowing in the wind, bulky in his flying jacket. 'Yes, sir.' He began to walk towards the aircraft again, and said in more conciliatory tones, 'If you climb in again, sir.'

Thurston got in, started to fasten the straps. Reynolds said quietly, 'If you were still eighteen and wet behind the ears, I'd say you'd just had a bust-up with your girlfriend. I don't want to know what's bugging you this morning, but while you're here, forget about it. *I* might be able to fly when my mind's on other things, but at your stage flying needs your undivided attention.'

Reynolds was perfectly right, of course, and perhaps the air had cleared a little, as the next two landings were considerably better.

There were more merchant ships in the Clyde each day, some visible from *Crusader*'s deck, others in the distance from the cockpit of the Tiger Moth. It would not be long now. The Commander (E) was aware of that, and had given up the idea of doing any long-term repairs.

In the late afternoon Thurston went ashore, found Kate in the lounge of the hotel.

'Hello.'

Kate put down the newspaper she was reading. 'Hello.' There was a teapot in front of her, milk and sugar, a plate containing a small assortment of biscuits. He sat down alongside her, unsure what to say, the chair creaking alarmingly under his thirteen stone. The room was largely empty, a neglected piano at one end, a few women spread around the small tables at the edges, a scatter of men, mostly in civilian clothes.

'How long have you got?' Kate asked, breaking the silence.

'A bit over an hour. I'm going to be picked up from here instead of the docks.'

He was already dressed to dine with the Admiral: mess undress with miniature medals, stiff shirt, watch chain arranged across the front of his waistcoat, black leather wellingtons which Spencer had spent a good part of the afternoon working on, an ensemble incongruous amid the drab wartime setting. 'I wasn't sure whether I'd find you here.'

Kate smiled. 'When I woke up this morning I decided I wasn't going home without seeing you first.'

'I've been thinking,' he began.

'Why don't you have some of this tea, and then tell me.'

He signalled to a passing waitress, asked her to bring some more tea and another cup. He was glad of a brief interlude, to sort out what he was trying to say.

The service expected much of its members, and much also of their wives. There were the long separations, the appointments elsewhere at a few hours' notice, the all-pervading ethos, drummed if not beaten into the naval cadet from the moment he arrived at Dartmouth, or Osborne in his day, that the service came first, last and always. The wife was important only when she was useful, and was more usually regarded as an encumbrance and an unnecessary distraction; Thurston had been told himself that to marry at the age of twenty-five was professional suicide and that he would be 'no damn use to the service for the first two years at best'. Until shortly before the war the Navy had not paid marriage allowances to its officers, unlike the other two services, and provided accommodation only in cases where a house went with a particular appointment. If an officer wished to have his wife and family with him on a foreign station, he was required to make his own arrangements and pay for their passages out of his very modest pay. There was one of those hoary old jokes, which like many such conveyed an underlying truth: the rating who asked for compassionate leave at the time his wife was giving birth was informed by his Captain that while his presence was of course essential to the laying of the keel it was quite superfluous at the launching. And the demands were likely to be greater as the husband rose in rank; an able seaman with a domestic problem would readily be given compassionate leave, but a senior officer might well be held too valuable to be spared, and his wife left to manage as best she could.

He looked around him, saw that the other people in the hotel lounge were lost in their own concerns, took a deep breath, then took both Kate's hands in his.

'Kate, it's not that you don't matter to me.' There was the contrast between Kate's hands, smooth and elegant, with the wedding and engagement rings on one finger, and his own, which were large and uncompromisingly square, calloused in places, their backs scattered with black hairs. 'If I tried to tell you exactly what I mean I don't think I could.'

There was the double pull, one part which began at Osborne, perhaps much earlier through the example of his father and grandfather, the other which only came in on marriage, the perpetual need to satisfy the two conflicting demands, which perhaps could only be dealt with by keeping them rigidly separated. Kate drank some tea and waited for him to continue.

'Do you remember Uriah the Hittite?'

She thought for a moment. 'In the Bible? Didn't David seduce his wife?'

'Bathsheba.'

'And make her pregnant. And then David calls him back from fighting the Philistines so that he can blame the child on him. Yes, I remember now.'

'My father's quite keen on that one. It appeals to his sense of propriety. David gave Uriah special leave, expecting him to go straight home and celebrate with Bathsheba, but Uriah wouldn't. It's what he told David that's important here. It just about sums up what I mean. "The ark, and Israel and Judah, abideth in tents, and my lord Joab, and the army of my lord, are encamped in the open fields. Shall I then go down to my house, to eat and to drink and to lie with my wife? As thou livest and as thy soul liveth, I will not do this thing." '

'I can see why your father likes it.'

'But do you see what I mean?'

Kate went off into a peal of laughter. 'Oh Bob, only you could justify the way you carry on by quoting Uriah the Hittite at me! What happened in the end? Didn't David marry Bathsheba?'

'He did. When he realised that all his scheming wasn't going to work – he got Uriah drunk, but he still wouldn't go near his wife – he gave up. He let Uriah go back to the front, and sent a letter to Joab by the hand of Uriah saying, "Set ye Uriah in the forefront of the hottest battle, and retire ye from him, that he may be smitten and die." And that's exactly what Joab did. I've never had much time for David since I found out about that. And what about you?' He was grinning broadly. 'Is there something I don't know about this baby?' Kate was laughing again. The tension between them was broken. 'How is he today? There, you see, I am interested.'

'How can we be sure it's a he? It might be a girl.'

'Boys run in my family.'

'And girls run in mine. But your father didn't have a son in the Guides, and George was only ever interested in the Navy, so he wants me to produce another grandson, though the way things are going in India there may not be any Guides for him to join. Perhaps it's time you Thurstons did something more peaceful. He's getting an introduction to the oboe tonight. Mrs Hodgson's coming with me. I met her at lunch-time and we had a good moan together. She has just the same trouble with the Chief. She's hardly seen anything of him because he's so busy with his boilers, and when he does get ashore he's so tired that all he can do is fall asleep in a chair. It must be hard for him at his age.'

'He wouldn't have it any other way. He doesn't have to be at sea; he could have a shore job if he wanted it.'

'So could you. Mrs Hodgson was telling me that he was in the water for an hour when he was sunk, and was only spotted because he had a torch.' She shuddered. 'And yet he stays at sea, and so do you after *Connaught* and everything else that's happened.'

'Gluttons for punishment. And I wouldn't want to lose Chief. He's too good at his job. And he's good with the men. With all the young lads we've got on board he's a steadying influence.'

'Did you know that Chief is going to be a grandfather.'

'No, he hasn't mentioned it. And you've got babies on the brain.'

'Mrs Hodgson says she doesn't know which he's more pleased about: this grandchild, or his other son getting a command – in the Merchant Navy. Isn't that sweet?'

Another waitress approached. 'Excuse me, sir. There's someone waiting for you in reception.'

She had found him unerringly. 'The one with the VC,' the Admiral's driver would have told her.

Kate squeezed his arm, looked him up and down. 'You men. You go on about us and our dressmaker's bills, but you're all such *peacocks* at heart.'

Manning-Wilson proved to be quietly satisfied with *Crusader*'s progress. 'You're still having these technical failures, but at least you're doing something about them instead of limping back to port every time. Arthur Canning put up a good show with that petrol business. Not in the face of the enemy, so I can't get him a DSO for it, and I don't think he did quite enough for an Albert Medal, but I wouldn't want to see him fobbed off with a mention. Could you let me have an OBE recommendation?' Over the brandy the Admiral turned, inevitably, to his matrimonial troubles. 'Never have thought it, not after twenty-one years. I met the fellow. Liked him even. Colonel of Engineers, about your age, but never seen action as far as I could make out. I suppose if I hadn't been working late so much I'd have started to wonder where she was going in the evenings, but the first I knew was when I got back one night and found the note on my shaving mirror. She'd hopped it. She's asked me for a divorce, but I'm hoping she can be talked out of it, for the usual reasons.' An officer who became involved in divorce proceedings, in whatever capacity, was expected to submit his resignation from the service. 'Legal separation and some sort of financial settlement, if she'll agree to it. I've got my solicitors working on it.'

It was three days before Christmas and the spell in harbour was ending. A signal summoned Thurston to a convoy conference at 1600 and he knew as he went out to Abbotsinch that morning that this would be the last time for at least three weeks. The buzz had got about; the Admiral had remarked about his joining the intrepid birdmen, and this morning there were two or three of *Crusader*'s pilots drifting about the hangars

162

and trying rather ostentatiously to look as though they were there for a purpose.

Engine failures and emergency landings this morning. 'Once you get below two thousand feet with a dead engine, start looking for a field. Better to land in the next field and have to buy a round of drinks in the mess afterwards than finish up spread over the hedge like strawberry jam because you tried to make it back.'

Thurston was surprised that Reynolds had decided to take him through emergency landings when he seemed as far from mastering ordinary landings as ever. Commander (Flying) had asked him earlier how things were going, and told him not to get disheartened after he admitted that he was beginning to think he should have stuck to horses. 'Most people, unless they're natural pilots, and there aren't many of those around, have trouble landing to start off with. It's the most difficult single thing to get the hang of, and remember that you're starting a good deal later than most. According to Reynolds the rest of your flying is all right. Some time soon you'll just suddenly twig it.'

The allotted hour came to an end. The audience began to disperse, walking back towards the administrative buildings and the messes with tea and coffee in mind.

'Can you stay a bit longer today, sir?' Reynolds asked casually. 'I think we're near to cracking this landing problem of yours, and it would be a pity to leave things like this when you're going off to sea.'

'How did you know?'

'I had a jar with John Sterling last night, sir. He dropped the odd hint. And he also said that Royal Navy captains are very big noises and I had better show you some respect because he's got to live with you. We'll just do a few circuits and bumps. You know what you're supposed to do, so I'll keep quiet and leave you to see if you can get your eye in.'

Round again, the whole thing routine now, with a pang of envy for the Seafire pilots who took off, retracted their undercarriages when still only a few feet from the ground and disappeared on more exciting errands. He had done five or six circuits and landings which were still bumpy at best when Reynolds told him to switch off and began to climb out. Thurston released his straps to do the same.

'No, sir. Stay where you are, and remember she'll come off the ground a bit quicker without my weight on board. Your landings may be a bit rough, but a couple of feet above the ground is a darn sight safer than a couple of feet too low. Off you go, one circuit and landing, and don't break anything.'

It felt strange to be alone in the cockpit, without the back of Reynolds' head breaking the line of the aircraft's nose in front of him. Reynolds had taken the stick out of the front cockpit, taken out his cigarettes and walked away towards the hangar. Thurston suddenly felt very lonely.

Get on with it. Taxi into wind, weaving to port and starboard as usual. Open the throttle, the bumps smoothing out as the aircraft picked up speed, the ground beginning to fall away a little sooner than before. Climb to five hundred feet, turn to port and continue in a steady climb. Turn to port again at a thousand feet, with a familiar hedge junction beneath. Level out and let the speed build up to eighty-five, re-set the trim until the weight was off the stick. The sun had come through the broken cloud and was shining on the hangar roofs, which gleamed wetly from the overnight rain. It had all become automatic, the small movements of stick and rudder to keep the aircraft on a straight course, the occasional glances at the instruments and the listening to the engine note to keep the correct speed. Turn crosswind, stick forward a little and begin to descend. Look around, a Seafire just taking off, nothing else in the circuit. Check that the landing area was clear. The final turn into wind, close the throttle, re-set the trim for sixty-five. There was a subtly different response without Reynolds' weight on board, or was that just his imagination? A single figure standing at the edge of the tarmac apron who must be Reynolds. The starboard wing dropping a little, touch the stick to level it. Watch the speed. A hundred feet, green airfield all around. Closer, closer, nothing but damp grass ahead. Ease the stick back and let the nose come up. The aircraft bounced, once, then a smaller bounce, and then she was bumping over the uneven grass, slowing, coming to a stop.

An almost sexual exaltation at having done it, comparable with the euphoria after coming down from the mast at Osborne for the first time, feeling solid earth beneath once more and looking back at the place you had come from, knowing that you had done it, and conquered something to do it. He must be grinning all over his face, resting his elbows on the cockpit rim. Reynolds was running up, throwing his cigarette away, encumbered by his flying kit.

'Well, you gave me far enough to run.' Reynolds, panting a little, pulled himself up onto the lower wing root. 'A bit bouncy, but at least you got her down in one piece. Take her back up and do a couple more, and you owe me a double gin. Should be beer, but you fish-heads . . .'

Reynolds signed Thurston's log book with an illegible flourish, calculated that it had taken him nine hours and forty minutes to get off solo. 'Bit on the high side by normal standards – you'd be just about due for a CFI's check and remustering as a navigator, but considering you're twice the age of most of my pupils, that's really not too bad. And you didn't freeze up without me there. I had one pupil who went off solo in just over seven hours – the first of his course. He got up there, and he didn't want to come down. Flew round and round for the next hour until the fuel ran out and he had to land. Nothing wrong with the landing, but he remustered pretty quick. Became a bomb aimer and was killed on his first op in a Stirling.' Reynolds too was pleased with himself. 'I told John Sterling last night I'd get you off solo today. He owes me a few drinks as well. But,' he grew more serious, 'all you've learnt up to now is how to go solo. *Now*, sir, is when you start to learn to fly, so if you want to get on to me the next time your ship's in Greenock.'

'Told you, sir,' Commander (Flying) said triumphantly.
'I think I owe you a drink.'

He told Scott he would be sleeping ashore that night, left the hotel telephone number with him in case anything came up. He and Kate went once more to the cinema, afterwards made love lingeringly until sleep overcame them. For the first time in months the dream came. He was back in *Warrior*'s forward turret, a glistening tide of entrails spreading from the body of the man next to him, a severed head on the turret floor, rolling from side to side in time with the ship's motion, both his feet jammed under something so that he could not move, warm blood running into his eyes, and the deck growing hotter beneath. An effort to break free, and he was lying on his back beneath the weight only of blankets, pyjamas clammy with sweat. He had been shouting and his throat was dry and painful. Kate was awake, turning over beside him and stretching to switch the light on.
'Was it Jutland?'
He nodded. His breath was still coming out in gasps. Kate rolled over, put an arm across his shoulders, moved in close against him. But at these moments he didn't want Kate, or anybody else. He pulled himself away, got out of bed and put his greatcoat on over his pyjamas. 'I'm going for a drink of water.'
Kate tried to persuade him to come back, but he went out onto the landing, lit now only by a single low-wattage bulb which cast a dim yellowish light over a few feet of wall. The hands of Kate's travelling

clock had pointed to a few minutes after four and it was the dead time of night, when the last of the revellers had made their way home and the early risers had yet to wake. Even aboard *Crusader* there would only be a skeleton watch on deck, though a few minutes ago a full complement would have mustered in the engine room to raise steam.

But the night was not quite dead. A head appeared out of the next door but one, with tousled hair sticking up around a bare expanse of cranium. 'Anything happening?'

'No one's been murdered. Go back to bed.' Thurston kept his tone studiedly casual.

The man seemed about to say something, then, seeing the Captain's shoulder straps, he contented himself with a brief goodnight.

Thurston walked to the end of the landing, rested his hands on the rail and looked down into the stairwell. He was all right, he told himself fiercely. Recently he had been able to forget that he had ever cracked up. He had done the things required of him; he had been able to establish his authority over Canning and anyone else who might have thought to dispute it, and dealt with the various minor emergencies – the steering jam at Argentia, the petrol leak – with hardly a second thought, the training taking over once more. But this was an uncomfortable reminder of the deeper current beneath, and of what had gone before, not just the direct hit on *Warrior*'s forward turret, but the crackup itself. Forget it!

He had been having the dream ever since the event it replayed in its distorted form, perhaps twice a year in normal times. The trick cyclist in Alexandria had told him to look on it as a kind of safety valve, at least while it came occasionally, 'but you can consider it as a warning sign that you're under strain when you get it anything like as frequently as you've been doing recently, and you should try to reduce that strain.' He almost laughed aloud. He had been bombarded with medical advice about getting plenty of rest, eating regular meals, getting plenty of fresh air, and leading a quiet, well-ordered life, all of which was a dead letter when commanding a ship in wartime, with the exception of the fresh air. Since they had started flying round the clock he never got more than two hours' sleep at a stretch, and even in his bunk he was five seconds from the bridge, up and on his feet at the opening click of the buzzer next to his head.

Kate turned the light off, rolled over towards him. 'Come here.'

He hesitated still. Her movements made the springs creak, the mattress undulated beneath her weight. Her body stretched itself against

166

his. She was very warm, soft now with pregnancy where she had been firm.

'All right now?'

Half of him wanted to resist a surrender, but the lure was too strong. Kate was stroking his hair, one finger tracing the scar left by the glancing splinter that had laid his forehead open in the instant when well-drilled efficiency and eager anticipation of battle exploded into pain and carnage and animal terror.

'What time are they calling you?'

'Six.'

'You're itching to get away from me,' Kate teased.

'The tide's just after nine, and aren't you getting the seven o'clock train yourself?'

'I've a long way to go and I'd like to get back in time to sleep in my own bed, rather than spend another night in a compartment with five subalterns on their way to a Commando course.'

He unfastened a button on her nightdress, slid his hand over her belly. 'Young Thomas seems to be asleep.'

'Sensible child. I suppose you want to wake him up.' Kate's hand moved inside his pyjamas. 'I thought so. You sailors!'

'How many more do you know?' He pulled the nightdress aside and buried his face in her breasts.

'You won't be able to do that soon.'

'Thanks to this little blighter here. Then I'd better make the most of it while I've got the chance.' In any case he probably wouldn't see Kate again until after the baby was born. *Crusader* would sail with the tide, and in a little more than an hour he must put on his uniform and be the Captain again, but for that hour there was urgent need, the nagging sense at the back of the mind, as always at these times of parting, that this might be the last time, an end then to war and pain and death as their bodies came together and apart, and together again. He thrust himself blindly into the deepest parts of her, Kate's internal muscles gripping so that he felt himself huge within her, then lost all control and found another kind of fulfilment in shooting his seed into his wife's body, into the womb which held their child.

'Do you love me?'

'Of course I do. Haven't I just proved it?'

'Then tell me.'

'All right.' He pulled himself up onto one elbow, switched on the light to look down at Kate, curled naked beside him. 'You look like the cat that got the cream.'

'You're trying to wriggle out of it.'

'No, I'm not. I love you. Are you satisfied?'

'Robert Thurston, I do believe you're blushing.'

He shivered a little in the cold air of the room – the fire had burnt its way through the meagre ration of coal and gone out hours ago – and slid down between the blankets once more. This was one of the things he was supposed to try to make sense of. In Alexandria Surgeon Commander Campbell used to pose those awkward psychiatrist's questions, which seemed to bear little relation to what was happening at the time, or to the label of combat fatigue that had been pinned on him, and had once asked him, without any preamble, whether he could ever remember either of his parents hugging him. The truth was that he could barely remember his mother at all, as Campbell well knew, and his father had just never been that kind of man. He had told Campbell then, quite seriously, that the old man was really only demonstrative towards horses. But Campbell's question had set him thinking afterwards, which was perhaps the purpose, wondering whether Campbell's idea was correct, whether that had had some effect on him since.

He could remember that when he was four or five, when they were still in India and his father was still in the army, his father would pick him up to put him aboard one of his polo ponies as an occasional treat. But that was as far as he could remember the old man ever going, and it was as serious a business as anything else he concerned himself with. Sit up straight, arms folded, look ahead, up Raschid's arching stallion's neck and between the mobile chestnut ears, while the syce led him and his father walked alongside. Once something startled Raschid, or, as his father had admitted years later, there was a mare in season nearby, and he took off before Azheruddin could try to hold him. When they caught Raschid his father put him back aboard, saying simply, 'Horsemen must learn to fall,' but perhaps his mother said something, because his father never put him on Raschid again, and waited to teach him to ride until his legs had grown long enough to grip properly, though again there was the same theme. No reins, no stirrups, bumping along at the sitting trot on the end of a lunging rein, and when you fell off, you gritted your teeth and got back on, and kept falling off and getting back on until you found your balance.

'You will be careful.'

'As careful as I can be,' he promised.

'Which means not careful at all,' Kate sighed.

'I'll be all right.'

He had grown fatalistic about his chances. This was his second war,

168

and neither his brothers nor the majority of his Dartmouth term had survived the first. He was, in a sense, living on borrowed time, and had been since Jutland, or at least since *Connaught*. If a bullet had his name on it . . . But let it be quick, and not in the guts or the privates.

The knock on the door came. A head appeared, told him it was six o'clock. He slid out of bed, shaved and dressed, took a final hungry kiss of Kate's lips.

'Take care of yourself. And the baby.'

'Don't do anything stupid.'

But the talk soon turned to mundane matters.

'Have you got everything?'

'Of course I have. And there's a taxi coming for half past.'

Now the time had come, he was impatient to be away, so as not to prolong the parting, a sense once more of slotting one part of his life back into its compartment, to be taken out again at the right time and place. He looked at his watch. 'Better get myself to the ship.'

Outside it was raining, and the raw cold of a dead early morning. He fastened his greatcoat collar and strode away into the darkness without looking back.

19

The convoy sailed with the morning tide, to be joined during that first day by others from Liverpool and Londonderry. Three days out the news came through that the Home Fleet had sunk the *Scharnhorst* while acting as covering force for a convoy to Russia, far up beyond the Arctic Circle. Five days after that the youngest rating aboard, an ordinary signalman who had only joined *Crusader* at Greenock, rang sixteen bells, eight for the old year and eight for the new. Thurston, as Senior Officer Escort, made a brief signal to the effect that everybody wished everybody else a Happy and Victorious New Year, and two Swordfish landed and two more took off on the first patrol of 1944.

On the first full night of 1944 Lieutenant Higgins had the middle watch. It was a black night, starless and with heavy cloud, and Thurston had wondered whether he should stay on the bridge throughout Higgins's watch. But he told himself that his vague sense of unease about Higgins's competence was simply the result of his having started on the wrong foot, and in any case he was dog tired after eight days at sea with no more than two hours away from the bridge at a stretch. So he went below after the first air patrol had safely taken off, and he had impressed on Higgins that he must be called immediately if the visibility got any worse, stretched out on his bunk and fell instantly asleep.

For the first hour things were quiet. The convoy was zig-zagging to the pattern it had followed for the past eight days. Four minutes on the base course, turn twenty-five degrees to port for eight minutes, then a fifty-degree turn to starboard for eight minutes. Back onto the base course for four minutes, then twenty-five degrees to starboard, fifty degrees to port and start again. Down in the plot the Meteorological Officer called up each alteration of course, the ships which could be seen were in their allotted stations, and the rest were small bright blips on the radar display. The two Swordfish were somewhere overhead, and so far there had been no reports of U-boats in the vicinity.

Higgins relaxed. *Crusader* was in her box at the rear of the convoy, with sufficient space to turn into wind and so well clear of the merchant ships on three sides of her. Astern there was only a single corvette, currently invisible in the darkness. Higgins grew bored and the damp cold had worked its way through his layers of clothing, so that he would not be warm again until he got below to the cabin he shared with Vincent, turned on the electric fire and stripped off so that the heat could play over him. He stamped his feet in an effort to restore the circulation, began to think about the Wren he had met in Greenock.

Carol was very pretty, a little plump, with blonde hair which curled enticingly beneath her sailor cap, an upper lip which did not quite cover her teeth, and a luscious pink and white skin, and she melted most obligingly each time he kissed her. She had let him undo a couple of her shirt buttons when he took her to the cinema, but slapped his hand when he tried to go further. But he would soon persuade her, if he could just find somewhere to take her. That was the problem, there was nowhere they could be sure of being on their own. He could not take her aboard *Crusader*, nor could she sneak him into the Wrennery, where in any case she shared a dormitory with eleven other girls. At this time of year the park was too cold and wet, and Carol would reject out of hand any suggestion of going into an unoccupied air raid shelter.

Higgins was still musing when the Meteorological Officer called up the next alteration of course. Wondering whether he could afford to book a room in a hotel and whether he could then persuade Carol to spend a night there with him, he missed out the first turn to starboard and went straight back onto the base course. At the same time Higgins had failed to notice that the visibility had deteriorated a little further, so that a Polish merchantman, lacking radar and unable to see the ships around her when in her proper station, began to drift into the empty space on her port side. For ten minutes nothing happened. *Crusader* made the second turn to starboard in the pattern and ran for a time on a slowly converging course with the column to starboard, but was still on the starboard leg when the merchant ships turned onto the base course in the correct place.

The radar operator yawned and scratched his head. One of the blips was getting a bit close. He reported it to the bridge.

'Signalman, tell them to watch their station-keeping.'

The signalman picked up his Aldis lamp, but before he could begin the message a more solid blackness loomed out of the black night.

'By Christ, she's going to hit us!' the signalman shouted. The lamp dropped from his hands.

Higgins knew that he should be doing something, putting the helm over, stopping engines, calling the Captain, something, but he found he could only stand there transfixed, as the other ship came on, seemingly oblivious to the danger, her shape becoming apparent, a few points of light visible where the deadlights over her scuttles did not quite seal.

171

He was aware of the signalman and lookouts watching him, waiting for him to react, but still he could not move.

On the deck below Thurston started out of sleep, sat up sharply. Fully dressed as he was he had only to swing his feet down onto the deck and start to run. He clattered up the ladder, burst out onto the bridge, bareheaded, duffel coat flying behind, saw what was happening and shoved Higgins out of the way in the same instant, shouted into the voicepipe, 'Hard a port. Close all watertight doors.'

'Hard a port, sir. Close all watertight doors, sir,' the quartermaster checked back quite calmly. A pause while he spun the wheel. 'Wheel's hard a port, sir.'

In the interval before the helm went over and began to bite, the Polish merchantman came still closer. Thurston could see a surprised white face looking up from her decks, heard, or perhaps imagined he heard, someone cursing in Polish. Then *Crusader* began to swing to port.

'She's going to hit us, sir!'

'We might just do it,' someone else breathed.

The merchantman must have seen them at almost the same moment they saw her, for she began to heel away starboard, showing a lighter area of red lead below the dark grey of her flank.

Someone's breath came out in a long gasp. 'Bloody close!'

There was silence for a moment, then Higgins picked himself up from the deck where he had gone sprawling.

'You mutton-headed idiot! What the hell do you think you were playing at?'

Higgins was standing there stupidly, obviously trying to think of an explanation. Thurston turned away from him once more, put the helm amidships and concentrated for several minutes on conning *Crusader* clear of further trouble and back into the safety of the box, then establishing with the plot what point in the zig-zag she should be on.

It was not difficult to work out what had happened. Collisions and near misses while zig-zagging were hardly uncommon, and it only needed a moment's inattention to turn the wrong way or miss out a leg completely. A sister ship of *Connaught*'s had been lost with most of her crew a few months before and the buzz was going round that the *Queen Mary* had hit her while zig-zagging.

Higgins was still standing there, looking down at the deck. Thurston wanted to shake him, seize him by the lapels and shake him until his teeth rattled.

'Mr Higgins, you are relieved.'

Higgins looked up, pale in the darkness, biting into his lower lip. Without replying he moved slowly towards the ladder, disappeared down it.

Thurston, suddenly weary now that the danger was over, fastened the toggles of his duffel coat, sent the bridge messenger for his cap and night binoculars. The Navigator arrived, having woken when the helm went hard over and come to find out what was happening. Thurston told him in a few short sentences. Higgins would have to go, not because of the moment's carelessness, but because in an emergency he had frozen. There was no need for a court martial; a request to Manning-Wilson for a replacement, and a recommendation that Higgins should not serve at sea again would suffice. He and the Navigator would have to divide Higgins's watches between them for the rest of the trip. It would mean little rest for either of them, but Beveridge at least was competent, and radiated a silent reassurance about his abilities.

Thurston saw Higgins in his sea cabin after breakfast, told him that he would be leaving the ship as soon as *Crusader* returned to the UK. Higgins was embarrassingly contrite, declared that he had learned his lesson and that it would never happen again, begged him to reconsider. But someone who had frozen in such an emergency could not be trusted again. If he had done something, even if it was the wrong thing, he might have had second thoughts about his decision, but someone who could only stand there and do nothing was too much of a danger. He thought he should have felt sorry for Higgins, certainly if this had been Vincent he would have, but he could not, and it was a relief when Higgins finally went away in dejection.

Of course, it was only a matter of hours before the buzz went round that the Old Man had second sight.

'Never saw anything like it. Mr Higgins was just standing there gawping, and the skipper suddenly appears, like he *knew*, shoves him out of the way and gets on with it.'

'I'd no idea what it was,' Thurston said to the Commander. 'I just had to get up there.'

The premonition had shaken him a little. He did not tell the Commander that something like it had happened before, that he had been halfway up the ladder when the first of two torpedoes hit *Connaught*. There ought to be a rational explanation, but . . . *There are more things in heaven and earth, Horatio, than are dreamt of in your philosophy.*

To his surprise, Canning understood. 'It's a funny business, sir, but it does happen, and too often to be just coincidence. Friend of mine was watchkeeping in a cruiser one night, called the Captain and all he could say was that he thought he should call him. The Captain was busy bollocking him when the ship hit a mine and blew the bows off.'

The Commander had seemed more relaxed, less as though he was watching his back, since the business with the petrol fumes. Perhaps he too had had something to prove to himself, and in pulling two men out of the bedding store at risk of his own life he had succeeded.

But the near miss proved to be the start of another lean spell. The next afternoon one of the Seafires held off too high on landing, bounced hard so that the undercarriage collapsed and the aircraft slewed violently round to port. The nose went down onto the catwalk, and for a moment there was hope that it might stay there, but the aircraft's momentum carried it on over, so that the tail stood vertical for a second against the grey sky and then toppled, the rails tearing with whiplash cracks as the Seafire went into the sea. Thurston put the helm over to take the ship clear of the pilot, and one of the corvettes bustled up, but there was nothing to be seen beyond a slowly widening circle of foam.

Lieutenant Newell also smashed his undercarriage on landing, and ploughed into the barrier on his belly. He had released his straps, pushed back his canopy and was standing on his seat to climb out when the thin stream of petrol which had begun to run down the wooden deck ignited. The petrol tank, almost empty now and filled with vapour, exploded, set off hundreds of rounds of 20mm cannon ammunition in their magazines in the wings, sending streams of coloured tracer in gentle arcs into the water ahead of the ship.

Newell got clear of the cockpit, hands flung up to his face to protect his eyes, jumped off the port wing towards the rear. His flying boots slipped as he landed and he sat down in a patch of flame. One of the flight deck party ran up, pulled Newell away by one of his hands and rolled him on a clear patch of deck to put the flames out. Newell's heavy flying gear had protected him from the worst external burns, but the fire had scorched his lungs and he died as he was being carried below. The flight deck party got to work, but their efforts only showed the inadequacy of the equipment they had been provided with, and the wreckage of the Seafire burned on for a long time, the bright blobs of tracer going off over *Crusader*'s bows.

Nothing left to show that two pilots had lived, beyond the personal effects which would be parcelled up and sent to their parents, after any girlie magazines, contraceptives and questionable love letters had been disposed of, so as not to cast any doubt on the bright clean image of the dead warrior. Nothing left of Davidson, who had gone into the sea with his aircraft, nor of Newell after the brief ceremonial of burial at sea, and nothing to show how they had died, except the scorch mark which Newell's burning aircraft had left on *Crusader*'s wooden deck. For a day or two the flight deck party showed an almost superstitious reluctance to move aircraft across the blackened area, but after Leading Airman Quinn insisted that the men in his charge manoeuvre a Seafire across the patch, the spell of it was broken. The aircrew ready room was quieter for a little, and the empty places at the wardroom table were taken note of, in silence, but only for a time. Deck landing accidents were accepted as the main hazard of carrier flying, a greater killer than enemy action.

The convoy made the rendevous with the Canadian escorts, and *Crusader* and the British group turned south to meet the eastbound convoy from Halifax. Unlike the ships of the outward-bound convoy, which made the Atlantic crossing in ballast, these were deep-laden, loaded below their Plimsoll marks, some with deck cargoes secured by ropes and tarpaulins, creating strange new silhouettes: railway sleepers, iron, crated aircraft, tanks. The laden ships were a more inviting target for the U-boats; one ship might carry several weeks' tea or sugar ration for a sizeable portion of the British population, or vehicles to equip the army units now pushing their way painfully up from the toe of Italy. The U-boats could establish a patrol line and wait for the convoys to reach it, and laden ships sank more easily.

Eight days out from the Clyde Lieutenant Thwaites, Midshipman Roberts and Leading Airman Prentice picked up a U-boat on radar, tracked her to the point at which radar became useless, but could not sight her in the cloudy January darkness. They set off a flare, and caught sight of the U-boat, less than two miles away, then had to endure the frustration of seeing her dive and disappear into the safety of the depths before their slow and heavily laden Swordfish could get close enough to make the attack. The escort group commander detached *Deveron* to investigate, but her asdic found nothing. *Crusader*'s men could remind themselves that, while submerged, the U-boat could make eight knots at maximum and must fall behind the convoy, but merely preventing U-boats from attacking was not the same as sinking them. The same thing happened to one of the other crews a couple of nights later. The flare went up, giving enough light to make an attack by, but all that could be seen was the white foam rising over the U-

175

boat's saddle tanks as she began to dive, and the Swordfish did not have the speed to reach her before she submerged.

For Thurston life had settled into a pattern. Every two hours a patrol had to land and another take off, so that he had to be on the bridge. In some of the spaces between he could sleep, but many times he was woken again by a report from one of the smaller escorts, that a merchant ship was out of station or had engine trouble, or someone had picked up an asdic contact. His world was the bridge, the grey sea all around and the great sky above, the sharp rain and biting wind of midwinter, and his sea cabin immediately below, where there was uneasy rest, and meals brought up on a tray: sandwiches, soup, stews which Spencer somehow managed to keep hot on the journey up from the galley. He could never be more than ten seconds away from the bridge while at sea. An athlete in training could run a hundred yards in ten seconds, but he did not have to rouse himself from sleep, get out of a bunk and climb a near-vertical ladder, all aboard a ship which was never still, where the deck beneath rolled and pitched unpredictably and was always slippery with water, while encumbered by seaboots and the layers of clothing required to maintain a semblance of warmth during the hours in the open air.

20

It was just one of those stupid things. It was a little after midnight, the ship pitching heavily in a head sea, which had made landing difficult for the two Swordfish which had come in. Thurston was on the ladder on his way to his sea cabin when a sudden pitch made him lose his handhold, the back of his head slammed against the right-angled metal sheathing of one of the rungs. The bows began to come up as the ship met the next wave, and the motion catapulted him clear of the ladder. He landed heavily on his knees, just had time to decide that this was a bloody silly thing to do, before he crumpled forward onto the deck.

He became aware of someone coming down the ladder, seaboots landing on the deck behind him. Someone was sliding something beneath his head. Thurston realised that there was corticene deck an inch from his nose, put his hand up to his head, found that it met warm wetness and a shallow furrow, but he was suddenly weary, and not very interested. Someone was telling him to leave the furrow alone, the voice coming from a long way off.

'Who's that?'

'Vincent, sir.'

'Aren't you supposed to be on watch?'

'The Navigator sent me down, sir.' Vincent was on his knees beside him, trying rather ineffectually to staunch the flow of blood with his handkerchief.

'How long has he been there?'

'He was there while you were on the bridge, sir.'

Vincent lifted the handkerchief away, parted the hair with his fingers and peered at the gash. 'You've just about split your head open, sir.'

'Bloody silly thing to do,' Thurston said after a moment.

Vincent stood up. 'I'll just use your telephone to ring up the PMO, sir.'

'I'll be all right in a minute.' He found himself giddy and sick as he lifted his head. It seemed immensely heavy.

'Don't move, sir.'

The sea cabin door was open and he could hear Vincent talking into the telephone, 'Yes, sir. He's bleeding quite a lot and I think he's concussed,' but it all came from a great distance.

Vincent came back. 'The PMO's on his way up, sir.'

'I'll be all right.'

'Better to make sure, sir.'

'Did I fall off the ladder?'

'Yes, sir.'

'And aren't the next Swordfish landing on in a couple of minutes?' He scrabbled for a foothold on the deck.

'Stay where you are, please, sir. The doctor won't be long.'

'Get back to your watch, Mr Vincent.' Pain shot through his head, the deck lurched beneath him, and he was almost relieved to subside once more. Vincent had not moved. 'Get back to your watch, Mr Vincent. Now!'

'I'm sorry, sir,' Vincent said diffidently, 'I think I should stay with you until the PMO gets here.' He was trying once more to stop the flow of blood from Thurston's head. 'I don't want to move you, sir, in case you've damaged something else as well.'

'I'm all right.' He was getting angry with Vincent.

'With respect, sir,' Vincent was polite, 'you've got a bad cut on your head, and probably concussion as well.' Vincent's voice had acquired the calm overlay which came from training.

'Have you done this before, Mr Vincent?'

'I have done a first aid course, sir, but,' Thurston could sense Vincent blushing, 'this is the first time I've actually used it.'

Surgeon Lieutenant-Commander Barnard arrived, deposited his medical bag on the corticene, pressed a wad of cotton wool against Thurston's head, and told Vincent to hold it in place. 'How did this happen?'

'The Captain fell off the ladder, sir.'

'I'm asking the Captain.'

'I fell off the ladder,' Thurston repeated dully.

'Well, you've given yourself quite a knock. Were you unconscious at all?'

'No. Just a bit groggy. I feel all right now.' He was surprised to find himself shivering.

'You don't look all right,' Barnard said unsympathetically. 'We'll have to get this stitched, quite apart from anything else. Would you give me a hand, Mr Vincent?'

Barnard and Vincent got either side of Thurston and hoisted him upright. The ship was still pitching, but there was a second motion added, making him giddy and sick once more, so that it was an effort to avoid being sick in front of Vincent. They got him into his sea cabin,

178

head hanging, the deck dipping and swaying beneath his feet. Spencer materialised in the doorway.

'Wait outside.'

'Sir?' Spencer looked at Thurston.

'Wait outside,' Barnard said more firmly.

Thurston wondered how Spencer had come to be there. 'Mr Vincent, I told you to get back to your watch.'

'Aye aye, sir.' Vincent went out.

The PMO snapped open his medical bag. 'At times like these you wish they'd light these places properly, night vision or no.' He pulled out a pencil torch, shone it into each of Thurston's eyes, the beam painfully bright against the dull red glow which came from the deckhead bulb. He grunted non-committally, then switched the torch off. 'Now I want you to follow this with your eyes without moving your head.'

'What's all this for?'

Barnard sighed. 'I am merely attempting to establish whether or not you are suffering from concussion.'

The slow movements of the torch made the sickness worse; the chair Thurston was sitting on tilted violently to starboard.

'Very interesting. They're going in different directions. However, I think you're going to live.'

'I'm glad to hear it.'

'Now is there anything else before I sew you up?'

'Banged my knees a bit, but they're all right.'

'Hm. Just let me see you straighten your legs out, and bend them again . . . That looks all right. I think if you'd broken a kneecap you'd know about it.' Barnard rummaged in his bag, then alcohol went into the gash, and sharp pain sliced through his head. 'That's better. Now I can see what I'm doing.' Barnard took out a pair of scissors. 'You're going to have a nice bald strip there until the hair grows again. Scalp injuries always look very messy, because they bleed so much, but they heal up well, and the scars usually disappear under the hair. This is what I tell hysterical mothers when their little darlings have fallen off their fairy cycles. All right, Spencer, you can come in now.'

Spencer glided in on noiseless feet, carrying Thurston's brass hat, which he replaced on its hook.

'Come here and hold this head still while I do the stitchery.'

Thurston pressed his forehead against the bulkhead, within the cage of Spencer's fingers, the hardness providing a cold counter-irritant as pain jolted from each movement of the needle, as if Barnard was forcing the point clean through the bony skull and deep inside, then groping

179

inside with his fingers to haul it out. He felt shameful tears gathering behind his lowered eyelids, heard Barnard's voice complaining about the lighting arrangements, that he couldn't be expected to do delicate work in these conditions, felt the ship's motion, the rising and falling as *Crusader* punched her way through and over the waves.

'That'll do,' Barnard said at last.

'How many?'

'Eleven.'

'What did you use? It felt bloody blunt.'

Barnard showed him a small curved thing resting in his palm, with a vicious one-edged cutting blade. 'Now I want you to get into that bunk and not to budge from it for the next forty-eight hours at least.'

Thurston digested this. 'PMO, I'm all right now that you've sewn me up, and I haven't the time to spend eight hours in my bunk, let alone forty-eight.'

'You've had a nasty bang on the head. You're concussed and you've lost quite a lot of blood from that gash,' Barnard said patiently.

'I've had worse clouts playing rugby and carried on.'

'And that was when you were young and foolish and also lucky that you didn't do yourself some serious damage. Head injuries aren't something to be treated lightly. If we weren't at sea I'd be sending you straight to hospital. You may think you're indispensable but I'm sure the ship can function without you for a few days. I'm not going to listen to any more protests. In any case, you're hardly going to be much use in your present state and you wouldn't be much use on the rugby field either. You can't even see straight, for heaven's sake!'

Thurston had become aware in the last few moments that he was looking at two Barnards, each clad in pyjamas and greatcoat, with the slight bulge of an uninflated lifebelt beneath, and that there were oilskins swaying on two cabin doors behind.

'The only thing for concussion, sir, is rest. I'll give you something to help you sleep.'

The 'sir' had come as a surprise. Barnard, perhaps to demonstrate his civilian loyalties, usually managed to avoid using the word. The PMO went off to his sick bay to fetch his drugs. Two Spencers materialised from the background.

'Give you a hand to undress, sir?'

Despite what he had said to Barnard, he was glad of Spencer's services as he deftly got him out of his clothes and seaboots and into a pair of pyjamas he produced from the drawers under the bunk.

'What are those doing there?'

180

'Never know when you might need them, sir. Now I'll just get you tucked in, and the doctor'll be back in a minute.'

Spencer sounded like a nurse from Barnard's children's hospital.

'I never thanked you for doing this the last time.'

'Oh, that's all right, sir. Odd bender does no 'arm, and you weren't no trouble.'

He had drunk himself senseless one night in *Marathon* and Spencer had had to put him to bed.

'Used to have to do it quite a lot for Commander Bishop,' Spencer reminisced. 'Every night there was a guest night. Couldn't hold his drink. And some other times. He wasn't married and I think he used to get a bit lonely. Anyway, he'd go wandering round the upper deck saying the Catechism. Used to get very religious in his cups – went with having a name like Bishop, I suppose. I didn't want him going over the side so I used to get him below. Then he'd say, "Thank you very much, Spencer. Goodnight," but he never managed to get himself turned in, so I used to do it for him. Don't know what happened to him in the end.'

Two Commanders appeared, duffel-coated and seabooted; Thurston was vaguely aware of giving them instructions, then the PMO returned, sent the Commanders out, gave him an anti-tetanus injection and bade him drink some whitish fluid from a glass.

'There you are, sir. What you need now is sleep. I'll look in on you in the morning.'

He came half-awake at intervals, whenever the damaged part of his head made contact with the pillow, and once he awoke sufficiently to notice the sounds of aircraft taking off from the deck outside, the engines running up, reaching full power, and then fading away as they flew clear of the ship. Merlin engines, which meant Seafires. It struck him that he had never before been below when *Crusader* was flying off her aircraft, then he rolled over, found a comfortable place on the pillow for his head, and fell back into sleep.

When he awoke again it was quite dark in the cabin, even the red light which Barnard had complained of was turned off, and there was silence. The ship's motion had changed, the sea now on her beam, so that she rolled rather than pitched. His head ached, and there was a foul taste in his mouth which must have come from the stuff Barnard had given him last night, or was it last night?

Spencer's voice came out of the dark. 'Are you awake, sir?'

'What time is it?'

'Just gone ten, sir, at night. The doctor said to leave you 'til you woke up.'

'Have I been out all that time?'

'Just about, sir. You did wake up once, and you talked a lot of nonsense in your sleep, but that was all.'

'Have you been here all that time?'

'Just about, sir,' Spencer said again. 'Charlie Metcalfe did take over for a bit, and the PMO's been in a couple of times.'

'Spencer, you needn't have bothered.'

'Thought you might have needed something, and the doctor said to keep an eye on you.'

There were creaking sounds as Spencer got up from the chair and picked up the telephone handset from above Thurston's head. 'The doctor said to ring him when you woke up.' He asked the switchboard for the PMO's extension. There was a click at the other end. 'This is Able Seaman Spencer, sir. The Captain's awake. Sounds all right, sir . . . Yes, sir . . . Aye aye, sir. Even if I 'ave to sit on 'im.'

'What was all that about?'

'He said I was to make sure you didn't start to get up, sir.'

'Very funny.' Thurston was aware of a growing need. 'But I'm going to have to get up, PMO or no PMO.' Barnard was an old woman, the Commander was quite right. But he found his legs quite ridiculously weak and unsteady, his knees aching sharply where he had banged them on the deck, and he had to balance himself against the furniture, moving stiff-legged and rather gingerly along the side of the bunk and grasping the door jamb as he went through. The nausea started again and he was sick into the lavatory bowl after he had relieved himself. Then there was the long journey back, his head pounding anew, and an unpleasant awareness of the ship's motion. His balance deserted him, and he found himself down on the deck once more, with Spencer moving to help him up, providing a shoulder to lean on and asking him whether he was all right.

The PMO arrived at the same moment. 'I thought I told you to stay in your bunk.'

'I had to get up.' Spencer's arm was round his shoulders. He was dizzy and pain was thumping into his head. He despised himself for his weakness.

'What do you think bedpans are for? Now get back into that bunk and *stay there* until I say you're fit to be out of it.'

Once Spencer had got him back into his bunk the world settled onto a more even keel. The PMO departed, leaving Spencer with a lot of

182

instructions and muttering that he had far less trouble with eight-year-olds. Thurston went back to sleep.

The Commander came to see him the next morning, brought him up to date with what had been going on in the thirty-six hours he had been out of circulation. *Mawddach* had picked up a submerged U-boat on asdic, depth-charged her and claimed a kill, 'but all anybody could see was oil, so it may be a bit doubtful.' *Crusader* had been sending up air patrols as usual and, touch wood, there had been no further landing problems. 'Everything's under control, sir.' He would say that; he had probably had orders from Barnard not to excite the patient, and it would in any case be a confession of his own unfittedness for command if he were to say anything else. 'How's the head, sir?'

'Feels as though someone's been trying to kick it off my shoulders. It was a bloody stupid thing to do.'

'It could happen to anyone, sir. But we'll manage until you're fit again.'

He was laid up for several more days, and it was a boring and frustrating period. As long as he stayed in his bunk with his head still and the light off there was little beyond the headache to remind him of the injury, but each time he stood up the world began to sway, the nausea re-emerged, and not infrequently he found that he was seeing two of everything. Barnard counselled patience, assured him that it was simply a matter of rest, quiet and freedom from worry, that nature must be allowed time to do its work, all the things he had heard before.

Spencer brought him a succession of invalid's meals, scrambled dried egg, milk puddings and various other bland offerings that he and Barnard seemed to consider appropriate, read to him from time to time, as did Scott. But mostly it was a lengthy tedium of lying in his bunk in the dark, with nothing to occupy himself beyond scratching the scabs of dried blood from his hair, finding himself a useless passenger aboard his own ship, wondering how the Commander was getting on. Of course the Commander should be able to manage; he was in the zone for promotion, for heaven's sake, but there was still the frustration of having his ship out of his own control, and all because he had slipped on a ladder.

'Everything's all right,' the Commander would insist, for so it seemed to be. The air patrols took off at their ordained times, and returned safely to land on *Crusader*, the ship zig-zagged with the rest of the convoy in accordance with the ordained pattern. There had been no losses among the merchant ships. Yes, the Commander was rising to

183

the challenge, and seemed to be enjoying the responsibility, but that knowledge did not ease Thurston's frustration.

On the morning of the sixth day, Thurston was finally able to get up, stand under the shower and wash the last of the blood from his hair, examine the gash with the aid of a couple of mirrors: a stubbly horizontal strip, a swollen ridge of tight black stitching, awkwardly placed where the rim of his cap would rest. It was strange to be back on the bridge, among the watchkeepers who had been there the night he fell from the ladder, to take up his usual place and say quietly to Sub-Lieutenant Vincent, 'I'll take the con now,' for going into harbour.

It was a bright morning, with only scattered cloud and a brisk wind to blow it inland, green hills on either side, and civilians visible through binoculars. A couple of cyclists following the undulating road along the north shore, a solitary golfer coming over a low rise and squaring up to take a putt, bringing ribald comment from the signalmen when he missed. The contrast between the battered, rust-streaked merchant ships which had battled their way across the Atlantic against both natural and human enemies and this civilian world was always noticeable. There was the usual talk of girls ashore – one of the lookouts was engaged to a local girl and being subjected to a good deal of ribbing by his comrades.

'Got someone fixed up to tell you what she's saying?'

'You don't need to know what she's saying. You just need to get in there and get her knickers down.'

'You do need to be able to check how long you've got. Not much fun if her mother walks in and catches you in the middle of it.'

As usual, Rear Admiral Manning-Wilson came aboard as soon as *Crusader* was secured to her buoy.

'What on earth have you been doing to yourself, Bob?'

'Fell off a ladder.'

'Very careless of you. Mind you, we've all done it. Damn near broke my neck coming off a ladder when I was in *Suffolk*. Back's never been the same since. How did Arthur Canning get on?'

The Commander had come a long way in the last few weeks. It was only a couple of months ago, when he was trying to have Shepherd court-martialled, that Thurston had seriously considered getting rid of him, and he would have done so if he had stepped out of line again.

'I'm glad to hear that. Those petrol fumes must have helped knock some sense into him, though I don't suppose knocked is the right word. He's in the zone, isn't he? Can you let me have a written assessment?'

This meant that the Commander was very much in contention for promotion, or would be if his captain's assessment was favourable. Manning-Wilson was generous with recommendations; he believed that credit should go where it was due, to the man who had earned it, rather than being attributed to that man's superiors. Aboard *Retribution* an inspecting admiral had remarked on the excellence of the ship's notice boards, and Manning-Wilson had afterwards sent for the carpenter who had made them and passed this on to him in person.

'Got some news for you, Bob. That report you and your chaps produced on night flying from escort carriers has excited quite a bit of interest. It seems nobody's actually done it before. So we're going to keep you off convoys for a couple of weeks so you can pass on your expertise. Show the rest how it's done. Have you managed to crack the illumination problem yet?'

'Not yet, sir. Flares are no good. They just alert the U-boat and she's dived before the Swordfish can get close enough to attack. The RAF have searchlights in the aircraft and their aircraft are fast enough to get over the target as she's diving. But we can't fit one of those to a Swordfish, or if we did there wouldn't be room for the radar in the first place, let alone any armament.'

'All the same, just your being airborne at night is going to make a difference. I've seen some of the interrogation reports on captured U-boat men, and they make interesting reading. Apparently they submerge as soon as they pick up radar transmissions on their Metox. All the thing does is pick up the transmissions; it doesn't tell them whether the aircraft is half a mile away or fifty. When you get close to them and they're still surfaced, either Metox isn't working or they've had too many false alarms recently. Even if you don't manage to sink them, they're going to get a fright when you get close enough to drop flares over them, which means they'll be that bit less likely to surface again in a hurry. And as long as they're submerged they can't keep up with a ten-knot convoy. I don't suppose your keen young lads will appreciate this, but just by being airborne they're making a real difference. Pity we can't get a few Liberators with Leigh Lights aboard escort carriers, but there it is.'

Manning-Wilson declined a second drink. 'Better not.' He patted his stomach. 'I'm trying to get rid of some of this. Blame it on my Wren cook. She seems to have made it her mission in life to keep me well fed.'

Manning-Wilson was one of the stocky kind who put on weight easily. He had managed to keep it under control at sea, but had grown much heavier since he had been ashore. He looked much older too, and tired. His might be a shore job, but it still involved long hours, and he was far from immune from the enervating business of being called out of his bunk in the small hours. Despite his refusal of a second drink, he seemed in a mood to linger, sitting in the armchair opposite Thurston nursing his empty glass.

'Of course,' the Admiral went on reflectively, 'we're not facing such a high calibre of enemy nowadays. Not like it was at the beginning when all their commanders were hand-picked regulars. The U-boat service has expanded so much that the quality's been very much diluted. They're having to use what manpower they can get. And we've managed to dispose of their really top men. Prien's dead, so are Schepke, Endrass, Mohr. Kretschmer's a POW, thank heavens. There are still some good ones around – Topp, Suhren, and that fellow Lauterbeck who had the Yanks very worried a couple of years ago, before they realised they were really fighting a war and blacked out their east coast and started to institute convoys. But chaps like that are spread pretty thinly nowadays, and a good thing too. We couldn't deal with a whole fleet of Kretschmers. You have to admire the professionalism of these chaps, even though you can hardly admire the system that pays them. The way Prien got inside Scapa, creeping in round the blockships, and actually reloaded inside after his first spread missed. Thank heavens there was only *Royal Oak* in there at the time.'

Then Manning-Wilson pulled out his watch, a heavy gold half-hunter which lived in his breast pocket. 'Better be going, or my Chief of Staff'll start wondering where I've got to. Jennifer's insisting on a divorce. Wants to marry this fellow.' He had got up from his chair, but still made no move away from it. He sighed, seemed abruptly to change his mind. 'If you don't mind, Bob, I think I will have that drink. But a lot of tonic, and not too much gin.'

'I'd still have her back, despite all this, if she'd just give up this Yank of hers. I don't know how many letters I've written her, but they've all come back unopened, and now her solicitors are insisting that any communication must be through them. She seems set on the idea of a divorce, so I've been on to the Second Sea Lord, and I'm going down to the Admiralty to see him the day after tomorrow.' He managed a bitter smile. 'It'd be ironic, wouldn't it, if I had to resign, since it's because of the service that Jennifer left me. At least that's what she

186

claims, though I don't suppose she'd have gone if it hadn't been for Lootenant-Colonel Charles Morton.'

'It would be unrealistic of the service to expect you to resign in wartime,' Thurston said slowly.

'Thanks, Bob, but you know as well as I do that the service is not always noted for being realistic. It all depends on the Second Sea Lord, and whether it's going to be possible to keep the thing quiet. We don't want a scandal, do we, Herbert, and we don't want to make difficulties between ourselves and our allies.'

'Just a minute. Jennifer deserted *you*, so you'd have to divorce her.'

Manning-Wilson smiled. 'It's not quite as simple as that. My solicitor thinks she could get a divorce on the grounds of cruelty. She could prove I'd neglected her sufficiently for that; she'd say I'd forgotten her birthday often enough, not shown her sufficient affection, apparently that constitutes cruelty in the eyes of the divorce courts. Then there's an affair I had a few years ago – before your time – which Jennifer knows about. It wasn't serious and it didn't last very long, and I thought she'd accepted it, but she could use it. So it looks as though she'll go ahead, and the best I can hope for is to keep it quiet, and at the moment I can't even promise the Second Sea Lord that. If I tried to divorce her she could defend on the grounds that I drove her into the arms of Morton, or she could cross-petition on the basis of my cruelty or my adultery and then the fat would really be in the fire as far as the service is concerned.'

Manning-Wilson ruminated in silence for a time, then took a long swallow of his gin and tonic and began speaking once more. 'Perhaps if we'd had children things might have been different. She wouldn't have been by herself as much. But we didn't. We had some rather embarrassing tests eventually, and it turned out that I was the one who was sterile. I had mumps when I was twenty-one and they seemed to think that caused it. Jennifer was very good about it at the time, but I'd be surprised if it didn't rankle. Women are funny about children. Never told anybody about that before. Only Jennifer and the quacks know.'

Outside, dusk had begun to fall and the cabin was growing dark. Only the desk lamp was switched on, and the dim light made the conversation more private still. Thurston found himself embarrassed by the intimacy of the revelations, coming from Manning-Wilson of all people. In *Retribution* days he had been a short, purposeful figure striding about his bridge and quarterdeck, demanding the highest standards of his officers and men. He could surprise any man among the twelve hundred on board by calling him by name, and he expected things to be done almost before they were thought of. He had once been the youngest post-captain in the service, and had been only forty-eight when he got his flag, but since then his career had stagnated in a succession of shore jobs and he would not fly his flag at sea now, something he must know.

His wife's desertion too had hit him harder than he was prepared to admit. And as was the lot of any commander, he had many people around him, but no one to whom he could turn in his distress, with always the demands of the service to override all more personal considerations. And for Thurston there was the frustration of being able to do nothing to ease the situation. When a man came to him on Captain's Requestmen to stop his allotment because his wife was being unfaithful, he could send him on compassionate leave in the hope that he could sort it out, but that was all he could do. He realised that he was looking at two Manning-Wilsons, screwed up his eyes for a moment and opened them to find that the two had again become one.

Manning-Wilson stood up for the second time. 'If I don't get back soon, my chief of staff will be sending out the search parties. Thanks for listening, Bob.'

'That's all right, sir,' and with that the intimacy was broken, and they were Admiral and Captain again.

Thurston saw him over the side and watched the Admiral's barge disappear over the dark water, its white wake breaking the smoothness.

21

Lieutenant Higgins left the ship the next morning, with hardly a word to anyone, his mess bills paid up-to-date, a rating accompanying him as far as the station to carry his kit. Sub-Lieutenant Shepherd also left, en route for submarines, proudly wearing the miniature brass oak leaf of a mention in despatches.

'Mind you don't go arguing with any more commanders,' Thurston told him.

'No, sir.'

'Good luck.'

For ten days *Crusader* kept a parody of office hours, in harbour during the day and moving out into the Firth at dusk for several hours of night flying exercises – 'clockwork mice flying' as the wags called it. The Swordfish came mainly from Abbotsinch and Machrihanish, a few from less familiar airfields in Northern Ireland. They appeared out of the darkness, circled the carrier anxiously for several minutes, made a couple of practice passes before attempting the landing itself. Round and round until Wings was satisfied, then they took off a last time and disappeared beyond the hills towards home. Then back into Greenock for a few hours, a brief period of shore leave in the afternoons, and grumbles from the mess decks that they only got ashore as the pubs were closing.

Thurston managed to make time to get out to Abbotsinch in the afternoons. He was aware that he was taking a risk. The PMO had warned him when he was taking out the stitches that he might feel the effects of the concussion for some time yet, but Thurston had not told him about the double vision which came upon him unpredictably when he was tired. He told himself it would be all right. He could get rid of it by shutting his eyes, and he could make sure that he only flew when he was fresh.

'No doubt you'll have forgotten it all,' Reynolds remarked, but proved willing to send him solo again after an hour's dual. Strangely, flying and even landing seemed much easier without Reynolds' presence in the front cockpit. It was enjoyable to be flying alone in the stillness of late afternoon, with the low sun shining across the hills to the south, and the sky in the west turning gradually to pink and gold, crossed by wisps of grey cloud. It was Wordsworth's bliss of solitude, even at a few hundred feet above industrial Clydeside, bumbling along in a clapped-out Tiger Moth. He had started to learn to fly for purely professional reasons, the need to have some personal experience of what his pilots faced, but he found himself going to Abbotsinch in order to fly for its own sake. Reynolds seemed to be happy to continue teaching him. 'I've got damn all work to do, sir, and it gets me airborne.'

Bernard Mann and his crew ditched. The aircraft came in well over to port, Mann did not correct sufficiently in response to the batman's signals, a sudden roll just as the wheels touched the desk sent the aircraft further over, the hook missed the wire which would have brought it up short, and it went over the side. Thurston put the helm over to starboard, and the Swordfish stayed afloat long enough for all three men to release their harnesses and get clear. The accompanying destroyer bustled up, saw the red lights attached to their Mae Wests and picked them up within a few minutes. It was the only accident of the entire ten days. Bernard Mann flew again the next night, but the batsman waved him off twice, and on the third approach he ignored the signal, bounced heavily and just managed to catch the 'Jesus Christ' wire and avoid hitting the barrier.

'Right, that's it,' Commander (Flying) said. 'I'm going to put my foot down. He's been mooching around like a wet weekend for weeks, and if he goes on flying like that he's for the chop. I'll have a word with the PMO in the morning.'

It was all done quietly and efficiently, the necessary letters written, a rail warrant made out, so quickly that Thurston could call Bernard Mann to his cabin before lunch the following day to make the proper farewells.

'I'm sorry about this, sir. It must be an infernal nuisance, having to find someone to take over in a hurry.'

Mann made his halting apologies, looking uncomfortable in his best uniform, with a handkerchief in his top pocket, the blue and white ribbon of the DSC standing out in solitary splendour above.

'It's not a nuisance. James can hold the fort until we get someone else. He's quite capable of doing the job, isn't he?'

'Yes, sir. He's good.'

Thurston said the usual things. He was sorry to lose him. He shouldn't go away thinking he had let the side down, it was just one of those things. He had the sense once more that he was playing a part,

190

this time the all-powerful father seated behind his desk, forearms resting on the blotter, large square hands clasped together. Mann sat opposite him, eyes downcast, black stains beneath from long sleeplessness.

He ran out of the usual things, stopped, picked up a pen and rolled it between his thumb and index finger before putting it down again. Mann watched him in silence, sitting on the edge of the chair, yet slumped in it. Thurston could guess at what he felt. Shame, and the sense of hopelessness which the twitch brought on, that there was no way out of the misery, and at the same time a sneaking relief that someone had stepped in and released him from the burden of responsibility. And in addition an embarrassment and discomfort at the way everyone was being decent, a desire to get away from everyone and be alone with the black canker that was eating away inside. After Thurston had been officially invalided from *Marathon*, the Commander had come to see him in hospital and said that the officers wished to row him ashore in the traditional manner. He was touched by the gesture, but he had to refuse, because he couldn't stand the thought of being among them again and on the receiving end of their respect and sympathy. No matter what Campbell and the rest kept telling him, he had failed to measure up, and forfeited the right to either.

He found himself speaking again. 'If I said I knew how you feel, you wouldn't believe me, but I do, because it happened to me.' Mann's head lifted momentarily in surprise. 'I left my last ship because I got twitch. By rights someone should have stepped in and put me ashore long before I did go, but it wasn't until I keeled over completely that the powers-that-be realised the state I was in and anything was done. The PMO knew, but like a bloody fool I didn't listen to him and insisted on carrying on, which was neither brave nor clever of me because I wasn't in any fit state to do my job properly. And that's the important thing. You've no doubt heard all about Stonehenge, how we got the ship back after the torpedo blew half the bottom out. But I'll never know whether we might not have been hit in the first place if I, or whoever was in command, had been fully up to the mark. We lost sixty-six men then, and the ship's still refitting. You're being grounded because if you carry on flying the way you have been, you're going to kill yourself, and, what is more important, you're probably going to kill your crew in the process.' The last words were brutal, but the only words which were likely to get through.

'Yes, sir. I know.'

There was another silence. Thurston found himself embarrassed by

191

his admission, wondering as many times before just how many people aboard knew about his breakdown. The razor scar on his wrist began to itch in sympathy, just where it was crossed by the buckle of his watch strap. He found himself cloaking the embarrassment in more words, anxious now to get rid of Bernard Mann as quickly as he could. 'You're going ashore for a rest now, and once you're fit you'll go back to flying, because the service can't afford to leave experienced flyers sitting on their backsides.'

'No, sir.'

They stood up, and shook hands, and Bernard Mann left. Thurston found himself vaguely frustrated and unsatisfied, though Mann would no doubt say in time to come that the Old Man had been very understanding. He took off his watch, put it into his side pocket, unfastened the shirt cuff to expose the purplish ridge which, flanked by a line of stitch holes on either side, ran in a gentle diagonal curve across the wrist and disappeared up the sleeve. There was a small square indent were the buckle had rested; he scratched at it with a fingernail and found relief. He picked up the pen from the desk top again, went through the precision movements of the thumb and fingers which the surgeon's skill had restored. The point of the razor had missed the radial nerve by a fraction, so that the loss of use of the hand had been temporary, while he had his arm in plaster, but there had been several weeks of having to manage everything with one hand only.

It was one of the tenets of Campbell's hospital regime that his patients, however twitch-ridden, remained naval officers, and they were therefore required to be washed and shaved and correctly dressed in uniform between the hours of 0730 and 2200. The sick berth attendants would cajole and had carte blanche, occasionally utilised, to pull out onto the floor any laggard who would have preferred to nurse his despair in bed for ever, but were forbidden to offer any assistance in getting up. So every morning there was the awkward fumbling business of getting his shoe laces tied with one hand, and he could only knot his tie by getting down on his knees and jamming the thin end in a drawer.

He could see the reasoning behind that now, that a man whose responsibility for his ship and other people had been taken from him, often forcibly, had to be forced to recognise that he still had a responsibility for himself, and to preserve some vestige of pride in himself. All of them had fought a losing battle against the cancer which they referred to, with a curious lightheartedness, as the twitch; they arrived in Campbell's ward having lost their way and their purpose in life, and it was Campbell's stated intention to get them back to seagoing duty as soon as possible, by what proved to be a mixture of compassion, insight, and plain, old-fashioned bullying. In the beginning Cambell had been gentle with him, gradually drawing him out on a variety of subjects; later he had begun to go in harder, so that the daily hour tended to develop into a verbal sparring match, with Thurston finding himself pushed continually onto the defensive and fighting a losing fight to keep the psychiatrist at arm's length. And finally Campbell broke through his guard and began to probe relentlessly at the raw wound of *Connaught*'s sinking and his own survival when almost all his men had died, set him blubbering uncontrollably and finding shameful relief in the crying, and put his arms round him and held him as a father might, but his own father never would.

A letter came from Midshipman G. R. W. Thurston, Royal Navy, announcing that he was shortly to leave *Duke of York* for three months' destroyer training, 'but I still don't know which ship I'm going to yet.' There was a letter from Crag Farm House, Langdon, Northumberland: '*My dear Robert . . . Your affectionate Father, Henry Maitland Thurston.*' Crates of warm clothing arrived and the rumours started. Some saw this as a bluff, and claimed that *Crusader* was headed for somewhere hot – one party favoured the Mediterranean, others the Indian Ocean or the Freetown escort force, 'where all that'll happen is you'll pick up a dose of footrot to last the rest of your life.' Others argued that bluff was beyond the wit of Their Lordships of the Admiralty, and agreed with the philosophic few who detected an elaborate double bluff in believing Russia to be their objective.

'S'pose our fucking neck or nothing skipper's after another VC,' Sutcliffe said to Metcalfe. 'The gilt's worn off the one he's got. Done anything about your will yet, kid?'

22

'D'you hear there? This is the Captain speaking. We are heading for Loch Ewe . . .' The Captain did not need to say anything more. Loch Ewe was where the Arctic convoys assembled; Loch Ewe meant Russia. Few listened to the remainder of the broadcast; there was a palpable tension in the air, men stopped what they were doing, or ostentatiously continued. Metcalfe set a steaming fanny of tea on the narrow table which ran between the two rows of triple-tiered bunks in his mess, watched the contents slop to and fro with the ship's rolling. Russia had been spoken of almost in whispers since he joined the Navy; there was fear, also a desire, half-hidden in the fear, to experience this for himself, so that he could say afterwards that he had been on a Russian convoy. He wiped his damp hands on his trouser legs, sat down on the backless bench and got himself a mug of tea.

'Russia, kid,' Sutcliffe said. 'Aren't you sorry you didn't get inside your Dottie's knickers when you had the chance?'

Metcalfe reddened, looked across the table at Sutcliffe's laughing face. 'Oh, sod off.'

''Ark at him. Did she tell you yours wasn't big enough to bother with?'

Metcalfe pushed the tea away, manoeuvred himself over the bench and towards the door.

'Am I embarrassing the poor little squirt?' Sutcliffe said loudly. He shrugged, and pulled the untouched mug of tea towards him.

Metcalfe went up the ladders towards the deck, wishing that he could finally be free of Sutcliffe and his taunting. 'You want to find yourself a caboose,' Spencer had said, 'quiet spot to sling your 'ammock.' It was all right for Spencer, who had installed himself and his kit in the Captain's pantry, an unofficial perk of his position as the Captain's body servant. But there wasn't room in there for two, and all the convenient little spaces seemed already to have been filled by other ratings in search of the privacy which was impossible to find on the crowded messdecks. Spencer knew about Sutcliffe, of course, and had offered to deal with him for him, but if Spencer didn't succeed his efforts would only make things worse. He could ask to go to another mess, but that still wouldn't get rid of Sutcliffe entirely. And it was true that Dottie wouldn't let him do it to her.

He reached the catwalk below the flight deck, felt the cold wind and the night rain in his face. He hadn't got his duffel on and he shivered. He had been home on a week's leave after basic training, spun a few yarns to those of his mates who were still civilians, about chasing a German pocket battleship all over the North Atlantic – it hadn't been in the newspapers because it was all secret. He waited for Dottie every evening outside the office where she worked – she was a shorthand typist – and took her to the pictures, then bought fish and chips to eat on the way home, keeping a weather eye open for the Military Police. She let him kiss her on the lips the first night, and by the end of the week he had unfastened her bra and squeezed her nipples, and she had rested her hand tantalisingly on the flap of his trousers. But she pushed him away when he tried to go further. 'No, Charlie, we mustn't.' She was scared about having a baby, of course, even though he'd told her he could get something to stop it happening, and then his leave was over and he had to join *Crusader*.

Then, a week ago, he had gone ashore by himself – Spencer had decided to say aboard, and anyway he just wanted to get away from the ship and be by himself. A woman had asked him for a light for her cigarette, and somehow he had ended up going back to her flat. Fifteen shillings, five days' pay, but he had been paid that morning and had it on him. Her place wasn't up to much – his mam would have been shocked at the yellowed net curtains, the pots in the sink and the film of dust on every surface, and she wasn't very clean either, her thighs greyish from ingrained dirt once she took off the nylons that some Yank must have given her, a rank smell coming out of her underclothes. But she had his fifteen bob and he was loath to waste it, and he did not feel he could ask for it back. He could not have been in the flat more than ten minutes. She rubbed him with one hand, pulled up her skirt, took off the nylons and lay down on the rumpled bed. He came almost before he was inside her. If that was all it was like, then why the fuss?

And in the last two days he had grown more and more sure that he had picked up a dose of the clap. The PMO's lectures made things perfectly clear. You weren't supposed to get it in the first place – there were sheaths available from the sick bay and if you had a woman you were expected to use one – and if you did they would stick a barbed instrument up your cock and drag it out again, as Sutcliffe had once described to him in graphic detail, they would pump gallons of pink liquid into you the same way, you would be banished to a separate

195

mess, euphemistically known as Rose Cottage, until you were adjudged cured. And the Captain would hear about it and he would lose his job as Captain's messenger, and Spencer's friendship with it. But the PMO's slides also showed what would happen if you didn't get anything done about clap. He shivered. Perhaps he could find a civilian doctor once they got back from Russia, if he saved all his pay, and perhaps the civilian doctor would keep quiet for him, but could he do that before the disease had done its work? And first there was Russia.

Loch Ewe was a kidney shape scooped out of Scotland's Atlantic coast, perhaps eight miles long, with a couple of small islands to provide comparative shelter in their lee. But this morning the wind came straight through the entrance and whipped the waters of the loch up into waves and white foam, so that the ships gathered there worried at their anchors, one or two moving in search of more secure berths. The shore was cloaked in rain, and grey mist hid the hills to the west. Before the war this had been a sparsely populated place; a few farmers, and a transient summer population who came for the fishing. There was a small hotel, a shop and post office, and a few houses on the edge of the loch, a couple of grey farmhouses visible ahead of the mist on the lower slopes. The war had added a huddle of Nissen huts next to the jetty, and a few dozen men permanently stationed there, but like the summer visitors, the bulk of the wartime population was transient, men and ships waiting to begin the voyage to Russia, having at Loch Ewe their last contact with the British mainland, some only for four or five weeks, others for ever.

Crusader's boat nosed up to the jetty. 'Lie off. I'll be about an hour.'
    'Aye aye, sir.'
    The boat rolled gently. Thurston judged his moment to make the step across to the wet wooden structure, its planks worn smooth and slippery with use and weather, joined the scatter of men making their way up the slope beyond, heads down against the rain and wind, which had eddied unpredictably and now came back in their faces, hands thrust into greatcoat pockets, on their shoulders the four rings and diamond of captains in the Merchant Navy, or the executive curl of the Royal Navy and varying numbers of stripes, but all with responsibility for a ship and her men. The track had been roughly metalled at the time the Nissen huts were built, but rainwater coming down the slope had worn much of the surface away, so that there were now small islands of black tarmac rising above wet brown sand, and at the edges

196

deeper streams where the water had worked downwards through yielding earth, long fronds of green grass providing colour against the brown earth and brown water.

'Miserable day,' someone said.

'Won't be any better where we're going.'

The building where the convoy conferences were held stood by itself above the Nissen huts. It must have once been the village hall, and had the look of one still, though armed sentries in gaiters stood outside, a petty officer came forward to check identity cards and to tick off names against his list.

'Captain Thurston, sir? Aye aye, sir.'

Inside there was a stage where in days gone by the locals had performed their Gilbert and Sullivan, now occupied by a table at which sat a commander from Naval Control of Shipping in Glasgow and a Wren second officer. The side walls bore tattered posters which had been there since their slogans and images were new: a group of senior officers, drinks in hands, within earshot of a Marlene-Dietrich-like figure reclining on a chaise longue: *Careless talk costs lives!*

The rows of chairs had filled up and there was quiet conversation, sailors' talk, about shifting cargoes, and navigation problems and dragging anchors, conducted in a variety of accents, mostly British, but there was a huge, granite-faced Norwegian, turning round over the back of his chair to talk to a fellow countryman, a destroyer lieutenant-commander with Canadian flashes, a Belgian speaking in rapid French to the Pole alongside him.

The door opened again and the Commodore came in, followed at a couple of paces by the Senior Officer Escort, Captain (D) of the destroyer flotilla which would sail with the convoy. Thurston and Stewart Grant had been promoted on the same day, but G came before T in the Captains List, which made Grant the senior. He was a Scot from Forres, several years older than Thurston, having got his fourth stripe at virtually the last chance, and a salt-horse destroyer man, who had been on the Russia run for as long as anyone still alive. The Commodore too was an old Russia hand, with three previous round trips behind him. Thurston had a sense of being a newcomer in a very exclusive club, that he might have spent years in the North Atlantic and Mediterranean, but that was as nothing now.

The briefing followed the usual pattern. The Commodore, Stewart Grant, the naval control service Commander, and another Commander from the staff of the Admiral commanding the cruiser covering force stood up by turns and said their pieces. The Wren officer took notes, her chair pushed back and the shorthand pad resting on her knee. The legs which protruded below her skirt were long and shapely, rather like Kate's. Thurston found his attention wandering, thinking about Kate instead of concentrating on the instructions for merchant captains which the naval control service Commander was giving, but they were familiar enough, keep in station, obey the Commodore's signals promptly. If the baby decided to arrive early it might be born before he got back. No, that was ridiculous; there were still a couple of months to go. Someone was passing a crumpled paper bag along the row. Thurston dug his fingers in when it reached him, found boiled sweets, took one, and passed the bag on to the Canadian sitting next to him. It was cold in the hall, the radiators on either wall could not banish the damp chill, and everyone in there had kept his greatcoat on. The rain rattled on the tin roof, ran down the windows, so that all that could be seen outside was greyness. Stewart Grant stood up, announced that he was pleased to say that they would have an aircraft carrier with them on this occasion, went through the orders for the escorts.

The main briefing came to an end. The Commodore asked if there were any questions. The Polish captain asked about rescue ships. The naval control service Commander muttered something about, 'Bloody man doesn't understand English,' and repeated very slowly, 'for Captain Bzrezinsky's benefit,' what had been said earlier, that there were two rescue ships with the convoy, both large trawlers specially converted for the job, and they, and no others, would deal with survivors in the event of any sinkings. 'No stopping for survivors, the rest of you. You'll only put your own ships in danger, not to mention the rest of the convoy. Your best defence, against U-boats and against aircraft, is to keep in your stations and leave the escorts free to concentrate on dealing with the enemy, instead of having to nag you.'

The Pole turned to his Belgian neighbour once more. Thurston wondered whether the Commander had spent much time at sea. Perhaps not. He seemed to be treating the whole business as a Staff College exercise. 'Take twenty assorted merchant ships with vital cargoes and get them to the Kola Inlet with the minimum possible losses.' But at this time of year the only route to Russia was a narrow corridor between the northern tip of Norway and the southern margin of the polar ice, a corridor patrolled by a cordon of U-boats and covered by fighter and bomber aircraft from airfields less than an hour's flying time away. In that it was like the run to Malta, but unlike the Mediterranean there was darkness for twenty hours in twenty-four, some of the stormiest seas in the world, and cold which would kill within minutes any man who was forced to jump overboard to escape his sinking ship.

And there was the *Tirpitz*, badly damaged by the midget submarine attack in the autumn, but now, according to intelligence, almost ready for sea once more. The *Tirpitz* had almost never left her Norwegian fjord, but the mere threat of a sortie had led a former First Sea Lord, now himself dead after a series of strokes, to order the scattering of a convoy and the withdrawal of its escorts back to Scapa. The *Tirpitz* was out for a few hours only, and did no damage in that time, but the lone merchant ships made easy pickings for aircraft and U-boats, so that of the thirty-seven which had set out, only eleven reached the Russian ports, some to be sunk in their turn on the return journey.

'Well gentlemen, I think we should be getting back to our ships,' the Commodore said.

The officers on the platform began to gather up their papers. The captains got up, separated into small groups and stood talking for a few minutes, before leaving. Thurston found himself separated from the rest, apart from the merchant captains because he was of the Royal Navy, and denied the easy banter of the destroyer and frigate captains because of his rank. He had a brief word with Stewart Grant, who was standing in the middle of the floor with the naval control service Commander, who was fretting about the train he needed to catch to get back to Glasgow that day.

'Better hitch a lift in one of Captain Thurston's Swordfish,' Grant chaffed him.

The Commander looked out at the rain, and declined.

'Better get moving myself,' said Grant. 'Got to get back to Scapa to pick up my flotilla. See you in Murmansk.'

Thurston went out into the rain, saw *Crusader*'s boat lying off the jetty. By some natural quirk the eddy had disappeared and the wind was once again whipping into their faces. He heard the door bang behind him, turned to see the Wren officer, holding her tricorn hat onto her head with one hand.

'Filthy weather.'

'Yes, sir.' She smiled back. Dripping water and with her face alight she looked more attractive than she had when cool and composed a few minutes earlier.

Thurston came to a decision. 'Have you got a telephone I could use?'

'Private call, sir?' He nodded. 'I shouldn't really let you, but in the circumstances . . .'

He followed her towards one of the Nissen huts, the smooth leather soles of his shoes sliding on the wet path.

'It's just in here, sir.'

Her office was a quarter of the Nissen hut, opening off a narrow passage which ran the length of the hut. There was a desk, a shelf containing an assortment of mugs, glass jars labelled 'tea', 'cocoa' and 'sugar', a bottle of milk, kettle and an electric ring. On the window ledge was a plant in a pot. 'It's not doing very well,' she said ruefully. Then she was briskly efficient once more. 'The switchboard will put you through, sir. I'll wait outside.'

Kate answered almost at once.

'That was quick. You must have been right next to it.'

There was a pause, as if Kate was working out what she should say. 'Well, actually, I'm in bed.' There was a telephone on his side of the bed, which the previous tenant, a surgeon commander, had had installed. 'It's all right. There's nothing really wrong with me. Dr Heath just thinks my blood pressure is a bit high, and he told me to stay in bed for a couple of days, until it goes down.'

Kate insisted that she was all right, and that the doctor was making a fuss about nothing, reminded him that her sister Caroline had had the same thing with both her children, and everything had turned out all right. 'He seemed very concerned that I couldn't get my wedding ring on, but it was the same when I had George.' She laughed. 'It's very embarrassing when I'm this size.' He couldn't say much, the wall was thin and there were only three minutes before the civilian operator would cut them off. He couldn't tell her, even obliquely, that he would be sailing on a Murmansk convoy in a couple of hours.

'It's all a bit of a bore really. Mrs Crosby's having a lovely time fussing over me, and Helen went to the library and got me a pile of books, and I've got the wireless, but I'm starting to get awfully restless.'

'You look after yourself.'

'Oh, Bob, you are such a hypocrite. When the doctor tells *you* to take some rest, you immediately go out and do the opposite!'

'That's different. I'm not having a baby.'

'It would be very strange if you were.'

'Three minutes,' the operator called.

'I've got to go. I'll ring you . . . when I get back.'

The telephone went dead. Kate was cheerful enough, and making light of things, but as Thurston walked down the slope towards the jetty he felt a nagging sense of unease.

Dr Heath, highly recommended by a friend of Kate's whose daughter had been looked after by him during her pregnancy, had made it clear from the beginning that he considered Kate most unwise to be having a child at her age. 'I take it this pregnancy was unplanned, Captain Thurston?' He refused to give any reasons when pressed, except to say that 'difficulties' were more likely to occur in 'the older mother'. 'You will have to take life very quietly, Mrs Thurston.'

Petty Officer Pym brought the boat alongside the jetty. Once aboard, Thurston unlaced his shoes and turned them upside down, peeled off his sodden socks and wrung them out in his hands, creating a small puddle of dirty water which found the lowest level of the cabin floor.

'Dirty weather, sir,' someone said.

Grey sea, grey ships, grey land disappearing into the grey sky, only the ship's ensigns, blown stiffly from their staffs in the wind, to break the monotony. The white ensigns of the escorts, the red duster of the British Merchant Navy, the Norwegians' off-centre red cross bordered white; red and white, with the proud Polish eagle blazoned across, a solitary American stars and stripes on a Liberty ship making her first voyage.

There was *Crusader*'s flat top and asymmetrical superstructure, the tips of her Seafires' folded wings outlined against the sky. The deck park was doubled in size, more aircraft packed into the hangar below, for a complete second squadron had flown aboard the day before, so that there were new faces among the familiar ones of James, Wallace, Kornilov and the rest, newcomers bashfully finding their way around a strange ship, more men to be packed into the already crowded messdecks. But the greater threat on the Murmansk run came from aircraft and not from U-boats, so that the Seafires, as well as the Swordfish, would be fully utilised.

In the last few months the young fighter pilots, patrolling far out over the North Atlantic, had seen no enemy aircraft. For them the danger came at the end of each patrol, in the nerve-stretching business of landing a delicate high-performance aircraft which had never been intended for anything rougher than grass fields on the rolling, pitching deck of an escort carrier. One afternoon Thurston had flown the Tiger Moth over the anchorage, seen *Crusader*'s long narrow rectangle moored stem and stern and gone lower, keeping a wary eye open, for naval gunners were notoriously trigger-happy and their aircraft recognition proverbially bad. Even at a hundred feet the deck which seemed so large when standing on it was minute, scarcely wider than the aircraft's

201

wingspan, and restricted still further by the island, and by the barrier which cut the usable length by a third.

Manning-Wilson had been aboard the day before, a more cheerful Manning-Wilson than recently. 'The Second Sea Lord was quite reasonable about it all. Said there would be no question of my resigning provided the business with Jennifer is dealt with quietly. Apparently the thing to do is to give her the grounds to divorce me, and not to contest it, and make sure that Jennifer chooses some divorce court in the sticks where neither of us is known. That is apparently why Mrs Simpson got her divorce from Simpson in Ipswich, of all places. My solicitors have been in touch with Jennifer's, and it looks as though she's prepared to agree – after all, she's getting what she wants.' He smiled ruefully. 'So it looks as though it's going to be one of those ghastly weekends in Brighton with a woman unknown, and the chambermaid tells the court that she saw me having breakfast in bed with the woman. Brighton's a bit far away, so I'll make it Troon and perhaps I can get in a bit of golf at the same time. It's hardly what I want, but it seems as though Jennifer is determined to have a divorce, by whatever means, and the only thing I can do now is limit the damage.' He stretched his arms out forwards.

'Enough of my troubles, Bob. What about this ship of yours? Are you happy with young James as squadron CO? If you're not, it's a bit late to do anything about it before you sail.'

'I've every confidence in him.'

'Glad to hear it. Pity about the other fellow – Mann. I wouldn't wish that on my worst enemy, though you've proved yourself that it needn't be the end of the line.'

Thurston had started, put down the cup of tea he was holding with studied care.

'You thought I didn't know? Dammit, Bob, how could you think that? There aren't many secrets in the service. To be honest, I wasn't all that surprised when I heard about it.'

Thurston found that he had shifted towards the edge of his chair, the hand which had held the cup still flexed and held rigid.

'You always were a bit intense,' Manning-Wilson went on. 'Got too personally involved, even when you were a Commander. But I suppose that's a fault in the right direction.' The tone of voice changed again. 'And don't go thinking that I asked for you for *Crusader* because I felt sorry for you. I asked for you because I knew you were a bloody-minded young bugger and the best man for the job.'

25

As the convoy moved northwards the weather grew colder. A few hours after leaving Loch Ewe the rain stopped, the sky cleared and as the sun rose the next morning with the convoy abreast the Faroe Islands, a rime of frost whitened the grey metal surfaces. The morning was clear, but a bitter wind blew down from the north, raising great mounds of grey water all around.

'Goin' to get plenty worse than this,' Spencer remarked to Metcalfe. 'You been to Russia before?'

'No, but when we was in *Connaught*, me and the Old Man, we spent most of the time up the Denmark Strait. This is a millpond compared to that. All the weather coming down from the Pole gets funnelled through, and you've never seen seas like them. And the cold. Gawd, it'd freeze your balls off!'

'Spence,' Metcalfe took a hasty look around him, 'I've got to talk to you.' The itching seemed to get worse the more clothes he put on, stinging and burning all over his crotch and resistant to all scratching.

'Okay, kid. Soon as you can get below.' Spencer's voice was casual, but there was an undertone of concern.

'Been poking your prick where you shouldn't, Charlie? Drop your trousers and let's have a look.'

Metcalfe stood bashful and shivering in the Captain's pantry with his trousers and underpants around his ankles, while Spencer got down on his knees and peered intently.

'Gawd, the pong! When did you last do any dhobi, Charlie? And don't you know what soap is?'

Metcalfe blushed several shades redder. Spencer nudged his thigh. 'Only joking, kid. But . . . Gawd, you can see them running about! They're having a lovely time in there. No wonder you got an itch.'

'What are, Spence?' He wished Spencer would tell him instead of making a joke out of his embarrassment.

'Crabs, kid. Dozens of 'em.' Spencer got to his feet. 'Don't worry. I got some stuff that'll shift 'em, easy. Hang on a sec and I'll get it.' He moved into a corner and rummaged inside his kitbag, threw out various articles, and finally produced a flattened tube of ointment. 'Thought I had some left. You just rub it all over, wait a few minutes, and they just brush out. If you go to the MO they shave your bush and cover you with iodine and all sorts, so I'm doing you a favour. Doin' us all a favour, 'cos it'd be short arm inspections for the rest of us. Stuff stings a bit, but it does plenty worse to the crabs. Can you do it yourself? There's some funny blokes like it done for 'em.'

Metcalfe blushed again.

'All right, Charlie, I'll wait outside. Shout when you're ready.'

'You got to be careful where you go screwing,' Spencer said when the job was done and they were sitting down with a cup of tea apiece. 'You can pick up all sorts. Fifteen bob? You were asking for trouble. You don't want to go with tarts, or if you do, save up a bit and go with the expensive ones. They're safer. Or you want to wait until you get back home, give your Dottie one too many in the pub and then have her. She wouldn't let you last time, but you can spin her a few yarns about going to Russia, and once she's had a few she won't know whether she's going to her wedding or her funeral. That's the way to treat 'em while you're young, but once you're older you want to get your feet under the table with someone like Rosie.'

Spencer was off again. Metcalfe had already heard more than he ever wished to know about Rosie and her multifarious virtues.

For three days it was like any other convoy, except for the increasing cold, and the shortening of the brief intervals of daylight. There were ships drifting out of station, ships making too much smoke, a ship with engine trouble, a ship whose Chief Engineer suffered a heart attack in his engine room. *Mawddach* transferred her Surgeon Lieutenant by jackstay, but there was nothing he could do which had not been done already. Off the north-eastern tip of Iceland a destroyer took the invalid off, and dashed into Laganes to land him ashore, and out again to rejoin the convoy.

Laganes marked their last contact with the land. Thurston watched the low rocky shore receding into the darkness, shivered, and stamped his feet. The weather was still clear, but the forecast which he held in his hand, brought up by the meteorological rating a few minutes before, promised heavy weather to come.

The convoy crossed the Arctic Circle and turned east. The first of the snow came, and the storm struck. The wind came from the east, piling up great mountains of water which bore down on the convoy in steady, almost monotonous procession. *Crusader* climbed sluggishly over one wave, to find herself faced by another still larger. The bows dropped into empty space, then the next wave broke over the flight deck as hundreds of tons of green water. Spray froze even as it was thrown up and hit the island as solid ice, sharp-edged enough to cut an exposed face to the bone. Flying came to a halt, the flight deck was pitching fifty degrees in each direction and half-submerged in water each time the bows went down. No man could move on that deck, the aircraft in the deck park had to be left to themselves, double- and triple-lashed, water swirling around their undercarriages.

'God knows what state they're going to be in when we get near enough to find out!'

Below in the hangar the aircraft were also doubled-lashed, and watched continuously for the first sign of a fraying line which would herald a Swordfish or Seafire breaking loose. Toolboxes and equipment skidded back and forth, men slipped and slithered between the aircraft, attempting to go on with the routine work of servicing and minor repairs.

On the messdecks all was chaos. Water had found its inexorable way around the edges of hatch covers, past the seals on scuttles, some of the welds which united the ship's plates had begun to leak. Water piled up at one end of each mess as the ship began to climb over the wave, and washed back to the other as the bows went down into the trough beyond, carrying a litter of broken crockery, clothing, photographs from home, letters begun and then abandoned as the weather changed, and a scum of vomit. Buckets had been overturned, and some men were so prostrated by seasickness that they could do no more than lean dizzily out of their bunks and spew on the deck below. It was impossible to sleep, even when lashed into a bunk. There was the conscious motion and the noise of the storm, the howling of the wind, the buffeting as the ship met each sea, the creaking and groaning of strained metal, and the curses of other men for whom sleep was equally elusive. Even with the heating full on, the temperature on the messdecks barely cleared freezing point, condensation ran off the steel bulkheads to soak bedding and add to the water running over the deck.

'Roll on my fucking twelve. Don't you wish you'd joined the army?'

While the gale lasted Thurston never left the bridge. For most of that time he sat wedged into his bridge chair, silent, watching the wind and the weather, and the Officer of the Watch who was struggling to keep the ship's bows on to the sea, occasionally getting up and stamping around the confines of the bridge to restore his circulation.

'Signal's just come through, sir. The Chief Engineer's dead.'

'Not our Chief Engineer surely?'

The visible parts of the Chief Yeoman's face were lashed red-raw by the wind. His teeth appeared in a wide grin. 'No, sir. The one with the heart attack that we landed.'

'Chief, I hope you're not planning to have a heart attack.'

'No, sir. I've no intention of having Wullie Duff take over yet. He's standing opposite me grinning, sir.' Chief sounded cheerful enough. 'We're managing, sir, and at least we're warm.'

From the open bridge, with the temperature many degrees below freezing and the wind making it colder still, wrapped in many layers of clothing in a vain attempt to keep out the cold, it was difficult to imagine that directly below him, a mere eighty or ninety feet away, the temperature topped a hundred degrees and men sweated in even the lightest overalls.

Daylight came slowly, and lasted only a brief time. The sky was dull blue-grey, the colour of a shotgun barrel, a partly obscured horizon ahead heralded the approach of more snow within the hour. The great swelling mountains of sea were the same colour, obscuring some of the ships of the convoy as they disappeared into the troughs beyond. But the weather was on their side. The U-boats would stay submerged for the most part, staying below the weather, and even when surfaced they would be less likely to find the convoy in the murk. And though enemy aircraft, unlike *Crusader*'s, might be able to take off and land from their well-equipped airfields, they lacked a radar which could detect ships, and were also dependent on the eyes of their crews.

Midshipman George Thurston stretched out one arm to steady himself against the bridge screen.

'If you can't take a joke, sir, you shouldn't have joined!' *Vittoria*'s Yeoman of Signals was a foxy little man with red hair and sideburns trimmed to a point, now entirely hidden by a large green balaclava helmet, on top of which was perched his uniform cap, which managed to stay in place despite the wind. The Yeoman was looking up at him, grinning hugely. ''Bout time for a drop of kye, I think, sir.'

The Gunnery Officer, Lieutenant Morse, had the watch. The Captain was sitting on his bridge chair on the starboard side of the binnacle, silently watching, until he came awake at the Yeoman's words.

'Mr Thurston, the Yeoman's quite right. Go and make Mr Morse and myself some cocoa. And if there are any biscuits left bring those up.'

'Aye aye, sir.'

Followed by one of the signalmen George went down the ladder to the galley, and busied himself with preparations. He had been looking forward keenly to this period of destroyer training, sure that it would mean greater responsibility, a chance to put all his Dartmouth training into practice, after eight months of being just one among a couple of dozen midshipmen in the Fleet flagship. But as in *Duke of York* a midshipman's duties seemed only to involve the making of cocoa and the running of errands, and acting as an extra pair of eyes on the bridge; he was expected to learn the ropes simply by watching and listening to those more experienced than he. This was the way it had always been done, and everyone had to go through it, but it seemed a waste of the eleven terms he had spent at Dartmouth, waiting impatiently to go to sea, and praying that the war would not end before he left.

'Careful, sir, you'll have that over,' the signalman broke in warningly.

'Thanks, Snodgrass.' He pushed the container further back onto the hob. He had been amazed to discover the day before that the signalman's name really was Snodgrass.

And *Vittoria* was not even a real destroyer any more, stripped of her torpedo tubes, director control, and two of her guns, to make room for extra depth charges, her speed reduced to twenty-five knots by the replacement of one of her boilers with long-range fuel tanks. Not a real destroyer, but a long-range escort, intended only for convoy work. Convoy escorts were important, of course, and even real destroyers, the most modern ones with 4.7 inch guns, torpedo tubes and speeds above thirty-five knots which he had envied back at Scapa, spent most of their time escorting convoys, but this just wasn't the same.

Of course, he reminded himself, he had only been on board a matter of days, and he would have to show that he could measure up before they gave him some real work to do. That was the way of the Navy, and had been made quite clear when he joined *Vittoria*.

'Thurston. Are you related to R. H. M. Thurston by any chance?'

'Yes, sir. He's my father.'

'And I see you were a chief cadet captain at Dartmouth.'

'Yes, sir.'

'That is all well and good, Mr Thurston, and remember me to your father, but you will find things aboard my ship rather different from a flagship, and it is your performance of your duties while you are aboard her which counts, not who your father is, or what you did at Dartmouth.'

'I understand, sir.'

'I hope you do. The First Lieutenant will explain your duties.'

The water boiled at last. He and the signalman upended the vessel over a fanny in which rested shavings from a large block of plain chocolate, the contents of a tin of condensed milk and a large quantity of sugar. The signalman stirred the mixture.

'Now let's see if we can get it back up there without losing the lot, sir.'

Snodgrass nursed the fanny up the ladder, some of the contents slopping over the rim and staining the front of his duffel coat as the ship rolled. George followed with a motley assortment of mugs strung on a length of wire.

'Ah, thank you.' Lieutenant-Commander Haldane took a full mug from him, held it in both hands and sniffed appreciatively.

'The first thing you need to know,' the junior Sub-Lieutenant, a chatty soul named Atkinson, had told him, 'is the skipper's name. Spelt *Haldane*, pronounced *Haddon*. At least that's what he calls himself, and he's very particular about it. He's sweating on his brass hat at the moment, and he's also the most fearful snob. As soon as I saw him I could see that I was less than the dust beneath the chariot wheel. RNVR, and from Manchester, of all places. You'll be all right. He'll be preening himself at the mere thought of having R. H. M. Thurston's son as his midshipman.'

Somewhere out there, separated from him by a mile of boiling sea, and unaware that he also was here, was his father. George had had no notice of his transfer to *Vittoria*, only sufficient time to get his kit together and persuade one of the other snotties to take him to Kirkwall to catch the ferry across the Pentland Firth to link up with the train south. He had been going to write a letter during the journey, but he had got into company with other chaps going to Liverpool, and somehow he had never got round to it. And then he had only just begun to find his way around *Vittoria* before she sailed.

'Never seen a carrier taking it green before,' the Yeoman remarked laconically.

Crusader looked impressive in a strange sort of way, burying her bows in the heavy seas, water coming back as far as the island, the aircraft standing forlornly on the deck, her lattice-work of masts and aerials standing clear above.

'Bloody unstable those things. Better off here. This old scow rolls a lot, but she's not top-heavy like that.'

It was almost a year since he had last seen his father, on leave after passing out from Dartmouth. Thurston had been sick, bad-tempered and in pain, and George had kept out of his way as much as he decently could.

'He's had a very bad time,' his mother advised. 'You'll have to bear with him.'

But this was something he could not comprehend, the sudden change in his father. There had been special occasions when he was younger and his father would take him aboard his ship, show him how to take bearings with the compass and plot them on the chart, and how to use a sextant, had even once sent him down several sets of ladders into the steering compartment so that he could steer *Retribution* herself, though admittedly with the Chief Quartermaster's huge gnarled hands on the wheel over his. He could not remember a time when there had not been ships, and when he had not wanted to go into the Navy himself.

The war had broken out the week before he went to Dartmouth; he went aboard *Connaught* before he left, full of bursting pride at being in the Navy at last, been taken over the ship by one of the midshipmen, been told to look after his mother and sister.

Then, in his sixth term at Dartmouth, there was the action with the *Seydlitz;* he was summoned from a maths lesson to the Captain's office to be told that his father had been wounded, but he would be all right, he was off the danger list, and was certain to be decorated. 'At least a DSO, I should imagine.' There was a dizzying period when he could tell people, yes, it *was* his father, and enjoy a little of the glory. Only two could go to the investiture at the Palace; Mother had to go, of course, he and Helen tossed for the second place and he won, so that he could watch his father standing tall and straight at attention as the citation was read out, the scar of his jaw wound still livid – 'though faint from loss of blood and virtually unable to speak, Captain Thurston continued to fight his ship with the utmost determination until the enemy vessel was finally sunk, refusing all but the most basic medical attention for his injuries . . .' – and stand alongside him afterwards to be photographed for the newspapers. And almost the next time he saw him, 'He's had a very bad time,' his mother kept saying. His father had taken him for a walk before he left to catch the train for Scapa, but said almost nothing to him.

Vittoria's bows disappeared into green water. Frozen spray came back at them once more. George wondered how long the storm could last. Only yesterday evening the weather had been clear, yet it seemed now that there had never been a time when he was not fighting a continuous battle to maintain his footing on the ice-slippery deck plates which never lay at the same angle for more than two consecutive seconds, surrounded by waves which seemed every moment to threaten to engulf the small destroyer.

Darkness came once more. The PMO came up from below, reported that he now had eight men in the sick bay who were prostrated by seasickness, 'and that's only the ones we know about,' another who had been catapulted off a ladder and dislocated his shoulder, and a constant flow of mashed fingers, cuts requiring stitches and other miscellaneous petty damage. Sub-Lieutenant Vincent had the watch, made diffident helm and engine orders to keep the ship bows on to the weather. Vincent was doing all right, Thurston thought to himself, but over all these months nothing had yet convinced him of his own competence. And there was a small dark core of Thurston's own mind which whispered to him that he was only going through the motions, that he might be doing that competently enough, but it could not last. That on the outside there was a shell of efficiency and experience, which did that which was required, but underneath there was no substance and that one day, not very far ahead, this truth would be revealed. This sense had perhaps always been there, but he had only become fully aware of it since his crack-up. Campbell would say that he was doing all right, Manning-Wilson would probably laugh, but he still had to find some proof of his fitness for command.

Spencer appeared at his elbow. 'Ready for some supper, sir?'

He considered for a moment. 'Can you do me another of those bacon butties of yours?'

'You're goin' to start looking like a bacon butty soon, sir.'

'Get away with you, you King's hard bargain.' Spencer grinned at the description. 'And don't look so bloody proud of it.'

'One bacon butty comin' up, sir.'

'Wait a moment, Spencer. Mr Vincent, are you in the market for a bacon butty?'

Vincent half-turned, one hand holding his binoculars. 'Er, yes, sir.'

'Make that two then, Spencer.'

'Aye aye, sir.'

Spencer's bacon butties were made with split bread rolls, toasted on the inside, spread thickly with butter which melted obligingly through the holes, and contained several layers of lightly crisped bacon, mustard, salt and pepper.

The bows dropped again. The gun's crews had been stood down, their positions untenable. For a moment the upper deck was a lake of water, then it washed away astern as the forepart of the ship rose once more above the horizontal. It was fully dark now, and they might have been entirely alone on the great ocean. Thurston thought suddenly of Kate. He had asked the PMO about it, as casually as he could.

'It's actually very common, sir, especially in a first pregnancy. But we don't as yet know what causes it, and we don't have a cure for it specifically. How old is your wife . . . ? Has she had it before? Hm. In a first pregnancy we don't worry too much about it, but in a third, when the woman hasn't had it before, it can be rather more serious.' Barnard began to hedge, like all doctors, Thurston thought a little bitterly. 'Well, sir, as you insist, it can lead to convulsions, even to ante-partum haemorrhage if the rise in blood pressure isn't checked. But that is only likely to happen if the problem isn't detected before the woman goes into labour. Your wife's been given exactly the right advice, to go to bed and stay there. It's very important that she does that. That's about all I can say, sir; my interest in children starts after birth, not before. Sorry I can't be more helpful.'

Thurston swore to himself. That was the worst thing, that there was nothing he could do about it. He couldn't have given himself compassionate leave, not at a time like this, and even if he had been able to go home, instead of taking his ship to sea, there was nothing constructive he could have done. All the same, he wished he could simply pick up a telephone and ask Kate how she was. Unless something went seriously wrong, sufficient to justify an official signal, he would know nothing until *Crusader* returned from Murmansk.

Spencer reappeared, armed with a covered plate and a large mug of cocoa, miraculously still nearly full.

'There you are, sir.'

Spencer was grinning.

'Enjoying yourself, Spencer?'

'Roll on my twenty-two, sir.'

Thurston bit into the bacon butty, getting a brief taste of leather gauntlet in addition, felt the melting butter run over his chin. Vincent was doing the same with his own, gripping it in one hand, stopping chewing for a moment to grin back at him, as if this represented something deeper, a unity between them, a belonging.

211

26

Slowly the wind began to drop. When the sun rose the next morning, though the seas remained huge, they no longer broke over *Crusader's* flight deck and the storm was past. The deck now was sheeted with ice, smooth in some places and hummocked in others, glowing dull red where the low sun shone on it. Ice filled the slots which contained the arrester wires, jammed every winch and windlass, coated gun barrels and the lattice of mast and aerials in white.

'And a Merry Christmas everybody! All we need is Father Christmas and his bloody reindeer.'

'Bit late!'

The flight deck party got busy with brooms and shovels. Steam hoses were led up from below and played over the guns and arrester wires, and the aircraft mechanics got to work on the deck park. But long before the flight deck was clear the first enemy aircraft appeared over the convoy, a four-engined Focke Wulf Kondor, circling provocatively just out of reach of the convoy's guns. They knew as they watched her that the respite was over, that she would already have passed a sighting report to her base in Norway, so that both aircraft and U-boats would know where to find them, and before long they would be facing not only the sea but everything the Germans could pit against them.

Meanwhile the solitary aircraft, circling just beyond their reach, was a challenge.

'Haven't you got that deck clear yet, Wings?'

'We're doing all we can, sir,' Commander (Flying) said defensively.

The pilots hung around a ready room heavy with cigarette smoke, playing cards in small groups, or trying to read the various dog-eared paperbacks which were doing the rounds. Occasionally one would appear on deck, watch the Kondor for a few minutes, the sun glinting off its wings as it banked into its turns, shiver, and go under cover once more.

'Deck's clear, sir.'

'About time. Pipe Flying Stations.'

Two Seafires were ranged on deck, the aircraft of the deck park trundled clear. Engines were started, coughing and sending thick billows of exhaust smoke up into the icy air. The pilots opened their throttles in turn, the aircraft coming up hard against their chocks, two mechanics bent double over each tailplane, battered and buffeted by the slipstream. The engines throttled back, the mechanics dropped to the deck, crawled forward beneath the wings. Thurston turned *Crusader* a couple of points to port to bring her directly into wind, took her up to her maximum seventeen knots. The green flag went down, the chocks were yanked clear of the wheels, the throttles opened once more and the two Seafires began to move forward. The ship pitched forward, so that for a moment it seemed the aircraft must fly straight into the wave which was rising up ahead, then they came clear of the deck, sluggishly, the undercarriage of the second seeming almost to brush the summit, and began to claw their way upwards towards safety.

'Dicey,' breathed Commander (Flying).

Dusk was already gathering, though it was little more than an hour after noon, heavy cloud lying close to the eastern horizon.

'Going to snow again,' someone said.

The Kondor must have seen *Crusader* turn into wind, and rapidly disappeared out of sight.

'They'll get her,' Commander (Flying) promised. 'Those things are bloody slow, and they've got no armour to speak of.'

'That was a near one,' Lieutenant James remarked to Sub-Lieutenant Gough, who was tucked into his port side. 'Still got your wheels?'

'Just!'

From five thousand feet the Kondor was a small dark patch in the great emptiness of sky, colouring once more with dusk.

'There he is!'

James brought his Seafire round in a shallow turn to starboard, pushed the throttle forward, glanced round to see that Gough was following.

'He's piling on the revs. Wants to get home for his tea.'

Strapped into the pilot's seat of a Seafire you moved with the machine, became part of it. The aircraft reacted to the lightest touch of the controls, instantly, almost without need for thought by the pilot. They were directly astern of the Kondor, closing her at a hundred and twenty miles an hour, two miles closer every minute. The Kondor had seen them and dropped lower, hoping to find more speed closer to sea level, a dark shape above the heaving grey water. James switched on his reflector sight, moved the knurled ring to adjust the graticules to suit the wingspan of a Kondor. Even inside his cockpit, with the Merlin engine developing eighteen hundred horsepower a few feet away, it was

213

cold. He took each foot off the rudder bar in turn and banged the heel on the floor. The Kondor was becoming large, filling half the sight. Without thinking, he moved the stick to port and applied a touch of rudder to bring his Seafire directly in line with the tailplane, remembered then that the Kondor had only one gun which could bear above and astern, eased the stick back to take himself a little higher.

The Kondor filled the sight. James pushed the gun button down with his thumb, felt the Seafire shudder with the recoil from her 20mm cannon, saw small red points appear on top of the Kondor's fuselage, then the Seafire's superior speed had carried him on past his target. He cursed, whipped round in a tight turn to starboard, remembered his mirror and checked again that Gough was still following. The machine gun in the German's dorsal turret was firing, so was a second from the window in the starboard side of the fuselage. James swept past, Gough following, made another tight turn to come round behind the Kondor once more.

'Get him this time,' muttered Gough.

James made the same approach in a shallow dive as before, throttled back, and opened fire. This time the German gunner was ready, his red tracer at first dropping away below James, then quite suddenly it was coming directly at him. Suddenly the armour plate around him and the huge Merlin engine in front seemed to have been stripped away. There was a sudden overpowering urge to duck below the level of his windscreen, turn blindly away, out of the German's line of fire. He felt himself curl tighter inside his straps, trying instinctively to reduce the target he made, saw his own tracer go harmlessly past. The Kondor was still obstinately flying as his speed took him past for the second time.

'Thought those buggers were supposed to fall apart as soon as you hit them,' said Gough.

Round once again, a sick chill of fear in anticipation of facing the gun again, but suddenly there were flames coming out of the Kondor's port outer engine, turning yellow and running back along the wing towards the root.

'Got 'im!' yelled Gough.

Too close! James pulled back his stick and shoved the throttle open, saw the German gunner's oxygen mask and a flash of white face above it, almost close enough to touch, turned to starboard and craned his head round to see the Kondor's port wing begin to separate itself from the fuselage, slowly peeling away from front to rear. The wing dropped away, the remainder of the aircraft cartwheeled downwards on the starboard wing. Gough's voice was shouting into his headset, in incomprehensible exaltation. A small dark thing appeared, falling away from the aircraft. A blob of white parachute streamed behind on its rigging lines, but the canopy had not deployed before the man smashed into the sea, a hundred yards below.

The sigh jerked Gough back to sobriety. 'Poor sod,' he muttered.

James released his oxygen mask and let it hang free for a moment, breathing the cold oil-and-cordite-smelling air inside the cockpit. Sweat streamed from where the mask had been, suddenly cold. He looked around, saw the empty sea, greyish-black now, spread out below, a vast expanse of sky above, streaked with many colours, pink, purple, red, grey where cloud crossed the bands of colour.

' *"The Assyrian came down like the wolf on the fold,*
And his cohorts were gleaming in purple and gold," ' he said into the radio.

'What are you on about?' said Gough in prosaic tones.

'Poetry. Come on, let's find that ship.'

It was growing darker every minute, the sky still light, but the sea already black. James called up the FDO, told him briefly that they had shot down the Kondor, asked for the ship's homing beacon to be switched on.

'You ever landed one of these at night?' James asked Gough.

'No. Have you?'

The exaltation was gone, their minds concentrated now on the business of finding the ship and getting down safely. James looked at his watch, surprised to find that it was only half an hour since they had taken off. When they caught sight of the carrier it seemed a century since they had left her, walked on her decks. It was so dark now that the flames from the Seafires' exhaust stubs were clearly visible, the ship no more than an indistinct rectangular shadow. James looked at his petrol gauge. Still all right, but it was the light which was the problem now. He dropped lower, noticed the landing lights on the deck, red to port, green to starboard. His mouth was dry. He was suddenly very cold.

'I'll go first and give you a lead.'

'Roger.'

James made his automatic movements, adjusted the trim for the landing speed, lined the aircraft up with the lights on the deck. There were the batsman's two yellow lights on the port side, slightly above deck level. The exhaust flames were becoming a distraction. The lights on deck were moving up and down as *Crusader* met successive seas.

The small automatic movements of stick and rudder. Watch the lights and do it automatically. Closer, closer, begin to move the stick back to level out, then suddenly the exhaust flames dazzled him, blotted out deck, batsman, everything. Instinctively he moved the stick back, opened the throttle to take him clear, level with the topmost aerials.

Gough's voice came over the radio. 'What happened?'

'Bloody exhausts. Couldn't see a thing.'

James looked down at the black water, and shivered. The FDO's voice came up, asking what was happening. He collected his thoughts, found his answer was surprisingly calm. 'The exhausts dazzled me just as I came in. The lights aren't strong enough to cancel them out.'

He and Gough were circling once more, five hundred feet up. James was thinking, you can't ditch a Seafire. Take her up to two thousand and jump, and pray a destroyer gets to you before the cold does.

On deck Thurston was pacing the narrow confines of the bridge.

'They can't see to land, sir.'

'Is there anything showing on radar?'

The Officer of the Watch knew he meant the enemy. 'No, sir.'

'Nothing at all?'

'No, sir.'

There could still be a U-boat in the vicinity, out of asdic range and at periscope depth, waiting for a sight of the convoy and an opportunity to get close.

'Put all the lights on. Tell Bats to make it snappy.'

'Aye aye, sir.'

The lights came on. The ship was suddenly naked and exposed. Men on deck stopped what they were doing. Someone crossed himself. They all waited, tensing themselves for an explosion.

'There she is. All lit up like a Brock's benefit.'

James began his approach, his eyes aching amid the unaccustomed light, the sudden contrast as he got close. There was the batsman, a dark shape with his yellow lights upraised. He lowered his undercarriage, checked that the wheels were down and locked. He drew the stick back, saw that area of warmth and light coming closer, filling his vision, the batsman's signals within it. Too high, stick forward, touch the stick and rudder a little to starboard. The lights were moving up and down with the motion. Ignore that, just watch the batsman's signals. The bats crossed. Cut! He shut the throttle. The Seafire dropped, picked up the first wire, the deck came up to meet him. The wire ran

216

out, the aircraft slowed and came to a stop. James released his straps, pushed back his canopy, breathing in the cold clear air, suddenly nectar.

'Down wires and barriers!'

The flight deck party were pushing his aircraft over the barrier, before he could summon up the energy to get out of the cockpit. Gough's aircraft came in, too high. Frantically the batsman waved him off.

'That's torn it,' one of the flight deck party muttered.

The Captain was taking a hell of a risk by turning the lights on, not only for his own ship but for the entire convoy. James remembered that Swordfish crew, months ago now, the Captain unable or unwilling to turn back because he considered the danger to the ship too great. Any minute the lights would be turned off, and Gough left to risk a ditching or a parachute jump. He got stiffly out of his cockpit, stamped on numb feet towards the huddle of aircrew who had appeared from the ready room.

'Put that bloody cigarette out,' someone shouted.

The offender looked surprised. There was so much light on deck that a glowing cigarette was academic. He dropped the cigarette onto the deck and ground it with his heel.

Gough came in once more, the pale undercarriage coming into view as the stick went back. He was too fast, bounced hard after picking up the second wire. The wire streamed out behind, brought him up short within a few feet of the barrier. The lights were turned off. There was a collective letting-out of indrawn breath, rising as white steam.

'Congratulations,' someone said.

It took James a moment to remember that he and Gough had indeed shot down the Kondor, that this was the first aircraft shot down by *Crusader*'s fighters, his own first kill, and the squadron's first kill. Someone slapped him on the back, as if he was an ordinary pilot again and not the acting squadron commander.

The first merchant ship was torpedoed that night, a U-boat having eluded the patrolling Swordfish and the shipboard radar sets, masked from asdic by the unpredictable cold and warm water layers of Arctic waters. There was an explosion halfway along the starboard sight, a gout of yellow flames rising above deck level. The ship – it was the Norwegian – slewed out of line, beginning to list. A signal flashed from the Commodore's lamp. There was a long interval, then a laborious reply.

'What's he saying, Yeoman?'

'EIW, sir. Damage is serious.'

The Norwegian ship was falling behind, listing more heavily. One of the tanks which formed her deck cargo began to move, first slowly and then more rapidly, trundled across the deck, broke through the guard-rails and went into the sea. A boat began to move down the starboard side, unevenly, the bow higher than the stern. Through his binoculars Thurston could see three or four men already on board, two more working frantically at the davits. The lamp flashed again.

'He's abandoning, sir.'

The ship was still moving, deeper in the water, clouds of steam rising from her funnel. The fire was still burning, lighting up a tangle of fallen mast and rigging lying across the upperworks. The stern of the lifeboat stopped moving, the bows were still going down.

'Bloody fall's jammed,' someone said.

The bows touched the water, met a wave. The boat was swamped, the men in it flung out, arms outstretched, trying to save themselves. Three heads appeared in the sea, small dark shapes in the pool of yellow light shed by the fire. More men were climbing over the rails and jumping, each hesitating before he committed himself. The ship gave a lurch, the starboard rails dipping under the water. One man was standing by himself on the bridge. Thurston did not need to see the line of gold oak leaves on the cap peak to know who it was, remembered the Norwegian captain at the convoy conference, resting his huge hands on the back of his chair and laughing with a fellow countryman behind. Patches of burning oil were spreading from the torn hull. The ship's stern reared up, she seemed to hang for a moment, then slid, bows first, her captain still upright on his bridge. Thurston counted eleven heads. When he looked again there were eight, and by the time the rescue ship, a converted trawler, bustled up from the rear of the convoy, there were five. Two corvettes made a slow and painstaking search with asdic, but the U-boat had disappeared.

The air attacks began in earnest with the dawn. Twin-engined JU 88s, packed in a tight defensive formation, fighters weaving above them. *Crusader*'s Seafires got in among them, shot down two, and the convoy's guns disposed of a couple more. There was no damage among the ships. But this was only the beginning. Through the short hours of daylight the attacks kept coming. *Crusader* kept four Seafires constantly airborne, and the remainder at five minutes' readiness, the pilots strapped into their cockpits, their aircraft ranged ready for take-off, but the storm had rendered nearly half the Seafires unserviceable, and constant flying in extreme conditions began to wear down the rest. The hangar party, fitters, riggers, mechanics, toiled round the clock, but as fast as one aircraft was cleared to fly, another seemed to become unserviceable. Darkness brought a respite from the air, but *Crusader*'s anti-submarine patrols continued in a regular monotonous routine. Take-off from the heaving deck, fly in straight lines back and forth, thirty miles either side of the convoy, the observer staring at the flickering green of his radar display, the points of light dancing before his tired eyes, occasionally peeling off his outer gloves to make a minute adjustment to the set, then the cold-pain and shoving the hand inside his Irvin jacket to try to warm it.

The cold made men sleepy, brought a strange sense of detachment which must be fought against. You had also to fight the tendency to let the mind drift to other matters, the simple thought of being warm again. The gunner fired an occasional burst from his Vickers gun to keep its working parts from freezing, maintained a listening watch on the radio. Time crawled by, and then at last they could send the ship a brief signal that they were returning, and make a final turn back towards the convoy. There was the beacon to guide them back, and *Crusader* was not difficult to detect on radar; the convoy showed up as a rectangle of regularly spaced blips, each the same distance from the next, except, inevitably, where a ship had drifted far enough out of station to break the symmetry, but towards the rear of the convoy there was empty space, two columns deep and three ships long, a single blip in the centre of the space, which was the carrier. Then a landing, a climb out of the cockpit on frozen legs and feet too numb to register the contact with the deck, debriefing, the miraculous arrival of a cup of steaming cocoa, and the beginnings of the thaw in front of the electric fire in the ready room. Then fall asleep, theoretically until the next launch, but more usually until the next call to action stations.

For Thurston there was also a routine. On the bridge for take-offs and landings, a brief respite at night while the Swordfish patrols were airborne, when he could fall onto his bunk and find exhausted sleep, broken by a call to action stations or the voice of the Officer of the Watch in his ear. Through the daylight hours he was on the bridge, or occasionally below in the Ops Room.

27

'Radar reports large formation of enemy aircraft bearing green three-oh, sir.'

'Sound Action Stations. How many Seafires have we serviceable?'

'Four on CAP, sir. Five at readiness. The CAP have got twenty minutes' fuel left.'

'All right. Scramble.'

'Look at them. Bloody hundreds of them!'

There were the JU 88s, camouflaged in dull green and grey, above them the shark-like ME 109s in pale blue.

'In we go.'

It was close to noon, the sky the same pale blue as the 109s. Don't bother with the fighters, go for the bombers. But the enemy fighters were between them and the bombers, coming at them out of the sun. James selected his target, the aircraft at the left front of the formation.

'Tally ho!'

He pushed the throttle forward, put the Seafire into a shallow dive. The bombers maintained their formation, seemingly impassive. Like the convoy, their main defence lay in keeping their formation and putting up a defensive barrage with their guns. He pulled his goggles down over his eyes, wriggled a little inside his straps. The 88s were firing, tracer coming up, but too far away to be any danger. A 109 appeared in his windscreen, he pressed the firing button to get off a brief burst, but it went harmlessly past the German's starboard wing. There was another, coming at him head-on. Another burst, bits flew off the 109's nose and he dropped below James's line of vision, trailing black smoke. James had forgotten the other Seafires; he was alone among the enemy. There was the bomber. His burst went through the glass nose and something fell back inside, the muzzle of the single machine gun dropped towards the sea. The pilot was jinking, pushing his nose down in an effort to get away, then the Seafire's speed had carried James past, and machine guns from other 88s were firing at his tail.

'Look out, Ken!' shouted into his headphones.

He jerked his head left and right, saw nothing, then remembered the mirror. Something buffeted his Seafire, he glanced into the mirror, saw the pointed spinner of a 109 and its swirling propeller filling it, the flash of its nose cannon. He forgot everything but the enemy on his tail, jerked the Seafire to port and starboard and back again, no finesse in the handling, only a rapid movement with the stick and a thrust forward of the boot against the rudder bar. The 109 went out of the mirror, but within half a second he was back, the black spinner, and the yellow flame coming from it. At some time James had pushed the stick forward, now the altimeter was unwinding and the sea coming up. He pulled the stick back, levelled out at two hundred feet, still turning. Turn, always turn; a normal Spitfire was faster than a 109, but a Seafire was hampered by the weight of its arrester hook and the strengthening required for deck landing. The propeller was still there. Desperately he pushed the throttle lever forward to emergency boost, felt the wire gate break. Ten minutes on that, and the engine would seize solid. He whipped the Seafire round to starboard, directly into the low sun, shutting his eyes momentarily, then pulled the nose up and went into a climbing turn the other way. If he had dazzled the German sufficiently he might just get away.

The mirror was clear, he swung his head in both directions, the muscles of his neck pulling hard as he did so. His beard felt damp; he must have sweated buckets in the last few minutes. Then he was frightened again. Where was the 109? He craned his neck again, saw nothing, then at the same moment felt something slam into the underside of the aircraft beneath his feet. A cannon shell passed through his pelvis, bladder and bowels, impacted against the instrument panel in front of him and exploded. Splinters of glass and metal came back into his face, blinding him. Streams of petrol from the ruptured tank began to run around his legs. He remembered very vaguely that he must get out, pulled with weakening fingers at the safety pin of his Sutton harness, tried to get a purchase on it, but it would not move. Above the petrol reek there was the stench of his own foulness, and then the petrol around his legs ignited. He let go the stick, and found the strength to scream as he died, while the aircraft fell the last four hundred feet into the sea and the tormenting flames were extinguished.

'Radar reports a further large formation of aircraft, bearing green six-oh, sir.' The CAP aircraft had landed on, their fuel expended, and petrol hoses were snaking across the deck as the flight deck party laboured to get them airborne once more.

'Haven't we got anything else that will fly?'

'No, sir.'

In the Air Plot the FDO was already guiding the remaining Seafires onto an interception course, but they would take time to arrive, too long to prevent an attack on the convoy. Tin hats went on, nervous fingers fumbled with the chinstays, cotton wool was stuffed into ears.

'For what we are about to receive,' muttered Commander (Flying) in the familiar blasphemy.

'Like a swarm of bloody locusts,' said the Chief Yeoman as the black shapes stippled the sky to the south-east.

'Can't see a damn thing!' Thurston put a hand up to shield his eyes from the sun. 'Metcalfe, go to my sea cabin and get me my sunglasses.'

Glad of something to do, Metcalfe scuttled away.

In one way it was the same as coming under air attack in *Marathon*, the separation of the brain into two parts, the one dealing coldly and logically with the situation as it developed, calculating and carrying out the avoiding action, the other detaching itself in tension and high excitement, which someone had once described to Thurston as 'better than coming'. But he missed the familiar and satisfying crash of *Marathon*'s eight 5.25 inch guns and the crisp orders of the Gunnery Officer to his guns. There was the rapid rattle of the 40mm pom-poms in their twin mounts along *Crusader*'s hull, and the sharper sound of the 20mm cannon. And there was *Crusader*'s vulnerable expanse of wooden deck, a perfect target for any German bomb-aimer who got it into his sights, the four Seafires standing isolated on it, the men tending them having taken cover at the alarm, and the hoses with their gallons of highly inflammable hundred-octane aviation spirit left in place.

A dark shape in the sky directly above, the stick of bombs falling from the belly. The professional half of the mind making its calculation, noting the relative position of the nearest ship – she was well clear – ordering a turn to port.

'Port thirty, sir,' from the quartermaster three decks below.

The tension and sudden wave of fear before *Crusader* made her sluggish response, then the bows began to swing, and there was a wave of relief as the bombs expended their force harmlessly in the water alongside, sending spray cascading over the starboard side of the deck. A bomber trailed black smoke, and dived vertically into the water, perhaps a cable off *Crusader*'s port bow.

'Midships.'

'Midships, sir. Wheel's amidships, sir.'

Metcalfe reappeared from below, handed him the black metal case containing the sunglasses. Then another aircraft above, the bombs falling away. Another instantaneous calculation.

222

'Port thirty.'

'Port thirty, sir.'

The nearest ship had turned to starboard to avoid a stick aimed at her. This turn would take *Crusader* close. Relief as the bombs again exploded harmlessly clear, then he was turning her again to avoid a collision.

'There they are!'

There was a brief glimpse of elliptical wings, and *Crusader*'s Seafires were in among the bombers, splitting their formation, driving them away. Two more JU 88s went down, too low for a parachute to open, and then, quite suddenly, the attack was over, the ships' companies drawing breath, realising that their vessels were still afloat and undamaged. Thurston unclenched his fists, found that he had been gripping the sunglasses case for most of the attack, barely noticing that it was there. The flight deck party reappeared and went back to work.

'Get those things refuelled and back in the air as fast as you can. We can't have that happening again. We'll have to make sure in future that we've always got something in reserve and ready to take off, even if it means we can only scramble a couple of aircraft.'

Commander (Flying) nodded in agreement. 'We made the mistake of committing all our reserves. It won't happen again, sir.'

They were learning, from bitter experience.

'The OC got it. I saw him go in. When we were dealing with the first lot.'

'I'm just about out of juice.'

'So am I.'

Crusader lay below them, steaming away from the convoy to allow the CAP to take off, for the wind had turned northerly.

'Wonder what we'll get for tea?'

'Tea! We haven't had any lunch yet.'

'It just feels as though it should be teatime. It's starting to get dark already.'

'Wish they'd hurry up down there.'

One by one the CAP Seafires took off. *Crusader* was a rectangle on the ocean, with a needle shape off her starboard beam which was her escorting destroyer.

'Home, sweet home,' someone said.

The five surviving pilots continued to cast anxious glances at their petrol gauges, and at the sea below.

'Looks bloody cold down there.'

'At last,' the senior of the survivors, Sub-Lieutenant Mould, said when the FDO's message came through. 'Who wants first go?' He kept his voice casual, but his eyes crept back once more to the petrol gauge, now reading only a little above empty. Only one aircraft could land at a time, and the others must orbit the carrier while the flight deck party cleared the landing area.

Three Seafires went in, each in its turn, and bumped safely along the deck. Then Sub-Lieutenant Grimshaw. His petrol lasted until his final approach, then cut abruptly. He moved the stick back, stretching the glide until he was over the carrier's stern. His landing was several feet too high. He missed both wires, went over onto his nose and ploughed forward into the barrier. The flight deck party came running up. He spurned the proffered assistance, unfastened his harness and got himself out of the cockpit, walked away from the aircraft like a man in a dream, then sat down against the base of the island.

'Come on, sir. You'd better come down to the sick bay.'

'I'm all right,' he began to protest, then suddenly the world began to slide. He moved his head to one side and was sick down the front of his Irvin jacket and Mae West.

'Come on, sir. I'll just mop you up and get you below.' It was one of the engine mechanics, whose face and name he struggled to remember, pulling a petrol-smelling rag out of his pocket and wiping away the already half-frozen mess on his Mae West. 'Do you want to stay here a bit longer, sir?' Grimshaw did not know, or care, what he wanted. He let the man hoist him to his feet, put an arm around his shoulders and support him on his tottering legs away from the wreckage of his aircraft.

In the last aircraft Sub-Lieutenant Mould watched with mounting horror as the flight deck party struggled to distangle Grimshaw's aircraft from the barrier. The needle rested on the bottom of his petrol gauge, yet the Seafire's Merlin engine roared on reassuringly. He had throttled back as far as he dared in order to save fuel, so that he was flying only a little above the stalling speed, the four CAP aircraft circling with him, a reassurance, though there was nothing practical they could do for him.

'What the fuck are they doing down there?' someone burst out.

Mould did not answer. He did not feel like talking now. From three thousand feet it was impossible to see the movements on the carrier's decks. The FDO's voice came over the radio, telling him that they were going to put Grimshaw's aircraft over the side, as soon as they had got it free, his tone reassuring, like a family doctor. 'Just this little operation, Mrs Bloggs, then everything will be all right.'

The engine coughed, ran again for a moment, coughed once more, then cut out. Training took over. Push the nose down a little, take her to windward of the ship and bail out. The destroyer would pick him up, if he lasted that long in the water. He shuddered, then, relic of a Catholic education, crossed himself. The Seafire responded more slackly, more sluggishly, without its engine. He banked round to port, passed over the carrier, still steaming hard into wind, a little smoke rising from her vents and hanging in the still air. The altimeter was dropping, passing through two thousand feet. Release the harness, push back the canopy, then flick her upside down and just fall out.

He took a deep breath, pulled out the safety pin, felt for a moment strangely naked without the harness. He pushed back the canopy with both hands, holding the stick between his knees. The slipstream was knifingly cold. He pushed the stick forward, and fully to the right. The Seafire rolled obediently, then as his hand let go of the stick the nose dropped, the aircraft went into a vertical dive inverted. Mould pushed with his hands to get himself out of the seat, got part of the way, then the slipstream forced him back, and the canopy slid shut once more. He scrabbled with his legs to find a purchase, found his feet scrabbling on the instrument panel, his body doubled up, his fists punching uselessly at the perspex which imprisoned him. One of his feet knocked the radio onto transmit, so that in the other aircraft and aboard *Crusader* they heard his screams.

'Turn that thing off!'

No one moved.

'I said turn it off,' Thurston snapped.

Someone moved to switch off the bridge loudspeaker, which was, as usual, set to the flying frequency, but the aircraft hit the sea before he reached it, so they heard Mould's death screaming come to its abrupt end.

No one spoke. Thurston found himself looking at Commander (Flying), a small figure bulked out by his Arctic clothing. Seven pilots had flown off in search of the German bombers a little more than an hour before. Now there were three more names for the FDO to wipe off his blackboard.

'Pilot.'

'Sir?'

'Plot me a course back to the convoy.'

'Aye aye, sir.'

They would call him a cold fish, those who saw and heard him, those who did not know. They had been his men, for whom he was responsible. It was all part of the mystique, the imperturbable facade which must both conceal and protect the vulnerable individual beneath. Spencer knew, of course. Spencer had seen him when the mask slipped, had heard him shouting in his sleep for many nights in succession before the Stonehenge convoy, and found him blubbering over the condolence letters he had to write on the day he finally keeled over, but those were things not to be spoken of.

28

Crusader and the destroyer with her had been left a long way astern of the convoy by the time the last of the Seafires had landed on. With her maximum speed of seventeen knots she could close the gap only gradually, and before long her engines began to protest. Commander Hodgson came up to the bridge, correctly turned out as usual, brass hat on his head, wing collar showing between the lapels of his greatcoat.

'What brings you from your engine room, Chief?' Thurston kept his voice casual, but the Chief's appearance at other than the times he normally reported to the bridge could only mean that something was seriously wrong.

'The thrust bearing on the high-pressure turbine is running a bit hot. The temperature was up when Wullie Duff did his routine check at the beginning of his watch. We've kept an eye on it and it's still rising. It's probably the shock of that near miss we had earlier that's done it. Could easily have unseated the bearing.'

'Can you do anything about it?'

'We'll have to slow the shaft right down, sir. If we keep it turning at this speed then that bearing is going to run. I've only once had to deal with a run bearing, and I wouldn't like to do it again. We were stopped for twenty-eight hours while we got it out, and a new one fitted and in place.'

They had moved into the corner beside the chart table, their voices automatically lowered.

'How much speed can you give me?'

'Four knots, to give the thing a chance to cool down. If it does, we can start to build the revs back up and see what the bearing will take. I've left them rigging a hose to spray it, which should take some of the heat out.'

Thurston had heard enough. He remembered sufficient from the three months he had spent in *Oudenarde*'s engine room as a midshipman to appreciate what was wrong, and the likely result if the problem was ignored. Beneath the bearing shells was a layer of soft, lead-like white metal, separated from the rotating shaft by only a thin film of oil. If the supply of oil was insufficient, the temperature inside the bearing would gradually build up to a point where the white metal would melt or 'run' and the ship would be brought to a halt until the bearing could be replaced, a job which would take at least twenty-four hours, even if the necessary spares were on board.

'All right, Chief. Four knots. Keep me informed.'

At four knots *Crusader* would continue to fall astern of the convoy. She would be unable to operate her aircraft, with insufficient wind over the decks to allow a fully laden Swordfish to take off. Even if the catapult was used, the aircraft would not be able to land back on. Not for the first time he cursed *Crusader*'s builders, who had given her only a freighter's single screw, and a freighter's unarmoured hull which would offer no resistance to a torpedo. But she had never been intended to be a warship, the men who designed her had not envisaged that she would be requisitioned for the Royal Navy and turned into an aircraft carrier. There were two Swordfish in the air now. They would have to ditch, unless they preferred to attempt to reach a Russian airfield on their remaining fuel.

Crusader's way fell off, her motion changed, so that she rolled more heavily, less able to resist the swell. It was a calm night, the storm now only a receding memory, clear, starlit and very cold. Too bloody clear; Thurston would have welcomed fog or snow which could blanket them from enemy eyes. Sub-Lieutenant Vincent came to take over the watch. Spencer brought Thurston his supper, some rich thick soup of his own creation, with a hot undertone of curry powder beneath and promised syrup pudding to follow. 'Won't bring it up yet, sir. Don't want it freezing solid before you eat it.' Thurston ate the food without tasting it, sat for a long time looking down at the dark sea. No one spoke for long intervals. The Navigator and Navigator's Yeoman came up to take the evening star sights, a lengthy process as Beveridge had to take his gloves off to adjust the micrometer scale on his sextant, and found his fingers growing too numb to move the small knurled screws. It took several attempts at each of the three sights before he was satisfied, and retired to the chartroom to make his calculations. Vincent was a nervous shadow alongside Thurston. It shouldn't be such a bloody clear night; no moon, but thousands upon thousands of stars, some bright, others smaller, fainter and further away. There was Orion, easy to pick out in the southern sky, the head and horns of Taurus bending to charge him.

Vincent must have been looking at the same thing. 'I always like to see Orion, sir. When I was younger it was the only one I could recognise.' He gave a brief laugh.

The Chief Yeoman looked up in surprise, and the silence fell again. Thurston got up from his bridge chair, stiff from long stillness, and went into the Ops Room. The convoy was a regular pattern of blips on the radar display.

'About thirty miles away now, sir. There's *Vituperate.*' The operator indicated a separate, much closer blip. The destroyer was circling *Crusader*, a mile or so off, her radar and asdic alert for U-boats.

'Nothing else?'

'No, sir.'

'Set working all right?'

'Yes, sir.'

He looked into the asdic cabinet, where the two operators were sitting with their headsets aslant, one ear uncovered so that they could hear what was going on around them. There was the familiar monotonous pinging, which went on unceasing all the time the ship was at sea, almost unnoticed in normal times, but now unnaturally loud, and however much anyone tried to ignore it, one ear and part of the brain were waiting for the echo to begin.

In the Air Plot next door Commander (Flying) was sitting at one of the desks, a brimming ashtray beside him, in the act of placing a fresh cigarette in his mouth, taking a match from the box on the desk, lighting it, and leaning back to exhale a cloud of smoke.

'You ought to get your head down, now you've got the chance.'

'So should you, sir.'

Like him, Wings had to be on the bridge for take-offs and landings, so that his periods away from the bridge were broken every two or three hours all the time flying was going on. This was the seventh night at sea, and during the storm there had been no rest for any of them. And now, like him, Commander (Flying) could not tear himself away from his place of duty, even though there was nothing he could do for the present.

On to the chartroom, where Beveridge, his work completed, silently indicated *Crusader*'s position on the chart, and began to unroll his sleeping bag on the chart table. Like any Navigator, Beveridge had made this his domain. There were oilskins hanging on the back of the door, a second pair of seaboots in one corner, the coarse, oiled-wool seaboot stockings trailing out of them, a Thermos flask on one of the shelves, among the pilot books and copies of Notices to Mariners. Nothing to say here either. He knew, because it was in Beveridge's file, that Beveridge had been Third Hand of a submarine which had collided with a corvette while on training exercises off Tobermory. Fewer than half the men on board had got out, trusting themselves to their flimsy escape apparatus in ninety feet of water. Beveridge had requested a return to General Service afterwards and this was something he did not talk about.

Thurston grinned at him. 'Everything all right, Pilot?'

'Yes, sir.' A slightly strained grin back.

Somewhere below there was a sudden clatter, where someone in the hangar must have dropped one of his tools. The echo off the metal bulkheads seemed to last for ever.

Thurston went back to the bridge. No change, only the vast sky of stars, the dark shape of *Vituperate* a mile off the starboard quarter.

'Anything to report, Mr Vincent?'

'No, sir.'

The Commander came up. 'All quiet below, sir. Cold, isn't it?'

The Commander, up from the comparative warmth below, shivered. Thurston thought for a moment, made up his mind. 'Do you want to hold the fort while I go and take a look at this bearing for myself?'

The Commander did not reply immediately, surprise written across his face. It was unusual; virtually unheard of, and highly irregular at the very least. While the ship was at sea the Captain's place was on the bridge, or seconds away from it in his sea cabin. But there was nothing he could do on the bridge which was beyond the Commander's capabilities, and he knew that even if he did go below to his bunk he would not be able to sleep.

'Sir.'

'Straight there and straight back, Arthur.'

'Aye aye, sir.'

He slid down the ladder, Metcalfe at his heels. There was the hangar, with the dark shapes of lashed-down aircraft, their folded wings disappearing into the deckhead shadows, a few men working on them, moving slowly and carefully on rubber soles, passing instructions in low tones. One man's hands were inside a toolbox, searching for something, bringing each item out and laying it carefully on the deck alongside, whereas in normal times he would have rummaged noisily until he came to the thing he was seeking, pulled it out with more noise, and piled everything else back into the box.

In the passages below the hangar many men slept, as close to the outer air as they could manage, lying on mattresses brought up from their bunks, heads pillowed on their lifebelts, half-inflated and then doubled over and tied with string, blankets thrown over them. One man was snoring gently, another curled into a foetal position, knees drawn up almost to his stomach, hands thrust between his thighs for warmth.

He looked very young, fair-haired and smooth-faced. Perhaps he did not need to shave yet.

'Jumper Collins, sir,' Metcalfe said. 'He's in my mess.'

Collins stirred for a moment, opened his mouth and muttered, curled his position tighter. Thurston was stepping carefully over and between the sleeping bodies. All these men, he thought, boys really, whose names I don't know, no older than my son.

'Good evening, sir.' Chief, too, could not let go.

'Should have told you I was coming down, Chief. How's the bearing?'

'Cooler than it was, but I'd like to leave it as it is a bit longer. Get the heat out of it, before we put some higher revs through it.'

The faulty bearing looked, to Thurston, as any bearing always did, except for the seawater hose that was playing over it.

'Stand back, sir, or you'll get your feet wet.'

Water was rebounding off the bearing in all directions as the shaft continued to turn, running in discoloured grey streams through the metal gratings below. One of the junior engineers was standing just out of range with a notebook, patches of water on the front of his overalls, his sleeves rolled up and black oil making glistening streaks on his forearms.

'Knowles here is keeping an eye on things.'

The Chief smiled at Knowles. Knowles smiled back. There was a sense of mutual trust and reliance between them, unspoken but none-theless valid. Another junior engineer was crossing the engine room, carrying an oil can, humming an unrecognisable tune through his teeth.

'Just going to take a look at that sticking diaphragm.'

Chief was standing by, looking quietly satisfied, wearing overalls for the first time Thurston had ever seen, without his cap, his thinning hair rumpled. 'Good lads, sir.'

The engine room was a vast open cavern below the waterline. If a torpedo were to come through the ship's side, through that half-inch of plating a few feet away, none of them would get out. But it was something they had pushed to the back of their minds, and simply carried on with their jobs.

'Yes, Chief. Anything else to report while I'm here?'

'We've got a bit of a leak in the stern gland again, but we can mop that up. The Yanks were penny-pinching when they built this thing. Used greenheart instead of lignum vitae to pack the topside of the gland. It saved them a bob or two, but there's always been a bit of a trickle in there, and those near misses we've had today didn't help.'

Chief pursed his lips, his professional pride affronted at such poor workmanship.

'I'll leave you to it, Chief.'

'Aye aye, sir.' Chief pulled out his watch from his breast pocket. 'Give it another four hours, and then we'll see what the bearing will take.'

Thurston went back to the bridge, once more stepping over the sleeping bodies. It struck him that he had not been so far below decks at sea since *Retribution* days before the war – she too had temperamental engines and he could not have seen men asleep in the passages like this since the last war, before Metcalfe and most of these men were born. Spencer produced mugs of cocoa for all.

More time passed. He stamped his feet, worried for a time at a thread of meat which had lodged itself between a wisdom tooth and the molar next to it. Four knots, and falling four miles further astern of the convoy with every hour. The quietness was unreal, a quietness which could be ended without warning. He explored the horizon with his binoculars, seeing the points of starlight reflected off the calm water. Midshipman Elder finished his cocoa, put the empty mug down out of the way, then, turning, caught it with the sleeve of his duffel and knocked it with a clatter to the deck. The echo seemed to go on and on, and the mug rolled noisily back and forth until it came to rest against the base of the monkey's island around the binnacle. Thurston opened his mouth to shout at Elder, in a sudden flare of temper, then shut it again.

29

Deprived of the extra protection of *Crusader*'s air patrols, the convoy had taken a mauling. A U-boat had been stealthily shadowing for two days, remaining just below the horizon and prudently submerging each time her Metox picked up a radar transmission. Far to the south, at Brest on the French Atlantic coast, U-boat High Command had responded to her signals, and to those from the Luftwaffe in Norway, and thrown a cordon of U-boats across the convoy's line of advance.

In the grounds of a requisitioned stately home in Buckinghamshire, watches of ATS girls monitored the German frequencies and took down the meaningless strings of morse dots and dashes which came into their headsets. Every hour a Royal Signals despatch rider took the latest transcripts to another Nissen hut nearby, where an eccentric and determinedly unmilitary assortment of university mathematicians, chess players and crossword solvers worked to decode the messages the Germans believed to be secure. At times this Ultra intelligence, whose source was known only to a carefully vetted few, became available sufficiently quickly for a convoy to be routed away from a U-boat concentration in good time, but on this day a series of minor delays meant that the location of the U-boat cordon did not become known at Bletchley Park until after it had struck. And the strange and shifting warm and cold layers of the far northern seas did their work in confusing the escorts' asdic sets, so that the first signal of the enemy's presence was a torpedo which struck the American Liberty ship in the second column shortly after 2100. The ship settled and began to sink, two corvettes were quickly on the scene, pursued a faint asdic contact for a time, dropped a couple of patterns of depth charges, but the U-boat must have found a warm water layer, for the contact faded out.

An hour passed, and then the U-boats struck again. It may have been the same one, or perhaps another, but the effect was the same. She came in on the surface, appeared suddenly as a blip on the radar displays. The escort commander sent a destroyer to investigate the contact. Then there was the explosion, a lighting-up of the sky as the stricken ship's oil fuel began to burn.

'There she is,' one of *Vittoria*'s lookouts shouted.

'What? Where?' growled Haldane. 'Make your report in the proper manner.'

'Aye aye, sir,' said the crestfallen lookout. 'Conning tower bearing green six-oh, sir.'

There it was, clearly visible through binoculars, the upright conning tower and the 'bandstand' at its rear, the flat expanse of foredeck emerging just above the water.

'Get her before she submerges,' muttered Haldane. 'All guns load.'

The order rang around the ship. 'All guns load, load, load.'

Two 4.7 inch guns were left after *Vittoria*'s conversion to a long-range escort, both of which must fire in local control after the removal of the director equipment. B gun was directly ahead of and a few feet below the bridge. George Thurston watched with mounting excitement as the 4.7 inch round and its cartridge were rammed into the breech, heard the First Lieutenant's shouted order from alongside him. 'Target bearing green five-oh. Range two-five-hundred. Open fire!'

'Shoot!' from the Sub-Lieutenant who was Officer of Quarters.

A crash, a sudden burst of light which momentarily dazzled him, and a cloud of cordite-tasting smoke which came back from the gun. The breech was already open, a second shell being rammed home, another man standing by with the brass cartridge. A tall narrow column of water on the far side of the U-boat's bow.

'Over!' cursed Haldane.

'Down four hundred!'

More quick movements by the layer and trainer on either side of the breech.

'Ready!'

'Shoot!'

The U-boat was still there, bow wave creaming back over her deck. The second round landed short, as intended.

'Bracket!'

'Get off another before she submerges,' muttered Haldane, head down, legs propelling him over the three or four paces in each direction that the dimensions of the bridge allowed.

'She's diving, sir.'

'Damn!'

The U-boat's bows had disappeared, white foam lapping around the base of the conning tower. The distant figures on her bridge were disappearing.

'Ready!'

'Shoot!'

Then there was only spreading foam, and the waterspout from *Vittoria*'s round rising out of it.

'We'd have got her that time,' someone said.

'Asdic!'

The asdic cabinet was a wooden structure at the rear of the bridge. The Anti-Submarine Officer's head, crowned with earphones, appeared from the open door. 'In contact, sir. Echo bearing one-four-three degrees. Range two thousand.' Had the target moved that far already? Then George remembered that the gunnery bearings had been relative to the ship's bow; asdic gave compass bearings.

'Steer one-four-three. Revolutions for eighteen knots.'

Eighteen knots, as fast as the ship could go before water noises blanked out the asdic.

'How's the echo?'

'Firm, sir. Moving slightly to starboard.'

The seconds and minutes went by, far too slowly, the asdic echo coming gradually faster as the destroyer closed the U-boat, the asdic officer calling out changes of course as the target moved gradually to starboard. George cast a brief look to either side. There was the burning ship, falling away astern, a single boat, crowded with men, visible in the light, one man standing up, shading his eyes in the bows.

'Have to wait until we've dealt with this lot,' the First Lieutenant told him.

'Stand by depth charges set to a hundred feet.'

They waited tensely, the pinging sounding in their ears, praying that the echo would not suddenly disappear, as it had done on earlier occasions. On the other side of the convoy there was another explosion.

'More of the bastards. Let's do what we can with this one.'

'Target bearing one-four-nine. Range one hundred.'

Another small alteration of course, a slowing to fifteen knots.

'Instantaneous echo, sir.'

'Stand by – Fire.'

The asdic officer pressed his firing buzzer. The depth charges rolled over the stern. Another wait, as they drifted down to their set depth. A hundred feet was pure guesswork. Asdic gave no indication of the target's depth. The hunters could go only by experience, and the limited knowledge of a U-boat's capabilities. The explosions under water, men's heads appearing briefly over *Vittoria*'s rails. But no debris, or even oil, only white foam welling up from below, and another tense wait while the water settled enough to allow the asdic to operate once more.

'Target bearing three-five-two, sir. Range nine hundred.'

'Went underneath us. Steer three-five-two.'

Vittoria turned in a tight semi-circle, increased speed once again to eighteen knots. This time the U-boat captain had woken up to the danger, and began to twist and turn, never holding the same course for more than two consecutive minutes. They were beginning to cross the columns of the convoy now.

'Cunning. That'll upset the asdics.'

'Merchant ship to port, sir. She's altering course towards us in her zig-zag,' the First Lieutenant said.

The merchant ship was looming up. She was going to be close.

'Ring on full speed. Starboard ten.'

'Starboard ten, sir.'

Vittoria swung to starboard, water coming up over the rails on her starboard side.

'Lost contact, sir,' came the asdic officer's voice, oblivious to the danger close at hand.

Just in time. The merchant ship's bow seemed only feet away, her bow wash closer still, then they were past her, and breathing again.

'Target regained, sir.'

But the U-boat captain was good, and kept turning, so that it was many more minutes before they could get off another pattern of depth charges. Then there was the wait for the water to settle, and he was astern of them, moving back towards the convoy. *Vittoria* came round in another tight turn, the distance between them began to reduce, and then the echo disappeared.

'Gone deep, or he's found a warm layer. Carry out lost contact procedure.'

The escort commander ordered *Vittoria* to rejoin the convoy. It was a dejected ship's company which sighted the other escorts an hour later and eased back into their place in the screen.

'Anything on hydrophones?'

'Engine noises fading, Herr Kapitän,' the Petty Officer Telegraphist reported.

'Good.'

The air in U–686's control room was stale, laden with old cabbage, diesel oil and unwashed humanity. In the pale light shed by the deck-head bulbs the faces of the crew were pale, damp with sweat, the lower parts obscured by ragged, half-grown beards. Most of the faces were very young; some only eighteen or nineteen years old, able to grow only downy fluff, or, in a few cases, remaining smooth.

'Take her up to periscope depth.'

The hydroplane operators pressed their electric buttons and U–686 began obediently to rise.

'Eight metres, Herr Kapitän.'

'Up periscope.'

Another button was pressed, a motor hummed and the periscope rose smoothly from its well. The Captain grasped the handles on either side, put his face to the eyepiece. He bent his knees, let the periscope down a little.

'A metre too high, Chief.'

A quick circuit, then a second, much slower, methodically searching each sector of sea and sky in turn. No sign of the British destroyer. He allowed himself a small smile, unseen by the men around him. He was an old hand, with the wiliness born of long experience, which was why, after four and a half years of war, he was still alive. His left leg began to ache, a gnawing inside the shin bone, where a bullet from a Coastal Command Sunderland had hit him eighteen months before. The wound had taken a long time to heal and even now, in the cold, damp confines of a U-boat, when the knee was bent for any length of time, his shin ached like the very devil. This time it had been a destroyer, and he had kept the British captain guessing, so that he had only been able to get off a couple of patterns of depth charges. But there had been long intervals when the destroyer's asdic pulses scattered like pebbles on the hull, and all the manoeuvring, all the ruses of which he was capable, could not shake the British off. It had been a frightening experience for his crew, for most of whom U–686 was their first boat, and this their first patrol. Finally he had taken her deep, below the level to which the asdic impulses could penetrate, an unnerving experience in itself. The Type VIIC U-boat was tested only to ninety metres; many had gone far deeper, but nobody knew at what depth the hull would give way and the water pressure all around crush the submarine flat. The asdic had been scattering on the hull at precise intervals, he had given the order to go down, and keep on going down. The asdic got fainter, further away, then the hull itself began to creak and groan with the pressure, the needle on the depth gauge, watched tensely by every man in the control room, kept on rising; a hundred and ten, a hundred and thirty, then a hundred and sixty. The asdic disappeared, but the tortured sounds of the hull went on, louder now in the silence. At a hundred and seventy metres they levelled out, waited another twenty minutes before the Captain found himself satisfied.

Down periscope.

'Stand by to surface. Lookouts stand by. On oilskins.'

'Surface!'

The Chief Engineer took over. 'Foreplanes hard-a-rise, afterplanes up five. Blow main ballast.'

Compressed air hissed, forced the water out of the ballast tanks.

'Equalise pressure.'

The excess pressure inside the boat dwindled. If this was not done, the first man out would have shot out like a cork as soon as the upper hatch was opened. The Captain was up on the ladder inside the conning tower, pulling back the clips which secured the lower hatch. The bridge broke surface. The upper hatch opened, water drenching the Captain and the lookouts waiting below. Below, the engines coughed as they started, settled gradually into normal running.

'Blow to full buoyancy with diesel.'

The engine exhausts began to blow the last of the water from the ballast tanks, until air bubbles began to appear along the boat's sides.

'All main ballast tanks blown. Fall out from diving stations. Patrol routine.'

The Captain raised his binoculars, passed a handkerchief over the eyepieces to get rid of any condensation, put them to his eyes. The convoy had vanished over the horizon, and only a patch of still-burning oil remained to mark the passing of U–686's first victim, and two lifeboats, crowded with men, a couple of miles off.

The crew of the *Maiwand* had been in their boats two hours, most of them thankfully dry-shod, but already chilled to the marrow. One Lascar fireman had been caught by a rush of escaping steam and lay moaning on the bottom boards, his hair, eyebrows and most of his face scalded away. Another Lascar had been hurled down a ladder by the force of the explosion and landed with his right leg contorted awkwardly under him. The Captain had got busy, using a lifetime's experience and the instructions half-remembered from *The Shipmaster's Medical Guide* to roughly splint the leg with a length of shaft from a broken oar and strips torn from a fireman's overalls, covered both the invalids with all the blankets available and began silently to pray. There was a rescue ship with the convoy, but in the midst of a U-boat attack she had been unable to stop for them, and now they could only hope that the rescue ship or one of the escorts would come back for them before the Arctic cold began to kill them. The burnt fireman would not last long, nor would the man whose thigh was broken in two places. The two boats rocked back and forth on the waves, fifty yards apart, some of the men already beginning to sink into a stupor of cold and exhaustion.

'There's something out there, sir.' It was the junior apprentice, a boy of fifteen making his first trip.

The Captain roused himself to look in the direction the apprentice was pointing. For a moment he nursed the hope that it could be the rescue ship, but it was the wrong shape entirely.

'Shit!' someone said.

The U-boat came on, long and angular, with the conning tower rising vertically above.

'Are they going to shoot us?' the apprentice asked in sudden realisation.

'The bastards!' breathed someone else.

There were sidelong glances at the dark water. *Between the devil and the deep blue sea*, the Captain thought, managing a half-smile at the accuracy of the metaphor. They were all awake now, the burnt man groaning on the bottom boards, someone else feeling in his pockets. 'Can't find my rosary. Can't find my fucking rosary.'

They could see the men on the U-boat's bridge, bulky forms in many layers of clothes, the outlines of their faces blurred by beards. There also were the guns, more men standing ready on the bandstand beside them. The Captain felt in his coat pocket. His gloved fingers closed round the service revolver which was in there. Not much use against the U-boat's cannon, but in a strange way it made him feel better.

The U-boat's engine note changed, and she came to a stop a few yards away.

'Which ship?' came a German voice.

The Captain said nothing for a moment, then remembered that the ship's name was painted on the bows of both lifeboats, and clearly marked on the lifejackets they were all wearing. 'The steamship *Mai-wand*, of Liverpool,' he shouted, in defiance, and as a valediction for the ship he had lost.

'What was your cargo?'

'I'm not telling you that.'

'I did not think that you would.' The speaker's English, though accented, was excellent. He was a stocky man with a fair beard, standing on the base of the periscope standard, so that he was a little above the rest, his battered cap bearing the white cover worn only by U-boat captains. 'I am going to come closer, but do not be afraid. You have wounded men?'

'Two.'

'You murdering scum,' someone muttered under his breath.

'So. I have something for them.'

The Captain could hear the German giving orders in brisk tones. The U-boat began to move again, its bow coming gradually onwards. She stopped again, to leeward of *Maiwand*'s boats, so that they drifted towards her and their keels bumped on her ballast tanks. A German seaman came down the ladder from the bridge, stood on the narrow strip of deck alongside the conning tower, then edged his way sideways onto the broader foredeck. There was a white-painted Donald Duck stencilled on the grey of the conning tower, wearing a German-style sailor's cap, much broader in the crown than the British version, the long ribbon flying jauntily behind.

'There is a First Aid kit, and there is a chart. You have a compass?'

'Of course.'

'I have marked your course to the nearest land on the bottom of the chart. It is German land, in Norway, but . . . it is better than to be dead in the sea.'

The rating leaning out from the U-boat's rails, holding on with one hand, stretching out the other with a canvas bag marked with a red cross. 'The chart is inside the bag. There is also a bottle of cognac.'

'Thank you,' the Captain said, despite himself.

'If you find your own people, you will tell them that some of us still have our honour.' The U-boat Captain smiled, showing white teeth inside his beard.

The ship's Captain was on his feet, taking the bag and holding it in both hands. 'I should like to know who it was sank my ship.'

The German smiled again, and said in the German fashion, 'I am Lauterbeck, Korvettenkapitän. I must go now. Good luck.'

The rating climbed the ladder, swinging each leg over the bridge surround in turn. There were more brisk orders in German. The U-boat went astern, moved slowly away, hatches slammed shut, and in a few minutes there was only foam to show where she had been.

30

An hour before dawn the Commander (E) came back to the bridge.

'I think we're ready to start to inch the revs up. We'll have to take it very gently, virtually a rev at a time, and just see how much that bearing will stand.' Commander Hodgson was sixty-three years old, and had been continuously in his engine room and on his feet for the last twenty-four hours, but still he was freshly shaved and immaculately turned out to report to his captain.

'All right, Chief; you know what you're doing.'

It was a maddeningly slow process, and as tense as the long hours of steaming at four knots had been. The ship's speed would increase, by half a knot or less each time, there would be a wait of fifteen minutes or so, every ear cocked for the buzz of the telephone, before the Chief reported from the engine room that he was satisfied. Then another increase, a slight but perceptible change in the ship's motion, another wait, the speed going up very gradually in half-knot increments. Dawn came, streaking the sky ahead of them with pink and gold.

'How much more speed do we need to start flying?'

'We can't get them off in less than ten knots, sir. The Swordfish that is. Pity there isn't a bit more wind. We found at Salerno that you can't get a Seafire off safely with anything less than twenty-five knots over the deck. There we had no wind to speak of, and this thing was busting a gut to do eighteen knots, and you've never seen so many bits of Seafire cluttering up the deck.'

Vituperate lay off *Crusader*'s port bow. Even in her bastardised form as a long-range escort she could still make twenty-five knots, and overhaul the convoy in four hours or less, but she was tethered to her plodding charge as long as *Crusader*'s engine troubles lasted and, like her, easy meat.

A few men from the flight deck party, bored with the long wait for flying to start, had piled a few duffel coats at either end of the deck as makeshift goals and begun a game of deck hockey, shouting noisy encouragement to each other, their breath coming out as steam. One man slipped, slid for several yards on his backside before he came to a halt, and got up laughing, his heavy clothing having prevented any damage.

'Makes me feel tired just watching them,' commented the Gunnery Officer, who had the watch.

'Terrible confession to make at your age,' Thurston said.

'One way of getting warm, at least,' said the Navigator.

'Warm?' said the Gunnery Officer, raising his eyes to the empty blue sky. 'I've forgotten what being warm is. Would somebody mind telling me?'

There was some good-natured ribbing of the Gunnery Officer, and advice on doing something to get rid of his incipient middle-aged spread. Watching the men on the flight deck, Thurston wished he could put all this out of his mind as easily as they could, chasing a rope quoit around the deck like these men young enough to be his sons.

Noon approached. The Navigator went below and returned with his sextant, taking it carefully from its box, shaped and padded inside for protection, and removing the yellow dusters in which it was wrapped to save it from moisture. He passed the sextant to his yeoman, peeled off his heavy leather gauntlets, then two layers of silk inners, thumped his hands on the skirts of his duffel before taking the instrument back. The yeoman took a stopwatch from his pocket, frowned at the face. Beveridge straddled his legs to give himself a firm platform, made some small adjustments, cursing soundlessly as his fingertips made contact with bare metal.

'Ready.'

'Ready, sir.'

The sun was a golden orb riding above the southern horizon, behind a wisp of grey cloud, still rising towards its zenith. Beveridge screwed up his eyes, deepening the crow's feet at the corners into a mass of wrinkles, followed the sun as it moved to its highest point and hesitated for a second before beginning to drop once more.

'Now!'

The yeoman pressed the stopwatch. Beveridge moved the sextant's mirror to bring the sun down to the horizon in a smooth practised action. The yeoman moved closer to him, read the angle off the scale on the side of the instrument. Beveridge handed the sextant over, blew on his fingers and rubbed them on the front of his duffel before busying himself with his gloves and going below once more. In a little while he would return to the bridge to report the ship's position, the angle of the sun above the horizon at noon giving the latitude from a set of nautical tables, and the difference from Greenwich Mean Time the longitude.

An hour later *Crusader* reached ten knots.

'Pipe Flying Stations. Time we started earning our keep again.'

The goalposts were hastily dismantled. Two Swordfish came up from the hangar, one on each lift, were manoeuvred to the stern to give them as much space as possible.

'They should get off all right at this speed with the rockets,' said Commander (Flying).

Ten knots, plus a five- or six-knot wind, it was little enough for an aircraft laden to its limits with fuel, depth charges and the vital radar. The 'bandstand' just aft of the bridge, which provided a convenient 'goofing platform', filled up with off-duty aircrew whose turn to fly would come later. The first Swordfish moved heavily up the deck; as she reached the bows the rockets fired and she lumbered into the air, followed a minute later by the second. There was a small cheer from the flight deck party, some ironic clapping from the goofing platform and a brief, bright signal from *Vituperate*.

'Somebody should be pleased to see them.'

Commander Hodgson came up once more. 'That's going to be the best I can give you, sir. She'll take twelve knots, with the hose going on her, but as soon as we try to take her above that she starts to heat up again. Best we can do, until we get into harbour and have a proper look at it.'

At twelve knots they could operate the Swordfish and begin to over-haul the convoy, but, even taking the calculated risk of not zig-zagging, it would be a good twelve hours before they finally caught up, and went back inside the comparative safety of the escort screen.

It was one of the two Swordfish which sighted the *Maiwand*'s boats, as two miniature blips on the radar display. The scalded fireman had lived less than an hour after the meeting with the U-boat. The Captain had given him some of the brandy, pulling him away from the bottom boards with an arm around his shoulders, and putting the bottle to the blank hole among the bandages which covered his face. He remembered that the Lascar was a Muslim, but reflected that Allah would probably be merciful in the circumstances. The man screamed with pain at the movement, tried to push the bottle away, but after the spirit had gone down he was quieter, gradually drifted into stupor and then uncon-sciousness, and did not wake. The Lascar with the broken thigh was hanging on, but night was coming on and the cold deepening further. The boats' lockers were fully stored with chocolate and biscuit and other food sufficient to keep the survivors going for several days, per-haps weeks if strictly rationed, but the fresh water in the tanks had proved on inspection to be frozen solid. The Captain and the Chief Officer, who had charge of the second boat, had chivvied the men into getting the sails hoisted, then when the wind turned and would have blown them nearer to the polar pack ice, split them into watches and had them row, more for warmth and occupation than for its practical value, but the nearest inhabited land was the desolate north of Norway, and the cold and lack of water would have killed them long before they reached it.

One of the quartermasters in the Chief Officer's boat sighted the Swordfish, flying sedately eastwards at a couple of thousand feet. He scrambled for the locker which held the signal flares, fumbled with frozen fingers to get one out, tear off the tarred paper which concealed the striker. The flare would not ignite.

'Give it here.'

The man holding the flare tried again. A second European quartermaster lunged towards him, half knocking a Lascar aside, half scrambling over him in his efforts to reach the flare.

'Give it here, for God's sake! They'll be gone in a minute and they'll never have seen us.'

The boat rocked dangerously with the movement. 'Keep still!' the Chief Officer shouted.

All the men, numb and half-stupefied with cold a moment earlier, were awake now, shouting and waving in several languages, scrambling over each other.

'Sodding flare must be wet!'

The quartermaster dropped the offending flare in the bottom of the boat, started searching inside the locker for another. The Chief Officer pushed up his sleeve, exposed his wristwatch and swivelled his body round so as to catch the low sun on the glass. There was a flash as he found the angle, then more as he began to work his wrist back and forth. At the same time, in the other boat, the Captain had got a Verey pistol out of one of the lockers, found to his relief that it was loaded, and pulled the trigger. The red flare soared up into the darkening sky. The Captain tore his gloves off and began frantically to reload. The Swordfish came lower, dipped its wings. 'They've seen us!' Several of the Lascars began prayers of thanks to Allah. An Aldis lamp blinked.

'*Hang on. Destroyer coming.*'

'Two boatloads of survivors in this position here.' The Navigator indicated on the chart with the point of a propelling pencil. 'Twenty-seven miles by my reckoning. We should pick them up on radar any minute.'

He got busy with a parallel ruler, wrote some figures on the edge of the chart. 'There's our course to pick them up, sir.'

Thurston looked down at the chart, at the pencilled crosses which marked the dead reckoning positions of *Crusader* and of *Maiwand*'s boats, and at the line which was the convoy's track, with Beveridge's estimate of its current position. A little more than two hours' steaming to the boats' present position, plus the time it would take to pinpoint them in the dark, even with the Swordfish circling overhead and radar to guide, and the time it would take to pick them up, and a fourteen-degree alteration of course. *Vituperate* would do the picking-up itself. But they were still several hours behind the main convoy, until they rejoined they were vulnerable; altering course to pick up survivors would delay them further. He could detach *Vituperate*, which could get to the survivors in half the time, and then rejoin, but in her absence *Crusader* would be left still more vulnerable.

Beveridge was watching him in his habitual silence. Whatever order he gave Beveridge would carry out, with the silent efficiency with which he did everything, but Beveridge expected him to make that change of course. The Swordfish's signal had included the name of the sunken ship; Beveridge had remarked that she was a Brocklebank ship and Beveridge had done his Merchant Navy apprenticeship with Brocklebanks; he might well know some of the *Maiwand*'s officers.

This was a decision in which personal feelings could not be allowed to intrude, nor the private opinions of *Crusader*'s officers. Yet Thurston too had been a survivor, alive today only because a corvette had by chance sighted *Connaught*'s raft while searching for a straggler. *Connaught*'s Officer of the Watch on the night she was torpedoed had also come from Brocklebanks; Thurston had found him in the water, floating in his lifebelt, head clear of the surface but his neck broken. He had never asked Beveridge whether he had known Galbraith, the wound still went too deep. Yet also he had declined to turn back for that Swordfish which ran out of fuel. Objectively there was no difference. Beveridge was still standing next to him, one hand resting on the edge of the chart table, the other bringing out a large blue-edged handkerchief to blow his nose.

'All right, Pilot. Alter course to oh-seven-three.'

'Aye aye, sir,' Beveridge acknowledged, without a flicker of emotion.

It was shortly before dawn on the next day when *Crusader* sighted the convoy once more.

'From Senior Officer, Escort: *I thought we'd lost you.*'

'From the Commodore. *Nice to see you back.*'

The weather had changed again. Heavy snow had begun to fall while *Vituperate* was picking up the *Maiwand*'s survivors from their boats, gritty powder snow quite unlike the large soft flakes of most English winters, snow which, carried by a biting wind coming down from the north, could reduce a man's exposed face to raw meat. When the sky could be seen it was blanketed by leaden cloud, blown by the wind a few hundred feet up. But the weather grounded the Luftwaffe once more, and shielded the convoy from the eyes of the lookouts aboard the shadowing U-boats. *Crusader*'s Swordfish managed to get off, rather precariously after the flight deck party had cleared the take-off area of snow each time, and the crews tried in vain to keep warm in their open cockpits for the long hours of patrolling, but hour after hour they, and the radar operators aboard the escorts, could report only blank displays. There was a perceptible lightening of mood. The flight deck party and men off watch began snowball fights, but found the snow refused to pack together, and contented themselves with pursuing each other around the deck and hurling shovelfuls.

31

'I thought Murmansk wasn't supposed to ice over,' said Beveridge. 'According to the pilot book it's the only Russian Arctic port which doesn't.'

'Someone can't have read the book.'

The convoy was moving slowly up the Kola Inlet, threading its way along the narrow twisting channel between the ice floes, with occasional heavy grinding noises as a ship's bow found a stray piece of ice and forced it aside, the sound thrown back by the low hills on either side. It was snowing intermittently, the whirling grit descending without warning to blot out the land and even the ships immediately ahead and astern, so that a lookout with a field telephone had been stationed right forward in *Crusader*'s bows, and another in her stern. Foghorns sounded their heavy booming notes, and the escorts' radar sets remained switched on. *Crusader*'s bow hit a detached piece of ice, cut through it and sent the fragments floating back along her sides.

'Here's hoping this doesn't get any thicker. I don't suppose she was designed to be an icebreaker.'

The water between the floes looked black and uninviting by contrast with the greyish whiteness of the ice. The hills on either side were blanketed with snow, the monotony broken in places by stands of densely packed fir trees, themselves looking black at this distance. In a sheltered anchorage on the convoy's starboard beam lay a couple of old cruisers and half a dozen destroyers, each with a general air of dilapidation, rails hanging loose, deep snow on the flat surfaces of their decks, the red hammer-and-sickle flags streaming grubbily from the mastheads.

'Polyarnoe,' someone said. 'Used by the Russian Northern Fleet, which has hardly been out of it since this lot started.'

'Some of them look pretty much like museum pieces.'

'They've been so busy building their socialist utopia since the Revolution that they haven't done anything about building up their fleet.'

'It's a funny thing, isn't it,' said Bruce, who was Officer of the Watch, 'we come all this way with munitions for the Russians, and all that time we haven't seen a single Russian ship, or Russian aircraft, come to that.'

'Now you come to the real nub of the argument,' said the Chief Yeoman. 'They keep on demanding the stuff from us, but they won't do a hand's tap for us in return. You'll see when you get ashore.'

Crusader reached her allotted berth, and her anchor dropped into the water with a splash as the cable rumbled out. Ashore there was a rough wooden jetty, piled untidily with boxes of various shapes and sizes, a huddle of wooden roofs, brown streaks of trodden-down snow where the roads must be. Armed sentries in pudding-basin helmets and ankle-length greatcoats stamped up and down, their bayonets fixed, eighteen-inch blades bright against the snow.

'Don't look very friendly, do they?'

'Is this what we came all this way for?'

'This is the most godforsaken hole I've ever had the pleasure of serving in,' the Captain from the British Naval Mission told Thurston when he came aboard. 'The only reason that there's anything here at all is it's ice-free. Or it's supposed to be. Archangel, which is quite an interesting little place, is iced solid at this time of year. The only way out is by the railway, and between us and Leningrad there's six hundred-odd miles of nothing. The line is single track and the Germans spend a lot of time trying to cut it. Incidentally, the front line is less than fifty miles away and we get raided morning and evening. If your chaps are thinking that they're going to be able to try out the great cuisine of Russia, they're going to be disappointed, because about the only things available are black bread and cabbage soup, and not very much of either. Oh, and dried fish, for which Murmansk is apparently famous, or rather notorious. The place stinks of it in the summer, because they hang it all outside to dry. Warn them that if they do go ashore they'd better not go wandering about on their own. The sentries are all over the place, mostly to prevent the starving populace from looting what little food there is, and they usually shoot first and ask questions afterwards. Most of them are Mongolians and don't even speak Russian, let alone English.

'We've had quite a lot of nasty little incidents. Chap met a girl in the street and got her address or something. Went off to meet her that night and walked into one of the Mongols. There wasn't much of his head left. Your chaps can go to the Red Fleet Club, under escort, and if there happen to be any politicians or war correspondents about, the Red Navy will get in their choir to sing, but otherwise there's nothing much about the place to recommend it.'

The Captain accepted a second gin and continued. 'The Russians are, basically, an unfriendly lot of buggers, particularly the political officers who are there to make sure that nobody gets tainted with Western capitalist decadence. Whenever you're trying to discuss anything with one of their top brass, there's always a political officer standing over him and whispering in his ear, so it's hopeless trying to get anything out of them. And bloody inefficient too. Most of the stuff you bring just stays here. They do manage to move it away from the docks, but the stuff stays piled up at the railhead for months. Crates, tanks, everything, just left to rot, and if they do actually use anything they don't maintain it properly and wreck it inside five minutes. And they go on demanding more.'

The Captain paused in what was obviously a well-practised diatribe. Thurston took the opportunity to ask if there was any news of his two missing Swordfish. 'Ah, yes. We have located them. They managed to get to an airfield about ten miles away, and seem to have landed quite safely.' He shifted uncomfortably in his chair, studied the level of gin in his glass. 'Problem is that the Russians don't want to let them go, and they won't let anyone see them. We only found out where they were through strictly unofficial channels. Leave it with us, and we'll try to have them back before you sail.'

'You better had,' Thurston said with a flash of impatience. He remembered with unease that one of the radar operators was Petty Officer Kornilov. It would be him.

Paymaster Lieutenant Scott came into Thurston's cabin with a large pile of cards.

'What have you got there?'

'Bluenose Certificates, sir. I've been working on them ever since we crossed the Arctic Circle. Six hundred and eighty of them, for your signature.'

'Do you honestly want to go ashore, kid?' Spencer was in the midst of his dhobi, scrubbing with a nailbrush at one of his blue-jean collars which was spread out over the Captain's washbasin. 'There isn't nothing to see ashore. Worse than bloody Hvalfjord. At least there's a few mountains to look at there. And the place is full of Russkies!' Spencer made a particularly vicious attack on a small portion of the collar, and was rewarded by a white froth of soap suds rising from it. Metcalfe looked crestfallen. 'Yeah, Charlie, I know. You want to see a bit of Russia, so you've got something to tell your mum and your Dottie about when you get home on leave.'

'Spence, man . . .' Metcalfe began.

'All right. I'm just teasing. But if you want to go looking for some Russian crumpet I s'pose I'll have to go with you. You're not safe wandering off on your own. Look what happened the last time.'

Metcalfe blushed scarlet. 'I won't be doing that again.'

'Should 'ope not. Mind, I don't suppose you'd find any crabs to pick up round here. Too fucking cold for them. And it don't look like you're going to get a box of caviar for your mum and Dottie. All they get to eat ashore is mouldy bread and cat's-piss soup.'

'Sir, Midshipman from *Vittoria*, with some papers.'

'Show him in.'

Thurston glanced up from the files spread open on his desk as the midshipman came through the door and halted in front of him. There was a grin which was almost a smirk, hair which had been determinedly combed into place at some time, but had begun to escape rebelliously once the cap was removed.

'What the blazes are you doing here?'

'Hello, Dad.' George's familiar, rather cocky grin was spreading from both sides of his mouth. 'I haven't got any papers for you. I thought I'd give you a surprise.'

'More a shock than a surprise.' And then he too was laughing, coming out from behind his desk to shake George's hand, and making the necessary introductions to Scott, who seemed to be enjoying the situation as much as they were.

'He wouldn't tell me his name, sir. Said you would know him.'

'Why on earth didn't you write and tell me you were in *Vittoria*?'

'Sorry, Dad, I just didn't get round to it. It was all a bit of a rush. I did get a letter off to Mother though.'

It was snowing again, and George's seaboots were beginning to leave large damp patches on the deck, more water running off his duffel coat as the snow granules on his shoulders melted. Spencer appeared, unbidden, from the pantry. 'I'm just getting a brew on, sir.'

George was still standing in the centre of the cabin, dripping water.

'Oh get those things off and sit down before you ruin my carpet.'

George was sitting in the armchair opposite him, a mug of tea and a second large hunk of fruitcake at his elbow, his long legs stretched out in front of him, encased to the knee in coarse, oiled-wool seaboot stockings, a vast polo-neck sweater in grey specked with black emerging above and below his battledress blouse.

250

'I got a pierhead jump to *Vittoria* for destroyer training. Only a couple of hours' notice,' he explained between mouthfuls of cake. 'We sailed on this convoy the morning after I joined, and here I am. I had to take the Old Man ashore in the boat to see someone there. He won't be back for hours so I thought I'd come and find you instead of hanging about at the landing.'

Physically, George was all Thurston; already, at a month short of eighteen, as tall as his father, with powerful shoulders which looked a little ungainly now, but would be balanced out in a few years when he reached his full growth, dark hair which had by now escaped into full rebellion, and the steely blue eyes he had inherited from his grandfather. His face was familiar, but not quite as Thurston remembered it, losing its child's smoothness and becoming leaner, more angular. He and George could not be other than father and son, but in temperament they were quite unalike.

George was a noisy, gregarious boy who had thoroughly enjoyed his prep school, and then bounced cheerfully through eleven terms at Dartmouth, putting his abundant energy to good use in the three or four sports at which he had represented the College, and finishing his career there as one of the two Chief Cadet Captains, though he remained well down the term in work, steadfastly doing only the mini-mum necessary, even after a warning early in his Dartmouth career that if his grasp of engineering did not improve he would not be remaining there. 'But, Dad, what's the point? I'm not going to be an engineer.' He had taken George for a walk – it had been one of those odd occasions when the tail end of his own leave coincided with the beginning of George's – and tried to explain to him that it was not that the College was trying to make an engineer of him, but a competent seaman officer must have some understanding of what it was that got his ship to where it was needed, and an efficient Captain must at least be able to understand what his Chief Engineer was talking about when the Chief Engineer asked him to reduce speed, or whatever. He didn't know then whether he had got through to George, but his report the following term showed sufficient improvement to put him clear of the danger zone.

Watching George, and listening to his talk of the convoy they had just completed, Thurston was reminded of the other George, and the last time he had seen him, on leave at Langdon after Gallipoli. His older brother had turned up unexpectedly on embarkation leave, having attained the maturity of eighteen and a half years and been ordered to

251

France with a draft, after kicking his heels at the Depot since the autumn.

'I told the CO that even my brattish little brother was out in the Dardanelles as a midshipman, but he wouldn't make an exception.'

They had sat on George's bed yarning until their father banged on the door and enquired of them what time they intended to allow the household some sleep. And the next morning, one of those harsh bright February mornings with a biting easterly coming off the sea, so that you could never get properly warm, they had ridden out to Bamburgh, and up the beach there. The tide was far out, the sand just sheened with water, the Farnes and Holy Island rising mistily out of the sea, the great rectangular bulk of the castle brooding on its rock above the dunes. He had no idea what started it, but they chased each other up and down the empty beach in a glorious spontaneous game of tag, a last homage to boyhood. Rocket was smaller and handier than George's grey, Falcon, would whip round on his hocks like a polo pony at a slight pressure of the reins against his neck, and use his weight against Falcon when Thurston brought him close to ride George off, his black mane flying back in the wind. Fooling around and laughing, manoeuvring Rocket at the gallop with his knees and left hand alone, going fetlock deep into the shallows before stopping at last to draw breath and let the horses cool off. Walking back, one arm through the reins, carrying Rocket's saddle and watching the steam rising from his back, sensing the stillness of the place, despite the wind, the vastness of sea and sky, its timelessness and separateness.

'Have you had a woman yet, brat?'

He didn't answer. He had been telling George the night before about Gallipoli, with a little of the superiority of the professional naval officer over the temporary subaltern, and about shore leave in Malta, Gibraltar and Port Said, shown him the tattoo on his arm from the night *Hyperion*'s midshipmen had gone for a meal in Valletta and decided after a few drinks on a grand gesture of brotherhood, even Tommy Tuck, who hated needles and had once fainted in the queue for jabs.

'I paid a woman for a fuck the last time I was in London. It wasn't all it's cracked up to be, but at least I'm not going out there without doing it.' George bent down and picked up a flat pebble from the sand, with a flick of his wrist sent it spinning into the water. It bounced once and disappeared. 'Had to have a woman before they get me. They say it's bloody murder out there, but I'm bloody glad I'm going. Getting out of the Depot at last. Place is full of old majors – some of them are even older than Father, and subalterns who were gazetted after me.

Kids.' Then he put aside his sombre mood just as suddenly. Come on, brat, let's find something to eat.'

They went into Seahouse, thawed out in front of a huge log fire, and demolished a piled plate of steak and kidney pie each. George made up to the waitress, asking her whether she was working that night, with an air of showing off towards his younger brother.

The next day, very early, Thurston had gone with George to catch his train, in half-darkness with a promise of snow in the heavy cloud, saluted him for the first time and received a military salute in return, then shook hands with the formality of eighteen-year-old subalterns and sixteen-year-old midshipmen. 'See you in Berlin, Admiral.' The snow began as he rode Rocket home, with Falcon bumping against his leg, sharp gritty snow, which swirled around them in the wind, turned the horses' manes to white.

When the news came through, and after the Captain had finished with him, he climbed up to the roof of the foretop, the highest place in the ship, familiar from punishment watches, but one of the few places where he could be certain of being alone. He did not feel like facing the other chaps yet, with their questions and awkward sympathy. It did not occur to him, despite the Captain's reassurances, that he might well have been taken prisoner, or be unconscious and unidentified in some dressing station; here in the wide silence of Scapa Flow there was only the quiet and numbing certainty that George was dead. The dinner hour had begun, so that work had stopped; there was only a solitary picket boat making her way back to *Queen Elizabeth*, the next ahead, leaving a rippling wake on the smooth water astern, and occasional sharp gusts of wind which threatened to dislodge him from his perch. He grasped the lightning conductor to steady himself, took his cap off, let the wind blow through his hair.

'Dad?' Thurston jerked back to the present. 'You haven't been listening to half what I've been saying.'

'Sorry, George. Miles away.'

He invited George to dine with him that night, but George was on duty, so it would have to be the next night. George looked at his watch, decided it was time he got his boat back to the landing to pick up his captain, and left.

Spencer was not impressed with the Red Fleet Club.

'Only went 'cos Charlie Metcalfe wanted to see a bit of Russia, sir,' he told Thurston next morning. 'Thought I'd better keep an eye on the kid. Don't want him wandering off by himself in a place like this. When we got to the quay, there was a great crowd of Russki matelots there, with rifles and fixed bayonets. I used to think the crushers in Pompey were bad, but these were hardly what you'd call friendly. They frog-marched us up there through all the snow, and we was thinking this had better be good after all this. But all there was when we got there was a bloody film, if you can call it that. Supposed to be about Alexander the Great, but you'd never have known. It kept breaking down, and they were having to stick it back together again, and it must have been made about 1912 anyway. And all they gave us to drink was a cup of bloody tea, and even that was stone cold. Charlie Metcalfe's seen all he wants of Russia now, thank God. Do you want your battle-dress today, sir? Be a bit warmer than the good stuff.'

32

British Naval Headquarters had no news of the two Swordfish.

'We're working on it, but the Russians seem to have dug their toes in this time. They're not even admitting they've got them, officially, which makes things more difficult. It looks as though they're trying to hang on to the radar. They haven't any of their own, and they depend on us for it. We haven't let them have any ASV radar – there isn't enough to spare – so that's what they want. Not that they'd use it if they had it. Their Arctic Fleet does precisely nothing. But we'll make sure you get your chaps back, as soon as we've got this sorted out.' Thurston finally lost patience, told the Captain to find him an interpreter and he would go and treat with the Russians himself.

'Steady on, old boy. You don't know these people. You'll probably just put their backs up even more. Leave it to us. We're far more used to dealing with them. What's the hurry? You can't sail until the return convoy's ready for you.'

Thurston said, very slowly, spacing out his words to make his meaning absolutely clear, 'One of my men is called Kornilov. He's a White Russian exile.'

'I see.' The Captain said nothing more.

The interpreter was a bespectacled, fiftyish Lieutenant RNVR who introduced himself as Ross. 'I was born in St Petersburg,' was the surprising reply when Thurston asked him where he had learned his Russian. 'My grandfather came out to build the railway from Petersburg to Moscow, married a Russian, and stayed. My father worked for the Petersburg end of an export company, married the daughter of an English family out here, and I was born here. After the Revolution I left Russia but worked in the Baltic timber trade, so I've had plenty of practice at negotiating with Russians. The war came, I offered my services to the Admiralty and ended up out here.' His English was accentless, but indefinably foreign, perhaps in the placing of the pauses. Ross turned to the matter in hand. 'I think we should go and see Colonel Yeremenko, sir. He's the local Air Force commander. I've dealt with him before and he's one of the more reasonable ones. At least, he's not afraid of his political officer.' Ross was deferential, but firm. 'If you leave me to do the talking, sir. What is your father's Christian name – for the introductions?'

'Henry.'

'It would be. There's no Russian equivalent. There's no letter "h" in Russian. Ah well, if in doubt fall back on Ivan.'

There was no petrol to be had so Thurston and Ross were walking throught the hard-packed snow in Murmansk's streets, a low afternoon sun colouring expanses of ice dull red. It was already growing dark, though it was only a little after two. There were few civilians in the streets, so heavily muffled in greatcoats that they were distinguishable from the omnipresent soldiers only by their lack of weapons. Perhaps there were no women, or perhaps they were indistinguishable from the men.

They were walking up the road which ran parallel with the railway line, past an untidy sprawl of piled crates, their outlines blurred and softened by deposits of snow. Soldiers were patrolling up and down, each covering a beat a few yards in length, his bayonet fixed, his flat Mongolian face expressionless. More men stumbled among the crates, moving items from one patch of snow to another, apparently without purpose. They were wretchedly thin, some without boots, their feet bound up in old rags, the sleeves of their shapeless greatcoats pulled down to protect their hands, here and there part of a face showing the dead white signs of frostbite.

'Convict labour,' Ross said. 'German POWs or political undesirables.'

They had passed the final pile of crated stores when a clatter behind them made them turn round. One of the prisoners had dropped a box, which had landed against one of the crates and broken open, so that fresh new glass and metal gleamed against the snow. One of the sentries came up, unslung his rifle and knocked the man sprawling with the butt. The man tried to get up, his rag-bound feet scrabbling in the snow for a foothold. The rifle butt came down on his shoulders, once, then again. He fell back into the snow, tried again to rise. He was on his hands and knees, the wrappings on one foot unravelling so that a couple of naked toes appeared, blackened and gangrenous from frostbite. The rifle butt smashed into his mouth. He dropped once more, bright blood coming from his mouth. The sentry kicked him, twice, under the ribs so that he rolled over onto his back, then reversed the rifle once more, raised it high, and drove the bayonet into the man's stomach. He twisted the bayonet through ninety degrees, put his boot on the man's chest to pull it out, and then wiped the blade almost fastidiously on the snow, an expression on his face which might have been a smile. The other convicts had stopped working and stood still. Now one of them crossed himself, said something to the man next to him. The remaining rifles were trained on them, and the soldiers began to move, clubbing the prisoners back to work, dragging the dead man's body out of the way and shouting hoarsely in their unintelligible language.

The sentry who had bayonetted the man must have seen the two British officers for the first time. He came forward, crashed to a halt a few yards from them, and saluted smartly. Thurston, sickened, turned and walked rapidly away, without returning the salute.

'Ukrainians,' Ross said. 'At least, that one was speaking Ukrainian. The regime is particularly anti-Ukrainian as a lot of captured Ukrainian soldiers have gone over to the Germans.'

It was only a few minutes later that they reached Colonel Yeremenko's headquarters, a single-storey wooden building with a large hammer-and-sickle flag flying above it and more armed sentries outside. A wall of heat hit them as soon as they went through the door. Thurston quickly pulled his trouser legs down over his seaboots as Ross spoke in Russian to a young man with epaulettes on his shoulders who seemed to be an officer.

'Colonel Yeremenko will see us, sir.'

The young Russian officer threw open a door. Inside, a large, clean-shaven man lazily removed his feet from the desk on which they were resting. Despite the heat which was being thrown out by the stove which occupied a quarter of the floor space, he was muffled in a large fur coat, and smoking a foul-smelling cigar which added to the stuffiness of the atmosphere. He put the cigar down in an ashtray made from the base of a brass cartridge case, and stood up.

Ross began speaking in Russian. Thurston caught only his own name. '*Kapitan pervogo ranga Thurston, Robert Ivanovich*,' then in English, 'Sir, Colonel Sergey Alexeyevich Yeremenko of the Red Army Air Force.'

He shook the proffered hand, and sat down when Ross prompted him. Ross began a long speech in Russian. Yeremenko listened in silence. Thurston began to grow impatient at his lack of Russian which prevented him from following what Ross was saying.

Ross finished speaking. Yeremenko said nothing for a little longer, then jumped up from his chair and flung open the door. 'Volodya!' he shouted into the passage. A young Russian soldier, shaven-headed, appeared with an ancient field telephone, placed it on the desk and cranked the handle several times. At last he passed the handset to Yeremenko, who began speaking in rapid Russian.

'He's ringing the airfield commander. This looks promising.'

'Ah, Ivan Ivanovich.' Yeremenko's tone changed.

'He's got through, at any rate.'

There was a long one-sided telephone conversation, peppered with Ivan Ivanoviches, in which Thurston heard a mangled version of his own name several times. Ross whispered a commentary into his ear. 'Ivan Ivanovich is having trouble with his political officer.' Yeremenko shouted into the telephone. 'That could be translated as, "Damn your political officer!"' Ross seemed to be enjoying himself.

Yeremenko slammed the telephone down, beaming.

'He says you will have your aeroplanes back today,' Ross said. 'He'll probably offer you vodka now, sir. If he does, for God's sake drink it!'

Ross was correct. Yeremenko stood up, crossed to a cupboard and brought out a bottle and three small glasses, pouring a measure into each.

'Colonel Yeremenko salutes his brave comrade of the British Navy.'

Yeremenko drained his glass in a gulp. Thurston took a deep breath, poured the vodka down, gasped, felt tears spring to his eyes. 'Tell the Colonel I salute my gallant ally.'

'To the glorious British Navy.'

'To the ever-victorious Red Army,' Thurston said carefully, remembering the dead Ukrainian beside the railway line. He was uncomfortably hot inside his greatcoat.

'King George!'

'Stalin.' Thurston replied uncomfortably.

'The Colonel wishes to know whether you have sunk many German ships.'

'German and Italian ships.'

Ross translated.

'*Khorosho!*' said Yeremenko.

'And have you killed many German sailors?'

This was getting ridiculous. The room had begun to swim, the vodka less fiery with each glassful.

Yeremenko stood up, extricated himself from his coat and from the thin shirt he was wearing underneath, to reveal an ugly puckered scar across his stomach. 'Kursk!'

'The Colonel wishes to say that he was not always a desk soldier.'

The Colonel was clearly waiting for another toast.

'The heroic defenders of Stalingrad.' But wasn't it the German Sixth

258

Army which had been defending Stalingrad? He couldn't remember. Yeremenko did not seem to care.

Thurston got up, waited a moment for the room to settle onto one plane, then said with a drunken man's careful gravity, 'Tell the Colonel I regret that I must return to my ship.'

Yeremenko uttered what appeared to be an expression of regret, then came out from behind the desk, grasped him by the shoulders and pulled him towards him to plant a bristly kiss on both his cheeks. 'Robert Ivanovich!' He launched into a further flood of Russian.

'The Colonel,' said Ross, by now very pink and blinking behind his spectacles, 'says that he and his brave comrade Robert Ivanovich will always remain brothers, and the ever-victorious Red Army will drive the treacherous Germans into the sea, where the British Navy will destroy them utterly.'

Thurston and Ross got out of the building, gulping in lungfuls of glorious cold air, and made their slightly uncertain way back to the docks.

'It was really quite funny looking back, though it wasn't at the time,' said Wallace that evening. 'The Russians were *very* surprised to see us. I don't think any of them had seen a Stringbag before, and they must have thought we were Germans because they started shooting at us. Fortunately they were rotten shots, because I had to put down on the field because I was down to my last teaspoon of petrol – in fact, once I did get down there wasn't enough left to taxi – and Bennett didn't have much more. We managed to convince the Russkies we weren't Jerries. We kept saying "Royal Navy" very slowly and showed them the crowns on our buttons, and they got the message eventually. It would probably have been easier if Petty Officer Kornilov had let on that he speaks Russian, but he wanted to keep that quiet. Then once we'd got that sorted out, they frogmarched us off to separate cells, had us strip off and searched us.'

'I was a bit worried about what they'd do when they found out my name,' said Kornilov. 'I managed to palm my dog tags, but I forgot about the name tags in my clothes until the fellow was poking through them. I'd just decided that I was going to tell them my grandfather had fled from Russia to get away from Tsarist persecution when I realised the fellow wasn't taking any notice of them at all. Couldn't read English script.'

'Probably couldn't read at all,' said Powell.

When Thurston got back to the ship, Spencer had taken one look at him and produced black coffee and Alka-Seltzer. That, and a couple of hours in his bunk, had got rid of the worst effects of the vodka, and he had woken to a report that the two Swordfish had returned. Now the six crewmen were in his cabin, all trying to tell their own version of the story at the same time.

'Then they put us all in the one cell, and it was so bloody cold that none of us slept a wink.'

'You did,' put in Powell. 'You snored all night and the rest of us didn't sleep a wink.'

'Of course, Petty Officer Kornilov didn't let on that he speaks Russian, and kept his ear to the ground, but he didn't manage to pick up anything. The sentries were all Mongolians, and he couldn't catch any of it. The next morning various Big Noises turned up and we were all trotted out for them to see. Of course, we didn't know what was happening or what they were going to do with us, and we were trying not to let on about Korny. Then the Chief Big Noise arrived.'

'With an enormous retinue of hangers-on, all bowing and scraping.'

'He was a Major-General of Engineers,' said Kornilov.

'We were frogmarched out to the Stringbags so that we could explain the ASV to the General. The rest of us just left it all to Korny and he was absolutely brilliant, completely blinded them with science.'

'I got the feeling that the General didn't know much about radar,' said Kornilov, 'so I went into a really complicated explanation of how it worked, which had the interpreter completely baffled. Then I told them that we had had nothing but trouble with the sets, that the sparking from the wave guide quite frequently set the aircaft on fire, and we'd lost quite a few that way. Then I got aboard and switched on, and twiddled a few knobs to put the set off-tune. I made a big show of tuning it with the General looking over my shoulder at one side and the interpreter at the other. I let them look through the eyepiece every now and then, and the interpreter was trying to explain it all to the General, and a crowd of commissars who had turned up as well. But his English wasn't much better than any of the others, and he was really tying himself in knots. I had a terrible job to keep my face straight. I nearly gave myself away a few times.'

'Then the General wanted to go up in one of the aircraft and see for himself how it worked in the air.'

'Or rather didn't work,' said Kornilov.

'We'd thought about that and worked out that we could follow the coast round to Murmansk and find somewhere to put her down, and hope that the General's sense of direction wasn't too hot. We'd probably have got him in, sitting on Powell's knee, but we'd never have got the interpreter on board as well, and it rather looked as though the head commissar wanted to come too. Anyway, Bennett's kite would still have been stuck on the ground, though we did think of telling them that we had to have two aircraft working together because we could only get a fix on a U-boat by cross-bearings, and of course we weren't too happy about leaving Bennett and co with the Russians while we waltzed off with their General. So we told them we were sorry, but there wasn't enough room in the aircraft.'

'Then this is the best bit,' said Bennett. 'Korny told them very casually that exposure to short-wave radiation makes you sterile, and of course we were getting double pay to compensate.'

'It took the interpreter a minute or two to realise what I was saying, then when he did he jumped back about three feet, and when he'd translated it the General just turned on his heel and walked away as fast as he decently could, with all the hangers-on following. The chaps who'd been guarding us couldn't wait to get away either, so they doubled us back to the cell, which we were quite glad to see by then, and apart from bringing us food three times a day – if you can call it food – they left us alone after that.'

'Then when we were waiting for the lunch to arrive, or what passed for lunch, one of the Big Noises turned up with the interpreter and told us we were free to go.'

'I noticed that they kept well clear of us. Must have decided the sterility was catching.'

'Careful. We don't yet know that it *doesn't* cause sterility,' Wallace said, looking down at Kornilov.

It was good to see them, each with a glass in his hand, their youthful spirits undimmed by what must have been an unpleasant few days in the hands of a highly suspicious ally.

'So we persuaded the Russkies to let us have some petrol, got the engines thawed out, and got ourselves back here before they changed their minds.'

'We were a bit worried about getting the engines going again. They'd been sitting outside all that time without even a tarpaulin over them, but the Russki mechanics lit a fire underneath them for us, and they actually started first go, once they'd found a starting handle that fitted.'

'You should have seen Powell's starting handle imitations, sir!'

'It took ages for them to get the message,' said Kornilov. 'I nearly gave myself away. I was just itching to say starting handle to them.'

There was another gale of laughter, then Wallace wondered aloud what had induced the Russians to let them go when they did. Thurston said simply, a curl of his upper lip betraying his distaste, that it had cost him a thick head and a kiss on both cheeks from a drunken Russian colonel.

George came aboard for dinner that night. There was soup, roast lamb and apple pie, and rambling conversation centred on George's experiences since leaving Dartmouth. It was pleasant enough, but underneath there was a vague sense of dissatisfaction. Thurston would have liked to be closer to his son; from the time when they were newly married and Kate had first told him that she was expecting a child, he had been determined that things were not going to be as they were and had been between his own father and himself. But it hadn't worked out as he had intended. Yes, he had taught George to swim, got down on his knees to take him through the basics of boxing, and taken him out with a gun later on, but something indefinable was missing between them. It might have been because he had been away so much when George was younger; he had gone to China for two years when George was four months old, and then for another two and a half years when he was five, and soon after his return George had gone to his prep school so that he only saw him in the school holidays. Or perhaps it was simply the difference in their temperaments. 'He worships you,' Kate had once told him, and that increased the sense of dissatisfaction. George saw only the outer trappings, the uniform, the red ribbon, he had no knowledge of the man beneath. Thurston had been secretly relieved that George was back at Dartmouth for his final term when he arrived from the Mediterranean on sick leave, and at the same time ashamed of the relief. He had hoped to be fully fit and back on duty by the time George came home on his passing-out leave, but in the event he was sick and depressed after the failed tendon graft, and bad-tempered with the pain from it, and George had, not surprisingly, avoided him. But the illusion remained. He had taken George for a walk the afternoon before he caught his train to Scapa, told him jocularly not to try to be a hero. George had stood stock-still, gaping at him. And now there was to be another child, perhaps another son, and perhaps it would be the same with him.

George, as Kate had predicted, found the whole idea of another child faintly disgusting. But he supposed he would have reacted in much the same way if, when he was George's age, his own father had told him that his stepmother was having a baby. At the time of his father's second marriage there had been a good deal of surreptitious discussion between himself and his brother on the question of whether 'Father is going to do it to Mrs F', and a degree of indignation at the thought that someone as old as that (the vicar was fifty-four) even contemplated such a thing. Arthur Hancock, who was Thurston's closest friend at Osborne, increased the disquiet by informing them that his parents, who were very nearly as old and had been married for years, were still doing it.

'Every now and then you see them gazing into each other's eyes and holding hands.' Hank put on a swooning female expression by way of demonstration. 'And they start calling each other darling, and disappear upstairs. In the middle of the afternoon too!'

George looked at his watch and said that he had to get back to *Vittoria*. Thurston told the Officer of the Watch to call away his boat and went up onto the flight deck with him, wanting obscurely to stretch out the meeting a little.

'Look, Dad, the northern lights.'

The sky had cleared while they had been below and the blackness to the north had changed to layer upon layer of colour, shading from white and palest pink to purple and then back again by infinitely subtle steps, overlaid by a pale glow reflected off the polar pack ice a few dozen miles to the north, the few stars palely insignificant by comparison. Powdery snow crunched beneath their feet. The deck was empty except for a few men who had had word of the display and come to see it for themselves, heads in their peakless caps cocked skywards, hands thrust into coat pockets against the cold, feet stamping occasionally. Most of them were by themselves: the subtly shifting display was something to be watched in solitude.

At length Thurston tore himself away. 'Better not keep Pym waiting for you any longer.'

Down the ladder from the unreal light above decks to the darkness of *Crusader*'s enclosed quarterdeck, almost claustrophobic by comparison. They shook hands.

'Goodnight, Dad.' George came to attention, snapped off a salute.

Thurston raised his right hand to his cap to return it. George clattered down the accommodation ladder, returned Petty Officer Pym's salute as he stepped nimbly into the waiting boat. Thurston went back up to the flight deck, but the glory of the lights was ending. He remained watching a little longer, then went below to his cabin to undress.

Aboard U–686 Korvettenkapitän Lauterbeck went below to his bunk a little more than an hour later. His second lieutenant, like most of the men, was on his first patrol, and needed to be kept an eye on, but he also needed to be left to grow accustomed to responsibility. So Lauterbeck had stayed on the bridge for a time, then gone below to the control room for a little longer, then made another brief appearance on the bridge before going below to his cabin. A cabin in name only, simply an alcove separated from the wardroom by a hanging green curtain. There was no privacy aboard a U-boat, where forty-eight men were crammed into a vessel two hundred and twenty feet long and a maximum of twenty-two in beam, the pressure hull smaller still, and having to accommodate the two diesel engines which powered the boat on the surface, and their fuel, sufficient for seven thousand nine hundred miles at ten knots, the two electric motors which powered her when submerged, and their huge, many-celled batteries, charged by the engines when the boat was surfaced, and the five torpedo tubes which were U–686's reason for existing, four in the bow and one in the stern.

The men lived in the space which was left; the bulk of the ratings in the fore ends among the reloads, a few having to sling hammocks as there were insufficient bunks for all of them, even with two men sharing, and changing places at the change of watches. There was one lavatory on board, and one washbasin to serve the needs of all the forty-eight men, so that after five weeks at sea, a distinct sour reek of stale sweat and unwashed bodies mingled with and overlaid the eternal U-boat smell of diesel oil, boiled cabbage, and damp wool and leather.

Lauterbeck sniffed the familiar smell and smiled to himself, unfastened the front of his leather jacket and scratched at his chest hair through the red-checked shirt he was wearing. He pulled off his seaboots, knelt down beside his bunk and fingered the rosary in his trouser pocket, a gift from his wife before he sailed on his first war patrol. No doubt it had become known among his crew that U–686's Captain knelt in prayer each night, but no one had made any comment about it, and he did not care if they did. At length he rose from his knees and climbed into his bunk, with a glance at the photograph on the bulkhead at the foot.

He had known Helga all his life. They had been born and grown up together in the same Bavarian village, where his father had been the schoolmaster until he was called up as a reserve officer and killed at Verdun. There had been friendship between them, nothing more, until he came home to Pahl on his first leave from the merchant service, and suddenly realised that Helga was a very pretty girl, who made him laugh and turned him shy at the same time. He completed his cadet's training

264

in the merchant service and found a berth as a junior officer with the Hamburg-Amerika Line, no less. Then in 1932, when he had just been promoted Third Officer, the sinking of the sail training ship *Niobe* cost the German Navy almost the entire officer cadet intake for the year. Lauterbeck, and a large number of other young merchant officers, found themselves being pressed to transfer, with two years' seniority on commissioning offered as an inducement. It was not an offer to be accepted without thought. He had his Master's ticket, and could look forward to a command in a few years if he stayed with the Hamburg-Amerika Line. The Versailles Treaty limited the German Navy to 15,000 men, and forbade it modern battleships to replace the venerable *Schleisen* and *Schlesvig-Holstein*, now suitable only for training; submarines or aircraft, and a transfer would mean beginning at the bottom once more, at the relatively advanced age of twenty-five. It was in part Helga who swayed him, or rather the unwelcome attentions of a young officer of the SA who had begun to pay court, and there were whispers that Germany would not subordinate itself to the Versailles Treaty for much longer.

Lauterbeck had emerged as a Leutnant zur See from two years' training and a further year at sea as a midshipman just as Germany's new U-boat arm was coming out into the open. U-boats offered better pay, earlier responsibility, and the kudos of belonging to an élite within the service and so, newly engaged to Helga, he applied again to transfer and was accepted. By the time war broke out he was in command of a three-hundred-ton Type II coastal U-boat, having been successively second lieutenant and first lieutenant in other boats of the same flotilla. In the four and a half years since, he had commanded two more boats beside this one, sunk fourteen British and American ships totalling eighty-two thousand tons and been awarded the Iron Cross first and second class and the Knight's Cross of the Iron Cross. He had, finally, married Helga, on a forty-eight-hour leave shortly after the fall of France, and fathered two sons eighteen months apart. Lying in his damp blankets, a few inches from U–686's steel bulkheads, his left shin began to ache. His previous boat had been on passage home from a second patrol in American waters, during which they had sunk five merchant ships, easy pickings, unescorted and close inshore, silhouetted against a coastline which the Americans, believing that three thousand miles of Atlantic Ocean put them beyond reach of any enemy, had neglected to black out. The U-boat was still six hundred miles out from Lorient when the RAF Sunderland found her. One bullet from her machine guns cut the First Lieutenant's throat, another smashed Lauterback's leg below the knee. One of the lookouts unceremoniously pushed him through the conning tower hatch just as the boat began to dive, so that he landed with the leg twisted agonisingly beneath him. The same man got him to his bunk, someone else shot him full of morphine, and the Second Lieutenant took over, but in the five days it took to limp back to Lorient infection set in. The doctors ashore operated, and operated again, and eventually saved the leg, but for a long time the wound festered and would not heal, so that he was still in hospital, taking his first unsteady steps on crutches, when the news came through that his boat, with her replacement officers, was presumed lost with all hands. Doenitz had offered him a shore job, command of a training flotilla in the Baltic to go with his third stripe, but he had preferred to go back to sea.

To the untried crew of U–686, and the equally inexperienced officers, most of whom had been pressed into the U-boat service from decom-missioned surface ships, Lauterbeck must have seemed a survivor from a vanished age; a contemporary of Kretschmer and the long-dead Prien and Schepke; and much had changed in his eighteen months ashore. Even the slow convoys were now heavily escorted; there were aircraft and there was radar, more powerful asdics and better depth charges. Increasing numbers of U-boats failed to reach their patrol areas, being picked off by the RAF while crossing the Bay of Biscay at the very beginning of the patrol. Even in the Arctic waters where U–686 was based, and where the enemy were hampered in their hunting by the weather and by the unpredictable warm and cold water layers which blinded asdic, the row of photographs on one wall of the wardroom grew longer with every month.

And as men grew from green hands into veterans in the space of two or three patrols they became aware that the odds against them were rising, and that death would come for them, as it had for so many before them, somewhere in the depths of the ocean after the British with their depth charges had sent the boat plunging out of control far beyond its maximum depth, where the pressure of thousands upon thousands of tons of water crushed her hull like an eggshell, or perhaps slowly, from lack of oxygen, perhaps lying on the bottom, with the pressure hull intact but the boat too damaged in other ways to rise.

Lauterbeck shivered, pulled his blankets more closely around him, tried to find a more comfortable position for his leg. They would not understand, those green hands of his, why it was that he had surfaced and gone to those British survivors in their boats. They would not realise that it was part of a tradition far older than Nazism, which went back to Karl von Müller of the *Emden* in the last war, and had been carried on by Langsdorff of the *Graf Spee* and by Otto Kretschmer in this. He wondered whether those men had made it to land by now, or whether their own people had sighted them and picked them up.

33

A patrolling Luftwaffe reconnaissance aircraft sighted the convoy as it departed from Murmansk. A report was passed back to U-boat High Command in Brest, which ordered the five U-boats on patrol in the Barents Sea into position to intercept. Once more U–686 was working up and down a patrol line running north and south, up as far as the ice and back again, waiting, like the other boats, for the convoy to reach that line and present itself for attack. The atmosphere aboard was tense. Twice the Metox, a rough wooden crucifix bearing an array of wires which detected airborne radar transmissions, had given its warning, and Lauterbeck had hastily submerged, but neither the periscope nor the hydrophones had revealed the presence of a ship. Perhaps the convoy would not appear at all; on many occasions in the last few months BdU had thrown a patrol line across the track of a convoy, but the British had for some reason passed north or south of the line and escaped unscathed. But in these latitudes, with the ice now at its furthest extent, the British could not outflank the line. U–686's men waited for a sighting, or a sighting report from one of the other boats, forgetful for now of the retribution by depth-charging which must follow once their attack had betrayed their position.

The sighting report came as those off watch were at their evening meal. The Petty Officer Telegraphist, half his mind on the dog-eared thriller he was reading, started awake, noted down the meaningless string of letters which came from his headset, then tore off the sheet and passed it out into the passage where the Second Lieutenant was waiting, also roused by the sudden burst of morse. A space was cleared among the plates on the wardroom table for the Enigma machine, and the Second Lieutenant set to work to decode the signal, tapping out each letter painfully slowly with the index finger of his right hand. The task completed at last, he passed the signal to the Captain, who stood up silently, leaving his meal unfinished, went to the control room, conferred for a moment with the Navigator, then ordered a change of course.

'Masthead on the starboard bow!'

A warship's mast, so the ship was one of the escorts, screening the convoy from attack. As on the outward convoy they must get inside that screen in order to get within range of the merchant ships, evading the unseen eyes of radar and asdic. Lauterbeck gave the order to dive and U–686 slid smoothly beneath the surface once more.

'Periscope depth,' he told the Chief Engineer, Lieutenant Knopf, who was standing in his position beside the depth gauges.

The U-boat levelled out as the Chief adjusted the trim, pumping water fore and aft until he was satisfied.

'Periscope depth, Herr Kapitän.'

Lauterbeck moved up the conning tower ladder to the periscope. 'Up periscope.'

With a whirring of its electric motor the periscope rose from its well. Sitting on the saddle seat, feet on the pedals which moved it from side to side, Lauterbeck swiftly rotated it through three hundred and sixty degrees, sighting the single masthead once more.

'Down periscope.'

Submerged, U–686's maximum speed was reduced to seven and a half knots, less than that of the convoy she was shadowing, but the convoy was zig-zagging, and sooner or later the zig-zag would bring the enemy ships across the U-boat's path.

'Propeller noises, zero-eight-zero, drawing nearer,' reported the Petty Officer Telegraphist, who had now moved to the hydrophones, the only other man aboard with direct access to the outer world.

'Up periscope.'

Lauterbeck took another quick glance round. There were other masts now, the unmistakable smoke pumped out by coal-burning engines rising into the night sky. He looked at his watch. It was just after 0330, nine hours since the sighting report had come through. Still no asdic. The hydroplane operator reported reciprocating engines, a steady thump-thumping sound, quite distinct from the turbines of the warships. Below Lauterbeck in the control room, and unseen by him, all was silence and expectancy, each man in his own place, concentrating on his own task in an effort to distract himself from the tension; the Chief watching the depth gauges, the planesmen making minute adjustments to keep the boat level, the Second Lieutenant waiting at the 'fruit machine' to receive the firing data Lauterbeck would pass down.

Still no asdic, the turbine noises growing fainter, and moving aft.

'Flood Tubes One to Four.'

They were inside the screen, able now to choose their targets.

'Up periscope.'

For the first time Lauterbeck saw the carrier, turning towards him as he watched, two biplane aircraft visible on her deck. He made up his mind.

'Tubes One to Four ready. Bow caps shut.'

'Pass the word that we're going for the carrier. Flood Tube Five.'

Tube Five was the stern tube.

'Tube Five ready. Bow cap shut,' came the report.

Lauterbeck moved the periscope lever to lower the head a little, so that the next wave washed over it, temporarily blinding him. His shin had begun to ache. He moved his foot from its cramped position and worked it up and down while he waited for the lenses to clear. The carrier had come out of her turn, her bow wave creaming ahead, a thin plume of smoke rising from her vents, then streaming behind in the slipstream. One of the biplanes was beginning to move up her deck. She had changed course so that she could fly off her aircraft.

His voice, when he spoke, was quite steady. 'Open bow caps, Tubes One to Four. Enemy speed sixteen. Depth three. Angle on the bow five-zero left. Range two thousand.' The enemy's speed was guesswork, so he was going to fire a spread to make sure of hitting her; an aircraft carrier, even a converted merchant ship like this, was worth it.

In the fore ends men cranked the bow caps open. The Second Lieutenant punched the firing data into the fruit machine, producing angles which would be passed automatically to the torpedoes. Once it had been necessary to aim the entire boat, now it was all done by the machine.

'Tubes One to Four, bow caps open,' came from the fore ends.

'Tubes One to Four ready,' reported the First Lieutenant.

The carrier was inside the periscope lens, moving slowly towards the cross-wires. Lauterbeck's mouth was dry and his shin was beginning to cramp unbearably. Any second the British could sight the unmistakable wake of white foam left by the periscope head, or the invisible asdic pulses could fall on U–686's hull. The carrier's bow wave stood out in the darkness of the night, the biplane moving up the deck, then a burst of light as the take-off rockets fired, and she was airborne, rising away into the sky. Lauterbeck's hand moved to the firing lever, which would set off a red light in the fore ends to signal the Torpedo Gunner's Mate to fire. At last the carrier's bow cut the cross-wires. He yanked the lever towards him.

'Tubes One to Four, *los!*'

There was a whoosh as one by one the torpedoes left their tubes in a rush of compressed air. A moment later their electric motors would start and propel them at thirty-five knots towards their target.

'Tubes One to Four fired.'

'Shut all bow caps. Down periscope. Shut off for depth-charging. Sixty metres.'

The watertight doors slammed shut, dividing the boat into a series of separate compartments. U–686 began to descend. The Chief had not yet managed to catch a trim after firing and she was reluctant to level out at the required depth. Better a little deep, though, than to rise out of control to the surface because the boat was suddenly five tons lighter. The seconds ticked away. The hydrophone operator took off his headset, an explosion would have blasted out his eardrums.

The third torpedo of the spread struck *Crusader* on her port side, just forward of the boiler room, tearing a hole a few feet below the waterline and exploding inside one of her merchant ship's open holds, now partially divided and used for stores. The force of the explosion was carried upwards, so that from *Vittoria*'s bridge and from the Swordfish which had just taken off, the first indication was a flash of yellow fire and a column of debris rising from the flight deck abreast the island. *Crusader* was making seventeen knots, and the remaining torpedoes passed harmlessly ahead and astern, to sink unnoticed on the other side of the convoy.

Thurston, dazzled and half-deafened by the explosion, felt the ship's motion change, the steering becoming sluggish and imprecise as the hold flooded and she began to go down by the head.

'Pipe Emergency Stations. Close all watertight doors. Ask for some damage reports.'

'Aye aye, sir.' Vincent reached for the telephone.

Flames were crackling around the edges of the hole in the flight deck, men, stunned and immobile a moment ago, beginning to move towards it, beginning to run, hoses unreeling behind them, goaded by shouts from the flight deck chief petty officer.

'Come on. Don't just stand there! Fight that fucking fire!'

The second Swordfish was still on deck. The crew were scrambling hurriedly from their cockpit, the observer brought up short by the g-string which secured him to the aircraft and which he had forgotten to release.

In the hangar there was chaos, men dazedly picking themselves up from the deck plates to which they had been flung. One aircraft, and the men who had been working on it, had disappeared completely. A

Seafire had been blown off its undercarriage and hurled against the deckhead, then skidding up the deck in a screech of tortured metal before it came to rest on one of its folded wings.

For a moment after the explosion there was silence, and then someone began to scream. All the lights had gone out, and the remaining men could not tell where the sound came from, as it reverberated around the steel bulkheads of the compartment, slicing through their fuddled eardrums and into their brains, going on and on.

One man began to crawl across the deck plates, dazedly seeking the source of the screaming, noticed that something was running into his eyes, put his hand up to his head, and licked his finger to find that the stuff tasted salt. It took a long time for him to realise that it must be blood. He went on, pausing every few moments to wipe his eyes, and finding that he kept blundering into things which seemed not to be in their proper places any more. The fires that were burning lit up the hangar, but also cast deep shadows amid the litter of wrecked aircraft, so that his search took a long time. He hardly heard the Chief Air Fitter shouting at them all to find the fire extinguishers and get on with fighting the fire, all he heard was the screaming. It seemed to get no nearer, but quite suddenly, in one of the patches of shadow alongside the starboard bulkhead, he found the source. There was a bare foot sticking out from beneath the wrecked Seafire's wingtip, very pale in the shadow, then a couple of inches of pulped and bloody shin before the rest of the leg was lost beneath the wing. He looked up, and saw one of the engine mechanics, his legs and pelvis crushed beneath the wing, more of the wet, salty stuff spreading in a wide pool over the deck. He realised muzzily that he could never lift the aircraft off the man by himself, that he must go and find the Chief Air Fitter and tell him.

'Stay here,' he told the man, and began to crawl away once more, but the blood loss from his own wound had weakened him and before he had moved more than a few feet he settled gently onto his face in another patch of shadow.

The explosion had strained the bulkhead which divided the boiler room from the hold where the torpedo had struck, and the sudden inrush of water into the hold made the bulkhead bulge ominously for a moment, and then split through six feet of its height, so that a sudden torrent of freezing water poured into the boiler room. The Senior Engineer's first reaction was to tell his men to start shoring it up, but he realised at almost the same moment that none of them could work long enough

272

in water of that temperature to get any sort of shoring into place, and shouted at them to get the pumps going, in the boiler room itself. Then the Chief Engineer arrived, wearing pyjamas beneath his overalls, his hair rumpled from the pillow, and, to Duff's relief, took charge.

On the bridge the telephone buzzed. Vincent moved to answer it. 'Captain, sir, it's the Commander (E).'

'Captain, sir. This is Chief. I'm in the boiler room. The forward bulkhead in here's leaking, and I don't like the look of it at all. Could we slow right down to take some of the strain off it?'

'How bad is it?'

'Bad enough. It's over my knees already and the thing's bulging pretty ominously. I'll keep things going in here as long as I can but I don't think we can stay here much longer.'

There was the noise of rushing water in the background all the time Chief was speaking. If that bulkhead went the ship was lost. If it held, then even without power they could keep her afloat and get her back to Murmansk under tow.

'Revolutions for three knots,' he told Vincent. 'Bring her round to two-seven-two.'

'What about those two Swordfish, sir?' asked Commander (Flying), who must instantly have regretted his question as he changed immediately to uncharacteristic silence.

'Tell them they'll have to ditch.'

There was the fire still burning on the flight deck, men with hoses silhouetted against the dirty yellow flames, the heat in Thurston's face sharply contrasted with the icy air at his back, and for yards around the fire the flight deck was hummocked with splintered wood. There was little hope for the two Swordfish crews in a ditching; no Captain would risk stopping his ship while there was at least one U-boat inside the escort screen, and they could never reach land on the fuel they had left.

Stewart Grant came up on the TBS. 'Is that you, Bob? Are you all right?' Thurston found that, as before at such times, some circuit of his mind had switched off and the trained reflexes of thirty years in the Navy had taken over. He was thinking the problem through as he spoke. The U-boat was still out there, making up to sixteen knots if on the surface, eight if submerged, possibly reloading and positioning herself for a second attack at this very moment. *Crusader* was reduced to three knots, for as long as the boiler room staff could remain there; at the same time her steering was becoming erratic because of the weight of

273

water in the flooded hold. He remembered that petrol for the aircraft was stored in tanks in the ship's double bottom. The explosion had not touched it, but if the fire reached it the leaking bulkhead would be academic.

'I think we can keep her afloat, but it's going to come to a tow. How does she look from where you are?'

'Down by the head, and your flight deck looks like something by Henry Moore. Can you make Murmansk?'

'We can try.'

'All right, Bob, but don't try too hard. Get your men off if you need to. I'll leave *Vituperate* and *Vittoria* with you. That's all I can spare.'

It reminded Thurston uncannily of *Marathon*'s torpedoing fourteen months ago: the convoy gradually drawing away into the darkness, leaving them behind, with three hundred miles of ocean between them and safety, and the enemy bombers less than an hour's flying time away. But *Marathon* was not a cockleshell converted merchant ship, and she did not have several thousand tons of explosive and highly inflammable aviation spirit filling her double bottom.

Commander (Flying) finished speaking into his microphone. 'They want to try a landing, sir.'

Thurston thought for a moment. All the damage to the flight deck was ahead of the barrier, and the crews' chances, even on a landing approach made out of wind with the ship reduced to three knots, would be better than in a ditching. 'All right.'

Commander (Flying) began speaking to the Swordfish again. Somewhere to starboard there was another explosion, as a second torpedo found its target, a merchant ship in the outermost column. Was that the same U-boat, or was there a second inside the screen? Damn those bloody water layers!

'They're coming in now, sir.'

The fire on the flight deck was dying, but the night scene was still lit up, the batsman on his platform on the port side, the aircraft of the deck park which had been pushed hurriedly clear, the men still fighting the fire and, further off, the other ships of the convoy, a red pall of fire hanging over the torpedoed merchantman. The first Swordfish came in awkwardly, blown off her course continually by the crosswind, the batsman signalling frantically for her to move over to starboard. He waved her off, but she came in all the same, one wheel hitting the deck before the other so that the tyre burst, taking her still further over to port. The batsman threw himself into the nets alongside his platform.

The aircraft bounced, came down a second time in a splintering of undercarriage, and pitched forward onto her nose. The crew half-climbed, half-slithered out, the gunner turned aside to be sick, the vomit freezing instantaneously. The flight deck party rushed up, began to manhandle the wreckage over the side, one man cheekily climbing up into the cockpit to seize what he could of the instruments, even in these circumstances, the flight deck chief petty officer roaring at him to come down.

Circling at one thousand feet, Sub-Lieutenant Wallace's crew waited tensely while the wrecked Swordfish was cleared away.

'Better hurry up. I don't fancy swimming for it on a night like this,' said Powell. 'And I don't fancy another trip to Russia either,' he added as an afterthought.

Kornilov was occupying himself with his radar, concentrating on the small sheet of green glass in front of him. Down below there was another explosion as a third ship was hit. Destroyers were swinging out of station, forsaking their shepherd's role to take up the hunt for U-boats.

'Looks a proper picnic, doesn't it?'

'And we're going to be down there in it in a minute.'

The exchange between Wallace and Powell had distracted Kornilov's attention from the radar for a moment. He concentrated once more, and there was a blip on the display that had not been there a second ago, right on the starboard side of the convoy, outside the larger blip that marked the burning merchantman.

'Bill, I've got something! Bearing oh-one-two.'

'Sure it isn't a lifeboat, Korny?'

Kornilov adjusted the gain, then minutely adjusted the tuning to find the best possible echo. 'It wasn't there just now, and it's the right size for a U-boat. Too big for a lifeboat, and moving too fast. How much fuel have we got?'

'About fifteen minutes. Do you think it's worth a look?'

'Anyway, I don't fancy landing crosswind with the cans on board, not the way you land this kite,' said Powell. He pulled himself up out of his seat, the freezing slipstream battering his upper body so that he had to brace himself against his Vickers gun with his hands. 'There he is! Trying to run for it on the surface. Just on the other side of that burning ship.'

'Sure it's a U-boat?'

'Of course I'm fucking sure!'

Wallace put the Swordfish into a sharp turn to starboard, pushed the throttle forward so that the old aircraft's speed began to build up

275

towards the maximum. 'Tell the ship we're attacking. We'll go in low, over the top of that lame duck, and hope he doesn't see us.'

Another of the escorts had swung out of position and was heading towards the U-boat from the other direction. Two others seemed to be co-operating in a creeping attack on a second with asdic. *Crusader*, marked out from the rest by her distinctive shape and the now-sunken fire on her deck, was falling behind the convoy now, a lonely sight in the vast expanse of the ocean.

The Swordfish swept over the burning ship, a hundred and fifty feet up. There was the U-boat, its course taking it directly away from them, the long foredeck knifing through the gentle swell and sending spray back towards the conning tower as she moved away at her maximum speed.

'Running for it,' muttered Powell.

Wallace kicked the rudder to bring it round a little to port, at the same moment as the cannon on the U-boat's bandstand opened up. A shell went through the fabric of the port wing, jolted the Swordfish from her course.

There was a gurgling noise in Wallace's headset, then a shout from Powell, 'Bill, Korny's hit!' He glanced round, saw Kornilov slumped against the side of the cockpit, head hanging over, dark blood coming from his mouth. Coldly, Wallace straightened the aircraft out. There was another jolt, a lurch downwards as something else struck the engine and hot oil spurted back into his face. He pushed his goggles up, shifted himself to one side, but the oil had found its way into his eyes and he couldn't see. The U-boat was still firing, in counterpoint to the staccato rattle of Powell's machine gun. Something else hit the aircraft. He was blinking continually to try to clear his vision, rubbing his eyes with the sleeve of his flying jacket. There was the U-boat, filling the sights, barely visible through the oil. His thumb pushed the trigger home, the aircraft leapt as the depth charges fell away. He pulled the stick back, trying to climb away from the U-boat, but the engine was firing unevenly now, clanking as its oil supply ran away, and would not respond. He glanced round again. Kornilov had not moved, his head lolling back and forth in the slipstream, blood frozen in trickles on his chin and on the yellow scarf he was wearing at his neck. Powell was standing up, leaning out to fire his Vickers past the tailplane. Wallace's eyes were full of oil and tears, stinging painfully from the oil so that he automatically screwed them shut, dreading the moment when he would have to open them again.

'Bill!' Powell was shouting into his headset.

276

Blindly, Wallace pulled the stick back, trying desperately to get the Swordfish into the right attitude for ditching. For a few seconds she skimmed inches above the wave crests, then the main wheels hit the water, and the aircraft flipped over onto its back. Wallace found himself suddenly submerged beneath the icy water, upside down, still strapped tight into his seat. His hand groped for the release box of his harness, but already his fingers were too numb to feel it. The aircraft was sinking, carrying him down, the water turning grey, then to black around him.

Powell had released his G-string as the Swordfish hit the water. His head struck the butt of the Vickers gun, swinging wildly now that his hands were no longer there to steady it. The shock of the cold water jerked him back to consciousness. He began to claw his way out, realised vaguely that the aircraft was upside down and he must go down before he could go up, but he did not know which way was down. His legs seemed to be caught under the cockpit coaming. He kicked, finding that his flying boots made holes in the fabric, struck out with his arms. The aircraft was moving up and down with the motion of the sea, so that nothing was in the same position for more than a second. His legs came clear, he struck out towards the surface, but the cold was paralysing his limbs, and his heavy clothing hampered his movements, and down beneath the dark water he could not tell where the surface was. But the water's buoyancy carried him upwards, and at last, when his chest seemed about to explode, his head broke surface, alongside the wrecked aircraft. By blind instinct he reached out, got an arm across the fuselage, steadying himself while he gasped in great lungfuls of air, then began very slowly, his flying boots slipping back all the time, to claw his way onto the fuselage and up towards the tailplane, still standing out of the water. He kicked out, made holes in the fabric, found precarious footholds on the cross-members as they were exposed, the tail bucking up and down, moving further down towards the water under his weight. With a last effort he got one forearm over the tailwheel, then the other, hung on, and found himself praying.

'Lost contact with Wallace's aircraft,' Commander (Flying) reported. 'He said he was attacking, then nothing.'
   'Keep trying.'

Still maintaining his precarious hold on the Swordfish's tail, Leading Airman Powell saw with mounting horror the U-boat surface a hundred yards away, and her gunners spill out of the hatches, take up their positions, and the gun barrels themselves elevating. He wondered whether he should simply let go, and give himself up to the sea, but something kept him holding on, and it was not from the U-boat that the gunfire came. A round landed in the water on the other side of the U-boat, sending up a column of spray, starkly white against the dark of the night. The U-boat's guns were training, coloured blobs of tracer emerging from their muzzles. There was another waterspout, this time at his back. The British ship was finding the range, bracketing the target and then halving the bracket with each round. The next round would go over him, but the one after that would probably get him, even if the fire from the U-boat didn't.

'Captain, sir. There's something out there!' George Thurston shouted.

'Of course there is. There's a bloody great U-boat out there and I'm going to sink it!'

The Officer of Quarters on *Vittoria*'s forward gun dropped his night binoculars onto his chest, turned to shout towards the bridge, 'Sir! It's that Swordfish, and . . . There's one of the crew there, sir. Hanging onto the tail. Permission to cease firing, sir?'

'What do you mean, cease firing, *Mr* Cronin?' Haldane shouted back. 'You want me to let that U-boat get away?'

'No, sir. But,' the young officer's voice rose higher as he wrestled with conflicting demands, 'we can't go on firing with our man there.'

'Don't you argue with me, Mr Cronin! Carry on firing and I'll deal with you in the morning!'

Cronin stood still for a moment, facing his captain, one hand on his binoculars, torn in two directions.

'Carry on firing, Mr Cronin, or I'll see you hang!'

Cronin stood stock-still, jaw set. The gun's crew at his back had turned round, intent on the confrontation between Captain and Sub-Lieutenant. George tore his eyes away for a moment, threw a glance at the dark blob clinging to the Swordfish's tail, suddenly filled with relief that the responsibility to continue firing or not to fire was not his.

'Making water in the fore ends, Herr Kapitän!'

'Making water in the motor room, Herr Kapitän!'

The damage reports were coming through, all of them damning. U–686 could not dive, only one of her diesel engines had started when she surfaced, there were leaks being reported from every major compartment. And there was the British destroyer out there, finding the range, getting closer with every round. She lurched, the damaged bow dropping away. Lauterbeck shouted an order down the voicepipe, trying to keep her on a straight course, trying to build up speed to get out of trouble. But the British destroyer had the legs of a U-boat even when the U-boat was not damaged and with only one engine serviceable. Knopf had gone aft to see if anything could be done with the damaged engine. Now he appeared on the bridge, his overalls soaked to the waist.

'No good, Herr Kapitän. She's going.'

'She's definitely going?'

'Jawohl, Herr Kapitän.' Knopf's heels came together.

Another round landed, much closer this time. Lauterbeck could see the white-faced English boy still clinging to the wreckage of his aircraft, his own gunners, expertly hosing tracer out of the dark sea towards the destroyer, another destroyer coming up, muzzle flash coming from her guns.

'Making water in the control room, Herr Kapitän!'

His mouth was dry, his mind filled with regret as he gave the order. 'Abandon ship.'

Knopf turned towards the hatch. 'Scuttling charges, Herr Kapitän.' He dropped away down the ladder, even as the rest of the crew began to come up.

The impact of another explosion threatened to shake Powell from his perch. He clung on, despairing now. It wasn't fair, being killed by his own people like this. It just wasn't fair.

'Get me a white flag!' U–686 was sinking, listing over to starboard, her bow going down all the time. Knopf was setting the scuttling charges which would ensure she did not fall into enemy hands. His battle was over, it was time now to save his men. 'Get me a white flag!' he shouted into the conning tower hatch, then remembered his own gunners were still firing.

'Cease firing!'

The petty officer commanding the gun crews looked at him as though he was mad, then discipline asserted itself once more. He came to attention, the loader on the bandstand aft straightened up, one end of the ammunition belt still in his hands, the brass of the rounds gleaming dully. Men were coming up out of the hatches. Lauterbeck moved aside to let them past him. Someone pushed a large white bundle into his hands.

'Wardroom tablecloth, Herr Kapitän,' he said breathlessly. 'All I could find.'

Lauterbeck extended his arms, so that the cloth opened out in front of him, then raised it high so that the brisk wind tugged at it, tried to pull it from his hands. On the white cloth he could see many dark stains, marks of spilled coffee, tomato juice, the trivial accidents of U-boat life. He lashed the cloth to the periscope standard by its corners, watched it stand out straight in the wind. He remembered the precious Enigma machine, shouted down the conning tower for someone to bring it up.

He smelt chlorine gas, sniffed deeper to make sure. There was sea-water in the batteries, reacting with the battery acid to create the choking gas. The men were jumping into the sea around him, some preferring to cling onto the casing until the last possible moment, the First Lieutenant standing in front of him, nursing the wooden box containing the Enigma machine against his chest. The First Lieutenant rested the box on the bridge surround, wrenched the machine out of its housing, took it in both hands and dropped it into the sea, then hurled the spare code wheels overarm as far as he could.

'Permission to fall out, Herr Kapitan?' Then he was swinging his legs one by one over the surround and dropping straight down into the water. The tide of men was diminishing. He did not know how many men were in the water, how many on the casing, how many might still be trapped below. He put his head down into the hatchway, took in a lungful of chlorine which made his eyes water, shouted at Knopf and the Petty Officer Telegraphist to come up. He realised that the firing had stopped, that the two destroyers were steaming straight towards him from different directions, and were much closer now.

The telegraphist appeared, bare-headed, hair neatly slicked down with brilliantine, or was it wet with seawater? 'I got the signal off, Herr Kapitän. Told them we'd hit the carrier too.' Then he too was gone, and Lauterbeck found himself counting heads, heads in the water, men crowded together on the casing, their ankles covered by water. But no Knopf. He shouted into the conning tower again.

'Chief, are you there?' Knopf was more than just a good chief engineer. He and Lauterbeck had grown up together in the same Bavarian village; Knopf had gone into the regular Navy while Lauter-beck had joined the Merchant Service and become one of only a very few men to work his way from ERA to a commission. Lauterbeck had pulled strings shamelessly to have him appointed to U–686, he could not leave him now. 'Franz!' he shouted this time, but still there was no answer. He could hear splashing below him, but was it Knopf coming back, or merely the sound of the water coming in? He pulled the towel that was round his neck up over his nose and mouth, dropped into the conning tower, landing in eighteen inches of water. In the control room the emergency lighting was still on, casting a ghostly red glow over the rows of smashed gauges and the rising level of water. The watertight doors were open, flung back and swinging gently on their hinges. He splashed his way towards the first of them, and then saw Knopf coming through, staggering, like a drunken man. Wordlessly, Lauterbeck grabbed him by the shoulder, propelled him towards the ladder, then got behind him, desperately pushing him up from below. Knopf was very heavy, all the time swaying backwards on the ladder and threatening to fall back on top of him. But at last Knopf's head broke through the upper hatch, there was a final shove at Knopf's backside and a great indrawn lungful of fresh night air. Lauterbeck pushed Knopf over the side and into the water as the boat gave another lurch and began to settle by the bow. One of the destroyers was close by now, moving slowly through the water, scrambling nets hanging down her side, towards the wreckage of the Swordfish which still floated above the surface, the solitary airman still stubbornly clinging on, some of his own men swimming towards her, shouting in a mixture of German and the few English words that some of them knew.

Powell was so numb now from cold and exhaustion that he did not move from the tailplane when *Vittoria*'s bow nosed in alongside him. Someone reached out from her rails with a boathook, there was a tearing of fabric for inches along the fuselage before the head caught on one of the cross-members. A man leant out from the scrambling net, then jumped onto the fuselage below Powell, a line round his waist, got his knees on either side of the fuselage, waited a moment for the slack in the line to be taken up, then deftly passed a bowline beneath Powell's arms, pulling him away from his precarious hold to get the line around his chest which was hard up against the tail wheel. Powell shifted, tried to push him away with his elbows, but the man held on, got the line round him at last, gave a quick thumbs-up signal to the party at the rails.

Powell felt something try to wrench him away from the fuselage, redoubled his efforts to hold on, but his fingers had lost the last of their strength, scrabbled at the aircraft's fabric skin to no effect. He found himself dangling in the air a few feet above the sea and the Swordfish's tail which had been his refuge; he screamed, and then he was scraping against the rough hemp of the scrambling net and willing hands were taking his arms, grabbing handfuls of his clothing and pulling him the last few feet over *Vittoria*'s rails. He could hear shouting below him, shouting which he realised blearily was in German, saw other men in the water, dark mounds of inflated lifebelts around their chests, arms upraised, mouths open.

There were the men in the water, the U-boat captain in his white-topped cap stepping out from the casing, then the stern of the U-boat rising vertically as the enemy vessel made its final plunge, the twin screws on their spindly shafts standing out from the hull. A couple of miles away *Crusader* lay stopped and listing, the fire burning on her flight deck. George Thurston remembered his father, wanted very badly to know whether anything had happened, wished he could simply pick up the Aldis lamp and flash the quick message, *Dad, are you all right?*

Lieutenant-Commander Haldane was watching the scene in silence, hands thrust into his pockets, a tight-lipped smile of satisfaction on his face. A red-faced Sub-Lieutenant Cronin was standing in a corner of the bridge, waiting for Haldane to decree his immediate fate.

Haldane must have remembered George's presence, for he turned his head towards him. 'Go down to the iron deck and start sorting those prisoners out, Mr Thurston.'

'Aye aye, sir.'

George slid away down the ladder, found himself projected into a scene of chaos. There were men from *Vittoria* going down on the scrambling nets to haul the Germans up, the men in the water shouting in German and in broken English, men collapsed on the deck plates, gasping for air and shuddering in the cold air, the young British airman struggling to fend off the man who was trying to get him onto a stretcher.

'Gangway, sir!' someone shouted at his back. He stepped aside, let a stretcher go past, an oil-covered man who must have been a German lying on it on his side, knees drawn up to his chest, a small bright crucifix hanging out of the open front of his overalls, a scanty fluff of beard coating his cheeks.

'There's the skipper,' someone said.

The U-boat captain was treading water, his white cap still on his head against all the odds, but streaked black with fuel oil like his face, one of his arms round the chest of one of his men who seemed not to have a lifebelt. Someone flung a lifebuoy from *Vittoria*'s rails. The thing landed on the water just beyond the U-boat captain's fingertips. George saw him reach out with that hand, grasp the line which was attached to its rim.

'Right, haul him in!' a petty officer shouted.

Someone began to haul the line in, the U-boat captain's face disappeared behind a small bow wave of white spray, but he was still holding onto the other man. Two men went down on the net, twisting their feet through the hemp ropes before they leant outwards from one arm to grab a fistful of sodden clothing and start to pull them up. The other man was coming up, the Captain clinging to the lowest rungs, someone else going down to help him clear of the water.

'Come on, easy does it.'

But the other German was very heavy, and he was slippery with water and oil. One of the men on the net lost his grip on the man's hand, felt it slide out of his grip. He made another grab for him, caught a lump of his overalls, but the German had already gone from the other Englishman's grasp and he went on falling outwards, went into the water with a tremendous splash and did not come up. The other men were more careful with the U-boat captain, got their arms around his shoulders and climbed back up the net with his body slumped between them.

'Is that all of them, Mr Thurston?' Haldane called out from the bridge.

'Yes, sir, I think so.'

'Then get them below. I don't want them littering my decks any longer.'

Nothing was left of the U-boat now beyond a scatter of wreckage, and a patch of calmer water where the oil leaking from her tanks had spread. George wondered if this was the same boat that had torpedoed *Crusader*, which reminded him again of his father. Was he all right, or was the carrier already sinking, in which case he would be reduced, in a few minutes, to the same state as the German survivors now huddled into heaps of sodden clothing on *Vittoria*'s deck. He shuddered, thought that this was something that had never been voiced at Dartmouth.

'All right. Everybody out.'

The water in the boiler room had reached waist-height. Stoker Petty Officer Green spun the wheels which opened the boiler release valves to allow steam to escape and would prevent an explosion as the freezing water made contact with the hot boilers. Commander Hodgson picked up the telephone from its bracket and dialled the bridge extension. 'We're pulling out. I'll give you a full report when I get up.'

The ladder was on the far side of the compartment, standing vertically above the water. All the lights had gone out as the boilers were shut down and the only illumination came from a torch which someone had wedged into place on a platform above water level. One man was already on the ladder, pulling himself up it, away from the water, a second reaching out to grasp the lowest rungs.

Hodgson replaced the telephone and began to move, finding that the water had developed currents of its own as it surged through the machinery spaces, and was continually lifting him off his feet as he tried to wade through it. The water was shudderingly cold, its chill seeming to strike up into his heart. He reached out to grasp a length of pipe, hot a moment ago, but now stone cold, pulled himself forward, making his way along the side of one of the boilers and then round one end of it. But then there was a long empty space, perhaps twice the length of a man, with no handholds to steady him against the swirling water. Here too the water was higher, up to his chest now, because the compartments along the ship's starboard side had been flooded to bring the hole in the port side above the waterline. The cold was numbing his entire body, so that he could no longer feel the deck plates beneath his feet. The man ahead of him stopped, half-turned to one side, then a sudden pitch made him lurch and lose his footing, and the water swept him to the far end of the compartment. For a moment Hodgson could just make out his dark head in the torchlight; then he disappeared.

'Come on, sir!' a voice shouted from the base of the ladder.

Reluctantly, Hodgson let go of the pipe he was holding, which seemed now to be the only thing between him and the fate of the man he had just seen swept away. The current hit him at his second stride, trying to force him into the dark void to his left, where the stoker had just disappeared.

'Come on, sir,' the man on the ladder yelled. He was reaching out from the ladder, holding on with one hand, the other stretched out over the black water. 'Come on, sir. Grab my hand!'

Another step, the deck once more disappearing beneath him. He was spreading his arms out in front of him, trying to clear a way through the water.

'Come on, sir!' another voice shouted, and someone else was coming back down the ladder, stretching out towards him alongside the other. The ship rolled, and Hodgson was lifted off his feet, but the roll was to starboard and took him towards the ladder. Something grabbed hold of his collar, held him steady against the current, then something else came out and got hold of one of his hands, pulling him in against the ladder, then they were hauling him up, their breath coming out in sharp pants. 'By Christ, you're a weight!' The water reached the platform where the torch rested, and the last of the light in the boiler room was extinguished, but the dim glow of another torch was coming from the hatchway above. Hodgson's feet scrabbled for the rungs of the ladder, and he began to climb, the other two men above him, each with an arm around his shoulders to steady him. He was out of the water, climbing away from it, his numb hands also finding the rungs. 'Come on, sir. Nearly there.'

He could not see the man's face, but from the accent he realised it must be McCutcheon. 'Thanks, McCutcheon,' he said as his head came through the hatchway. 'Who's with you?'

'Murray, sir,' the other man said.

He was in the passage above the boiler room now. McCutcheon was pulling up the legs of his overalls and rubbing vigorously at the frigid flesh beneath. 'Thanks, McCutcheon,' he said again.

'Och, that's all right, sir. I dinna want to play a pibroch for you yet.' For some reason that made him feel like crying.

It was a little after 0500. Thurston, the Commander, Commander (E), Commander (Flying), Navigator and Warrant Shipwright were spread around the chartroom. It was the Warrant Shipwright who was speaking. He was a recalled pensioner in his fifties, a slow-speaking Lancashire man who had begun his working life as an apprentice farrier. 'I've had a look at that hole, sir. I haven't got a collision mat big enough to go over it. I could join two together but it's anybody's guess how long that bulkhead will hold.' He did not mention that he had gone over the side in a bo'sun's chair, and had several times been almost knocked out of it by the seas.

'Chief.'

'I agree with Mr Holmes, sir. That bulkhead could go at any time, and we can't get at it to shore it without pumping the boiler room dry. I've a diesel generator which I can connect up to get the pumps going, but that's not going to be much use unless Mr Holmes can get something over the hole.'

Whether the bulkhead would stand up to a tow would depend on the weather. Stopped, as she was, *Crusader* was a sitting target for another U-boat or for aircraft as soon as daylight came. The U-boat would have sent off a report, which would be passed to the Luftwaffe

285

at Kirkenes; even if it had not, the recce Kondor would be airborne and searching for the convoy as soon as dawn broke.

'Ask the Met Officer to come up.'

The ideal conditions would be a calm sea and low cloud, which would make it more difficult for the Luftwaffe to find them. But the Met Officer could only promise clear skies, with the wind rising towards Force Six within a few hours.

'Commander?'

'I don't know whether she'll tow, sir, but I'd rather not swim for it at this time of year.' There was a burst of laughter. He took a notebook from his pocket. 'Fourteen certainly dead, That's the number of bodies we've found so far. I haven't been able to do a muster yet, so there could be a good many more. All the fires are out. There are a couple of places which are still smouldering, but I'm having them watched, and I'm not expecting any more trouble from them.'

'Wings?'

'The one certain thing is that we can't fly anything off. We haven't enough deck left intact. One Swordfish still airborne, heading for Murmansk. She's got plenty of fuel so she should make it all right.'

Thurston was sitting on the chart table facing the rest, all unnaturally pale and ghostlike under the red lighting. The Commander (E), bundled up in layers of sweaters and an old pair of grey flannels, looked quite unlike his usual self. There was stubble on his chin, growing out white rather than grey, making him look like an old man. They were silent, all of them. They had all said their piece and the decision to be made was for Thurston as the Captain.

There were two courses open. He could signal the two destroyers to come alongside *Crusader* and start taking the men off, then when that was done have *Vituperate* which, unlike *Vittoria*, had not been converted as an escort and still had her torpedo tubes, sink her, and be steaming full ahead to catch up with the convoy before daylight brought the Germans back. Or he could try to get the ship back to Murmansk. *Connaught* had broken in two and gone down in three minutes, there had never been any hope of saving her. *Marathon* had stayed afloat through six days on tow, and survived a further air attack on the way, but she was a solidly built cruiser and still had steam to power the pumps. But *Crusader* was as valuable a ship as a cruiser, perhaps more so in the present climate, and even if only a converted merchantman was equally worth fighting for. And dammit, and there his professional detachment was lost, she was his ship, just as *Marathon* had been, and

286

he wasn't letting her go without a fight. He stood up from the chart table.

'We may not succeed, but we're going to give it a go. Jettison everything we don't actually need, and we'll get all surplus hands across to the destroyers.'

The work began in earnest. In the hangar the wrecked aircraft were one by one wheeled or pushed onto the lifts, and the lifts themselves raised painfully slowly by hand, several men on each of the vast wheels that powered them. On the flight deck more men manoeuvred them to the edge of the flight deck and over the side, to follow the aircraft of the deck park which had already gone. All over the ship men worked with a kind of maniacal glee to dismantle the equipment they had in some cases expended much labour over, carried it up onto the deck and threw it into the sea, their mattresses and bedding, the wardroom furniture, the ship's entire supply of aircraft depth charges. The boats too; there were enough Carley floats to take all the men if it came to it. *Vituperate* came alongside, *Vittoria* remained circling a couple of miles off, jackstays were rigged and non-essential personnel taken off, some with relief, others slightly shamefaced at departing to relative safety.

On the flight deck, a party under Mr Holmes's direction was at work on the collision mats, sewing them together with twine. There was no time for pretty or painstaking work. One man made a hole in the coarse fabric with a bradawl, a second shoved the needle through, moved his arm to its full extent to pull the thread taut. Another man followed close behind them, painting the join and the canvas on either side of it with hot tar kept molten by a brazier burning beneath the cask. It was a long slow job, made worse by the intense cold, which meant the men sewing the collision mats together needed to stop every few minutes to thaw their hands sufficiently to go on. Below decks the radar operators watched their displays, empty now that the convoy had moved away westwards beyond range of the sets, the asdic operators listened to the monotonous ping-pinging in their headsets, alert for the slightest suggestion of an echo, an echo which might simply come from a warm water layer somewhere beneath the surface, or from a U-boat manoeuvring itself into position to finish *Crusader* off.

'Cocoa, sir.' Spencer appeared on noiseless feet with a brimming fanny. 'I've been tellin' the lads not to worry, sir, you've 'ad plenty of practice at this.'

287

'That's not funny,' Thurston said in the quiet but incisive tone he rarely used towards Spencer.

'No, sir. I s'pose it isn't,' Spencer said after a moment of thought.

Spencer's mother had been bombed out a day or two before *Connaught* sailed for Gibraltar on her final convoy, and so Spencer had been on compassionate leave. Spencer had never asked Thurston about the sinking; it was something that went too deep.

'There's your cocoa, sir. You want to drink it while it's hot.' Thurston took the mug and raised it to his mouth, found himself yawning with weariness despite the twanging tension inside. Sub-Lieutenant Vincent was still on the bridge, though it was no longer his watch and Forrest had relieved him, standing against the bridge screen on the starboard side, paler than ever, his mouth set as though he was trying to hold something in. He looked back towards Thurston, past his shoulder and avoiding his eyes.

'It wasn't your fault, Mr Vincent.'

'No, sir,' Vincent said, for form's sake only, his eyes moving down to the deck plates.

'And this isn't your watch, and you can't stay here doing nothing, so go and get some more of the men working on getting the topweight over the side.'

'Aye aye, sir,' Vincent said, equally formally, then began to move away slowly, draggingly, towards the ladder and down to the flight deck.

34

Feldwebel Werner Hoffmann moved the Kondor into a gentle turn to port, then took his left hand off the control wheel and banged it on his knee in an effort to restore the circulation. From five thousand feet the surface of the sea, still dark grey in the pre-dawn light, was rippled like a length of grey cloth, flecked with white foam which made brief appearances and then disappeared.

'Nice morning,' commented Kurt Wagner, the Navigator, coming up alongside his pilot with his chart and a pencil. 'Pity it has to be so damn cold.'

'Won't be any warmer for the British.'

Wagner grinned. 'I should think Hans Lauterbeck's made it pretty hot for them. Wouldn't want to be in their shoes. Not once we've found them.'

'If they haven't sunk already.'

'They're sure it was that carrier?'

'Couldn't be more sure. They don't look like anything else floating.'

Hoffmann turned his head to look at the chart. 'That's where the U-boat got them?'

Wagner nodded. 'Our ETA ten minutes. Incidentally, Werner,' he glanced across the compass, 'you're half a degree off course.'

Hoffmann shook his fist at Wagner's retreating form. The crew had been briefed that Hans Lauterbeck in U–686 had torpedoed a British escort carrier during the night, and to be on the lookout for her in case she had not already sunk. It had been emphasised by the Intelligence officer, a bespectacled former lawyer from Frankfurt, that the carrier was a vital target, but Hoffmann did not need to be told. He had been flying long enough to remember the early days of 1941 when the Kondor had first been converted from civil airliner to long-range maritime bomber, and had for a few months ranged gloriously unchallenged over the Atlantic convoys. But the British had fought back, first building platforms onto their merchant ships and equipping them with rockets which would fire a clapped-out Hurricane into the air to deal with the intruder. Hoffmann could remember vividly the shock of suddenly seeing one of those Hurricanes in the air eight hundred miles out over the Atlantic, and even now had no idea how he had managed to evade the attack and get his aircraft home. Then the British had converted a captured German merchant ship, the *Hannover*, into an aircraft carrier. She was sunk by a U-boat on her second convoy, but more and more of them had been built, and their aircraft, and better anti-aircraft armament aboard the merchant ships and their escorts, had driven the Kondors from the Atlantic. Only here, in the far north, were they still operational, their role altered to long-range reconnaissance ahead of the bombers. Essential, but boring.

The sea was still empty, but reflecting the light of the rising sun as it came above the horizon. Hoffmann turned his head and saw Wagner clambering towards one of the windows. Wagner was a passionate photographer and had managed to get hold of a couple of precious reels of colour film with which he was trying to photograph sunrises and sunsets from the air. Hoffmann banked the aircraft gently to starboard to give him a better view, saw Wagner with one glove hanging from his teeth, making minute adjustments to the exposure, then a thumbs-up sign when he was satisfied.

'Did you get it?'

'I think so.' Wagner was zipping the camera carefully away inside his flying suit. 'Now let's find that ship.'

They were over the position from which the U-boat had reported the torpedo hit, but there was nothing to be seen. Of course, the ship had probably sunk by now, or the original position could have been wrong. The position given by the U-boat was merely the starting point. He turned the aircraft to port and began the square search, moving gradually outward from the position given. Time passed. He huddled deeper inside his flying kit, tried to stop his mind from wandering towards the leave he was due in a couple of weeks, the first in more than a year. He could cut a dash in his Luftwaffe blue uniform with its pilot's wings in front of all the girls in Celle, but how much more of a dash it would be if he could find the carrier and add an Iron Cross first class to the second class he already wore.

'Turn onto one-nine-zero,' came Wagner's voice in his headphones.

'Turning onto one-nine-zero.' He moved the control column to the left, pushed his left foot forward, too numb now to feel the rudder pedal beneath.

Ten more minutes crawled by, with nothing to occupy him except keeping the heavy Kondor on a straight course and making the ninety-degree turns to port in response to Wagner's instructions. It was becoming difficult to keep awake, he had stayed too long in the mess last night and the intense cold tended to fuddle him still further. He groped with one hand for his sandwich box, placed carefully against the hot air duct beside him, placed it between his knees and lifted the hinged lid, took out a large slab of bread and cheese and bit into it. He found his Thermos flask and poured himself a cup of coffee, ersatz coffee made from acorns of course – when the wing first moved to Norway it had been possible to get the real thing from Sweden, but no longer.

'Turn onto one-zero-zero,' Wagner's voice prompted.

Hoffmann gulped down a mouthful of coffee, wedged the cup upright beside the throttles, then began the turn. The port wing went down, the sun came into his eyes, flooding the cockpit with light. He moved his head sideways to escape the glare, screwed up his eyes. The glare distracted him, so that the aircraft skidded a little in the turn and a few drops of coffee spilled over the edge of the cup. He levelled his wings, glanced at the compass and touched the rudder to settle the Kondor exactly into her new heading. Then suddenly there was a shout from Hans Steiger in the ventral gun position.

'I can see oil down there!'

'Are you sure?' Steiger was the newest member of the crew, and hadn't got his eyes in yet.

'Of course I'm sure! Right underneath us.'

Hoffmann slid the aircraft a little to starboard, banked the port wing down. The surface of the sea was much lighter now, pale grey flecked with shifting gold. But there was something there. Over an irregular zone, perhaps a few hundred yards across, the underlying colour was black; there were lighter patches which might have been wreckage dotted about over its surface.

'Must've sunk,' someone said disappointedly.

'No Iron Cross for you this time, Werner,' said Wagner.

Hoffmann moved the Kondor back into the previous heading, but hardly had he done so than there was another shout from Steiger.

'There's more of it!'

This time there was no mistake. A long black streak, moving back and forth with the motion of the water, beginning quite close to the first, but disappearing away eastwards.

'Still afloat, and trying to make it back to the Kola.' Hoffmann altered course to line the Kondor up with the oil streak.

'There she is,' Hoffmann breathed.

There was the carrier's distinctive shape, listed over to port, the smaller form of a destroyer close by, a second destroyer circling further off.

'What sort of speed do you think she's making?'

Wagner screwed up his eyes and studied the carrier's wake. 'She's not making any speed,' he said in excitement. 'She's stopped. Absolutely bloody sitter.'

'What's our position, Kurt?'

But Wagner was already pencilling it down, then tearing off the sheet and carrying it aft to the wireless operator who unclamped his morse key and began tapping out the message.

It had taken longer than expected. Dawn was already coming by the time the patch was completed and ready to be manoeuvred into place. Then the Commander and his party had first to pass the bottom lines, lowering two weighted loops of line into the sea at the bow, and gradually working them aft below the keel, past various snags which had not been there before the torpedo struck. Then one end of each line had to be attached to a corner of the patch, and the patch gradually paid out over the port side into the sea while men hauled the lines in on the other side of the ship to manoeuvre it over the hole. It was slow work, with many false starts, and it was not yet near completion when the Kondor appeared, remaining mockingly out of range.

It would not be long now. The Kondor would have signalled *Crusader*'s position to the bomber wing at Kirkenes, and the Germans would be over them in an hour or less, even if they were not already airborne in search of the rest of the convoy. Thurston found himself glancing over the starboard side of the bridge at the grey-blue water directly below. How long did they say a man could survive in that? Three minutes? Five minutes? And not much longer on a Carley float in wet clothes in an air temperature forty degrees below freezing. Most of the men had already been taken off, thank heavens; there were only the guns' crews, some of the engineers and stokers, the shipwright's party and others whose services would be required if the ship was got going again, and apart from the engineers they were all on deck.

'Radar . . . Bridge.'

'Bridge.'

'Large formation of enemy aircraft bearing one-six-oh, sir.'

'Sound Action Stations.' Thurston found his voice was quite steady; the training again.

There was a small grim smile playing across the Navigator's face. '*Ave, Caesar, morituri te salutant.*'

'*Reddite quae sunt Caesaris Caesari, et quae sunt Dei Deo,*' and then, when Beveridge looked blank, '*Render unto Caesar the things which are Caesar's, and unto God the things which are God's.*'

Thurston lifted his binoculars, screwed up his eyes behind them to counter the glare off the sea. There they were, just crossing the horizon to the south, the laden JU 88s and the wicked little ME 109s which escorted them, though there was no need for fighter escorts now, he thought a little bitterly. 'Pipe all personnel on deck to take cover.'

The tannoy crackled into life. 'D'ye hear there. All personnel on deck take cover. All personnel on deck take cover.'

'Tell *Vituperate* to get herself clear.'

The Chief Yeoman picked up his Aldis lamp and began to flash the signal. *Vituperate* flashed a brief acknowledgement and heeled away to starboard, showing the black paint along her waterline and the red lead below it. Thurston had time to count nineteen bombers in a tidy rectangular formation, their twin engines making their familiar unsynchronised throbbing, quite different from the sound made by British aircraft and somehow far more sinister, the fighters weaving several thousand feet above them, just below the thin high layer of grey cloud which covered most of the sky.

The destroyers' 4.7 inch guns opened fire, but the enemy were still out of range of *Crusader*'s 40mm Bofors and 20mm oerlikons. *Vittoria*'s fire was ragged, each of her guns firing independently in local control. *Vituperate* still had director control and with double the number of guns was putting up a small but determined barrage, four flashes coming from the muzzles and four puffs of grey smoke appearing in the sky simultaneously.

'Open fire.'

'Open fire, sir,' Forrest checked back in clipped Dartmouth tones.

Crusader's anti-aircraft guns opened up with their distinctive rattle, throwing a curtain of fire into the sky above the ship. Thurston glanced over the side of the bridge to see a Bofors crew in one of the sponsons which bulged out from the ship's side beyond the overhang of the flight deck, tin hats and white anti-flash hoods obscuring their faces, the director layer at his gyro sight, other men guiding the ammunition belts which snaked across from the storage racks, the twin barrels tracking smoothly round to port and rising towards the vertical, Canadian voices passing orders. Despite the noise of the firing, Thurston was aware of a strange, almost unearthly quietness. The flight deck was empty of men, the carrier herself stopped, so that her only movement was a gentle rocking on the swell and all he could do was watch in impotence as his ship came under attack. Smoke appeared from the starboard engine of one of the leading bombers. A stick of bombs fell one by one from its belly and dropped harmlessly into the sea, then the aircraft banked sharply to starboard out of the formation.

Nobody on *Crusader*'s bridge spoke; there was none of the usual excitement mingled with relief at hitting one of the enemy, only clenched teeth and fear clawing with icy talons at the stomach, at the same time a desire to simply get this over with, whatever the result. Then the bombs began to fall, aimed now by an unknown German with his eye glued to his bombsight, not simply jettisoned from a damaged aircraft, falling vertically from the undersides of each aircraft. The guns were firing, and another bomber went down, but all that was far away; all eyes were on the bombs, the black cylinders, at first small, but growing inexorably larger, seeming to come straight for them until they went into the sea and exploded in columns of yellow water. The puffs of smoke from exploding anti-aircraft ammunition brought a slight sense of protection, but in the sky directly above *Crusader* there was nothing save the enemy. There was a near miss, a bomb which hit the sea a few yards from the already damaged port side, sending tons of water cascading over the empty flight deck and holing the ship's side above the waterline.

One of *Crusader*'s Bofors, or perhaps the round came from one of the destroyers, must have hit a bomber as it passed above the carrier, for there was a flash of yellow at the rear of her fuselage, a rush of black smoke, the tail broke away, and the remains of the aircraft dived vertically into the sea. Then there was another aircraft, its bomb doors yawning open and a stick of bombs dropping from its belly, seeming to fall for an age before they reached the ship, growing larger and larger. Then the bombs were exploding all around and water was crashing onto the decks. For a moment it was impossible to tell whether any had actually hit the ship, but there was smoke rising from a fresh hole in the flight deck abaft the island and almost as Thurston realised that a bomb had made that hole there was an explosion. *Crusader* gave a violent lurch to starboard, there was a flash of fire on the deck and debris shooting up from below, a wave of hot air in his face. As the noise of the blast dispersed there was the unmistakable sound of steel giving way somewhere beneath his feet and then tons of water forcing their way inside the ship, another lurch to port, and with that came the certain knowledge that they would not save the ship now.

'Pipe, "All hands muster on the flight deck. Prepare to abandon ship." ' But this raid might only be the first wave, so a caveat had to be added. 'Guns' crews stand fast.'

But there was a reluctance to give the final order, which would mean the end of the ship and, the thought which always lurked at the back of the mind, a court martial if he abandoned her prematurely when she could have been saved.

The explosion had cut off the ship's emergency power supply and below decks there was only darkness and chaos, the sounds of water coming in seemingly from every side, the ship canted over onto her port side, ladders blown away, hatches buckled, and nothing was in its usual place any longer, so that it was difficult even to know which was the way to the outer world.

Commander Hodgson, Lieutenant Duff and a party of junior engineers and stokers had been working in the engine room to keep the auxiliary machinery going, and shoring the bulkhead which divided them from the flooded boiler room and which had also begun to bulge outwards as the pressure of water against it increased. The ship's lurch to port threw Hodgson off balance, so that he went staggering crazily across the engine room in pitch darkness. He put out his hands to something, then recoiled as his palms made contact with hot metal. Another lurch, he half-turned, tried to recover, and then, completely disorientated now, went staggering off in another direction, finally fetching up against something solid yet quite soft. His arms went out again, wrapped themselves around the man in front of him.

'Who's that?' the man asked out of the darkness.

There was an odd kind of relief at finding someone else there. Hodgson drew back carefully, searched for and finally found a handhold against which he could steady himself. At the same moment he heard the first sound of water coming in, not a trickle, but far louder and higher pitched as it played over a bare metal surface somewhere around them. With the other hand he groped in his pocket for his torch, thought in a moment's despair that he might have forgotten to transfer it to this set of overalls a few hours earlier. But there was relief as his fingers closed around the torch barrel, then again as he pushed the switch forward and a thin beam of light came from it. Still holding onto the length of piping he swung the torch in a rapid arc around the compartment. The deck plates beneath them now lay at an angle of thirty degrees, the baulks of timber against the damaged bulkhead had shifted, so that a gap had appeared, from which was coming a thin jet of water, perhaps half an inch in diameter, at first horizontal, then curving downwards in a gentle parabola to meet the deck plates against which it continued to sing. Above the sound of the water was a continuous creaking as the shoring slowly shifted under the pressure from the other side of the bulkhead. From somewhere else came the hiss of escaping steam, and a couple of times his torch beam caught a column of white rising into the darkness above their heads.

'Everybody out,' he found himself ordering for the second time in a few hours.

Some men were already on the ladders, others, less certain of the situation, or perhaps frozen for a moment by the suddenness of the thing, had been waiting for orders. Most now began to move, others remained where they were, one continuing to stare at the gauge in front of him.

'Come on!' Duff shouted. 'Move!'

The ship shifted again, still settling, the jet of water suddenly doubled in size, reached Duff, forced him against a set of pipes which he had been standing next to. The creaking of the timbers rose louder for a moment, then a tide of white water forced its way through the bulkhead, coming in a waist-deep swirl all around the engine room, icy cold as it had been in the boiler room. The tide picked Hodgson up and the torch went out. He was carried several yards before he could stick out a hand to something and save himself. He found himself thinking, inconsequentially, that twice in one night was a bit much. The water was rising much faster than it had in the boiler room, the deck already gone from beneath his feet when he tried to find it again. Once more the engine room was pitch black. He had no idea where he was in relation to the ladder. He could hear shouting. The hatch had jammed and the men on the ladder were struggling to force it open, to attract the attention of anyone who might be on the other side.

Hodgson kicked off his boots, began to swim slowly and awkwardly towards the shouting, finding that machinery barred his way and he had to follow it by feel and to work his way around it. And all the time the cold was eating into his body, paralysing him, so that it would have been quite easy simply to let go and allow the tide of water to carry him away. Something washed up against him, carried by the water, something that could only be another man's body. 'Who's that?' But there was no answer, and in the darkness he could not see whether the man was trying to swim, or whether his face was in the water and he was already dead. Above him the other men were still hammering at the hatch, he could hear Duff's Aberdonian shouting above the rest, much closer now, because the rising water was carrying him inexorably towards the top of the compartment.

Someone began to scream and he heard a single brutal shout from Duff, 'Whisht, ye daft gype!' Then there was a rush of cold air on his face, and he realised dully that the hatch must be open. But he was almost too tired to care, even when the light came down into the compartment and began shining across the water around him, the last few rungs of the ladder rising above it, only a few yards away. He struck out, but then there was desolation as the light disappeared. The water was very near the top of the engine room, only a couple of feet from the deckhead, but the pressure of air trapped in there was holding the water back. A pair of white overall legs appeared on the ladder, then the legs disappeared into the water and there was a torso and a head. Someone was pushing himself off from the ladder and starting to swim. Hodgson found himself being grabbed from behind, turned over onto his back.

'Come on, Chief,' then the man was slowly towing him back towards the ladder. 'It's all right, Chief, I've got you.' He realised that it was Duff's voice, then his eyes closed, and he was vaguely aware of being hauled up the last few rungs of the ladder and out into the passage above, where once more there was darkness except for the bobbing beams of torches.

'Thanks, Wullie,' he managed to say.

Because of the power failure there had been no damage reports. Thurston had told *Vittoria* to come alongside and stand by to take the remaining men off. But it was difficult to tell how long they had; he could only listen to the noises from below, breathe the acrid black smoke which was welling up from the fire. The other men on the bridge were standing in their places, waiting for his orders, the guns' crews were still closed up, firing at the bombers' tails as they retreated.

A tall figure in drenched white overalls came up from below, his face streaked with black fuel oil. 'Engine room flooded, sir. I think's she's going.'

Thurston realised it was Duff. 'Where's Chief! Is he all right?'

'Ach, the puir old man. We're just drying him off, sir. He's all right.' Thurston turned to Forrest. 'Pipe "Abandon ship" then. Get some lines rigged and the rafts cut away. Chief Yeoman?'

'Sir?'

'Ask *Vittoria* to come alongside and start taking us off.'

An incongruous formal touch. *Vittoria* was someone else's ship, so you could only ask, not tell.

'Abandon ship' was being piped across the flight deck, petty officers shouting the words through cupped hands. The second time he had given the order, and the last time *Connaught* had already broken in two

297

and there had been time for only a few men to get away from her before she went down.

Vittoria was turning to starboard, her bow nosing in towards the carrier's side, inching her way underneath the overhang of the flight deck. Duff was still standing on the bridge, shivering violently as the Arctic wind cut through his sodden overalls.

'Get yourself and your men off, Senior. Well done.'

Crusader shifted again as the destroyer came up against her flank. Ropes dropped from the rails towards *Vittoria*'s decks, and men began to move down them, letting go and dropping the last few feet. The Warrant Shipwright appeared on the bridge. Thurston felt a moment's doubt about his decision.

'She is going, Mr Holmes?'

'Yes, sir. She won't last much longer. Once the bulkheads start to go.' He was silent for a second. 'The patch wouldn't have made much difference, sir, not with another bomb.'

'I know. But at least we tried.'

'Yes, sir.' Mr Holmes drew himself up to an immaculate salute, waited for Thurston to return it, and went away down the ladder.

35

'Off you go, Spencer. I shan't be needing you now. You too, Metcalfe.'

Metcalfe slid away down the ladder, relieved to be released, but Spencer stood still.

Thurston wondered whether Spencer had misinterpreted his words. 'I won't be needing any more of your cups of tea for the time being.'

'Sir,' Spencer said under his breath, so that the Navigator and Forrest couldn't hear, 'you're not goin' to do anything silly?'

He knew what Spencer meant, and glossed over it. 'Get a move on, Spencer. You're making the place look untidy.'

Spencer grinned, then patted the pocket of his duffel coat. 'I got your gongs and miniatures in here, sir. And your gold cufflinks. Been hanging on to them since that torpedo hit us. Just in case.'

'Thanks. But you needn't have bothered.'

'That's okay, sir.' Spencer reached into his pocket, pulled out the medals so that the dulled bronze cross rested in the palm of his hand. 'Don't want you havin' to go to the King and tell him you've lost it.' Spencer was still grinning, still maintaining his particular brand of humour even in these extreme circumstances.

'Get away with you, Spencer,' Thurston raised his voice to a mock quarterdeck roar, 'and get yourself over the side before I throw you overboard myself!'

'Aye aye, sir.' Spencer went away, still grinning happily.

There had been less than a hundred men left on board when the bombers came, less than a hundred alive; there was no way of knowing how many more might still be below, dead, or perhaps trapped in isolated compartments by the flooding or the fire. Most of the men still on board were on the flight deck, only the guns' crews and bridge personnel were still at their stations. The Kondor was still circling, just beyond range of the guns, continuing to report *Crusader*'s situation to its base, so this respite from the enemy would not last long. In all probability a second wave of bombers was already on its way. Thurston saw one man carrying something slung over his back, recognised Stoker McCutcheon with his bagpipes, watched him clamber over the rails, push the bagpipes out of the way with one hand, then take hold of the rope. Then all he could see was McCutcheon's head and upper body, almost horizontal as he braced his feet against the hull, then he disappeared entirely. A moment later the two ships came apart, and McCutcheon came into view once more, standing grinning on *Vittoria*'s foredeck, jerking a thumb at the men above him at *Crusader*'s rails, an ironic cheer coming up around him.

Metcalfe reached the rails, looked around for Spencer, expecting him to be following, but there was no sign of him. He wondered whether to go back to find him, then decided simply to wait until he arrived. He wasn't looking forward to this. He had always hated heights, had once ripped a large chunk of skin out of the palm of his hand sliding down a rope at school. Even with the ship listing over to port, it was a long drop onto *Vittoria*'s deck, a deck which was going up and down all the time, one moment hard up against the carrier's side, the next, leaving a chasm of cold black water opening up as the swell carried her away.

'Come on, you. Don't just stand there. We haven't got all day.'

Metcalfe, lost in thought, took a moment to realise that the petty officer was speaking to him. He opened his mouth to say he was waiting for Spencer, then thought better of it.

'Come on. Get on with it. You'll be wanting me to hold your hand next.'

Metcalfe looked around again for Spencer, but there was still no sign of him. The petty officer was watching, teeth set, ready to begin haranguing him once again. Reluctantly, he put one hand on the stanchion, one foot on the bottommost rail, swung the other over. The rope was below him, snaking across the flight deck from one of the rings set into the planking for picketing aircraft, then turning in a right angle and disappearing between his feet.

The petty officer put the rope into one of his hands. Now that Metcalfe was on the other side of the rails, about to make the descent, his tone became almost fatherly. 'All you need to do is get a good grip on the rope, get your feet braced, and just walk down the ship's side. Dead easy. Then you just wait until *Vittoria*'s underneath, and drop off the bottom. Got that?'

Metcalfe took hold of the rope with both hands, balanced on the lip. He felt a little sick, wished this was all over and he was safe aboard the destroyer. On either side of him other men were going down similar ropes, seemingly without trouble. He found himself envying them.

'Come on; the rest of us are getting cold standing here.'

Involuntarily, his eyes strayed downwards. How far below him was the water? Twenty feet? Perhaps more. *Vittoria*'s bow was gradually coming into his vision. That made him feel a little better. He leant his body outwards, so that the rope came taut, then moved one foot down. Another breath, and the other foot moved down from the comforting solidity of the deck edge.

'That's the way, son. Just keep on walking down and you'll be okay.'

But his seaboots had smooth soles and kept slipping on the wet steel plates, his gloves had always been a little too big for him and he found that the rope kept slipping through his hands. His head was below the level of the catwalk now and he found himself terribly alone, the whole world suddenly compressed into the wet rope in his hands, and the wet steel plates in front of him. A gout of spray came up as *Vittoria*'s bow nosed into the space beneath, soaking his legs and streaming down the ship's side, which had become concave and was moving inwards away from him. How much further? He looked up and saw faces clustered along the rails, Spencer's among them, but there was nothing which would have made him look down at the sea below him.

His feet slipped again, first one and then the other, and with awful suddenness he was swinging like a pendulum out from the ship's side and back again, trying to get his feet back onto the plates, but swinging away before he could find his footing. For a moment the swinging stopped, there was a second of relief, succeeded by terror as he realised that there was nothing but sea beneath him, then he felt his hands begin to slide. He tried to get a grip of the rope with his feet, work his way back up, as they had tried to teach him in PT during basic training. But the clumsy seaboots gave him no assistance, and the rope went on sliding through his hands, just as on that day at school, though this time he was wearing gloves and there was none of the tearing pain he remembered. He looked up beseechingly at the men at the rails, but they were too far away to offer any aid. His feet went off the end of the rope, and he could only hang on with his hands, but they wouldn't hold him either. He opened his eyes in mid-air, saw the high grey sides above him, moving ever closer as the sea brought the two ships together, a shaft of bright sunlight between them. Then the sun was blotted out, and there was an instant in which the whole world turned to pain, so that he never felt the icy cold as he hit the water.

The ship's list to port was increasing all the time, and the brisk wind was blowing the flames and smoke from the fire towards the island, so that the bridge was becoming untenable.

'Tell the guns' crews to fall out.'

One of the petty officers began going round the gun positions, moving awkwardly crabwise on the steeply heeling deck. Most of the men clustered at the rails had gone, there were only a few petty officers left. The starboard side guns' crews came up from their positions; most of the men from the port side had only to judge their moment and drop down from their sponsons, *Vittoria*'s deck only a few feet below them now.

The Commander came up from below.

'No one left below, Commander?'

'No, sir.' There was an uncharacteristic pause. 'Nobody whom I could find.'

Below decks the ship had been deserted, empty of men, and eerily silent. Canning had found himself bracing all the time for the moment when the silence would end, with the rending of metal and inrush of water which would mean the last bulkheads had started to go. But there was only the echo of his own footsteps, a watertight door left open and swinging heavily back and forth, coming up with an irritating clunk against the edges of its hatchway, the sounds of water far off, the only light the beam of his torch, producing strange shadows as it reflected off the bulkheads. In many parts of the ship there was no damage, but only signs of hurried departure: bunks in disarray, with blankets hanging from the metal frames, an open ditty box, with a scatter of creased family photographs on the deck alongside, a seaman's jumper with a good conduct badge half sewn on, the needle pushed into the blue cloth beneath and the loose thread wound round it.

The black smoke was swirling around them, irritating the lungs, making it difficult to see properly.

'Clear the bridge.' *Crusader* might stay afloat for some time yet before the bulkheads began to go, but she was heeling over onto her port side now, and she was no longer a ship, but only a pounded hulk. Yet there was still regret at giving an order which acknowledged that there was nothing left but to abandon her. Beveridge picked up the weighted canvas bag which contained the confidential books, and which he had brought up from the chartroom some time earlier, followed Forrest down the ladder, awkwardly, since the ship's list had now carried the ladder over beyond the vertical.

Thurston found himself alone on the bridge in a sudden stillness. There was the Kondor circling low down, close to the horizon, the fire burning on *Crusader*'s decks, colouring the light an unearthly yellow through the smoke. The destroyer was still alongside, her signal lamp beginning to flash, more slowly than usual, since all *Crusader*'s signal-men had gone now. But the signal was clear enough. *Radar reports large formation of enemy aircraft approaching.*

'Captain, sir, are you coming?' a voice shouted from the flight deck. It was Beveridge, the canvas bag resting against his left foot.

His choice was quite straightforward. He could go over the side with the rest, or he could stay with *Crusader* at her end in the good old-fashioned way. Beveridge was standing there, legs straddled against the list, steadying himself with a hand on the rails. Dark shapes appeared in the sky above the southern horizon. The German bombers were coming back, the throbbing of their unsynchronised engines drawing closer.

There were Campbell's calm words, one morning in Alexandria. 'Of course, there's more than one way of looking at it. Some might say it takes guts to go down with the ship and deliberately sacrifice yourself, but it could also be seen as the easy way out, the final and supreme means of not having to face up to the consequences of your actions.' Dark shapes appeared above the southern horizon. Thurston slid down the ladder, weight taken on his hands. Something made him turn aside to his sea cabin, pick Kate's photograph off the table opposite his bunk and shove it into an inside pocket. The flat outside was quite dark, filled with the choking black smoke, which his torch barely penetrated. He bent forward, coughing uncontrollably, then straightened, breathless for a moment. There was someone else there, somewhere ahead of him in the smoky darkness, footsteps on the deck plates.

'Who's there?'

Silence for a moment, except for the sound of aero-engines overhead.

'Who's there?' he repeated, then the smoke started him coughing again.

It crossed his mind that he was imagining him, then the man spoke. 'Vincent, sir.'

'What the blazes are you doing here, Mr Vincent?' he said in a hot rush of anger. 'You should have gone hours ago.' He had sent Vincent across to *Vittoria* after the torpedoing, long before the bombing.

Vincent didn't answer, but it was not difficult to guess. Thurston moved a few steps forward, saw him through the smoke in the light of his torch, head bowed, huddled against the bulkhead. He grasped Vincent by one arm, propelled him out of the flat and onto the open flight deck, sinking his face into the neck of his duffel coat to get away from the worst of the smoke. The bombers were coming close, *Vittoria* heeling away from the carrier's side to give herself room to fire back

303

at the Germans. *Crusader*'s decks were quite empty now. Only he and Vincent were left alive. He wondered whether Beveridge and the Commander had got away safely. The two destroyers were firing, bright flashes coming out from the muzzles of their guns, the wind blowing cordite smells over *Crusader*'s flight deck. The deck shifted again, there were sounds of rending metal below and water rushing in. The bulkheads were going. His gloved hand was round Vincent's biceps, he was impelling him forward towards the rails. The bombs were starting to fall, the deck dipping downwards so that the portside rails were only a few feet above water. *Vittoria* was a hundred yards away, her two guns firing in their own time, the lighter anti-aircraft weapons flinging up their own barrage. His seaboots were slipping on the deck as the ship heeled a few degrees more. Vincent looked back at him, white-faced, almost like a child being frogmarched to his first day at school. The first of the bombers flew over their heads, the bombs falling away from its belly. It was impossible to believe that they could miss. The ship was settling all the time, her stern beginning to slide away beneath Thurston's feet. Over to port *Vittoria* was jinking in every direction, never holding the same course for more than a few seconds, which might prevent the bombers from hitting her but would also make accurate gunnery more difficult.

They reached the edge of the flight deck, dropped down onto the catwalk. He shouted at Vincent, who began to clamber over the rails. Bombs were falling all around, sending up their columns of water. One of them hit the ship, exploded over on the starboard side, the force of the blast passing close over Thurston's head, so that he ducked involuntarily below the level of the flight deck, his eyes shutting automatically.

'Sir!' Vincent was swaying crazily outwards, one foot on the topmost rail, both hands grasping the stanchion in an effort to save himself. Thurston lunged towards him, but the ship was heeling again. Vincent lost his hold on the stanchion, his arms were flung outwards and his eyes opened wide in horror, then he disappeared into the water. The ship was still going over, would turn turtle in a moment, the stanchions almost horizontal now, the rails hanging loose, broken in many places along their length. Thurston stepped out onto the nearest stanchion, arms outstretched to balance himself, then another long stride and he was falling into space.

The cold was greater than he had ever known. It grasped at his chest, shocked the breath from his body. His mouth opened involuntarily as his head went under, so that he swallowed a lot of water. His feet flailed uselessly for a moment, then there was relief as his seaboots came away and he came back to the surface. He gasped for air, started instinctively to swim, then remembered Vincent. He looked round for him, trod water, went round a complete circle and tried to shout for him: 'Vincent, are you there?' but no words would come. In the below-freezing air his eyelashes started to freeze together. He had forgotten to blow up his lifebelt before he jumped overboard and the duffel coat was dragging him down; he turned onto his back, worked himself away from the ship's side with his legs, used his teeth to get his gloves off, then began to fumble at the wooden toggles of the duffel coat, still turning his head to look for Vincent, water in his eyes, and oil, stinging salt working into the raw flesh of his face, freezing momentarily before the next splash washed it away and froze in its turn. One toggle came free; he started on the next, pushing away grimly with his legs to keep himself afloat.

Where was Vincent?

Crusader's rails dipped under the water, and her flight deck rose up above him. She's turning over, he realised, and worked frantically with his legs to get himself clear of her before she dragged him down. The duffel coat was holding him back. He started again on the toggles. The second came away but his hands were almost dead before he started on the third. There was a knife in one of his pockets but he knew even before he thought any further that he would never manage to get it out and then open. For the first time he wondered whether he was going to make it. The last of the toggles came free. He tugged at the cuffs of the duffel coat, went under, felt his head begin to burst, and terror, before he could wriggle free. He kicked the coat away, came up again, gasped in air once more. He turned onto his stomach, found his arms barely responded, wondered whether all that effort had been worth it.

Where was Vincent? He forced his eyelids apart with one hand, tried to remember where the destroyer was, then saw her, perhaps a hundred yards away, a long long way when the cold was draining away his strength with every second. There was a boat slowly descending from her davits, but how long had he been in the water? It must be more than the critical five minutes. He bumped against something, realising it could not be *Vittoria*'s side, got his eyelids apart once more. He sensed rather than saw another man, head barely above the water, pushed back and forth by the swell, no longer with the strength to swim. A fortunate wave pushed him towards Thurston so he was able to grab him. He turned automatically onto his back and got an arm across the man's chest, as taught in Osborne advanced swimming all those years ago. In the low sunlight he saw that it was Vincent, face

305

and hair glistening with fuel oil. He tried to tell Vincent that it was all right, he'd got him, but there were no words left. He tried to swim again, but there was nothing left there either. His legs and free arm moved sluggishly, but they had no power against the sea. He went under again, swallowed more water, and something else which must have been fuel oil. His head broke surface again in a trough, he tried once more to push towards the ship's side, to look about him for *Vittoria*'s boat, but his eyes were blinded by the oil and his body paralysed by the cold, and he knew that even if he let go of Vincent he wasn't going to make it, and it was more than anything the desolation of meeting death alone out here that kept his hold on him. He realised with sudden regret that he wasn't going to see the baby, then his mouth opened in a shout for the mother he had never had, but no sound came out, and only oil and cold sea came in.

Something pulling from behind, pressure on his throat, his shoulders bumping against something hard.

'This one's had it.'

'What about the other one?'

Something was pulling at him, trying to wrench his burden away from him, prising up his fingers one by one. He sank again, down once more into the dark, terror came again, that they thought he was dead and would let him go. Then hands under his armpits, his face scraping against something hard and splintery.

'Better have 'em both. The doc can sort it out.'

An icy blast of wind at his back, he was coming out of the water, bent over the boat's gunwale, crumpling into a protective huddle as he landed heavily on the bottom boards, and bringing his hands up to shield his head. 'Right, you buggers. Pull!' A change in the boat's motion as the oars found a ragged rhythm. 'Pull! You lot couldn't manage a piss-up in a brewery!' A hand went inside his jacket, feeling for the heartbeat. 'It's all right. We've got you. And your mate,' the voice added after a moment.

'Is your bloke breathing?'

'Dunno.'

Thurston wanted to tell them to look after Vincent, but all his strength had drained away. Hands turned him over, put him across one of the thwarts, pounded the base of his back so that he gasped out a sludge of water and oil.

'Check he hasn't swallowed his false teeth.'

His head was wrenched back by the hair, his mouth forced open and a couple of fingers shoved into his throat. There was warm tobacco-laden breath on his face. 'Come on, you lazy bugger! Breathe!'

The boat's motion changed again, then she was bumping against *Vittoria*'s side.

'Hook on. Hurry it up!'

The boat began to rise, swaying on its falls as the destroyer rolled. A voice in his ear, almost pleading with him, 'C'mon man. Breathe.'

The boat swung inboard, grounded gently on its chocks. 'Keep back. Give us some room.'

Hands lifted him out of the boat, laid him down. Something passed over his eyes, stinging its way through the numbness. There were several voices around him, all speaking at the same time.

'Got them both. I think that's all there were.'

'He wouldn't let go of the other one.'

'Got 'im by the neck with the boathook, just as 'e went under.'

'Reckon that one's had it.'

He saw a stretcher going away, then more hands were roaming over him, someone talking at a soothing pitch, faces clustered above.

'Stand *back* I say!'

His head slipped sideways; between a man's feet he saw *Crusader* half a cable away, right over on her beam ends, her flight deck rearing vertically into the sky, yellow flame still rising from her.

On *Vittoria*'s bridge, George Thurston had watched in an agony of restlessness as *Crusader*'s men came aboard. Of course, his father had not been among them and there was constantly lurking in the back of his mind the thought that there would not be time for him to get off. Then the carrier had begun to roll onto her side, and from that distance he could not be sure whether any of the few men left on deck was his father. He had seen two men picked up from the water, but even if his father was one of them, he might already be dead. Chaps didn't last long in water as cold as this.

'Well, we can't hang around waiting for that thing to sink,' Lieutenant-Commander Haldane was saying. 'Chief Yeoman, signal *Vituperate* to put a torpedo into her.' Haldane stalked to the starboard wing of the bridge, hands stuffed into his pockets. 'Get on with it, man, we've a convoy to catch up with!'

The Aldis lamp began to blink its message. *Vituperate* flashed a brief acknowledgement. George Thurston saw her begin to turn away, white foam rising about her bows as she increased speed. He looked over the bridge screen again, saw one man lying on the deck, quite still, a cluster of men around him, seemingly doing nothing to aid him. Suddenly, hardly realising what he was doing, he turned round sharply, made for the ladder.

'Mr Thurston!' he heard Haldane's voice shouting. 'Where do you think you're going?'

But George barely heard him. He was already on the ladder, sliding down on his hands, feet well up.

'Mr Thurston, I'll see you hang, you as well as Cronin!'

He was pushing through the group of men, wanting to know only whether the survivor was his father.

'Haven't they got any more stretchers?'

Thurston had started to drift, tired right through and secure in the knowledge that he was being looked after. Someone started to slap his face to keep him awake. 'You can have a sleep once you're thawed out.' The man stopped as he noticed the dull gleam of the stripes on his arms, drew in a long breath. 'Bloody hell.'

Someone else was pushing through the forest of legs around him, the legs parting unwillingly. What he saw in his last seconds of consciousness was his son's anguished face, coming down towards him again and again. 'Dad!' a voice was saying over and over.

'There she goes.'

Vituperate's torpedoes, fired at a stationary target from a range of a few hundred yards, struck *Crusader*'s stranded hull amidships. There were two explosions, separated by a few fractions of a second, then a brief silence, succeeded by a thunder of sound as her steel plates and members tore apart and she divided into two halves, each of which floated separately for a brief instant, one end still with its orthodox shape of bow or stern, the other an open void edged with grotesquely twisted metal, before it rose up vertically and began to slide down below the surface, with more noise as heavy structures broke free and crashed through bulkheads, and then more distant explosions as the boilers burst under the pressure of hundreds of tons of water.

He was lying on a table, looking up at the deckhead beams. His eyes stung again as someone passed a cloth over them, a smell of surgical spirit in his nostrils, and his eyes began to water. There was the blade of a clasp knife gleaming in the light from the deckhead as it cut away his clothes. His head was lifted up, someone coaxed him to take some hot soup from a large blue-rimmed enamel mug. His lips burned, the

308

effort exhausted him, the soup dribbled away from one side of his mouth. He tried to say something but his jaws were still frozen.

'It's all right. Vincent's fine. He's quite all right.'

He turned his head to look for Vincent, but could not see him. His trousers had gone, towels were rubbing at his feet and legs, seen but not felt. The knife swept up his body from waist to throat. Hands were pulling the soaking fragments of his clothes apart, a voice was reading out the details from his identity discs, a pencil scratching on a notebook close by, another voice checking back. 'Thurston? Same as snotty.'

'Don't bother with drying him. Just get him in the bath. Who've we got here?' The newcomer took the notebook, looked at it, and whistled. 'This is our night for bloody brass!'

The door opened. 'Out, snotty! You're supposed to be on watch. Or had you forgotten?'

'Sir, you've got my father in here!'

In the hours since the torpedoing Thurston had quite forgotten that George was aboard *Vittoria*. He tried to lift his head, moved far enough to see a blanket-covered form on the deck beneath the next table, felt his head swim, overbalancing, thought that he would go over on top of him.

'Outside,' *Vittoria*'s Surgeon Lieutenant repeated more gently. 'Just give me five minutes.' The door shut. 'Mills, have you got that bath run yet? Hundred and fifteen and no hotter . . . All right, take him through.'

He was lying in the bath, a scum of fuel oil coating the surface of the water, his chest bruised blue and streaked with more oil, his arms and legs hanging out over the sides.

'Wake up. You can't go to sleep yet. Not until you're thawed out a bit more. Let's have a drop more hot, Mills.'

Someone turned the hot tap on, so that the water level rose a little higher.

'Wonder how long it'll take us to catch up with the convoy.'

'Too fuckin' long! Don't ask such fuckin' silly questions.'

'And you can stop just standing there watching the rest of us work. Find a brush and start getting that oil off.'

Thurston realised that *Vittoria*'s engine note had changed, her motion was steeper as her speed increased and she settled onto a new course.

'Wonder how they're getting on with the other fellow?'

The doctor arrived, a youngish fair man with spectacles and wavy

RNVR stripes on the shoulders of his battledress, standing in the doorway and talking to the senior SBA.

Then, strangely, Thurston seemed to be looking down on them from above, seeing his body, bluish-white, being pulled from the water, tendrils of hair over the forehead, stipples of blood crusted across the face and the bridge of the nose. There was blackish stubble on his chin; he thought dreamily that he must have forgotten to shave that morning. The doctor was feeling the side of his neck, putting an ear to his chest. A grunted, 'Stopped breathing.' He saw himself sprawled on the corticine, dirty water pooled all around him, watched in detached interest as the doctor dropped onto his knees beside him, turned him over and began to bear down on his back, once, twice, grimacing with the effort. 'Come on!'

'One of the Jerries we had did that, sir. Couldn't get him going again.'

The other men were standing back against the bulkhead, leaving everything to their superior.

'Come on!'

A crash of pain through his chest, then another, and he was back in his body, gasping and coughing, staring with sudden surprise at the deck a few inches away, hearing the doctor's grunt of satisfaction.

'Don't do that to me again . . . All right, put him back in the bath and let's have another go.'

'How's the other one doing, sir?'

'Not very good. This chap's better built to take it. Got a bit more meat on him.'

'All right,' the doctor said at last. 'Wrap him up and get him to a bunk. I don't think he'll do that again now. Parrish, have we got any hot water bottles left?'

'No, sir. Used them all up on some of the others.'

'Then put one of the other survivors in with him. Someone who didn't get his feet wet.'

The doctor's five minutes became ten, and as the hands of his watch crawled round towards the hour George Thurston was still hanging round the sick bay flat among *Crusader*'s less injured survivors who were queuing for treatment. He was supposed to be on watch, and he should go back to the bridge and face whatever was due to him for deserting his post, and he could not disturb the doctor again, but he could not tear himself away from here until he knew. The survivors were silent for the most part, the lucky ones sitting on the deck with their backs against the bulkheads, the rest clumped together in a group which had to shuffle itself aside whenever anybody came out of the sick bay or went in.

'Next.'

The clump shifted, and a man with a bloody shell dressing on his head went in. Another came out, holding a brown envelope.

'Aspirins. He gave me bloody aspirins.'

The door opened again a little later, men shuffled out of the way once more. A stretcher came out, feet first, the boots still on, sticking out from beneath a grey blanket.

Oh God, don't let it be him. Please don't let it be him.

The stretcher bearers could not tell him who it was, and one of them casually pulled back the blanket, but the face belonged to another man.

Someone produced a crumpled packet of cigarettes, naval-issue ticklers, and passed it round.

'Go on, sir, you have one. Waiting for somebody?'

'The Captain's my father,' he said dully.

'Rough luck. Hope he makes it.'

Smoking below the age of eighteen was forbidden, but he had already committed the still more heinous offence of leaving his post, and he took the cigarette, and accepted a light from the seaman's antique-looking brass lighter.

'Good 'un, your dad. Not like some I've known, gongs or no gongs. No bloody flannel.'

Two more stretchers came out and on the second he saw his father, his eyes open, but grey and still as an effigy.

'Dad?'

'Don't suppose 'e'll hear you, sir,' the stretcher bearer said. 'Like frozen fucking meat still.' He noticed George's expression, tried to reassure. 'Don't you worry, sir. He's lasted this long so he ought to make it all right. We're just getting him to a bunk for now.' The SBA raised his voice. 'Any of you lot fancy a bunk for half an hour? Okay, you'll do. Now's your chance to satisfy all your perverted lusts by bedding down for the night with a four-striper.'

'Your father, ah yes.' The Surgeon Lieutenant's surname was Solomon, and despite his fair colouring he was Jewish. 'We've put him to bed, and one of the other survivors in with him. You see,' he hastened to explain, 'we have to be very careful not to warm them up too fast after they've been in the water, at least when it's as cold as this – the heart won't stand a sudden change in temperature, and there's also a danger that the limbs will turn gangrenous if they've been frostbitten. So what we do is put them in a fairly hot bath to begin with, which first of all stops the body temperature from falling any further, and then starts the warming process. After this first stage we've found that the natural body temperature – ninety-eight point four – is ideal, and the most effective way of providing that, as well as the simplest, is to pop another man in the bunk with them, even though it sounds a bit indecent. Once he starts to get cold, as he will, of course, we pop someone else in, and keep on doing that for as long as it takes.'

He was inside a cocoon of blankets, warm hairy flesh against him, a rough Glasgow voice close by. 'Man, they dinna give us much room. Nae more space than a hammock.' A beard bristled his forehead. 'Man, you're frozen through!' He started to shiver, top and bottom teeth rattling against each other, his body a moment later knotting up with cramp. 'It's aw reet, man.' He found he was crying and was ashamed of his weakness. 'It's aw reet, man.' The man was rubbing at his legs, trying to massage away the knots. His voice was almost a growl. 'Och, I nivver thocht I'd be sleeping wi' a pig.'

The spasm passed, but others followed it, his body twisting and contracting into tight knots of muscle. He would screw his eyes shut, set his teeth and bite the pillow to hold back the groaning, try to stretch within the cocoon to break free from the pain. As the spasms grew further apart, there came in the intervals between them a warm sense of thankfulness to this unknown man. Arms were about him, his head rested against the man's shoulder. 'Go tae sleep.' Dreams, the bombs falling once more; he was shouting orders to the quartermaster, but they brought no response, so that the ship held her course, and the bombs came ever closer to her decks, but they never quite exploded before he awoke out of the dream. Other dreams, in which he was trying to swim through slush which was freezing all around him, setting solid even as he tried to work his arms to find a way through.

'It's aw reet, man. Go back tae sleep.'

36

'Flags, could you get hold of Gieves' man and buy Captain Thurston a brass hat, and anything else he needs. Put it down to my account.' Manning-Wilson turned to Thurston before he could protest. 'I'm not having you get on a train in front of civilians in that thing. We'll sort it out some other time.'

Thurston smiled. Canning had lent him a brass hat ('Captain should have a cap, sir') but there was a long horizontal tear in one side, it was stained with oil and in any case it didn't fit. Otherwise, he supposed he looked presentable at least, in a shirt and battledress of George's, which Spencer had set upon with an iron, and begged, borrowed or stolen sufficient gold lace from *Vittoria*'s wardroom to put four stripes on the shoulder straps.

'I shan't keep you long,' Manning-Wilson went on when the Flag Lieutenant had gone out. 'You'll be wanting to get home to Kate. I rang her as soon as I knew you were safe, so she'll be expecting you. She told me to tell you she's quite all right, and the baby obviously has ambitions to be a gymnast.' He gave a brief guffaw, then brought his watch out from his breast pocket and cocked an eye at the sky through the window. 'Gin? Or have the quacks put you on the wagon?'

'Just a small one.'

'Abstemious as ever.' Manning-Wilson brought the necessary bottles out of the cupboard next to his desk, poured two glasses. 'How are you?'

'A bit sore still, and black and blue in parts, but nothing that won't sort itself out.' Most of the swelling had gone from his fingers now, but they were still tender, the knuckles scabbed and discoloured with bruising, so that he winced slightly as he took hold of the glass.

'You were very lucky.' The Admiral paused, and went on in slightly different tones. 'The young chap who was in the water with you, how's he doing?'

Vincent had been carried ashore and into a waiting ambulance as soon as *Vittoria* was alongside. The day after being picked up he was sitting up in his sick bay cot apparently almost recovered, but the same evening he had developed a cough which was more than simply his lungs ridding themselves of the fuel oil he had inhaled while in the water; before long pneumonia had set in and the doctors were shaking their heads over him. Thurston had gone to the sick bay to see Vincent, but *Vittoria*'s doctor would only let him look through the door at him. Even if he lived Vincent was unlikely to be fit for sea service again, and perhaps that was the kindest thing. He was a competent enough naval officer, but God had never intended him to be a fighting man.

The sun was shining through the window at the Admiral's back, so that Thurston had to look away a little to avoid being dazzled. The day had begun bright as *Vittoria* and *Vituperate* came up the Firth, sunny and with a promise of spring in the mild air though it was still only the beginning of March, the sort of day that looked as though it would not last the morning, but seemed now to be confounding expectations. Eight days ago he had been struggling in the sea four hundred miles north of the Arctic Circle, the water freezing on him, now the pavement he had walked along to get into the Admiral's headquarters was crowded with office workers, coats unfastened, enjoying the unexpected sun during their lunch hours.

Crusader's men had been crowded together on the destroyers' decks, some bantering, exchanging private jokes, others silently drinking in their first sight of the British mainland since the sinking. There too were civilians who could know nothing of what they had come from, children in school uniforms and carrying satchels on the road which wound round the northern bank, an early golfer sending up spurts of sand as he tried to extricate himself from a bunker, to ironic cheers when he succeeded.

'Don't know why you're all cheering *him*,' one man said sourly. 'Bastard's probably never heard of bloody Murmansk.'

There were all the familiar figures of the last months: the Commander, Chief, Wings, Beveridge, Duff, Leading Airman Powell, bandaged hands hanging uselessly at his sides, Stoker Murray, Able Seaman Dennis, RPO Slingsby. Most of the men had only the clothes they were wearing at the time of the torpedo hit, or had been given by *Vittoria*'s crew, and appeared in strange combinations of grease-stained overalls, old sweaters, duffel coats and football shirts, with here and there a man who had managed to abandon ship in what was recognisably a uniform, looking oddly out-of-place among his fellows. One or two lacked even basic clothing, and had little more than a blanket draped round their shoulders and plimsolls on their feet. Some men, better prepared, had private 'getaway' bags which they had managed to retrieve from their messdecks, and now nursed them as if they contained the crown jewels, anxious not to lose any of the few possessions they had saved from the sinking. And there were the missing faces: Metcalfe, Sub-Lieutenant Wallace and Pettty Officer Kornilov; James, whose promotion to Lieutenant Commander had come through too late.

The survivors would be sent back to barracks, kitted out afresh, given fourteen days' leave and split up among other ships, most of othem never to meet again. Addresses were being scribbled on odd scraps of paper, but few men would ever get round to writing. *Crusader*'s ship's company had found a unity for a short time only, and now the ship had gone that unity was at an end. Stoker McCutcheon had played as *Vittoria* came into harbour, first a pibroch for *Crusader* and her thirty-seven dead, a formless haunting sequence of notes, falling into the grey waters of the Clyde, then followed it with the swaggering defiance of 'Cock of the North'.

They were not the only survivors aboard *Vittoria*. The survivors from U–686 were crowded into the destroyer's forepeak under guard, and would not have emerged had one of them not died from wounds in the sick bay two days ago. The U-boat captain had given his parole on behalf of all of them in order to bury the man under his own flag and some of *Crusader*'s men had also attended the brief service, mainly, Thurston suspected, from curiosity, since this was the first time most of them could ever have seen their enemy. The Germans had been fallen in on one side of the quarterdeck, the British on the other, the canvas-wrapped corpse lying on the teak planking between them, draped in the swastika ensign which *Vittoria* kept on board, listening as the U-boat captain read the Latin service of the Roman Catholic Church, and one of the men stepped forward to play '*Ich hatt' ein Kamerad*' on a mouth organ which one of *Vittoria*'s men had lent him, some of the British almost disappointed in their first sight of men who had in four years of war destroyed untold millions of tons of shipping and killed thousands of other seamen.

The Germans had scrubby beards, and a wild assortment of filthy leather clothing, civilian shirts stained with water and oil, and many of them could have been no older than twenty. Yet they too still retained their pride, coming to attention and finally marching off with a parade-ground snap and heads held high. The U-boat captain had lingered a little, faced Thurston for a moment, taking in every detail of his appearance, the borrowed clothes, the scrapes and grazes on his face, the fuel oil grained into the creases around his eyes. He was a stocky fair man, with a seaman's watchful blue eyes beneath the battered white-topped cap, a Knight's Cross at his throat and a slight limp which he had not

315

been able to disguise while marching a few moments earlier. Not any U-boat captain, but one of the few surviving aces, a man who had disposed of eighty-two thousand tons of British and Allied shipping, and had put the torpedoes into *Crusader* which brought about her sinking. He did not speak, but at length clicked his heels and snapped to an immaculate salute. Thurston hesitated, and then slowly raised his hand to the Commander's cap in return.

The U-boat men had gone ashore from *Vittoria* first, each man blind-folded, with one hand on the shoulder of the man in front, the other clutching whatever small possessions he had managed to save, then *Crusader*'s survivors, for a time almost as lost in a strange world as they milled about the dockside in tight little huddles, wondering where they were supposed to go. Gradually order was created; they were taken away to a vast open shed and issued with rail warrants, an advance of pay and haversack rations, then driven to the station in relays of lorries. *Crusader*'s loss had struck Thurston forcibly as he came ashore from the destroyer. As he reached the gangway the bo'sun's mate began to raise the silver-plated call to his lips, then he paused suddenly in mid-movement, and his arm snapped back to his side, because Thurston didn't have a ship any more.

Manning-Wilson had been talking, and Thurston listening with only half his attention, his mind drawn back to *Crusader*. She, and he himself, had come a long way in the last five months. It was something difficult to recognise at the time, but in making *Crusader* work he had begun to restore his own self-respect. His breakdown had left him with some-thing to prove to himself, that he was a whole man again and still as capable as he had once been. He had started to be aware of the change while he was still in command, but it was only this morning, while he was standing on the dockside in the bright morning sun, that the realisation had struck him that the sinking itself formed part of his process of recovery. He could have remained with *Crusader* as she went down, but he had chosen to take the chance of survival, and in making that choice he had put the past behind him, and broken free from the shadow of the breakdown.

'Well, I take it you wouldn't object to a shore job this time,' he heard Manning-Wilson say. 'Matter of fact, Musgrave's tour is due to finish in a couple of months, so I'll be needing another Chief of Staff. You and I have worked together very well in the past, and I think we'd make a good team again. The job's yours if you want it. You've got your survivor's leave to come, so you can take your time to think about it. You don't have to make your mind up immediately.'

Thurston waited only a moment, took a pull at his glass of gin. 'No, sir. Thank you for the offer, but it's not the job for me.'

'Somehow,' Manning-Wilson was smiling, 'I thought you were going to say that. I suppose you want another ship.'

'Yes, sir, I do.' Not any ship, another carrier. The past was behind him, and he was going forward into something new.

'All right, I don't suppose I'll have much trouble finding a Chief of Staff. But for heaven's sake don't go and lose this one. One sinking is an accident, two is coincidence, but any more is just damned careless! And now I expect you'd like to talk to Kate. I'll have Charles Beasley get through for you.' Manning-Wilson picked up the telephone, spoke briefly to his secretary in the outer office.

Thurston finished the gin, found himself moving impatiently to the edge of his chair.

'Better not tell her you've just turned down a shore job. But I suppose she's used to it by now.'

Manning-Wilson was still talking inconsequentially. Thurston looked around him, noting the painting of Nelson's *Victory* hanging over the fireplace, the sun lighting on the sea on her port side. *When we get our next ship, sir*, Spencer had said in George's cabin earlier that morning, as he was looking around for something to pack.

'Must say, you're looking remarkably cheerful in the circumstances.'

Thurston waited for a long moment before replying. 'You might say,' he said slowly, 'that I've been on the road to Damascus.'

The telephone rang suddenly, the receiver vibrating a little on its rest.

The Admiral picked it up. 'Yes? . . . Thank you, Charles . . . Kate, it's Herbert Manning-Wilson. I've got him sitting in front of me.' He handed the receiver across the desk, then stood up and walked quietly out.

317